USA TODAY Bestselling Author

Laura Scott

and

New York Times Bestselling Author

Shirlee McCoy

Finding Justice

Previously published as *Battle Tested* and *Valiant Defender*

LOVE INSPIRED
INSPIRATIONAL ROMANCE

LOVE INSPIRED®

INSPIRATIONAL ROMANCE

Recycling programs for this product may not exist in your area.

ISBN-13: 978-1-335-53300-5

Finding Justice

Copyright © 2020 by Harlequin Books S.A.

Battle Tested
First published in 2018. This edition published in 2020.
Copyright © 2018 by Harlequin Books S.A.

Valiant Defender
First published in 2018. This edition published in 2020.
Copyright © 2018 by Harlequin Books S.A.

Special thanks and acknowledgment are given to Laura Scott and Shirlee McCoy for their contributions to the Military K-9 Unit miniseries.

This edition published by arrangement with Harlequin Books S.A.

For questions and comments about the quality of this book, please contact us at CustomerService@Harlequin.com.

Love Inspired
22 Adelaide St. West, 40th Floor
Toronto, Ontario M5H 4E3, Canada
www.Harlequin.com

Printed in U.S.A.

CONTENTS

Laura Scott is a nurse by day and an author by night. She has always loved romance and read faith-based books by Grace Livingston Hill in her teenage years. She's thrilled to have published over twelve books for Love Inspired Suspense. She has two adult children and lives in Milwaukee, Wisconsin, with her husband of over thirty years. Please visit Laura at laurascottbooks.com, as she loves to hear from her readers.

Books by Laura Scott

Love Inspired Suspense

True Blue K-9 Unit

Blind Trust

Military K-9 Unit

Battle Tested
Military K-9 Unit Christmas
"Yuletide Target"

Callahan Confidential

Shielding His Christmas Witness
The Only Witness
Christmas Amnesia
Shattered Lullaby
Primary Suspect
Protecting His Secret Son

Visit the Author Profile page
at Harlequin.com for more titles.

BATTLE TESTED

Laura Scott

The Lord is my rock, and my fortress,
and my deliverer; my God, my strength,
in whom I will trust; my buckler,
and the horn of my salvation, and my high tower.
—*Psalms* 18:2

This book is dedicated to all the men and women who have served our country and have paid the ultimate price in order to protect our freedom.

ONE

Two fatal drug overdoses in the past week.

Exhausted from her thirteen-hour shift in the intensive care unit, First Lieutenant Vanessa Gomez made her way down the hallway of the Canyon Air Force Base hospital, grappling with the impact of this latest drug-related death.

The medication both young men had overdosed on, Tyraxal, had been touted as the best new drug on the market to treat PTSD. Of course, no meds were risk free, but she was troubled by these two recent deaths. Not just because her young brother, Aiden, also suffered from PTSD, although he wasn't on that particular medication as far as she knew, but because she'd heard Tyraxal was highly addictive and it seemed these recent overdoses proved it.

The corridor lights abruptly went out, enclosing her in complete darkness. She froze, instinctively searching for the nearest exit sign, when strong hands roughly grabbed her from behind, long fingers wrapping themselves around her throat.

The Red Rose Killer?

It had been months since she'd received the red rose

indicating she was a target of convicted murderer and prison escapee Boyd Sullivan. She struggled against her attacker, wishing now that she'd brought Eagle, her protective attack Doberman, to work with her.

No! Dear God, please help me!

She kicked back at the man's shins, but her soft-soled nursing shoes didn't do much damage. She used her elbows, too, but couldn't make enough impact that way, either. Her phone was off, so she didn't bother digging it out of her bag. The attacker's fingers moved their position around her neck, as if searching for the proper pressure points.

"Why?" she asked in a harsh whisper as she tried to break his hold. She'd helped Boyd once after he'd gotten into a fight, tending to his wounds. So why was he intent on killing her? She clawed at his hands, but they were covered in plastic gloves.

"Because you're in my way..." the attacker said, his voice low and dripping with malice.

The pressure against her carotid arteries grew, making her dizzy and weak. Black spots dotted her vision.

She was going to die, and there was nothing she could do to stop it.

Poor Aiden, he'd be left all alone...

Her knees sagged, then she heard a man's voice. "Hey, what's going on?"

Her attacker abruptly let go just as the lights came on. She fell to the floor, wincing against the blinding brightness while struggling to breathe. The sound of pounding footsteps echoed along the corridor.

"Are you okay?" A man wearing battle-ready camo rushed over, dropping to his knees beside her. A soft, wet, furry nose pushed against her face and a sandpapery tongue licked her cheek.

"Yes," she managed, hoping he didn't notice how badly her hands were shaking.

"Stay, Tango," the stranger ordered. He ran toward the stairwell at the end of the hall, the one that her attacker must have used to escape.

"Hey, Tango," she whispered, stroking the golden retriever's soft coat and resting her forehead against his fur. He wasn't Eagle, her protective Doberman, but he was obviously well trained in offering comfort.

Hearing footsteps pounding in the stairwell, she quickly lifted her head and struggled to her feet. She slipped off her shoulder bag and wrapped the strap around her hand, the only thing she could use as a weapon in the event Boyd was coming back to finish the job.

The stairwell door opened revealing a tall, muscular man with wavy, sandy-brown hair. His expression was full of concern as he approached. "Sure you're all right?"

She nodded, her shoulders slumping in relief. "Yes. Did you see him? The man who attacked me?"

Her rescuer shook his head, his emerald green eyes heavy with remorse. "I'm sorry, but I didn't get a good look at him. Other than general statistics like medium height and build. He had a ski mask covering his head, so I can't even tell you his hair color."

Boyd Sullivan was medium height and build. Then again so were half the men on base.

But only Boyd Sullivan had sent her a red rose.

"Thank you." She drew in a deep breath, hoping to calm her racing heart. "I'm First Lieutenant Vanessa

Gomez. I'm one of the ICU nurses here. I'm not sure what would have happened if you hadn't chosen that moment to come down this hallway."

"Captain Isaac Goddard," he said, introducing himself. "I'm glad I was here to help. Do you think this is related to Boyd Sullivan?"

Vanessa grimaced, gingerly palpating her tender neck. No doubt she'd have bruises tomorrow. "Unfortunately, yes. I believe my attacker is the Red Rose Killer."

"I'm sorry to hear that." Isaac's expression turned grim.

"Me, too." Although she still didn't understand Boyd's motive for wanting her dead after she'd gone out of her way to help him.

"You need to call this in to the Security Forces, specifically to my buddy Captain Blackwood," Isaac said. "There were rumors that Boyd was seen recently on base, but this attack on you proves it."

She nodded and dug in her bag for her cell phone. She powered it up, her fingers still trembling from the aftermath of her attack. Vanessa sometimes turned her cell phone off when she was working in the intensive care unit. Obviously, she should have turned it on the moment she'd left the ICU, although the attack had been so unexpected, she doubted the phone would have been any help.

She shivered and punched in Justin Blackwood's number. She had his contact information from the ad hoc investigative team that had been put together months ago when Boyd had first sent roses identifying his next targets. As she waited for him to pick up, she marveled at how Tango stood right between her and Isaac, as if willing to protect both of them.

Justin didn't answer so she left him a brief message about her attack and the likelihood that Boyd had found her, and she asked him to return the call.

"Call the cops," Isaac said. "They need to take your statement."

"I'd prefer to speak directly to Justin." Vanessa glanced up and down the empty hallway. "It's not as if there are any clues here for them to find. He was wearing gloves, so there's no point in dusting for prints."

He looked as if he wanted to argue, but asked, "Where are you headed?"

"Home." She slipped her phone into her bag. "What about you?"

He shrugged. "I was going to stop by and see if Lieutenant Colonel Flintman was around, but that can wait. Right now, I think it's best if I walk you home."

Normally Vanessa considered herself a strong, independent woman, more than capable of taking care of herself. She'd needed to be strong, especially for her younger brother, Aiden, who was having a rough time since returning to base four weeks ago after his latest six-month deployment. But this vicious attack at the hospital, a place she considered her second home and immune to this type of violence, had put a serious dent in her confidence. "I'd appreciate that, thanks."

"No problem." Isaac fell into step beside her. Tango stayed at Isaac's left side, and she wondered about the dog's role in Isaac's life.

She could guess, considering Isaac had been heading to Lieutenant Colonel Flintman's office. She'd left the doctor a message earlier that afternoon about her concern about Tyraxal. The kindly psychiatrist might have some information related to the medication, so she hoped he returned her call, soon.

Isaac might be seeing Lieutenant Colonel Flintman for the same reason Aiden did.

Not that it was any of her business.

They stood for a moment waiting for the elevator, and Isaac must have picked up on her curiosity because he gestured to the dog. "I don't think I introduced my therapy dog, Tango."

She belatedly noticed that Isaac sported a pair of gold wings on his collar indicating he was a pilot. She smiled at the animal. "Tango is an amazing dog, so calm and reassuring. He's obviously good at his job."

Isaac shrugged. "Yeah, he's a great dog, but while I appreciate having him around, my top priority is to bring home Beacon, the dog who saved my life in Afghanistan. Beacon belonged to my closest friend, and I've been working day and night to get him back. After all this time, he's finally due to arrive tomorrow."

Instinctively, she reached out to place her hand on his arm. "I heard about your efforts to bring Beacon home, and I'm so glad it's finally happening."

"Me, too." He covered her hand on his arm briefly and she found herself liking the warmth of his skin. Then he moved away when the elevator arrived, breaking the connection. He held his hand over the electronic eye until she was safely inside, then stepped in behind her.

She told herself her reaction to Isaac was nothing more than misplaced gratitude for the way he'd saved her life with his impeccable timing. Yet she couldn't help sending him a sidelong glance, appreciating his sandy-brown hair, chiseled features, clean-cut square jaw and bright green eyes. She glanced away, telling herself to knock it off.

Outside, the October air smelled of pine trees and morning glories. She loved autumn in east Texas; it was her favorite time of year.

"Lead the way," Isaac said, when they reached the street in front of the hospital.

"I live in a small two-bedroom house about eight blocks from here," she said, turning left and taking the road that went past the church and veterinary clinic. "My younger brother, Aiden, has been staying with me since his return from combat four weeks ago. He's on medical leave, suffering badly from PTSD, and I'm at a loss as to how to help him."

Isaac didn't say anything for a long moment, then he finally spoke. "I'm working through my own issues, so I understand what he's dealing with." Isaac glanced at her, his eyes shadowed by the darkness. "I hope you realize he has a long road to recovery ahead of him."

"I understand," Vanessa said softly. "He's doing everything right so far, attending therapy sessions with Lieutenant Colonel Flintman and taking his medication as ordered. Aiden is also on the list to get a therapy dog of his own, but the first attempt didn't go well, and a second one hasn't been made available to him yet."

"I'll talk to him, if you think it may help," Isaac offered.

Vanessa was humbled by his willingness to put himself out there on behalf of a stranger. "Thank you, Captain. I'd be grateful for anything you can offer."

"Sounds good. Maybe you can introduce me tonight, if he's around. And please, call me Isaac."

"If you'll call me Vanessa," she said with a smile. Despite her recent attack, she experienced a surge of hope. She was so grateful for Isaac's willingness to help her brother, she could have hugged him, but managed to restrain herself.

Maybe Isaac was just what Aiden needed to turn the corner on battling his illness.

Maybe this was exactly God's plan.

Isaac couldn't believe he'd actually told Vanessa about his PTSD, something he rarely talked about outside of therapy sessions. For the first time in weeks, he didn't feel the urge to hide the truth about what he was going through.

Maybe this meant he'd turned the corner on his healing process.

The sound of a car door slamming shut made Vanessa jump and nervously glance over her shoulder. He reached out to capture her hand in his, recognizing she was still suffering the aftermath of her attack.

"It's okay, you're safe with me," he assured her. Would she end up having nightmares as a result of the near strangulation? He hoped not. "Tell me about Boyd Sullivan and why he wants to hurt you."

She grimaced and shook her head. "Nothing to tell."

Isaac chose his words carefully. "Vanessa, I know firsthand that talking through an event is better than keeping it bottled inside. And I'm willing to listen without passing any judgment."

They took several steps heading west on Webster Street, past Canyon Drive, where most of the base housing was located, before she let out a heavy sigh. "There really isn't anything to the story. Boyd holds a grudge against the Air Force for dishonorably discharging him and he's coming after people who he believes are responsible for his downfall."

He'd heard the same theories. The base had been on high alert for months now, and apparently with good reason. Sullivan was getting bold and impatient, judging by the way he'd sneaked into the hospital to attack Vanessa.

He cast a glance her way. She was beautiful, her long dark hair pulled back in a ponytail, matching her chocolate-brown eyes. Beside him, she was petite in her pale blue scrubs covered by a white scrub jacket. Her honeysuckle scent made him think of home, and he was glad he'd been in the right place at the right time for once.

"And what about you? Did he want a personal relationship with you?" he guessed.

"Not at all," Vanessa quickly denied. "In fact, I helped him one night while he was still in basic training, providing medical care for wounds he'd suffered as a result of a barroom brawl. He didn't want to go to the ER and get in trouble, so I provided first aid from the kit I carry in my car. That's why this attack doesn't make any sense." She paused, then added, "He told me that I was the first person to be nice to him without expecting anything in return. Does that sound like a rational reason to want me dead?"

"No, it doesn't," he agreed. "I wonder if he thought your being nice to him meant you were interested in something more." To be honest, Isaac couldn't imagine any red-blooded man not being attracted to Vanessa.

He was attracted to her. Not that he was going to do anything about it. He let go of her hand, reminding himself that he wasn't interested in another relationship. Been there, done that, didn't work out, end of story.

In his experience women thought they could help a guy get over his issues, yet when they learned they couldn't, they decided the guy wasn't worth the trouble and moved on.

And maybe he wasn't worth the trouble. He couldn't blame Amber for leaving him when his panic attacks prevented him from leading a normal life. He especially didn't appreciate her hovering over him. He used to think he'd get better and move on with his life, but he now understood PTSD didn't ever go away. There were strategies to deal with it, sure, but it wasn't like being treated for an infection that would be cured by a course of antibiotics.

No, this was more like having a chronic illness for the rest of your life.

"I'm sure he wasn't interested in me that way," Vanessa protested. "If he was, he didn't pursue anything." Then she added, "At the time I was drawn to him, not romantically, but in a maternal way. In a weird way, he reminded me of Aiden—young and a bit immature, yet trying to make something of himself. Silly now that I look back at it. Boyd wasn't interested in anything but placing blame for everything that happened to him on someone else. Nothing was ever his fault, oh, no. It was everyone else out to get him."

"Then why target you as someone who wronged him?"

"I have no idea." She was silent for another block, then added, "And just so you know, I was working the night shift the night the dogs were let loose from their kennels. I know everyone believes Boyd had help from inside the base, but it wasn't me. I'm not the one helping him."

Isaac was surprised by the sudden vehemence in her tone. "I didn't suggest you were."

"Well, that's something, I guess," she said, her tone faintly bitter. "There are others, including the anonymous blogger, who have made it clear they believe I sent the rose to myself to deflect suspicion. The latest theory is that Boyd is getting help from a woman on base."

He hadn't realized the depth of what she'd been going through over the past few months. "That's a tough break, but I'm a witness to the attack who will exonerate you once and for all."

She lightly rubbed her neck, wincing at the tenderness. "Pictures of the bruises likely to be visible by morning should help, right?"

The thought of her golden skin marred by bruises infuriated him. If he'd been a minute later… He clenched his jaw, unwilling to think about how he may have stumbled across Vanessa's dead body.

The level of hatred Boyd was carrying around with him was inconceivable. Must be that Boyd wanted more from Vanessa, a personal relationship of some kind. No other explanation made sense. She must have done something, or said something, that dented his fragile ego.

No point rehashing it now. She needed protection, and he intended to make sure Captain Blackwood provided it to her. Isaac wasn't going to leave her alone, not until a Security Forces cop was stationed outside her house.

They walked the next block in silence.

At the corner, Vanessa took a left, heading past a thick hedge separating two front yards. A movement in the shrubbery caught his eye at the same time that Tango made a whining sound in the back of his throat.

Not a growl, but still a sound of distress.

Vanessa stopped dead in her tracks, reaching out to tightly grab his arm. "Did you hear that?" she whispered.

"Yes." Isaac's pulse kicked up and he instinctively pushed Vanessa behind him in an effort to protect her. "Call the police."

The movement in the bushes increased and Tango strained on his leash as if desperate to rush over.

Was Boyd hiding in there? Did he right now have a gun trained on them?

For a split second, his mind went back to the moment his chopper had been hit by enemy fire, spinning helplessly out of control. Temporarily lost in the past, he let go of Tango's leash and the dog took off straight toward the bushes.

No! Stay focused on the here and now!

"Tango!" His voice came out in a strangled cry, but the golden retriever didn't listen. The dog disappeared into the bushes.

Leaving Isaac as the only protector for Vanessa.

TWO

Vanessa wasted several precious minutes fumbling in her bag for her phone. When she finally found it, she punched in the emergency number for the base police. "This is Lieutenant Gomez and I'm with Captain Isaac Goddard. We're on the corner of Webster and Viking and have reason to believe Boyd Sullivan is hiding in the bushes. Hurry!"

"I'll send someone over," the Security Forces dispatcher promised.

She kept the phone in one hand and gripped the back of Isaac's uniform with the other. Her entire body began to shake, and she abruptly understood a small part of what Aiden and Isaac went through while battling their illness.

The thought of coming face-to-face with Boyd Sullivan made her break out in a cold sweat. She'd never felt helpless and vulnerable like this, until tonight. First the attack, and now this.

"The cops from the south gate are closest," she said in a low voice. "I'm sure they'll be here soon."

"I know." Isaac's hands were fisted, his elbows

flexed at his side, as if he were expecting a physical fight.

Tango emerged from the bushes, tail wagging. He stood looking at them for a moment, then turned to duck back between the branches.

She frowned. "What was that about?"

"I'm not sure. Tango is a therapy dog, but he's still trained well enough to know when danger is near."

"So, Boyd isn't hiding in there?"

"Probably not. Stay here. I'll be right back." Isaac took a step forward, but she didn't let go of his uniform, choosing to go with him rather than remain on the street alone.

"Vanessa, you should stay here." Frustration was audible in his tone.

She shook her head. "Better to stick together."

Tango came out of the bushes again, gave a sharp bark and wheeled around to return to the brush. She relaxed her grip on Isaac's uniform, sensing the dog wanted them to follow.

Surely, the golden wouldn't lead them into harm's way.

"Call off the cops," Isaac said, parting the branches with one hand and using his flashlight app on his phone to illuminate the darkness. "False alarm."

She inwardly debated letting the police come anyway, since she needed to report her attack, but she would rather talk to Justin personally. Decision made, she called the dispatcher back, confirming there was no immediate danger and that the call could be canceled. She slipped the phone back into her bag, then crept closer, hearing the rustling and odd whimpering sounds before her eyes landed on a cluster of puppies.

"Did we find some of the lost dogs?" Six months ago, Boyd Sullivan or his accomplice had sneaked onto base and let nearly every single K-9 in the Working Dog Program out of their kennels, a little over two hundred of them. Over time many of the lost animals had been found, but there were still several missing, including three extremely valuable German shepherds named Glory, Scout and Liberty.

"I'm not sure. There are four pups here, but it's odd because there's no sign of the mother. I doubt the mother is one of the lost dogs or we would have found her by now. The puppies appear healthy and well cared for, so I don't think she abandoned them without a good reason."

"She must be one of the training dogs, don't you think? Maybe she was attacked by a coyote?" It was horrible to think of a pack of coyotes ganging up on the mom, who likely would have attempted to lure the predator away from her babies. "We have to try to find her."

"Agreed, although we need to get these pups to safety first." He gestured to the puppies. "These look to be a few weeks old—not that I'm an expert. And they're snuggled together to stay warm."

"My house is at the end of this block. Let's bring the puppies there and get them warmed up, then let the cops know what happened." Vanessa wondered how Aiden would like the puppies. Her brother tolerated Eagle, her Doberman, but didn't find any comfort in the animal. And while she was hopeful he'd connect with a therapy dog such as Tango, he'd already failed in the first attempt to match him up. Ruby, the first dog who'd been assigned to him, had been a loving Irish setter, but Aiden hadn't connected with Ruby on any level. Perhaps the adorable puppies might have a better chance of getting through to him.

Not that there was any guarantee that Master Sergeant Westley James, the lead trainer at the K-9 training center, would allow her and Aiden to care for them. Although if the mother wasn't one of the missing dogs, maybe he wouldn't mind?

She sent up a quick prayer, asking for God's grace and mercy in keeping the puppies and the lost mother safe.

"You take two, and I'll take two," Isaac said, gathering a couple of the puppies in his broad hands and handing them over. She cradled them against her chest, marveling at the softness of their fur and their adorable faces.

"When we get the puppies settled and you're safe, I'll come back and search for the mother," Isaac said. "I'll also check with the veterinary clinic. They might have an injured dog that may belong to these pups."

"All right." As her small ranch home came into view, Vanessa picked up the pace, suddenly desperate to see her brother. She'd been gone far longer than her normal twelve-hour shift, and Aiden didn't always handle being on his own very well.

The house was mostly dark except for a lone light in the corner of the living room. Awash with guilt, she shifted the puppies to one arm, and fished for her keys to unlock the door. Using her hip, she pushed the front door open and stepped inside.

"Aiden? It's me, Vanessa. I'm home."

Isaac followed her inside, but remained near the

doorway, instinctively giving her brother time to adjust to the presence of a stranger.

"Aiden?" She swept her gaze over the living room, then noticed her brother sitting on the floor in a corner of the room, his face buried in his hands. "I'm sorry I'm late," she said in a low voice. "But look what I found. Puppies!"

Aiden lifted his head, his gaze darting anxiously around the room, and instantly zeroing in on Isaac and Tango standing near the door. "Who is he?" Aiden asked harshly, his expression contorted in a mask of anger. "Why is he here?"

Her heart sank as she realized how Aiden had struggled in her absence. Eagle came out of the kitchen to greet her, but with her hands full, she couldn't give her canine protector the attention he deserved.

She stayed focused on Aiden. "This is Captain Isaac Goddard, and he helped me bring the puppies home. Maybe you could hold them while I find a box to put them in?"

Aiden's gaze remained fixed on Isaac for a long moment before he finally noticed the squirming animals in her arms. Her brother's expression softened and he rose to his feet.

"Where did you find them?" he asked in a hushed tone.

"In the bushes near Webster and Viking," Isaac said from the doorway. "Four pups. I'm sad to say their mother seems to be missing. We're hoping she's getting care at the vet."

She wished Isaac would have remained silent, concerned that Aiden would become upset again from simply hearing his deep voice, but she needn't have worried. Aiden's gaze locked on the puppies and he came over to take one of them from her hands, bringing him up to his cheek.

"They're so soft," Aiden whispered. He met her gaze. "There's really four of them?"

"Yes." She handed him the second pup and then stepped back, subtly swiping at her damp eyes. The way her brother responded so positively to the puppies was more than she could have hoped for. "I'll find a box."

"There's one full of old movies next to my bed," Aiden said. "Just dump them on the floor."

She took a moment to give Eagle a welcoming rub between the ears before hurrying into Aiden's bedroom to empty the box of movies. When she returned, she was shocked to see that Isaac had come farther into the room and was standing less than three feet from Aiden.

What was he thinking? Shouldn't he have stayed near the door? What if Aiden freaked out again?

"Found it," she said as she rejoined them. Isaac set his two puppies in the box first, then her brother did the same. When she realized she'd been holding her breath, she let it out in a soundless sigh.

Tango and Eagle sniffed at each other curiously, but both dogs were trained well enough not to growl. Tango in particular was a calm, sensitive dog, the kind she'd hoped to get for Aiden one day.

"The pups might be hungry." Aiden's expression was full of concern.

"You're right," Isaac said in a low, nonthreatening tone. "They'll need warm milk for starters, but I'm not sure if cow milk is good for them. Vanessa, why don't you call the training center to see what you'll need to do in order to care for the puppies?"

"Good idea." She picked up her bag and dug out her phone. The call to the training center was immediately picked up by Master Sergeant Westley James, the training center operations director.

"This is Lieutenant Vanessa Gomez. Captain Isaac Goddard and I found four puppies, without any sign of the mother. We're not sure what breed they are, maybe a cross between a Lab and a rottweiler. We'd like to foster them, if you'll allow it."

"Found them where?"

"Less than a block from my house on Webster." She glanced at Isaac, then added, "Captain Goddard is going to head out to find the mother, see if she's somewhere close by. In the meantime, would you like us to bring the puppies into the vet?"

"That would be good. I'll meet you there."

"Okay, but if you don't mind, Aiden would really like to help foster the puppies." She knew Westley was aware of Aiden's need for a therapy dog and how miserably her brother had failed with Ruby. "It would be a great experience for us. Please? Just tell us what you'd like us to do."

There was a pause then a sigh. "Okay, you and Aiden can foster them for now. But I'm warning you, it's a time-consuming process. Any idea how old the puppies are?"

"We're not sure," she admitted. "But they're bigger than newborns. Maybe a few weeks?"

"I hope you're right, because we have a better chance of success if they're at least three to four weeks old. Once we determine how old they are, you can get the appropriate commercially prepared puppy formula and instructions on how to start solid foods, along with how to housebreak them."

"We can do that. Thank you." The wave of relief was overwhelming. She disconnected the call and smiled at Aiden. "Westley gave us permission to foster, but warned me it's a lot of work."

"I don't mind." Aiden held the cardboard box in his arms as if he wasn't ever going to let it go, the expression on his face full of wonder and joy.

"Great. Then we've been ordered to bring them to the vet, and they'll provide everything we need."

"Okay." To her surprise, Aiden looked at Isaac. "We should probably take my sister's car, right?"

"Good idea."

Vanessa blinked the sting of tears away at Aiden's tentative acceptance of Isaac. Already they were bonded by the puppies and with that as a foundation, it was possible that Isaac's willingness to talk to Aiden would also help him learn better coping strategies.

Being attacked by Boyd Sullivan may have been the worst part of her day, but finding the puppies turned out to be the absolute best thing to have happened.

There was no doubt in her mind that these four tiny balls of fur were exactly what Aiden needed to help battle his illness.

And she'd do anything in her power to see her tormented brother relax and smile again.

Anything.

Isaac easily saw himself in Aiden's demeanor, from the tense anxiety emanating from the young man's very

being, to the fear and anger darkening his brown eyes, replicas of his older sister's.

The kid was young, barely twenty from his estimation, and suddenly Isaac wished that the minimum age to enter the military was older than a mere eighteen.

Not that he wasn't proud to serve his country, because he was. After all, he'd gone straight into the Air Force Academy in Colorado, and from there to flight school to become an Air Force combat pilot. By the time he'd served his first tour overseas, he'd been twenty-three.

Now that he was thirty, his first tour seemed a lifetime ago.

There was no way to prepare for being deployed, although the various branches of the military did their best. Logically, he knew it wasn't as if every airman, soldier, marine or seaman experienced combat, but still, the exposure to violence certainly took its toll.

Which was why he still hadn't signed the paperwork to reenlist. Returning to the air as a pilot wasn't an option now. He'd never risk other lives by flying with PTSD. Which left a huge question mark on his future.

But that was not a problem to solve tonight.

As they stepped outside to Vanessa's car, he did a quick sweep of the neighborhood, looking for any sign of the puppies' mother. Tango helped, but he came up empty-handed.

He climbed into the car beside Vanessa, and she drove directly to the veterinary clinic. The vet, Captain Kyle Roark, greeted them when they arrived.

"Westley called me about the puppies. I think I may have the injured mother inside. Someone turned her in a few hours ago. She suffered a rather serious animal bite that required surgery to repair. I think she'll be fine, but I'll need to watch her closely for the next few days for signs of infection."

"Is she one of the training dogs?" Isaac asked.

Kyle shook his head. "No microchip. But I'm concerned there may be a link between this dog and the person who let the others go."

Isaac didn't like the sound of that.

Kyle took the puppies into an examination room to assess their condition. He returned a short while later with good news.

"They're all surprisingly healthy, and they look to be about four weeks old." He glanced at Vanessa and Aiden as he continued, "I'll give you some supplies you'll need to foster them, okay?"

"That would be great," Vanessa agreed.

Isaac had noticed how protective Aiden was of the puppies, and hoped Vanessa was making the right decision allowing him to help foster them. Not that he thought Aiden would hurt them in any way, but Isaac knew how horrible it was to be separated from an animal you'd bonded with.

He missed Beacon with an all-consuming intensity. For several days, after Beacon had saved his life in Afghanistan by dragging him by the back of his flight suit away from the burning chopper, he and the dog had hidden together in enemy territory while waiting to be rescued. Losing his best friend and Beacon's handler, Jake Burke, had been horrible. During those endless hours after the crash, Beacon had been his only source of comfort. Although even Beacon's reassuring presence couldn't keep his guilt at bay.

Then the USAF search-and-rescue chopper had ar-

rived. The pilot had done a routine flyby, then circled around to land on a small level spot close to where he and Beacon had holed up. Getting into the chopper hadn't been easy, but by the time the rebels had begun firing at them, the pilot had gotten them airborne.

At first, he'd been overjoyed at being rescued, but when they'd landed in Kabul and he was separated from Beacon, his whole world had come crumbling down.

Not only had he failed Jake by crashing the chopper that caused his buddy's death, but he'd failed in keeping Jake's K-9 as he'd promised when they'd first begun flying together. Six months of red tape and politics and he still didn't have Beacon home.

But tomorrow was the day. Less than twenty-four hours and he'd have Beacon home where he belonged.

I'm trying, Jake. Just like I promised. I'll bring Be con home!

Before the crash that had taken his buddy's l he might have reached out to God for solace. Bu anymore. These days, he didn't feel much like ing to God.

"We're ready to go," Vanessa said, pulling hi his troubling thoughts. "Isaac? Is everything

He nodded and cleared his throat. "Yep. A

Aiden had obviously delegated himself the caregiver as he picked up the box of puppies a waited for Vanessa to get the door.

Vanessa's SUV had plenty of room for the t them and the two dogs Eagle and Tango, not to tion the box of squirming puppies. Aiden kept th on his lap the entire time, unwilling to let the pu out of his sight.

Interesting how the Doberman stayed close to Vanessa's side, obviously trained to protect her. If that was the case, why hadn't she brought the dog to the hospital with her? Granted, an intensive care unit probably wasn't an appropriate place for a dog, but surely under the circumstances an exception could be made for Vanessa's safety.

Aiden took the puppies inside and began feeding them, using the commercial formula provided by Kyle. He'd barely gotten settled when there was a sharp knock at the door. Vanessa answered it, looking surprised to see the head of the Security Forces standing there, his tall male Malinois named Quinn at his side.

"Why didn't you answer your phone?" Captain Justin Blackwood asked as he shouldered his way inside. Quinn stayed close, well trained enough not to react to the other dogs.

"Oh, I left my bag in the car while we were at the vet's office," she said with a guilty wince. "Sorry about that."

Justin scowled, glancing between Isaac and Vanessa. "Tell me what happened at the hospital."

Vanessa glanced over her shoulder, then gestured for the men to come into the living room. "I don't want my brother to hear this."

"Fine, but I need details," Justin insisted.

Isaac crossed his arms over his chest as Vanessa explained how she took a shortcut out of the hospital, going through the hallway containing offices to get to the other side of the building closest to the front entrance when the lights went out and strong hands grasped her around the neck.

Hearing her talk about the attack she'd suffered

made Isaac angry all over again. Justin's expression turned grim as he inspected the red marks around her throat, already beginning to bruise.

"Did he say anything?" Justin asked.

Vanessa nodded. "I asked why and he said, 'Because you're in my way.'"

"In the way?" Isaac repeated. "Doesn't make sense. In the way of what?"

She shrugged her shoulder. "I don't know. In the way of his mission to eliminate the people who wronged him?"

"Then what happened?" Justin asked, looking at Isaac.

He and Justin knew each other from when they'd attended the Air Force Academy, but at the moment, he understood his friend was in charge of the ongoing investigation.

"I heard what sounded like a scuffle in the darkness and called out to see what was going on," Isaac said, relating his side of the story. "I found the light switch and turned it on in time to see Vanessa fall to the floor and a guy wearing black disappear down the stairwell. I made sure she was all right and left Tango with her, before going after him. Unfortunately, he was long gone."

"No description?" Justin asked, his blue eyes intense.

"Medium height and build. He wore a ski mask that covered his head so I can't tell you his hair color." Isaac shrugged. "I wish I could be more help."

Justin raked his hand across his short blond hair and let out a heavy sigh. "No proof that Sullivan is the assailant."

Vanessa bristled. "Boyd sent me a red rose. Who else has a grudge against me?"

Justin lifted a brow. "You were the one who said that you helped Boyd by providing first aid to him. Why would he have a score to settle with you?"

Vanessa's dark eyes flashed with anger. "I don't know, but I didn't attack myself, Captain."

"Come on, Justin, you know she didn't," Isaac added. "I saw him. And if I hadn't shown up, she'd be dead."

Justin let out a heavy sigh. "You're right. The marks on her neck are for real, so that means somewhere deep in Boyd's twisted mind, he's decided to come after her."

"And nearly killed her," Isaac added.

"I know, I know." Justin sounded tense.

Isaac arched an eyebrow at his friend. "Can you offer her round-the-clock protection?"

"I can have someone stationed outside the house at night, but we're short staffed so I don't have someone available to follow her around all day."

"I can protect her during the day." The offer popped out of his mouth before he had a chance to consider the consequences.

"I'm not sure that's necessary," Vanessa protested.

"I'll take whatever help you can give us," Justin said, ignoring her protest. "I'll keep someone stationed outside the house from nineteen hundred hours until zero seven hundred." He turned toward Vanessa. "You're probably safe enough here at home with Eagle during the day, but don't go anywhere alone, and keep Eagle close, too. Dobermans are instinctively protective."

"Nessa?" Aiden's voice from the doorway drew their attention. The young man cradled a puppy in his arms and stared at his sister with fear in his eyes. "What's going on?"

"Nothing to worry about, Aiden." Vanessa crossed over to give her brother a hug. "Just extra protection for a while, no big deal."

Aiden didn't look as if he believed her, and Isaac didn't blame the kid. Vanessa was a lousy liar.

It was clear that Vanessa's life being in jeopardy impacted her brother in a big way. Isaac suspected if anything happened to her, Aiden wouldn't be able to handle it.

And even though he'd only just met Vanessa tonight, Isaac wasn't sure he'd be able to handle it, either.

THREE

"How are the puppies doing?" Vanessa crossed the living room to stand next to her brother. "We have to think of names for them."

Thankfully, Aiden's attention was diverted by the active pup in his arms as she'd hoped. "I was thinking about naming them after national parks. The two females could be Denali and Shenandoah, the males Smoky and Bryce."

"Those are awesome names." Vanessa stroked the puppy he held, wondering how they'd be able to tell them apart.

"You're in danger from Boyd Sullivan, aren't you?" Aiden asked abruptly.

She looked into her brother's mature-for-his-years gaze and knew she couldn't lie. "Yes. I'm afraid so. But Captain Blackwood is going to keep a cop stationed here at the house at night, so there's really nothing to worry about."

"You need to keep Eagle close from now on," he said, his tone full of reproach. "Even at the hospital."

"I will." She forced a smile, knowing that Eagle

wouldn't be allowed in an intensive care unit. "Do you need help feeding the rest of the litter?"

Aiden shook his head. "No, thanks." He looked at Isaac and Justin for a moment. "Make sure she's safe," he said, before disappearing into the kitchen.

"He'll be okay," Isaac said, reassuringly. "Just because he's struggling with an illness doesn't make him helpless."

"I know, but at twenty he's already been through so much…" Her voice trailed off as she glanced back at Aiden before joining the two men and the K-9 beside Justin. "Anything else you need from me?"

"Tell me more about this injured female dog that's at the veterinary clinic," Justin said with a frown. "It might be connected to our investigation."

"Captain Roark said she isn't from the training center," Isaac said. "The mother is a chocolate Lab, and the puppies appear to be a mix. Although he did mention there may be a link between this dog and the missing four from the training center."

"I have to agree," Justin said thoughtfully. "In speaking with Gretchen Hill, the newest trainer on Westley's staff, she thinks it's possible the Olio Crime Organization may be involved with the dognapping. Three dogs are still missing, but when Patriot was returned, her collar had the letters *POCO* engraved on it. It's probably not a coincidence that the last three letters stand for Olio Crime Organization. Maybe even Property of Olio Crime Organization. I wonder if the injured chocolate Lab belonged to them at some point."

Vanessa's stomach clenched. "We assumed she was attacked by an animal, like a coyote, and Captain Roark agreed based on her wounds. Besides, how would someone from the Olio Crime Organization get on base? Fake ID? Or help from someone inside?"

"Anything is possible," Justin admitted. "A stretch, but possible. After all, it's looking more and more like the missing dogs were taken off base." He shrugged. "Right now, I can't see how the injured Lab would be linked, but I need to keep an open mind. There could be a connection."

She shivered at the horrible thought. "I'm sure it's a coincidence. We know coyotes have gotten on base, so it's likely she was injured protecting her pups. I doubt her presence on base is the result of foul play."

"Yeah, you could be right." Justin's tone lacked conviction.

There was a moment of silence before Isaac glanced at his watch. "It's late, we should go."

Justin nodded. "Don't forget, Vanessa, you'll have a cop stationed outside your house at night, and don't go anywhere alone. I placed a call while you were speaking with Aiden, and someone should be arriving any minute now."

"Understood." She walked the two men and their respective K-9s to the front door, Eagle staying close at her side. "Thanks," she said, glancing at Isaac. "For everything you did for me tonight. If there's ever anything I can do for you, just let me know."

A hint of a smile played at the corner of Isaac's mouth. "You're welcome." He paused, then added, "If you're not working tomorrow, maybe you'd be willing to go with me to meet Beacon's flight. It's due to arrive at fourteen hundred hours."

"I'm off tomorrow and would love to go. The idea of sitting around my house all day isn't at all appealing." She was touched that he'd asked, although she told herself not to read more into the offer than what it was at face value. A friend inviting a friend along to meet a plane, nothing more.

"Great, I'll stop by to pick you up." Isaac smiled again, then turned and followed Justin out to the street, jumping into Justin's jeep beside him.

She stood in the doorway for a long moment, her hand resting on Eagle's silky head, watching as the red taillights of the jeep vanished into the darkness. She gave Eagle a few minutes out in the yard to do his business, then called him back inside.

A tall man with a Security Forces badge on his chest and navy blue beret on his head stepped up beside the doorway, offering a quick salute. "Everything okay, ma'am?"

"Of course. Good night." She returned the salute and ducked back inside. When Eagle joined her, she closed and locked the door behind her.

Aiden was still in the kitchen with the puppies, calling them by name as he worked on potty training. He took them out of the box and placed them on a spread of newspaper, praising them as they did their business.

"Good boy, Bryce. Denali, you're doing great, too. Shenandoah, stay on the paper, please. Smoky, you're a rock star. Nice job."

Watching her brother interacting positively with the pups filled her with hope and encouragement for his future.

Thank You, Lord, for answering my prayers!

"Are you going to keep them in the kitchen for the rest of the night?" she asked, when all four pups had been cared for and the newspaper mess cleaned up.

"I'll stretch out on the sofa for a while, keep the box nearby." Aiden didn't meet her gaze and she knew that he often slept in the living room with the light on in an effort to minimize the nightmares.

"Let me know if you need help," she said. "Otherwise I'll see you in the morning."

Aiden nodded. She turned toward her bedroom when he called out, "Nessa?"

She looked over her shoulder. "What?"

"That guy, Isaac, is he going to be hanging around often?"

She hesitated, unsure how to respond. "We're just acquaintances, that's all. I only just met him today. Isaac has been suffering from nightmares and flashbacks, too, Aiden, just like you. We're not going to get involved, if that's what you're asking. Tomorrow the dog who saved his life will be returning to base, so I'm going along to support him while he picks Beacon up. I hope you don't mind, especially since Isaac seems determined to protect me."

Aiden shrugged. "I'm glad you won't be alone, but I don't want him to hurt you, the way that Leo guy did."

She was surprised to realize Aiden had heard about her brief, misguided relationship with Leo Turner, an Air Force captain and one of the physicians she worked with at the hospital. She must have mentioned him during their FaceTime sessions while Aiden was overseas.

It bothered her that now that Aiden was back on base, he'd probably heard the rumors about Leo's multiple affairs. Her brother had enough to worry about without adding her welfare to the mix.

"Isaac and I are barely friends," she repeated firmly,

for her brother's sake and her own. "He just wants to help keep me safe, that's all."

Bad enough she'd become the laughingstock of the ICU because she'd been oblivious to Leo's antics, until she'd seen the evidence for herself.

She didn't know if Isaac was the kind of guy to cheat on his girlfriend. What did it matter? She wasn't interested in a relationship. And Isaac had enough going on in his life, between Beacon's delayed homecoming and getting better.

Anything more than friendship would only get in the way.

Isaac had thought for sure he'd have trouble sleeping, considering the way he'd witnessed the attack on Vanessa, but surprisingly, he slept the entire night through.

He scrubbed a hand over his sandpaper-rough jaw and marveled at how many times he'd slept through the night without being awoken from a nightmare. Months ago, they plagued him nightly. Now he only had them once a week, maybe less.

Logically, he knew that his issues weren't just because of Jake's death and the horrible experience of being shot out of the sky, but a culmination of several treacherous flights over enemy territory, always under fire, yet somehow managing to escape.

Until that last flight had killed Jake and his copilot, Kevin, leaving only him and Beacon.

He took several deep calming breaths to keep the memories at bay. Maybe he'd slept well because today was the day Beacon was coming home. The thought made him smile and he bolted out of bed to let Tango outside, then to shower, shave and dress.

As always, he took care of Tango first, providing the dog food and water, before grabbing a quick bite to eat. As he nursed a cup of coffee, his gaze fell on the reenlistment paperwork sitting in the center of the kitchen table. He pulled it toward him.

For several long seconds, he stared at the spot where he was supposed to sign his name. He'd have to pass a medical and psychological exam no matter what job he decided to do if he stayed in the Air Force, so why bother filling the stupid thing out? Maybe this was his time to get out of the military.

And do what?

He had no idea.

With a rough gesture, he shoved the paperwork aside. He still had several weeks yet before it was due. No point in dwelling on it now.

Today he only had one priority. Beacon.

After finishing his coffee, Isaac stared at Tango for a moment, then decided to take the dog for a walk. It was going to be a long day if he didn't find some way to occupy his time until Beacon's arrival.

Instantly, his thoughts went to Vanessa, Aiden and the four fostered puppies Aiden had named after national parks.

Nope. He shook his head. Not a smart idea to get too emotionally involved. Although, he had offered to talk to Aiden, hadn't he? And to keep Vanessa safe during the daytime hours?

Yes, he had.

She'd be safe with Eagle until he got there, so he took a quick walk around base to clear his head. He was secretly glad her house wasn't far from his as it would be easier to keep an eye on her.

He was thrilled when he'd found his place, located on a dead-end street not far from the veterinary clinic.

Dogs were known to suffer from PTSD, too, and he used the fact to argue why he was the best fit for Beacon. With Jake gone, he was Beacon's best chance. He'd even gotten Jake's younger sister, Jacey, who was also a dog handler currently deployed overseas, to add her support.

He and the dog were two wounded warriors who deserved to be together. And the powers that be within the Air Force had finally agreed with him.

He ran into Captain Kyle Roark outside the veterinary clinic and waved him down. "Hey, any news on the female dog you operated on last night?"

Kyle nodded. "So far, she's holding her own. I have her on heavy-duty antibiotics and I'm keeping her sedated because of the extensive sutures. In my professional opinion she was likely attacked by a coyote."

"I'm happy to hear she's recovering. And an animal bite is better than the idea of humans hurting her on purpose," Isaac said with a heavy sigh. "At least now there's no reason to believe there's a possible connection to the Olio Crime Organization."

Kyle grimaced. "I'm not sure they're entirely out of the picture. No one living on base has reported a lost dog, aside from the training dogs that are still missing. A person within the crime ring may have sneaked the dog on base because she was pregnant and they wanted nothing to do with a litter of pups."

"Why?" Isaac asked. "They could dump her anywhere."

"Who knows how these guys think?" Kyle shook his head. "It's just odd that she showed up here, that's all. Anyone on base would take better care of their pet."

"Maybe." Done with the discussion of the injured dog, he turned his attention to the topic that had him anxious. "Are you going to be around later when Beacon arrives?"

Kyle's face lit up with a wide smile. "Wouldn't miss it."

"Great. I'll see you then." Isaac waved and took Tango home.

He did some chores around the house for a couple of hours. By lunchtime, he decided he couldn't stay home alone any longer. He picked up three meals to go from Carmen's, his favorite Italian restaurant, and brought them over to Vanessa's house.

He walked up to Vanessa's front door and rapped lightly.

A series of high-pitched yips could be heard from inside, making him smile. Vanessa opened the door looking surprised to see him.

"Isaac, I wasn't expecting you for a couple of hours yet."

"I brought lunch from Carmen's," he said, lifting the bag as proof. "Enough pasta for all three of us."

Her expression softened as she realized he'd included Aiden. "Come in. Lunch will be a welcome break from the nonstop potty training going on around here."

"I can only imagine," he said with a chuckle. Inside, he nodded to her brother.

"Hey," Aiden greeted him cautiously.

"How are our four national parks doing?" he joked.

"They're awesome." Aiden placed the puppies back in their box. "Something smells good."

"Carmen's is always amazing." He set the bag in the center of the kitchen table as Vanessa and Aiden washed up at the sink. Vanessa was more beautiful than he remembered, with her dark wavy hair hanging loose around her shoulders. She wore her dress blues and he appreciated her delicate features.

Whoa, wait a minute. What was wrong with him? He'd been around plenty of attractive women before. Even since his former fiancée, Amber. None had even remotely raised his interest.

Until now.

Vanessa pulled out plates and silverware while Aiden fetched three bottles of cold water from the fridge. He opened the bag and pulled out the aluminum to-go containers of pasta, each still warm from the oven.

Vanessa took her seat, bowed her head and began to pray. "Dear Lord, we thank You for this food we are about to eat and for the friendship You have blessed us with. Keep Beacon and the puppies safe in Your care, Amen."

Despite his reservations about God and faith, Isaac thought of Beacon and found himself responding with a heartfelt "Amen."

"Amen," Aiden added, glancing down at the box of pups near his feet.

The spaghetti and meatballs from Carmen's were delicious, and as they ate, they discussed the puppies at length. Isaac was impressed at the responsibility Aiden was taking in caring for them, especially the way he'd found a way to identify each one by sight corresponding them to their name. Denali had a notch in her right ear and Shenandoah was the runt of the litter. Bryce had a small tan spot on his belly while the fur on the tip of Smoky's tail was black.

Vanessa seemed more relaxed, too, despite the bruises that darkened her neck. He was relieved to hear she'd used ice to keep the swelling down.

The time flew by and he soon realized they had to leave to avoid being late. He asked Aiden if he wanted to come with them, but the young man insisted on staying home to watch over the pups.

"I'm going to try some mash while you're gone," Aiden said with a wry grin. "Better that Nessa isn't here to watch, since Kyle warned me about how messy they'll get."

"Maybe you should feed them in the bathtub," Vanessa suggested, her expression half-joking. "That way you can contain the mess and go right into giving them a bath."

Aiden laughed at her suggestion. Vanessa looked so surprised, Isaac wondered how long it had been since she'd heard the sound of her brother's laughter.

Fostering the puppies was obviously a great job for him.

"I'll leave Eagle here with Aiden," Vanessa said. "I'm sure Beacon doesn't need the added stress."

Isaac hesitated, then nodded. "It's probably best."

"We'll take my SUV," Vanessa said. "I'll drive."

"Okay." After loading Tango into the back, he slid into the passenger seat beside her, wishing he was armed. But only Security Forces cops were armed on base, and as a pilot he couldn't carry one without special permission. As she drove, he kept a sharp eye out for anything suspicious.

Canyon Air Force Base was huge, covering over 600 acres. Roughly seven thousand people were on base at any given time, mostly military and some civilian. The airport runway was located on the north side of the base, a distance from the housing section.

Isaac swiped his damp palms against his jeans, unaccountably nervous. This was the moment he'd been waiting for since he arrived stateside.

Vanessa glanced at him. "Looks as if there's already a big crowd of people gathered there along with the media. I hope I can find a place to park."

Normally he wasn't a fan of crowds, but knowing Beacon would be getting off the plane in less than thirty minutes made the discomfort worthwhile.

They found a parking spot in front of the command offices and walked from there. With Tango at his side, he kept close to Vanessa as they walked, again keeping a keen eye on their surroundings. No easy task since there were literally hundreds of airmen and officers around.

Once they were situated at the front of the crowd, he shielded his eyes from the sun with his hands, scanning the sky for the plane. There! A surge of excitement hit hard, although he told himself not to get his hopes up too high.

It wasn't that long ago that he'd stood in this exact same spot waiting for another plane supposedly bringing Beacon home. Only it hadn't been Beacon on the plane, but some other K-9. He'd suffered a relapse that night, despairing over the possibility of never seeing Beacon again.

At least this time, Vanessa was with him. He glanced over at her, amazed at what a difference it made to have someone supporting him.

He enjoyed spending time with her. She was easy to be around. Not nearly as demanding as Amber had been, or maybe he was just in a better place now than he had been back then. Considering he'd only first met Vanessa less than twenty-four hours ago, it was crazy how much he'd come to depend on her.

Only as a friend, he reminded himself. Once he had Beacon home, he wouldn't need this weird connection he seemed to have with her.

As the sound of the plane engine grew louder, his heart beat faster with anticipation. The C-130 Hercules aircraft used for transporting troops emerged from the clouds, approaching the runway.

When the wheels hit the tarmac, he realized he was holding his breath and clutching Vanessa's hand tightly in his. He released her with an apologetic smile.

She rested her hand in a reassuring gesture on his arm. The C-130 coasted to a stop, then angled toward the hangar.

He couldn't stop himself from taking several steps forward, urging Vanessa along with him as they separated themselves from the crowd.

The cargo door in the rear of the plane opened and a short runway ramp was lowered to the ground. A man wearing his battle dress uniform emerged first, holding a leash, then he caught a glimpse of the familiar black-and-gold German shepherd.

Beacon!

He must have shouted the dog's name out loud because the crowd burst into spontaneous applause.

The dog stood still for a moment, nose quivering. The animal must have picked up his scent, because he abruptly wheeled toward him, ears perked forward as if in recognition.

"Come, Beacon," he said, taking a step forward to meet the dog who'd saved his life.

The loud crack of a gunshot rang out.

The entire area erupted into panicked chaos. The airman holding Beacon's leash yanked the dog hard, diving for shelter as people began running and screaming, dropping to the ground and desperately seeking cover.

Vanessa pulled him down beside her. "Are you all right?" she asked breathlessly.

"I think so." He was numb from shock, but checked himself for signs of injury. No blood? Good sign. Thankfully, he didn't see any injuries on Vanessa or Tango, either. "I have to get to Beacon."

He tried to pull away from her, but she hung on with steely determination. "No, you might put the dog in danger."

The possibility made him sick to his stomach. Was Boyd really out there shooting at them? Why would Beacon have been the target? It didn't make any sense for Boyd to come after the dog.

What in the world was going on?

FOUR

From her position low on the ground, Vanessa swept her gaze over the area, searching for any sign of injuries to the people near her. It wasn't easy, because most of them were running every which way, desperate to seek shelter from the gunman.

No evidence of bleeding wounds so far, but that fact was only slightly reassuring.

Boyd must have been the one who'd taken a shot at Isaac's dog. Who else would do something so crazy? But why? It didn't make any sense.

Unless Beacon hadn't been the true target. She shivered, despite the heat.

She remembered feeling something whizzing past her face. Was it possible the bullet was meant for her? She'd been standing in a direct line in front of Beacon.

"Beacon!" Isaac's voice was hoarse with fear. "I don't see him. Where did he go?"

She tightened her grip on Isaac's arm, determined to prevent him from running directly toward the plane. "The handler will keep him safe."

Isaac didn't look convinced. "I think Beacon may be hurt. It looked as if he may have hit the side of the

C-130 when the handler jerked him out of the line of fire."

"We'll check it out." She kept her tone calm, worried Isaac might suffer a relapse between the sound of gunfire and the crazed chaos surrounding them. The crowd was thinning so they couldn't stay here. They needed to move. The runway was clear, but what if the gunman was still out there? Better to try losing themselves in the crowd.

"This way." Isaac rose to his feet, clutching Tango's leash.

She nodded. "I'm with you."

Isaac gently propelled her protectively in front of him, toward a large group of people exiting the area, as if he'd read her mind. "We'll circle around to the other side of the plane."

"Understood." She continued to watch the people around her for injuries. Security Forces cops swarmed the area in search of the gunman. She hoped and prayed they'd find Boyd, or whoever the shooter was.

"Help me! Someone please help me!"

Vanessa stopped and turned toward the sound of crying. A woman was crouched on the ground, clutching her ankle.

"Isaac, hold up." She detoured toward the sobbing woman, kneeling beside her. "What happened?"

"I was crushed in the crowd." The woman swiped at her face in an attempt to pull herself together. "I was pushed down and someone stomped on my ankle." She sniffed and swiped at her face again. "Do you think it's broken?"

The ankle was swollen and starting to bruise, so

it was entirely possible. "You'll need to have that x-rayed."

Isaac dropped down beside them. "We better call an ambulance."

On cue, the wail of sirens rose above the din. "They're almost here." She glanced at Isaac. "I'll stay here with her, if you want to go ahead to find Beacon."

His gaze flickered with indecision, but then he shook his head. "I'm not leaving you alone. We'll make sure she's cared for first."

She flashed a grateful smile and then attempted to catch the attention of an ambulance that had just arrived. But she was just one person in a sea of people. Fortunately, one of the cops noticed her and ran over.

"Crowd crush injury," Vanessa told him. "I'm a nurse from the hospital. Do you know if anyone else is hurt?"

"Only minor bumps and bruises so far from what I can see." The cop's expression was grim. "Could have been much worse."

"I know." Vanessa silently thanked God for watching over the men and women on base. "She needs a lift to the hospital for X-rays."

"Understood." The cop jogged toward the ambulance, waving his arm. Two paramedics jumped out, grabbed a gurney and headed in their direction.

Once the injured woman was safely on her way to the hospital, she turned back to Isaac. "Let's go find Beacon."

He nodded, placing his hand on the small of her back, keeping her ahead of him.

Hyperaware of the heat radiating from his fingers, she did her best to stay focused. As they approached the opposite side of the runway, two cops identified by their dark blue berets stepped in front of them, blocking their path. They both saluted, then stood at attention.

"We need to get through," Vanessa said, after returning their salute.

"This is a restricted area, ma'am," the taller of the two said. "You both need to clear out."

Isaac frowned. "I'm Captain Goddard, and Beacon is my dog," Isaac said in an authoritative tone. "I need to make sure he's okay."

"I'm sorry, sir, but as I said, this is a restricted area," the taller cop repeated. "I'm afraid you'll need to make other arrangements."

She felt Isaac tense and tried to think of a way past these guys.

"Isaac?" A familiar voice caught her attention. She glanced over to see Captain Kyle Roark, waving at Isaac from behind the two cops. The vet sent him a reassuring smile. "Don't worry, I have it under control."

"Is Beacon all right?" Isaac asked. "He wasn't hit by gunfire, was he?"

"No, he wasn't shot. He'll be fine." A shadow crossed Kyle's eyes. "Try not to stress about this, Isaac. I'm taking Beacon to the clinic. You can visit him there later, okay?"

The hope in Isaac's eyes wilted away, replaced by panic. "The clinic? Why? What happened?"

Kyle made his way through the cops to face Isaac. "Beacon wasn't hit by a bullet or anything, but he does have a bad laceration and possible head injury."

Isaac went pale. Vanessa grasped his arm in an attempt to keep him grounded. "Did that happen when the handler jerked him out of the way?"

Kyle winced. "I'm afraid so. His head hit the edge of the plane. But I think he's going to be fine. This is merely a precaution, okay? I just want to watch him for a couple of days."

"Yeah, I get it." Isaac's shoulders slumped in defeat.

Vanessa's heart went out to him. She knew how much Isaac had been looking forward to being reunited with Beacon. Especially after all this time. Six months was a long time and now this latest issue was yet one more obstacle thrown into his path.

The vet turned and made his way back through the restricted area to care for Beacon.

"Come on, Isaac." She forced a smile. "Let's get out of here. Beacon is in good hands with Kyle."

"I know." Isaac's voice was low and rough. "I hope he's right about the injury not being serious. If anything happens to Beacon..." His voice trailed off.

She squeezed his arm. "It won't." She edged away from the two cops, unwilling to talk in front of them. Isaac and Tango followed. "Let's try to look on the bright side. Beacon is here, on base. Home at last. He'll be staying with you 24/7 in no time."

Isaac nodded, but the light in his eyes had been replaced with a dull acceptance.

They walked to her SUV in silence. She opened the doors and windows to let the hot air out, then cranked the air-conditioning.

"Do you want me to drop you off?" she asked, as Isaac stared blindly through the windshield.

"Huh?" He turned toward her. "No, I'm here to help keep you safe, remember? And after this latest issue, I think I need to stick close."

She nodded, put the SUV in gear and edged into

traffic. There were still a lot of people trying to get away from the landing strip, so there was no point in hurrying.

Isaac seemed to be concentrating on the area around them as she drove, and she was touched by his determination to protect her. She couldn't remember the last time any man had cared enough to do something like this.

It took a full thirty minutes to go five miles, but from there traffic thinned so that it was easy enough to reach her house. She hoped Aiden hadn't heard about the gunshot. She didn't want him to worry or to have a flashback.

Her brother had come so far in one day of taking care of the puppies. She'd hate to see him suffer a relapse now.

When she pulled into her short driveway, though, she was surprised to find Captain Blackwood and his K-9, Quinn, standing outside her front door. When Justin caught sight of her, he and Quinn loped over to meet her.

"Did you see what happened?" he demanded.

She suppressed a sigh and glanced at Isaac. He shrugged and slid out from the vehicle, letting out Tango. She came around the front of the car to join the two men.

"No," she said, belatedly answering Justin's question. "I heard the shot, and then everything went crazy. I thought I felt something whizz past me, but honestly, I can't even tell you what side of the landing strip the shot came from."

"I didn't see much, either," Isaac added. "My gaze was focused on Beacon. The handler reacted instantly, jerking Beacon out of the way, but the dog suffered a head injury as a result."

"The shooter must have been Boyd." Justin let out a frustrated sigh. "And he must have help on base, or I'm sure we would have found him by now."

"I don't understand why he'd shoot at Beacon," Isaac said. "That's the part that doesn't fit with what I've heard about the Red Rose Killer."

Vanessa straightened her shoulders and lifted her chin. "I'm not sure Beacon was the target."

Justin pinned her with a glare. "Who was?"

"Me." She lifted her hands, palms facing upward. "Boyd attacked me last evening. Why not follow me out to the airstrip to try again?"

"I don't know about that." Justin frowned.

"I was directly in front of Beacon." Vanessa touched the bruises on her neck. She felt certain, deep in her bones, that she was the intended target.

Only this time, she'd put Isaac, Beacon and hundreds of other innocent people in danger, too.

Isaac wanted to put a reassuring arm around Vanessa, but held back, loath to make her uncomfortable in front of Justin. Isaac cleared his throat. "Actually, it's possible I was the target."

Vanessa reared back, staring at him in surprise. "You? Why?"

He shrugged. "Why not? Beacon's homecoming has been in the news for months now. Everyone on base knew I'd be there today."

"Have you met Boyd? Talked to him? Interacted with him in any way?" Vanessa peppered him with questions. "Is there a reason for him to be upset with you?"

"No, I've never met him that I'm aware of," Isaac admitted. "I've studied his mug shot. His face doesn't ring any bells. But this guy seems to be offended at the smallest transgression. For all I know, he thinks I did something to him. Or maybe he doesn't like me stealing his limelight."

Justin crossed his arms over his chest with a scowl. "Boyd never made it out of basic training, so there's no reason for him to go after a combat pilot. Or your dog."

"What's your theory, then?" Isaac pressed.

Justin's lips thinned. "I don't have one yet. I prefer to deal with facts. Vanessa may have been the target, but at this point, all I know is that someone fired a shot in a crowd of people. I've heard from Security Forces that no deaths or gunshot wounds have been reported. That tells me the shooter isn't a Canyon sniper. Someone we trained wouldn't have missed."

Vanessa nodded slowly. "You're right. The shooter must be someone with less experience."

"Boyd fits the profile," Isaac said. "Considering he didn't finish basic."

Justin's smile was grim. "You're right, Boyd wasn't a good marksman. He could have been aiming for Vanessa and missed by a mile."

"Or he could have simply shot toward the dog out of spite," Vanessa offered. "Can't you see him sitting back and enjoying the sheer panic he'd caused?"

"I can." Isaac suspected Boyd had self-esteem issues; why else would he be lashing out at anyone who'd wronged him? He glanced at Blackwood. "You need to catch him, and soon."

"Tell me about it." Justin's tone was flat and hard. "He's making all of us look like idiots by being on the loose this long. Which is why I'm convinced someone is helping him." Justin shot an apologetic glance at Vanessa. "I'm sorry I ever suspected you. Since you helped him once before, I thought it was possible you did again."

Vanessa massaged the bruise around her neck. "I understand, but trust me. I wouldn't help him do something like this. I'm a nurse, so it's hard for me to ignore someone who is hurt." Her brown eyes were large and pleading. "That's the only reason I stopped to help Boyd all those years ago."

Isaac stepped closer to her in a show of support. "You're not a suspect anymore," he reassured her.

"No, you're not." Justin regarded her thoughtfully. "But it's clear you're next on Boyd's list. Be careful, understand? Keep Isaac and Eagle close."

"I will."

The front door opened and Vanessa's brother stood there, looking at the three of them uncertainly. "Something wrong?"

"Hi, Aiden. How are our national parks doing?" Vanessa dropped her hand from her throat and headed toward her brother.

"Great." There was a lack of enthusiasm in his tone.

Justin excused himself and headed to his vehicle with Quinn. Isaac moved toward Vanessa and Aiden, hoping she didn't close her brother out of the truth.

Suffering from PTSD was bad, but being lied to never helped. People thought softening the facts was the way to go, but he'd always hated it.

"Someone shot a gun into the crowd at the landing strip," Vanessa said. "But no one was seriously hurt. Beacon suffered a laceration and head injury, though."

Aiden's fingers closed into fists. "Boyd?"

"Possibly, but we don't know for sure." Isaac stepped forward. "I want you to know I'll be staying close in order to protect your sister."

Aiden's brown gaze, so much like Vanessa's, met his. "Thanks for telling me the truth."

"Always," Isaac said.

"I'm sorry about Beacon," Aiden added.

"Me, too. But he's in good hands with the vet." Isaac glanced anxiously at his watch. How much time did Kyle need to examine the dog? He needed to see Beacon up close with his own eyes, to know without a shadow of a doubt the dog would be okay.

"The puppies are doing okay?" Vanessa asked again.

This time, Aiden's smile was genuine. "They're great. They loved the mash I gave them. And I fed them in the bathtub, like you suggested. Worked perfectly. And they enjoyed the bath that followed."

"I'm glad." Vanessa gave her brother a one-armed hug.

Isaac was thrilled to hear Aiden was bonding with the puppies. He knew from personal experience how helpful it was to have that connection.

Like the one he had with Beacon.

"I'd like to head over to the clinic," he told her. "But don't want to leave you unprotected."

"I'll go with you," Vanessa offered.

He hesitated. It seemed that ever since he'd rescued Vanessa from Boyd's attack, he'd been leaning on her for strength and support. That wasn't what he'd intended. She was the one who needed his protection.

And staying here at her house with Eagle at her side

was probably the best way to keep her safe. Being with him at the airstrip hadn't worked out so well.

"It's okay," he said, averting his gaze. "I'm just going to pop in quick. I won't stay long."

"I'm coming with you," she said, as if she wasn't taking no for an answer. "You shouldn't be alone at a time like this."

He'd hated it when Amber had treated him like an invalid, but for some reason, he didn't have the same negative emotional response toward Vanessa. "Are you sure you won't feel safer here at home?"

"I'm sure. Justin said I could go out as long as I was with someone and had Eagle with me. I'd actually like to see how Beacon is for myself." Her brow puckered in a frown. "Especially since his injury is my fault."

"It's not," he protested. "If you want to blame someone, blame Boyd. He's the bad guy, not you."

Vanessa turned toward Aiden. "Are you okay here for a while longer?"

"Sure." Aiden glanced over his shoulder at what Isaac assumed was the box of puppies. "It's almost time for the next bout of potty training."

Vanessa laughed and Isaac found himself smiling in response to the joyous sound.

It had been a long time since he'd had something to be happy about.

"Come, Eagle," Vanessa called her K-9 protector out and came up beside Isaac. "This time, you're coming with us. Time to go."

"I'd rather walk, if you don't mind," Isaac said. He didn't trust himself behind the wheel since he'd been back on base. And especially now, after the recent gunfire.

Vanessa readily nodded in agreement, and the walk

to the veterinary clinic didn't take long. Isaac held the door open for her, then glanced over his shoulder, feeling as if someone might be watching them.

But of course, there wasn't. He told himself he had a right to be paranoid, but he also knew it was a side effect of his PTSD. Most of the time he was able to keep it under control.

Today had been a challenge. When the shot was fired, for a moment he'd gone back to the cockpit of the chopper he was manning when it had been struck by enemy fire. And though he'd tried to focus on Beacon, the dog had vanished from sight.

With Vanessa's help, he'd managed to stay grounded in the here and now. But it hadn't been easy.

"Can I help you?" a perky receptionist greeted them warmly when they entered the clinic. She eyed their respective dogs. "Do your dogs need a checkup?"

"No," Isaac said. "I'm here to see Beacon."

The receptionist looked confused for a moment. "Oh, you mean the shepherd that was just brought in by Captain Roark?"

"Yes. Will you please let him know Captain Isaac Goddard is here?"

"Of course, please excuse me." She disappeared, and it was all Isaac could do not to follow her back to find Kyle and Beacon for himself.

Thankfully she returned a few minutes later. "Captain Roark will meet you in exam room number three."

Finally! "Thank you."

He and Vanessa crowded into the small room with Eagle and Tango. He thought about Tango, wondering if Westley would reassign the therapy dog to someone else once Kyle discharged Beacon into his care. Tango was a great dog, and Isaac was sure that he'd be a wonderful companion to the next airman who needed him.

Two long minutes later, the door opened and Kyle came in carrying Beacon. The dog was large, so it was no easy task, but the vet gently placed Beacon on the exam table.

The laceration along the side of Beacon's head made the blood drain from Isaac's face. Vanessa grabbed his arm and moved closer.

"Hey, Beacon." Isaac eased forward and held out his hand for the animal to sniff. "Remember me?"

Beacon buried his nose in Isaac's hand, his tail thumping against the stainless-steel table. Isaac felt tears of relief burn his eyes, and he bent down to press his face against Beacon's fur.

"You're home now, boy," he murmured. "I'm not leaving you again."

"He's going to be fine, Isaac," Kyle said. "I did a CT scan of his brain and there's no sign of an intracranial bleed. Give me a day or two to watch over him, and Beacon here will be good to go."

Isaac nodded, knowing it was for the best that he stay at the clinic. The animal's health was all that mattered.

He felt Vanessa's hand on his back and between her comforting touch and Beacon being home, he knew he'd reached another milestone on his path to healing.

And for the first time in a long while, he silently lifted his heart and thanked God for everything he'd been given.

FIVE

The way Isaac hugged Beacon warmed Vanessa's heart. The bond between the dog and the fighter pilot was palpable. Clearly, after all this time, they deserved to be together.

Thinking of the reckless gunshot fired into the crowd at the landing strip earlier that afternoon made her temper simmer.

Boyd Sullivan needed to be found and arrested soon.

"Thanks, Kyle," Isaac murmured, stepping back from the exam table. "I appreciate getting a few minutes with Beacon, and everything you're doing for him."

"That's my job, remember?" Kyle pointed out with a smile. "But hey, I'm glad he's doing okay, too."

She dropped her hand from Isaac's back, suddenly feeling self-conscious about the warmth of his skin radiating through his shirt. "That makes three of us."

"Do you mind if I stop by again tomorrow morning?" Isaac asked.

Kyle hesitated, then nodded. "Sure, we open at zero nine hundred."

It was on the tip of Vanessa's tongue to offer to accompany Isaac again, but then remembered she was scheduled to work a twelve-hour shift. Besides, Isaac didn't need her assistance. Sure, he was supposed to protect her, but if she were honest with herself, she would admit she wanted to be with Isaac for purely selfish reasons.

Because she liked him. More than she should. They'd only just met, but she felt as if she'd known him for weeks rather than a couple of days.

They left the veterinary clinic, stepping back into the bright sunlight. Isaac paused to sweep his gaze over the area, taking his role as protector seriously. She looked at him curiously, and he shrugged, gesturing toward the Winged Java Café. "It seems safe enough. Would you like some coffee or sweet tea?"

His request caught her off guard, but her heart leaped with anticipation. "Sure."

They walked down the street with the dogs between them and claimed the first empty outside table shaded by a yellow umbrella. Isaac held out her chair for her, but remained standing. "What would you like?"

She normally didn't drink caffeine this late in the afternoon. "An iced coffee, but decaf, please."

"You got it." Isaac went inside to place their order. She felt funny sitting there waiting for him, as if this was some sort of date.

It wasn't. Isaac was just being courteous. The same way he'd been when he'd brought over lunch from Carmen's.

She went still. Was she wrong about what was happening here? Maybe Isaac was trying to be more than just friends with her.

The image of her ex-boyfriend Leo filled her mind.

He'd seemed nice, and protective and wonderful, too, but it had all been an act.

Leo liked women. Many women. She had no clue why he'd bothered to ask her out.

She pushed the memories aside and mentally reaffirmed she wasn't in the market for a relationship. Isaac was a nice guy who had not only agreed to protect her, but to talk to her brother. That was all that mattered.

To keep herself busy, she pulled out her cell phone and scrolled through her email. A notification from the anonymous blogger popped up. Ever since the blogger had put the idea that Vanessa was helping Boyd out there for everyone to read, she'd made sure to follow the blog so she could keep track of the ridiculous allegations.

Filled with dread, she clicked on the link to read what the phantom person had written this time.

Boyd Sullivan is back on base and obviously dumber than a box of rocks for continuing to come back to Canyon. He should be on his way to Mexico by now. That he's not means he's just asking to be caught!

"Are you kidding me?" she whispered in horror.

"What?" Isaac set down her iced decaf and then dropped his lanky frame into the seat beside her.

She gestured to her phone. "Have you seen the anonymous blogger's latest post?"

"May I?" He held out his hand for her phone. His emerald gaze grew tense and serious as he read the note. "Talk about waving a red flag at a bull."

"Right?" She sipped her iced coffee and shook her

head. "Why would anyone rile Boyd up like this? The man is already unstable. Something like this could easily send him off the deep end."

Isaac returned her phone. "I agree. I'm surprised Justin hasn't shut down the site."

"Freedom of speech, right?" She couldn't hide the hint of bitterness in her tone. "If Boyd was the one who took the shot at Beacon, or at me, then we know he's armed. He could decide to go on a wild shooting rampage at any time." The very thought made her stomach churn with nausea. "Do you know how many people he could kill before one of ours manages to take him out? Too many."

"He's had plenty of time to stage a mass shooting if that was his goal," Isaac pointed out. "In my opinion, he's enjoying this cloak and dagger stuff far too much."

"You're probably right," she agreed, but she couldn't shake the sense of despair. Over the course of the last several years there had been too many mass shootings to count.

Some people would do anything for a moment of glory. Was Boyd Sullivan one of them?

She truly didn't know.

Isaac changed the subject to comment on Aiden's progress with fostering the pups. "He's really doing great with them, isn't he?"

She smiled. "Yes, I'm amazed at the difference in just twenty-four hours. As much as I feel bad for the pups' mother being attacked by a coyote, I'm thrilled Aiden has been given this opportunity."

"I'm happy to keep checking in on him, if you think it will help."

She was touched by his offer. "That would be great.

I know Aiden still has a ways to go, but every step forward gives me hope for his future."

Isaac nodded. "It's the same for me, too. Knowing Beacon is close is a start, but…" His voice trailed off, then he softly continued, "I'm still not sure how much I'll be able to manage my symptoms."

She understood that this was his way of warning her there couldn't be anything romantic between them. That he didn't consider her anything but a friend. And she felt foolish that she'd thought, even for a minute, otherwise.

"I know, Isaac." She lightly brushed her fingers over his tanned forearm. "It's okay." She drained her iced coffee. "Thanks again, but I should head home. I need to encourage Aiden to eat something for dinner, and I have to work early in the morning."

Isaac stood, his brow furrowed. "You're going to take Eagle with you to the hospital tomorrow, right?"

She glanced down at her faithful Doberman and reluctantly nodded. "Yes, I'll take him. But it's not going to be easy to look out for his needs while also caring for my patients. He can't be in the middle of the ICU with me and patient care has to come first."

"I don't want you to go to the hospital alone, so I'll walk you over early in the morning. That way, I can give you a hand with Eagle during your shift," Isaac offered.

"All right," she agreed, understanding he was just fulfilling his role as her protector.

He walked her home. Her phone rang as they reached the door. She pulled it out, frowning when she didn't recognize the number. It began with the base exchange, so she went ahead and answered it.

"Hello?"

"Next time, you won't get away," a gravelly voice said.

"Who is this?" she demanded, looking at Isaac. She could feel the blood draining from her face. Holding her breath, she waited for a reply.

But there was nothing but silence on the line.

"What did he say?" Isaac asked.

She drew in a shaky breath. "'Next time, you won't get away.'"

"I think I need to sleep on your sofa tonight," Isaac said, his expression troubled. "I don't like this at all."

"I don't, either." Her fingers trembled as she slipped the phone back in her pocket. Had the voice belonged to Boyd? She couldn't say one way or the other for sure. She swallowed hard and tried to pull herself together. "There will be a cop outside my door starting at nineteen hundred hours."

"Then I'll wait." Isaac put his hand in the center of her back and escorted her into the house.

She was grateful for his presence. They helped with the puppies until nineteen hundred hours.

"Are you sure you don't want me to stay?" Isaac asked.

"I'm sure." She forced a smile. "We'll be fine."

He hesitated, clearly not happy, but reluctantly nodded. "See you tomorrow, then."

"Okay." She watched him walk away and the minute he was out of sight, regretted her decision.

Later that night, as she slipped into bed, she relived the phone call over and over.

Then she bolted upright in bed as a horrible thought

entered her mind. If the caller had been Boyd, how in the world had he gotten her personal cell number?

The next morning Isaac showed up as promised to escort her to the hospital. Vanessa reluctantly brought Eagle along, hoping it was the right decision to keep the animal inside for her twelve-hour shift. Dogs were not allowed in the intensive care unit, but her boss agreed that she could keep Eagle in the back nurses' work-room, away from the patients.

Still, it wasn't easy to concentrate when she was worried about how Eagle was doing.

Halfway through the day, Isaac arrived to take Eagle outside. She gratefully took him into the back room and handed him Eagle's leash. "Take him for a nice long walk, okay? I feel terrible that he's cooped up in here with me. It's not like Boyd is going to attack me while I'm in the middle of the ICU. Last time, he caught me in the hallway alone. Trust me, I won't make that mistake again." The more she thought about her agreement to keep Eagle here with her, the more upset she became.

"Okay, how about if I take Eagle back to your place, then bring him back here when your shift is over?" Isaac suggested. "That way he won't be cooped up back here, and you'll be safe."

"That would be great." She wanted to give Isaac a hug in thanks, but managed to keep herself in check. "If you're sure it's not too much of an inconvenience?"

"It's fine." He waved off her concern. "You're fin-ished around nineteen thirty, correct?"

"Yes, but just know that sometimes I don't get out right away," she cautioned. "Patient care comes first."

"Understood. Come on, Eagle, let's get out of here." Isaac took the dog's leash and left the critical care area.

Vanessa downed a quick bite to eat, then returned to her duties. After transferring one patient to the regular floor, she was notified of an impending admission.

A short while later, the ER brought up a young man lying unresponsive on a stretcher, with a breathing tube in his airway.

"Twenty-five-year-old white male found down outside the food services loading dock," the ER nurse informed her. "Suspected drug overdose, but tox screen is pending."

Vanessa frowned at the young man. "He looks familiar."

"Not surprising. His name is Joseph Kramer and he's a civilian employee working in the housekeeping department. He often cleans right here in the ICU."

"You're right, that's exactly how I know him." Vanessa began hooking the patient up to the monitor while the respiratory therapist connected him to the ventilator.

"He's a nice guy," the ER nurse said, her expression grim. "But it's not looking good. His shift started at fourteen hundred and he wasn't found until fifteen thirty." She shrugged. "No way to know how long he was down. Illegal drugs are really creating havoc in our society these days."

True, that. Vanessa began to assess her newest patient for herself. She was forced to agree; Joe Kramer's condition was extremely serious. One of his pupils was blown, and the other wasn't very reactive upon her exam.

She quickly called the neurosurgeon to let him know

of the deterioration of Joe's neurological status. As she injected the mannitol the doctor ordered to help bring down the swelling in his brain, her ex, Captain Leo Turner, strolled up to the bedside.

"Hi, Vanessa," he greeted her as if they were still on friendly terms. "I didn't hear about a new trauma patient being admitted."

She gritted her teeth and finished giving the medication. "That's because this patient isn't a trauma patient. He is being comanaged by pulmonary medicine and neurosurgery."

"What happened?" Leo asked, oblivious to her discomfort.

"Drug overdose," she admitted tersely. She dropped the syringe in the sharps container. Then she tucked her stethoscope buds into her ears, effectively shutting him out, and listened once again to her patient's breath sounds. She didn't like the way they were diminished in the bases, and wondered if her patient had aspirated while he was lying on the ground. If so, he might have pneumonia brewing.

Leo continued to stand at her patient's bedside, as if he had no place more important to be. Unfortunately for her, the trauma bay must be quiet this evening.

When she couldn't delay any longer, she pulled the stethoscope from her ears. She moved away from the bedside, even though her patient was not awake to hear them. "Do you need anything else, Captain Turner?" she asked pointedly.

Leo met her gaze full-on. "Do you want to get together after work?" he asked. "We could head over to Carmen's for dinner."

Seriously? Was he out of his mind? Seeking her out

at work? Asking her out after she'd caught him cheating on her? Talk about nerve! "No, thank you," she said politely, even though every instinct in her body wanted to rant and rave at him.

"Vanessa? Line one is the lab. They have a critical value on one of your patients."

"Excuse me." Vanessa gratefully latched onto the excuse to leave. She avoided the phone sitting on the desk near Leo in favor of taking the call at the unit secretary's desk. "This is First Lieutenant Gomez."

"We have a critical lab value on the drug screen that was sent down an hour ago on Joseph Kramer," the lab tech informed her. "The amount of Tyraxal in his blood stream is critical at four times the expected level."

"Four times the expected level," she repeated as her mind whirled.

This was now the third Tyraxal overdose in the past two weeks.

And why would a civilian janitor be taking Tyraxal anyway?

She'd already called the psychiatrist, Lieutenant Colonel Flintman, once, but he hadn't gotten back to her yet. She knew the kindly psychiatrist was busy treating patients, such as her brother, but this was important. Obviously, she needed to contact him again.

In her humble opinion, this latest and greatest PTSD medication was causing far more harm than good.

After bringing Eagle back, Isaac spent the rest of the afternoon with Aiden and the puppies. The kid really seemed to be doing great, and he hoped Vanessa's brother continued to make good progress.

Although, he knew only too well how easy it was

for the nightmares to pop up out of nowhere, holding you hostage in their dark and terror-filled grip.

He did his best to broach the subject of recovering emotionally after combat with Aiden, but the kid didn't want to discuss it. Refused to even look him in the eye, so Isaac dropped the issue and focused on helping to care for the pups.

At one point, Tango stretched out between him and Aiden, and he'd noticed the young man scratching the therapy dog behind the ears a few times and smiling when Tango licked his fingers.

Hadn't Vanessa mentioned something about Aiden not connecting with the therapy dog previously assigned to him? Now that Beacon was home, maybe he could convince Westley to shift Tango's assignment to Aiden.

He made a mental note to broach the subject with the master sergeant once Kyle had discharged Beacon into his care. It would be great to know that Tango's talents would be used where they were desperately needed.

Aiden cooked a pizza for dinner and afterward, Isaac cleaned up the dishes while Aiden took the pups out for another round of housebreaking.

"Aiden, do you mind if I leave Tango here with you?" Isaac offered Tango's leash. "I need to take Eagle up to meet your sister so we can walk her home."

"That's fine," Aiden agreed. The younger man met his gaze. "Don't hurt my sister. She's been through enough."

It was on the tip of his tongue to ask exactly what Aiden meant, but he swallowed the urge. For one thing, Vanessa should be the one to tell him if she was so inclined. And secondly, he didn't want to encourage her brother to break her trust.

"The last thing I want to do is to hurt Vanessa," Isaac said. "I'm not looking for a relationship and as far as I know, she's not, either. We're friends, okay?"

Her brother didn't look convinced. "That's what she said, too."

Ouch. That stung, more than it should considering he'd just told Aiden the same thing. He forced a smile. "See? We're both on the same page."

Isaac took the Doberman's leash, impressed at how well the dog walked calmly alongside. Considering the animal was trained to protect Vanessa, he'd expected a little trouble.

Maybe all the time they'd spent together over the past few days had smoothed things over. Eagle was already accustomed to having Isaac around.

He timed it so that he arrived at the hospital ICU right at Vanessa's quitting time. If she had to work later, that was fine; he didn't mind waiting around for her to finish.

Keeping her safe was all that mattered.

He didn't have to wait long. Ten minutes later, Vanessa came out of the ICU, swiping at her eyes. It took a second for him to realize she'd been crying.

"What happened?" He stepped closer, eyeing her with concern. "Are you hurt?"

"No, I'm fine." Her facial expression belied her words, especially when her eyes filled with tears.

Watching her silently weep shredded his heart. There had to be something wrong, but what? He instinctively pulled her into his arms, cradling her close. He half expected her to push him away, but she didn't.

Instead, she wrapped her arms around his waist and sagged against him as if she didn't have the strength to hold herself upright.

Eagle didn't like her distress, either, and he kept shoving his nose between them, as if trying to figure out what was wrong.

Vanessa pressed her face against his chest for several minutes before she dragged in a deep breath and lifted her head. "I'm sorry for getting your shirt all wet."

"Vanessa, my shirt isn't important, but you are. Talk to me. Tell me what happened."

She sniffed and swiped at her eyes again, then absently patted Eagle's head. "I lost a patient, a young man just a few years older than Aiden."

"I'm sorry," he murmured, lightly stroking a hand down her back. "It can't be easy to lose young patients like that."

"It's not just losing them, it's *how* we're losing them." A flash of anger glittered in her brown eyes. "He died from what the doctors are calling an accidental drug overdose."

His chest tightened as he remembered how difficult it had been not to succumb to drugs or alcohol after returning from Afghanistan. There was still the rare occasion that he was tempted to shut down the nightmares using artificial means.

"It's not easy to function when you're suffering from PTSD."

"That's just it." Vanessa tipped her head back and looked up at him with large red puffy eyes. "This is the third overdose of Tyraxal in the last two weeks, but the patient wasn't an airman or pilot who'd been in combat. He was a civilian working here in the hospital as a janitor."

He frowned. "That's odd."

"Isn't it?" Vanessa's gaze reflected her concern. "And it's worse because he shouldn't be taking PTSD meds. Makes me mad to think some guy is selling his prescription to make a few bucks."

"Maybe you should report this to Justin," he suggested.

"I will." Her shoulders slumped. "But that won't bring Joseph back. If you had seen his mother sobbing at his bedside…" Her voice trailed off and her eyes filled with fat tears. He wanted, needed, to comfort her, so he pulled her close and cradled her against his chest.

And when she lifted her head to look up at him, it took every ounce of willpower he possessed to fight the insane urge to kiss her.

SIX

Vanessa couldn't breathe, her lungs seemingly frozen as she stared into Isaac's incredible green eyes. Every sense was on alert, anticipating his kiss. When he took a step backward, releasing her, she was hit by an acute sense of loss.

She dragged in a deep breath and attempted to pull herself together. Isaac's embrace had distracted her from what really mattered. This wasn't about her growing awareness of the tall, sandy-haired and handsome combat pilot, but about the senseless death of a young man.

It was impossible to get the image of Joseph's mother sobbing at his bedside out of her mind. But she wiped the dampness off her face and squared her shoulders. The young man's death had hit hard, mostly because she kept thinking about how it would feel to lose Aiden.

There had been times she'd feared her brother would go down that dark and desperate path. Recently, Aiden seemed to be holding his own. Therapy with the base psychiatrist and fostering the puppies were working.

"Ready to walk home?" Isaac held out Eagle's leash, which she gratefully accepted.

"Yes." There wasn't anything more she could do about Joseph Kramer's death now. She'd left another message with Lieutenant Colonel Flintman to let him know about this latest Tyraxal overdose and the fact that the patient wasn't even in the Air Force. What she really wanted to know, but doubted the lieutenant colonel would tell her, is which one of his patients might be selling his prescription on the street.

No other explanation as to how Joseph Kramer had gotten the medication made sense.

"I wonder if the Tyraxal that guy had been given was laced with some other drug?" Isaac mused as they walked along the sidewalk. "Maybe a narcotic? For all we know, it could be some concoction put together by that Olio Crime Organization Justin mentioned."

"It's possible, but I'd think that drug would have shown up on the toxicology screen, as well."

"True." Isaac rubbed the back of his neck. "I still think you need to talk to the captain."

"I will, although I may wait until morning." She frowned, suddenly realizing that only one dog was between them. "Where's Tango?"

"Oh, I left him with Aiden." Isaac offered a crooked smile. "He didn't seem to mind."

Was it possible her brother was now emotionally ready to connect with a therapy dog? She'd secretly been a little worried about what would happen when the puppies no longer needed fostering. She doubted that Aiden would be allowed to keep all four of them. She'd been hopeful that maybe her brother would be able to keep one.

Something she'd intended to keep praying for.

"I was hoping that once Kyle releases Beacon from his care, we could arrange for Tango to be reassigned to your brother. The second time might be the charm."

She smiled. "Funny, I was thinking the same thing. Either getting Tango assigned or maybe being allowed to keep one of the pups."

"Both might be good options," Isaac said. "Tango is a trained therapy dog, so he'd be able to offer Aiden support right away. Meanwhile, it's possible Westley will assign someone to show Aiden how to train the puppies, too."

She stopped for a moment and turned to face him. "That's brilliant! Aiden would absolutely love it."

"I'm happy to put in a good word for him." Isaac's low, husky voice sent ripples of awareness down her arms.

"I'd appreciate that, and so would he." With an effort to ignore her out-of-control attraction to the man, she resumed walking. Eagle stayed close at her side. "It's highly competitive to be assigned to the dog handler program. Not sure an E-2 airman whose previous job was to do mechanic work on the fleet stands much of a chance."

"Is that what Aiden did in Afghanistan?" Isaac glanced at her curiously.

She nodded. "He doesn't like to talk about what happened, but I know that a suicide bomber was involved. A young local, barely old enough to drive, plowed directly into the fleet of parked vehicles. Aiden saw the whole thing, including the blast of the bomb and the death of his buddy."

Isaac winced. "How awful for him."

She nodded. "No worse than what you went through, I imagine."

"I flew combat for eighteen months straight, before our chopper was hit." Isaac shrugged. "I'd be dead if not for Beacon saving my life."

She rested her palm on his shoulder. His muscles tensed, so she quickly dropped her hand. They turned down Webster and seeing the veterinary clinic prodded her to ask, "How is Beacon doing? Did you visit him this morning?"

"Yeah, but unfortunately, his wound isn't looking great," Isaac admitted. "Kyle is going to switch antibiotics. If all goes well for a solid twenty-four hours, he'll consider discharging him the following morning."

"I'm glad to hear it." Vanessa felt awful about what had happened to Beacon, but she trusted Kyle Roark's instincts. If he wanted to watch Beacon longer, it was probably the right thing to do.

They approached the intersection of Webster and Viking, the corner where they'd found the puppies. She thought back, counting in her mind. Was it really just a few days ago? She shook her head in amazement.

It seemed she'd known Isaac for so much longer than that. She felt foolish for falling apart in his arms. Especially after he'd backed off, leaving an awkward silence between them. Obviously he didn't feel the same way.

Fine with her. Hadn't the debacle with Leo proven she couldn't trust her instincts around men? Was there something wrong with her that caused her to fall for men who weren't interested?

Enough of putting herself through the wringer for a man. She had her younger brother's mental health to consider. Along with staying focused on the patients she cared for.

The cop standing outside her front door gave a crisp salute as she and Isaac approached.

She and Isaac returned the acknowledgment with salutes of their own. "Thanks for walking me home," she said, taking a step up onto the porch. "Keep me posted on how things go with Beacon."

"I will." Isaac hesitated, then added, "I need to know if you're going to talk to Justin in the morning and what time. Or have you forgotten your promise not to go anywhere alone?"

The way her pulse jumped in anticipation was ridiculous. "I didn't forget."

"Great. Then I'll swing by at zero nine hundred," Isaac said. "Good night, Vanessa."

"Good night." She stood for a moment as he turned, then called out, "Wait. You forgot Tango."

He shifted toward her. "I guess I did."

It was telling that he wasn't nearly as connected to Tango as he was to Beacon. She slipped inside with Eagle, unleashing her protector. He ignored the golden retriever, who was stretched out on the floor next to the box of puppies pressed up against the sofa where Aiden slept.

She tiptoed in an effort not to disturb the sleeping pups. Tango lifted his head at her scent, his tail hitting the floor with a muffled thump in greeting.

"Come, Tango," she whispered.

The dog rose, stretched then trotted toward her. Eagle was slurping water from his bowl in the kitchen. She found Tango's leash, clipped it to his collar and took him outside.

"Thanks." Isaac took the strap from her hand, his fingertips lightly brushing against hers. Ignoring the tingle of awareness, she crossed her arms over her chest and stood for a moment, watching him head home.

Irrationally longing for something that could never be.

Isaac could feel Vanessa's gaze long after she disappeared inside the house.

He was losing what was left of his mind over her. He'd almost kissed her twice. And then in a rush to put distance between them, he'd almost forgotten Tango.

Yep, he was an unacceptable mess. Time to pull himself together and focus on what was important. Beacon, first and foremost, but then his career.

After Tango took care of business, he took the dog inside and glanced at the reenlistment paperwork sitting in the center of his kitchen table. It had been staring at him for days now, and he was still no closer to making a decision than he had been a week ago.

Not tonight, he told himself. Maybe he needed to make sure Beacon was over his ordeal before he could think about the future.

He didn't sleep well, but thankfully the nightmares weren't too bad. He'd had them, but each time he'd woken up, his heart pounding, he'd instantly known that what he was seeing in his mind's eye wasn't real.

A small step in the right direction.

The following morning, he took care of Tango, showered and then made himself a full breakfast, something he didn't do on a regular basis. He'd learned the importance of eating healthy meals even when he wasn't hungry, so he forced himself to make a full breakfast twice a week.

Bacon, eggs, hash browns and a tall glass of orange juice.

He was stuffed by the time he'd finished. A glance at his watch confirmed he had thirty minutes before he was due to head over to Vanessa's, so he cleaned up his breakfast mess and washed the dishes.

Not good that he was looking forward to seeing Vanessa again, as if it had been twelve days instead of twelve hours since he last saw her. But no way was he going to renege on his promise to keep her safe. He'd just have to get over it. Besides, he found himself curious about how a civilian janitor had overdosed on a PTSD prescription medication in the first place.

He wasn't sure why being with Vanessa was so different than what he'd experienced with Amber. But now wasn't the time to examine the reasons. Instead, he clipped on Tango's leash and headed outside. The October air held a distinct chill, but he didn't mind. The leaves on the trees were still 90 percent green, the colors only just starting to change.

In another week or two, the area would be glorious. By then he would have had to make a decision about whether or not to reenlist.

Later, he told himself. He'd deal with the paperwork later. As he approached Vanessa's place, he was surprised to see she was hovering in the doorway, waiting for him. When he came up the sidewalk, she hurried down with Eagle to join him.

"Hi. Are you sure Justin cares about these drug overdoses?"

"Why wouldn't he?" He glanced at her. "If it bothers you, it's important enough to report."

"You're right." She nodded, as if to dispel her lingering doubts.

He fell into step beside her, keeping the dogs as a buffer between them.

"I notice you like to walk," she said, eyeing him curiously.

He tensed for a moment, tempted to ignore the subject, then realized as a nurse she probably already knew. "Yeah. I don't want to drive until I know I won't have a flashback."

"I see." Her brow was furrowed. "Although I'm not sure how you'll know one way or the other until you try it."

She had a point; in fact, Flintman had encouraged him to drive, as well. "Maybe."

The walk to the Base Command took almost twenty minutes as the offices were on the opposite side of the base. When they arrived, they were shown into a large office and instructed to wait for Captain Blackwood.

"I hope that means there's news on the investigation," Vanessa said in a low tone. "We really need to capture Boyd before he can harm anyone else."

"I'm surprised the blatant note from the blogger hasn't spurred some sort of retaliation by now." Isaac shook his head. "Stupid move, taunting a killer like that."

"Maybe that's partially what Justin is working on," she agreed. "They're having enough trouble finding the guy without other people meddling in the investigation."

Fifteen minutes later, Justin and his K-9, Quinn, strode in. "Sorry to keep you both waiting. Please, have a seat," he said after they'd saluted.

"Not a problem." Vanessa dropped into the seat closest to the window, leaving him with his back to the door.

He didn't like it, but tried to ignore the weird paranoia that plagued him.

"Any news on Boyd?" Vanessa asked.

Justin's expression was grim. "Unfortunately not. I've had cops scouring the base from one side to the other, but no one has seen him." He paused, then added, "Or admitted to seeing him."

Vanessa leaned forward in her seat. "I have a concern about several drug overdoses that I've seen in the past two weeks. Three in total, and this last death was a civilian."

Justin's brows levered upward. "A civilian from where? How did he get on base?"

"He works as a janitor at the hospital. A better question is, how did a civilian noncombatant get ahold of the prescription PTSD medication known as Tyraxal?"

Justin stared at her for a long moment. "That is a good question. What are your thoughts?"

"I can only speculate that one of our airmen has sold his prescription. Tyraxal offers great benefits, but it's also highly addictive." Vanessa glanced at Isaac for a moment, and he figured she was speculating about whether or not he'd ever taken Tyraxal.

He hadn't.

"Have you shared your concerns with Lieutenant Colonel Flintman?" Justin asked with a frown.

"I have, yes," Vanessa nodded. "I'm hoping he'll get back to me today."

"Why are you bringing this issue to me?" Justin asked, sitting back in his seat.

Isaac picked up the thread. "You mentioned the Olio Crime Organization when we found the puppies. Isn't it possible they're dabbling in drugs, too?"

"You're assuming they aren't already up to their ears in dealing illegal drugs," Justin said drily. "They're likely involved in all kinds of criminal enterprises, but three overdoses involving a PTSD drug?" He grimaced. "Not sure how that would fit in with their master plan."

"You're assuming they have a master plan," Isaac joked. Then he turned somber. "Seriously, isn't it possible they're branching out? We believe they may have targeted the base by stealing four highly valuable dogs. Why not try to sneak their greedy tentacles inside this way, too?"

Justin nodded thoughtfully. "You have a point, Isaac. I can't afford to ignore any potential link to the Olio Crime Organization." He turned toward Vanessa. "Keep your eyes open at the hospital, okay? There may be other overdoses that were treated on days you weren't working that you're not even aware of."

"I know. I've already considered that." Her expression was troubled. "The thought of there being even more…" She swallowed hard.

The urge to comfort her was strong, but Isaac curled his fingers into the palms of his hands and stayed where he was. Because next time, he might not find the strength to keep himself from kissing her.

"Anything else?" Justin asked, looking a bit impatient.

"No, sir." Vanessa pushed to her feet. "Thanks for your time."

"I always appreciate being kept in the loop," Justin

said. "Don't hesitate to contact me if you find other anomalies."

"Of course," she agreed.

Isaac stood and turned toward the door, feeling the muscles in his back and neck relax as his tension eased. No one was watching them or hovering outside the office doorway.

Tango wagged his tail, and he bent to scratch the golden between his ears. The dog wasn't Beacon, but he was a good companion nonetheless.

Vanessa and Eagle led the way outside. As they walked back toward Canyon Drive, he caught a glimpse of the Winged Java. "Care for a coffee?"

She looked surprised and he mentally kicked himself for not thinking before he spoke. Hadn't he decided that spending time with Vanessa wasn't smart? So why ask her to share coffee?

There was a pause before she finally nodded. "Sure, that would be great."

He wasn't disappointed in her response, which only proved how far gone he was.

The café wasn't far and the tables outside were surprisingly empty.

"I'll buy this time," she offered.

It was the perfect way to put his impulsive invitation back on friendship terms, but he couldn't do it. People could call him a chauvinist if they wanted, but he wasn't going to allow a woman to buy him coffee. Especially not since he'd invited her.

"I'll take care of it. You want an iced decaf or would you rather go for the full load of caffeine?"

"Full load, please." She plopped down in the same seat they'd used yesterday, looking exhausted, as if she hadn't slept well. No doubt she'd been upset about losing her patient to a drug overdose.

"Hang on to Tango for a minute, would you?" He handed her the golden's leash, then headed inside the café. He took his place in line and after a few minutes placed their order. As he waited, he tried to think of a way to broach the subject of their friendship.

By the time their coffee was ready, he still hadn't figured out how to bring it up without looking or sounding like an idiot.

He carried the coffee outside and couldn't help but smile when he found Vanessa speaking to both Tango and Eagle as if they were her kids.

Don't go there, he warned himself. They weren't dating, weren't a couple and no way was he going to fall in love, get married and have kids.

He couldn't even be a combat pilot anymore, so what did he have to offer Vanessa? Or any woman for that matter?

Absolutely nothing.

He dropped into the seat next to her and set her coffee down. "Talk to the dogs often?"

She flashed a brilliant smile. "Of course, and don't act as if you don't do the same thing. I've watched you with Beacon, remember?"

"Guilty as charged," he agreed. "But that's just because for three solid days Beacon and I were alone on the mountain and he was the only one I could talk to."

"Oh, Isaac." Vanessa's gaze was full of sympathy. "It breaks my heart when you say things like that."

It was the truth, but before he could say anything more, a sharp retort rang out and it took him a split second to realize that the sound was gunfire.

."Get down!" He lunged forward, grabbing Vanessa's arm and dragging her to the ground, using the table for cover.

People nearby screamed and ran, while he did his best to cover Vanessa's body with his. The sound of panic hit hard, and his vision blurred as nightmares from the past threatened to drag him into the dark abyss.

SEVEN

Vanessa couldn't believe it was happening again. The situation outside the Winged Java was eerily similar to the events that had transpired during Beacon's homecoming.

The wail of sirens indicated help was on the way. She tried to ease away from Isaac's bulky frame, but he clamped his arms around her, keeping her in place.

"So much blood," he whispered.

Blood? Where? Vanessa, scanned the area around them, but didn't see any evidence of injury. She didn't think she'd been hit, but maybe Isaac had? She squirmed again, trying to get a good look at him. The vacant expression in Isaac's eyes reminded her too much of how Aiden looked after a flashback.

"Isaac? Are you hurt?" She prayed her voice would get through to him.

He didn't answer.

"Isaac?" She shook his arm. "The cops are on the way. Are you hurt?"

"No, I'm fine." His voice was a bit stilted, but at least he'd answered. But he didn't move from beneath the table until the Security Forces cops swarmed the area. "You okay?"

"I'm fine," she assured him when they finally crawled out from beneath the table.

"Good." His color was back, although she could still see beads of sweat dotting his brow. Because of the close call? Or his flashback?

"What happened?" Justin Blackwood pushed his way through the cops.

"We were sitting and talking, when suddenly I heard gunfire," Isaac reported. "The shot came from the east."

"The training center?" Vanessa frowned. "You think it was a random shot?"

"No way." Justin swept his gaze across the area, then stepped closer to the table. The top of the umbrella had an oddly shaped hole in it. "The bullet went through here."

"Seems strange, unless someone was standing up on higher ground?" Isaac asked.

Higher ground? Vanessa looked over her shoulder. The hospital was a five-story building not far from the training center. "Are you sure the bullet came from that way?"

"I'm sure." Isaac looked at Justin, who nodded in agreement.

"I concur. It makes sense based on the trajectory."

Vanessa shivered, despite the warmth of the sun. "I guess this proves I was the target before, on the tarmac, too."

"It looks that way," Justin agreed. "Did either of you notice anything else? Anyone or anything out of the ordinary?"

"No." Vanessa felt guilty that she hadn't paid more attention to her surroundings.

Isaac's phone rang, and his gaze widened in alarm when he answered it. "Are you sure? Okay, I'll be right there."

Vanessa put a hand on Isaac's arm. "Who was that?"

"Kyle Roark. Beacon has had a setback. Apparently he's suffered a small intracranial bleed."

"Oh, Isaac. I'm sorry."

"Yeah." He stared at the phone for a moment, before slipping it into his pocket. "Kyle still thinks he'll be okay."

"Try not to worry," she said, putting her arm around his waist in a half hug. She hated feeling so helpless. "Captain Roark is a great vet. We can take comfort in knowing Beacon is in good hands."

Isaac didn't say anything in response and she suspected he wouldn't feel whole until he had Beacon home with him.

After a few seconds, Isaac pulled away. "Thanks," he said in a gruff voice. "Justin, would you have a cop take Vanessa home? I need to head to the veterinary clinic."

"Wait, I'd rather come with you." Vanessa hated the idea of Isaac going alone.

He'd helped save her life, not just a few days ago, but now. The least she could do in return was stick by him through this added complication.

"It's not safe," Isaac protested.

She knew he was right but didn't like it. She spun around to face Justin. "Does this recent attempt mean I can't go anywhere in public? What am I supposed to do, sit home day after day? And what about my job?"

Justin let out a heavy sigh. "Okay, listen. For now, let's take added precautions. How about if I have a cop escort you both to the clinic and then home? He can hang out with you for a while, too. Will that work?"

She glanced at Isaac, who shrugged. "I won't argue."

"Works for me, too."

"Good." Justin gestured for one of the cops to join them. "Senior Airman Wade will accompany you to the vet and then see that you both get safely home."

"Thank you," Vanessa said.

The three of them were silent as they covered the short distance to the veterinary clinic. Senior Airman Wade held the door open for them, then stood off to the side so they could approach the front desk. Airman Fielding, Kyle's assistant, looked up as they entered.

"Captain Goddard? Captain Roark told me to expect you." She flashed a brief smile. "I'll let him know you're here."

Isaac stood stiff and straight at her side, his expression tense as if he were mentally preparing himself for battle rather than visiting his injured dog.

Maybe to him, it felt like the same thing. Especially after the recent gunfire.

She wondered if he was a believer and able to lean on his faith at times like this. Thinking back, she remembered how he'd said Amen after her premeal prayer, but since then he hadn't mentioned anything more about his faith or believing in God. Was it just because he didn't like to talk about something so private? Some worshipers were like that.

Please, Lord, look after Isaac's physical and mental well-being.

"Captain Goddard? You can follow me to room three," Airman Fielding announced.

"Let's go." She took Tango's leash from his fingers, keeping Tango on her left and Eagle on her right. Isaac strode past her into the exam room, where Kyle waited with Beacon on the stainless-steel table. She followed him inside, hovering at the back of the room, each dog sitting obediently at her side. Beacon wasn't as alert as the last time she'd seen him, but he thumped his tail in recognition when he caught Isaac's scent. Isaac crossed over and bent over the dog, awkwardly hugging him and whispering in his ear.

She met Kyle Roark's gaze and they shared a brief, sympathetic understanding of what Isaac was going through. Beacon had to make it through this, he just had to.

Isaac finally stepped away from the exam table. "You'll let me know if there are any changes?" His voice was low and hoarse.

"Of course. I promise to keep a close eye on him," the vet assured him.

"Thanks." Isaac turned away, his expression tortured. He moved past her as if she wasn't there, heading into the clinic lobby.

Vanessa hurried after him, still holding both dogs. Isaac nodded to Senior Airman Wade, then turned toward Vanessa. "It's time for us to get you safely home."

The reminder of how danger followed her like a shadow made her frown. She hated the thought of living in fear.

"I have an idea, Isaac," she said as the two men flanked her on either side. "You could stay at my house for a bit, to help Aiden with the puppies." The small

bundles of fur helped keep her brother grounded, so it made sense that they might be able to offer some solace to Isaac, too.

He didn't respond.

"Aiden has a therapy appointment tomorrow and wants to be sure I can manage the puppies on my own for a while, so he wants to go through everything with me tonight," she added. "Apparently, he doesn't trust me to handle them for a full hour. Maybe you could stick around to help."

Isaac finally shrugged. "Sure. I'll stay until the Security Forces cop arrives at nineteen hundred."

She refused to let his less-than-enthusiastic response bother her. At least he wasn't going to sit home alone, waiting for news. What else could she say to him that would offer hope about Beacon's ability to pull through this latest setback? She had no idea.

Senior Airman Wade cleared his throat. "My orders are to stay on duty at First Lieutenant Gomez's home for as long as she wants or until the night shift arrives."

"Glad to hear it," Isaac said.

Vanessa had the impression Isaac was relieved he had an excuse not to stay. Maybe the puppies would change his mind.

As they approached her house, they found Aiden knee-deep in another housebreaking session. There was a large square of newspaper stretched out on the grass, where the puppies were encouraged to do their business.

"Hey," Aiden greeted them distractedly. Vanessa was relieved that her brother seemed unaffected by the sound of the gunshot just a half mile away. "I think they're finally starting to get the hang of this."

"That's great news." Vanessa unleashed Eagle and watched as the Doberman went over to sniff at the puppies. No easy task as they left the newspaper to romp around the yard, keeping Aiden busy chasing after them. Her brother must have been frustrated, but she was impressed by Aiden's good-natured humor about the whole thing.

"I'm planning to feed them more mash," Aiden warned. "But don't worry, I'll use the bathtub trick again."

"Good idea. Stick with something that works," she agreed.

Her brother apparently just noticed the Security Forces cop standing near the front door. "What's up with the guard?"

"Oh, well…" She hesitated, then remembered her promise not to lie to her brother. "There was another gunshot near the Winged Java, so I've been offered additional protection."

Aiden's gaze widened in alarm. "You're okay?" He glanced at Isaac then back at her. "Both of you are all right?"

"We're fine," she reassured him. "But it's best to take the puppies inside now, just to be safe."

Isaac chased one determined pup, Denali based on the notch in her right ear, scooping her up before she hit the sidewalk and cuddling her close for a moment before returning her to the cardboard box in the middle of the yard.

Just when she thought maybe the puppies were beginning to help soothe his frayed nerves, Isaac abruptly turned away. "You should get them inside. I'm heading home."

"Wait!" She rushed to his side. "Are you sure it's a good idea for you to be alone right now?"

He avoided her gaze and shrugged. "I have Tango."

Tango was a good therapy dog, but Isaac had already confided in her that he didn't have a connection with the golden the way he did with Beacon.

"Please stay."

"I can't."

She couldn't force him, as much as she wanted to. Finally, she relented. "I'll keep you and Beacon in my prayers, Isaac," she softly promised.

He let out a harsh sound. "Don't bother. God hasn't listened to me in a long time. I doubt He'll start now."

"Isaac..." Her heart ached for him, but he didn't acknowledge her as he walked away.

She stood long after he was gone, wondering what she could do to help the man who'd turned his back on his faith.

"What's with him?" Aiden's voice broke into her thoughts.

"Isaac is upset because Beacon had a setback."

Aiden winced. "I'm sorry to hear that."

"Me, too." Since there wasn't anything more she could do for Isaac at the moment, she walked back toward Aiden, picking up Shenandoah before she could leave the yard. "Okay, let's go inside so you can show me what I need to do to care for them."

Safely inside the house, with the cop stationed outside, Aiden went into a detailed description of what he'd been doing to care for the pups, but she was only half listening.

Deep down, she couldn't tear her mind away from

Isaac's suffering. Or the implication of the most recent attempt to harm her.

Sunday church services were only three days away. She was scheduled for a twelve-hour shift on Saturday, but thankfully had tomorrow, which was Friday, off, and again on Sunday.

Her safety was in God's hands and those of the cop stationed outside her door. She could pray for Isaac, but longed to do more. Maybe Pastor Harmon had something to offer. The man had an uncanny way of knowing just what his parishioners needed to hear.

But for that to be successful, she needed to convince Isaac to accompany her to the service.

Based on this most recent interaction, she was afraid that might be an impossible task.

Isaac stared blindly out the window at his small backyard, battling a feeling of emptiness. He knew that sitting in his house alone wasn't smart. But he hadn't been able to stay at Vanessa's, either. He told himself he wasn't betraying his promise to keep her safe, because the task had been handed over to Senior Airman Wade.

Besides, watching the puppies play had only reminded him of the gap left behind in Beacon's absence. Logically, he knew the dog was getting the best care possible by Kyle Roark, but that didn't mean he liked being here without him.

The reckless gunman, likely Boyd Sullivan, was responsible for Beacon's injury. And he had taken a second shot at Vanessa. He knew Justin was determined to get the guy, but he wanted to help.

Restless, he rose to his feet, wishing he could find a way to track down Boyd Sullivan. Not that he thought he could manage to accomplish what Justin Blackwood's team had been unable to do.

He paced, and when that didn't work, he clipped a leash onto Tango's collar and headed back outside. In the past, walking around the base had helped keep him focused.

Steering clear of Vanessa's, he walked past the church, his steps slowed as Vanessa's words echoed in his memory.

I'll keep you and Beacon in my prayers, Isaac.

For a moment, he regretted his harsh response. He'd only spoken the truth, but the shocked expression on Vanessa's face confirmed he'd been too blunt about it.

He hadn't attended church services since he'd been back on base. When he and Beacon had been stranded on the mountain in Afghanistan, he'd prayed day and night for rescue. And the search and recover team had eventually found them. He'd thanked God for that, but in the ensuing months, as he'd been plagued by nightmares while unable to get Beacon returned to him, his faith had vanished.

His career was in shambles and Beacon had been injured by a nutjob with a gun.

Where was God now?

With resolute determination, he strode past the church. He didn't have a destination in mind as he walked past the officers' club and the airmen training facilities. When he reached the helipad, he stared at the choppers for a moment, mourning the loss of his career, then turned and headed past the hangar to Canyon Drive.

He walked in a circle around the base, eventually returning to his house.

Tango had willingly kept pace with him as he walked for miles and miles. When he returned home, Isaac felt bad for him and made sure to provide the golden with plenty of food and water, along with a special doggy treat. Isaac wasn't hungry, but forced himself to eat a grilled cheese sandwich that tasted like cardboard.

After dinner, he stretched out on the sofa, exhaustion weighing him down. Tango stretched out on the floor beside him, but he barely noticed.

"Delta one-five, do you read me, over?"

Isaac could barely hear their command center over the rat-a-tat-tat of gunfire.

"Delta one-five, what's your twenty?"

The bird jerked beneath the stick and it was all Isaac could do to keep the chopper airborne. "This is Delta one-five, we are under heavy artillery fire. Repeat, we are under fire!"

A bullet found its mark and the chopper tilted sideways, sending his passenger and best friend, Jake Burke, and his K-9, Beacon, slamming into the side of the bird.

Sweat rolled down his face beneath his helmet, and he held on to the stick with every ounce of strength he possessed, doing everything possible to keep the chopper in the air, while his copilot had been keeping track of their location.

"Mayday, Mayday. We're hit." He squinted at the landscape below, desperate for a place to land. "Repeat, we're hit. I'm going down."

There! He glimpsed a small field and aimed the

nose of the chopper in that direction. Another jerk as the bird took more gunfire.

Then they were falling, falling...landing with a jarring thud. A tree branch had poked through the window, piercing his copilot in the chest. Isaac yanked off his safety harness and checked for a pulse, but found nothing. Then he scrambled back to check on Jake and Beacon.

Beacon stood protectively near his handler. Jake's chest was *covered* in blood. Isaac ripped off his helmet, intending to do CPR, silently screaming when he realized his efforts were futile. The chopper jerked again and a large explosion filled the air. He saw the bright ball of flames shooting from the engine, seconds before the force sent him reeling backward.

He saw Jake's lifeless eyes...then nothing but darkness.

Noooo!

Isaac awoke to a sore, hoarse throat and the sound of his own screams. Tango whimpered, his paws on his chest, attempting to lick his face.

For a moment, he gathered the golden close, burying his face against Tango's glossy coat. His heart pounded in rhythm with the rat-a-tat-tat of gunfire that continued to echo through his memory.

He lifted his head, and pressed a hand to the center of his chest in an effort to slow his pulse. It had been months since he'd had this particular nightmare. Lately, he'd managed to wake himself up before the crash landing.

Before he gazed first into his copilot's slack face and then Jake's lifeless blue eyes.

Feeling shaky, he gently moved Tango to the side so he could get up off the sofa. He padded into the kitchen and downed a glass of water, willing himself to stop trembling.

He knew it was ridiculous to have this kind of response to a nightmare. Especially over something that had happened six months ago.

The clock on the microwave read zero one thirty. The need to see Vanessa was strong, and he tamped it back with an effort.

No sense in waking her up in the middle of the night, especially since he had no clue if she was scheduled to work the next day or not.

Again, he paced the length of the house, unable to release the nightmare's grip on his subconscious. Later, when he closed his eyes, he found himself right back in the cockpit, fighting to keep the bird in the air.

While Jake lay bleeding to death right behind him.

Enough. He couldn't stay inside the house a moment longer. Sitting here alone wasn't going to work. He needed to get out. He glanced down at Tango. "How about it, boy? Up to taking a walk?"

Tango wagged his tail.

After clipping a leash to Tango's collar, he headed outside, breathing deep. The cool night air provided a balm for his ragged nerves. He instinctively turned toward Vanessa's house. He wouldn't bother her, but would walk past, make sure things were fine.

Aiden might be having trouble sleeping, too. Lots of combat veterans suffering from PTSD didn't sleep through the night. Maybe if Aiden was awake, they could talk for a bit. He knew Vanessa wanted her brother to open up to him.

But when he approached her home, the hairs on the back of his neck stood on end and a wave of apprehension washed over him. As he came closer, he could see a body lying in a crumpled heap against the side of the house.

The cop stationed outside her door was injured!

He bolted forward, leaning down to feel for a pulse along the side of his neck. The beat of the cop's heart was reassuring despite the thin trail of blood that ran down the side of his temple.

Vanessa!

His heart lodged in his throat as he rushed through the front door hanging ajar, the frame cracked from where it had been forced open. He hurried, hoping and desperately praying that he wasn't too late and that Vanessa wasn't already dead at Boyd's hand.

Why hadn't he brought his phone? He wanted to kick himself for not being better prepared.

He swept his gaze over the darkened interior of the house, searching for signs of an intruder. The TV was still in the corner, and he noticed a laptop sitting on an end table. Clearly, robbery wasn't the motive.

Moving silently and with extreme caution, he made his way through the living room, toward the kitchen. He wished he'd grabbed the injured cop's duty weapon.

A masked man stood near the back door, holding a cardboard box awkwardly against his chest. Even from where Isaac stood several feet away, he could hear a whimpering sound inside.

The intruder had grabbed the puppies? Why?

"Hey! Stop!"

The masked man jerked at the sound of Isaac's voice. Isaac lunged toward the guy at the exact same time the intruder threw the box of puppies at him and pulled out a knife.

Isaac instinctively caught the box, risking a quick glance inside to see that the four puppies were okay. He set the box on the floor and confronted the masked man, his combat training instinctively kicking in. He settled in a fighting stance keeping his arms loose at his side. Without warning, he abruptly lashed out with his booted foot, aiming squarely for the wrist holding the knife.

The blade clattered to the floor.

His surge of satisfaction faded as the intruder immediately turned and escaped through the back door.

Isaac took off after him. No way was he letting Boyd Sullivan get away!

The guy was smart, taking a zigzag path through the trees and leaping over bushes. Isaac easily kept pace, and pushed himself to close the gap between them.

Boyd would not get away!

The masked man glanced over his shoulder in time to see Isaac closing in. He instantly changed directions, running directly out onto the two-lane road leading toward the south gate.

Isaac didn't slow his pace, hoping the cop on duty at the gate would see the masked man, too. A sudden squeal of brakes shattered the night, followed by a loud thump-thump.

Stumbling into the clearing, he stared in horror at the body of the masked man lying off to the side of the road in a boneless heap.

The truck driver slid out from behind the wheel. "He came out of nowhere, running right in front of me! I couldn't stop!"

"I know, it's okay." Isaac crossed over and checked for a pulse.

Nothing. The man was dead. Just like Jake.

No, don't go there. He gave himself a mental shake and looked up at the driver, who was on the phone with the cops.

Isaac hesitated, then reached down to remove the mask. He'd expected to see a familiar face staring up at him.

But the dead man wasn't Boyd Sullivan. He was someone Isaac had never seen before.

EIGHT

The sound of a shout followed by several loud thuds brought Vanessa out of a dead sleep. Worried about her brother, she ran into the main living area, searching wildly for Aiden.

He was crouched next to the box of puppies on the floor, attempting to soothe them.

"What happened?" she asked.

"I came out of my room to see Isaac running outside and the box sitting in the middle of the kitchen." Aiden's gaze was troubled. "I left the puppies in the living room when I went to bed and can't see why Isaac would move them."

Vanessa didn't understand it, either. Why would Isaac have been there? She heard a moan from the front of the house and quickly responded. When she saw the cop propped against the side of her house, she dropped to her knees, her nursing training rising to the forefront. "Senior Airman McDonald, are you okay?"

"Someone hit me." The cop touched the right side of his temple with a wince. "I'm sorry, ma'am. I shouldn't have been caught unaware."

"It's not your fault." Vanessa glanced around her

front yard, shivering in the cool night. Then she focused on the injured cop. "How long were you unconscious?"

He shrugged his shoulders. "No idea."

She didn't like being out in the open like this. What if Boyd Sullivan or his accomplice was out there watching them right now? "Let's get you inside, okay? I'll call for an ambulance."

"I need to contact my captain." Senior Airman McDonald didn't look happy with the idea of reporting in. It probably wouldn't be easy to admit someone had sneaked up on him, knocking him unconscious. "He needs to know what happened here."

She couldn't disagree. And where was Isaac? Aiden saw him running away. Had he chased the intruder? Was it possible he'd already caught Boyd?

She hoped and prayed he had.

Propping her shoulder beneath McDonald's arm, she helped him upright. As they made their way inside, Isaac rushed through the house, stopping abruptly when he saw her, relief filling his eyes.

"I'm glad you're okay," he said. "Can I borrow your phone? I left mine behind, and we need to contact Captain Blackwood ASAP."

She assisted McDonald into a kitchen chair, then went into her bedroom to fetch the mobile phone she routinely charged at night.

She wasn't sure why Isaac had shown up in the middle of the night, but was grateful for his impeccable timing.

"Here." She handed him the phone. "What happened? Did you catch the man who hit the senior airman?"

Isaac shook his head. "I chased him, but he ran out onto the street directly in the path of a truck. I think he hoped to get past it as a way to lose me, but his plan didn't work." He hesitated, then added, "He's dead."

"Boyd is dead?" she repeated, torn between horror and relief that the nightmare might be over.

"Not Boyd," Isaac corrected. "Some guy I never saw before in my life."

"What?" Vanessa didn't understand.

"He was trying to steal the puppies. He threw the box at me, then pulled a knife. I managed to disarm him, and when he took off, I chased him."

"He hit a cop to steal puppies?" The whole scenario didn't make any sense.

"I don't understand it, either." Isaac turned away and spoke into the phone. "Justin? You need to come to Vanessa's place. It's an active crime scene."

Vanessa couldn't hear the other side of the conversation, so she focused on the cop. She pulled a bag of frozen peas out and handed it to McDonald. "Use this as an ice pack."

He gratefully accepted the frozen peas, pressing the bag to his temple.

She peered into his eyes, assessing his pupils. They looked equal and reactive to light. "Do you feel dizzy? Confused? Sick to your stomach?"

"I have a headache, that's all."

She wasn't sure she believed him; Security Forces cops didn't like to admit to weakness. "Don't lie to me, Senior Airman," she warned. "Head injuries are no joke. You could die from bleeding into your brain."

He stared at her for a moment, then admitted, "A little dizzy and sick, but nothing serious."

That's all she needed to know. "Fine. I recommend you go to the emergency room for a CT scan."

McDonald didn't argue, which only convinced her he was hurting far more than he'd let on. She glanced at Aiden, who was trying to hold all four puppies in his arms at the same time, his expression laden with guilt.

"They're okay, Aiden." She placed a reassuring hand on her brother's shoulder.

"I should have either slept on the sofa the way I usually do, or taken them into the bedroom with me," Aiden said.

"It's not your fault."

"I almost lost them!" Aiden's voice rose in agitation. "Isaac said that man tried to steal them away from us. Who would do such an awful thing?"

"I don't know." Vanessa couldn't make sense out of any of it. "What matters now is that the puppies are safe, and Senior Airman McDonald will be okay, too."

Unfortunately, the masked man was dead.

If not Boyd, then who was he? And why did he want the puppies?

Justin Blackwood and his K-9, Quinn, along with two more cops, arrived at the same time as the ambulance. Vanessa gave a brief update to the medics about McDonald's condition and then stepped back so they could get him to the hospital. Then she crossed over to join Justin and Isaac.

"You just happened to be walking by Vanessa's house and noticed the injured officer?" Justin asked in an incredulous tone.

"Yes." Isaac met his gaze squarely. "If you must know, I had a nightmare and couldn't sleep. I decided a walk would help clear my head."

"Without your phone?" Justin pressed, clearly upset with how the situation had been handled.

Vanessa instinctively moved closer to Isaac.

"Yes, without my phone. The nightmare knocked me off balance. It was a stupid move. I should have been better prepared."

"Isaac isn't the bad guy here," she pointed out.

"I know." Justin let out a heavy sigh. "Go on. You were walking past Vanessa's house when you noticed the injured cop. You didn't have a phone so you made sure he was breathing, then went inside."

"I needed to make sure Vanessa and Aiden were okay." Isaac glanced at her, then continued with the story about how the intruder was near the back door, holding the box of puppies.

"Why would he take the puppies?" Justin demanded. "A shot at you earlier, then this? It doesn't make sense."

"I know," Vanessa admitted.

"It's definitely weird. When he saw me, he threw the box and pulled a knife. I disarmed him, and he took off running." Isaac hesitated, then shrugged. "I thought it was Boyd, so I kept after him. Then he tried to cross the road in front of the truck, I assume in an attempt to lose me. But he was hit instead. I believe he must have broken his neck on impact." The words were carefully articulated and she sensed it wasn't easy for him to talk about this. "I removed his mask and confirmed he wasn't Boyd Sullivan."

"Who was he?" Justin asked.

"Some guy I've never seen before."

"Walk us through the path you took," Justin ordered taking Quinn by the leash and stepping forward.

Vanessa didn't want to leave Aiden alone, but there

were two cops standing by, so she pulled on a rumpled Air Force sweatshirt emblazoned with the motto "Aim High, Fly, Fight, Win" and followed Isaac and Justin outside.

The masked intruder had taken a jagged path through the base neighborhood and when they emerged from the trees, she saw the truck sitting in the center of the road, the apparent driver speaking to a couple of cops she assumed had come over from the south gate.

An ambulance stood by, waiting for direction. There was obviously no rush to remove the deceased man. Vanessa had the distinct urge to verify for herself that it wasn't Boyd lying there.

It wasn't.

And like Isaac, she'd never seen this man before in her life.

"I don't recognize him," Justin said thoughtfully. "We'll need his fingerprints to verify he's not military."

"Can we take him to the morgue?" one of the medics asked.

Justin examined the front of the semitruck, likely making note of the new dent. The two cops from the south gate crossed over to join them, greeting the officers with a sharp salute.

"Did you see what happened?" Justin asked.

"Yes, sir." The airman first class named Steele stepped forward. "I caught a glimpse of a man running into the road in front of the truck. The semitruck couldn't stop in time and made contact with the pedestrian. He flew up in the air and landed at the side of the road on his head."

The airman first class's account validated Isaac's statement, so Justin gestured at the medic. "Go ahead and take him to the morgue." Then he turned toward Airman First Class Steele. "I want to see your report first thing in the morning."

"Yes, sir." The airman first class saluted again, then turned away.

Vanessa glanced between Isaac and Justin. "Is it possible this could be linked to the missing dogs and the Olio Crime Organization?"

"I don't see how," Justin admitted.

"I stand by my earlier theory," Isaac said. "I believe it's possible members of the Olio Crime Organization are attempting to infiltrate Canyon Air Force Base. Maybe they returned to steal the puppies back?"

"Why would they?" Justin countered. "What value is there to the puppies? Besides, why try to infiltrate the base at all? There are easier places, dozens of other cities in the area, in which to organize crime."

"Maybe it's military related," Vanessa pressed. She was sure there was something else going on, something other than Boyd's killing spree, which really was bad enough. "You must know something about what they're involved in."

Justin hesitated, shrugged. "I'm really not at liberty to say. Base Command hasn't given me clearance to discuss it."

Vanessa tried not to show her impatience. "This masked man attacked a cop, broke into my home and tried to steal four puppies, and you're not allowed to discuss it with me?"

Isaac put a reassuring hand on her arm. "He's just following orders."

Vanessa had been in the Air Force for six years, going in right after she'd graduated from a four-year

nursing program. She knew that the command struc-
ture was hierarchical and teams often worked in silos.
But this issue impacted her on a personal level.

Shouldn't that count for something?

"You brought me in when I received a red rose from
Boyd. I've been attacked twice, maybe a third time if
you assume I was the shooter's victim at the airfield
the other day. Why shut me out now?"

Justin's expression was noncommittal. "I'll discuss
your concerns with our Base Commander Lieutenant
General Hall."

Great. That would help about as much as placing
a bandage over a brisk arterial bleed. Isaac's arm slid
around her waist and he steered her away from Justin
and Quinn, back toward her house.

She leaned against Isaac, grateful for his support.
When they were out of Justin's earshot, she glanced up
at him. "I'm glad you were there to protect us."

Isaac gently hugged her. "Me, too."

It was scary how much she was coming to depend
on Isaac. And how much she cared about him on a
personal level.

Keeping their relationship on friendship terms felt
impossible.

Despite being burned in the past by Leo, she wanted
more. Much more.

Isaac paused outside Vanessa's back door, fighting
the urge to kiss her.

Not just because he was relieved to find her safe and
sound, but because he needed her.

Yet at the same time, it wasn't easy to trust his instincts. These circumstances were anything but nor-

mal, and he knew that feelings were amplified in crisis situations.

He was grateful to have been able to prevent her from being harmed yet again. When he'd thought she might be lying inside the house, injured or worse, he'd prayed to God that he'd find her in time.

Praying had felt right, and it occurred to him that maybe he'd been wrong to shy away from his faith.

Maybe God was watching over them.

The thought brought him a sense of peace.

"I'm so glad the puppies are safe," Vanessa said, flashing a relieved smile. "Losing them would have been a huge setback for Aiden."

"I know. Just like Beacon's head injury has set me back." Was that why the nightmare had returned with such vengeance? It was as if he'd been right there, living the experience all over again. "I think that's why I was plagued by a recurring nightmare tonight."

"Oh, Isaac, I'm sorry about Beacon and your nightmare, but thank you so much for arriving in time." Vanessa lifted up on her tiptoes and brushed his rough cheek with a light kiss. Before he could haul her into his arms for a proper kiss, she moved away and went through the back door into the kitchen.

He followed her inside and found Aiden corralling the puppies from the wet newspaper. The young man glanced up at his sister with a hesitant smile. "Even as scared as they were, they didn't make a mess in the box."

"I'm glad to hear it." Vanessa helped dispose of the soiled newspaper and then washed her hands at the sink as her brother followed suit.

"Aiden, will it bother you too much if I camp out on

the sofa for what's left of the night?" Isaac asked. "I don't want to leave you and your sister alone."

"I don't mind." Aiden tightened his grip on the box. "But the puppies are staying in my room with me."

"Understandable," Isaac agreed. "I don't want to make you uncomfortable, either."

Aiden glanced at his sister, then back at Isaac. "I'd feel better having someone to protect us here, inside the house," he said frankly. "It's obvious having a cop stationed outside isn't good enough."

Isaac silently agreed, although he suspected Justin would take issue with the young man's assessment. "Great, thanks."

Aiden nodded and headed down the short hallway to his bedroom, disappearing inside.

"That's settled," Vanessa said. "I'll find a spare blanket and pillow."

Before he could tell her not to bother, she left him alone in the kitchen. He crossed over to the adjacent living room, and stood for a moment, feeling uncertain.

Every cell in his body wanted to stick close to Vanessa after everything that had transpired, but deep down, he knew staying here wasn't smart. He was already too close to the edge, desperate to move beyond friendship, seeking something more.

He scrubbed his hands over his face, weary of trying to make sense out of his feelings. Emotions weren't logical, so there was no point in trying to dissect and analyze them.

"Here you go." Vanessa returned with a light blanket and a pillow, setting them both in the corner of the sofa. He stared at the flowered pillowcase, wondering if it smelled like her.

If that was the case, he'd never get any sleep. Not that he was expecting much shut-eye anyway.

"Thanks," he said. "You should try to get some rest, especially if you work in the morning." Glancing at the time—nearly zero three hundred hours—he winced. "In a few hours, I mean."

"I don't, but am scheduled on Saturday." She hesitated, then added, "I'm off Sunday, too. I was—um—thinking, or um, hoping, you'd consider joining me and Aiden at church services. I don't know if you've heard Pastor Harmon speak, but he does an amazing job."

His initial instinct was to refuse. It had been too long since he'd crossed the threshold of a church, much less found solace in one. But remembering his promise to protect her, he nodded in agreement. "Yeah, sure. I'd like that."

"You would?" The sheer joy radiating from Vanessa's dark eyes almost did him in. He was suddenly willing to do anything—stand on his head or turn cartwheels—if it made her this happy.

"Yes." He offered a hesitant smile. "I don't know Pastor Harmon, though. I haven't been to church services since I've been back on base. Between my flashbacks and fighting through the red-tape bureaucracy, I felt completely alone, with the military red tape in getting Beacon home dragging me down." He took a step toward her, silently pleading for her to understand. "But then, I came here in time to prevent the masked man from stealing the puppies. I prayed, desperately and reverently, for your safety and Aiden's. Now that you and Aiden are safe, it makes me think God must have been watching over you. Over me, too." His voice dropped to a whisper. "I was wrong to stay away for so long."

"I'm so happy to hear you say that." Vanessa smiled tremulously, looking as if she might cry. "It's during times of stress that we need Him the most. And I'm extremely grateful God brought you into my life, Isaac. Not just because of your incredible timing, but because I've never met someone like you. Someone who bravely faces adversity with steely determination."

"Vanessa." Her name came out as a groan. She moved toward him at the same time he reached for her. Then she was in his arms, where she belonged, and he was kissing her the way he'd longed to do from the moment he'd realized she was safe.

"You're so beautiful," he murmured, reveling in her softness.

"You're not so bad, yourself," she whispered, tipping her head back to look up at him.

He stared at her dainty features, as if to memorize the expression of desire on her sweet face and moist lips. Yet at the same time, he knew that this couldn't go anywhere. He forced himself to move backward, putting space between them. "You need to get some sleep. Good night, Vanessa."

"Good night, Isaac." She pulled out of his arms and moved away, disappearing down the hallway leading to the bedrooms.

He stood where he was for several long moments, telling himself he'd done the right thing. She deserved someone better. Someone whole. Someone with a future.

And none of that applied to him.

He finally stretched out on the sofa, ignoring the blanket but resting his head on the pillow.

Breathing deep, he inwardly groaned. The pillow carried Vanessa's honeysuckle scent.

Tormenting him with what he'd never have.

NINE

The incessant ringing of her phone dragged Vanessa awake, blinking groggily in the sunlight streaming through her window. Squinting against the glare, she fumbled for the phone. "Gomez," she answered in a hoarse voice.

"This is Captain Blackwood. Lieutenant General Hall would like to see you and Captain Goddard at zero nine hundred hours."

"Uh, okay." She pushed her hair behind her ear. "What time is it now?"

"Zero seven thirty. See you then." Justin disconnected the line.

She had just over an hour, which wasn't a lot of time, especially when she was still exhausted from her eventful night. Sleep hadn't come easily, especially after Isaac's toe-curling kiss.

He'd called her beautiful. And unlike Leo, who called everyone gorgeous, she sensed he'd really meant it.

Or maybe that's what she wanted to believe. Shaking her head at her foolishness, she ducked into the bathroom, showered and then changed into her dress blues. She idly wondered why Isaac's attendance was required, then figured it must be because he had first-hand information about the attack that she didn't.

The formal request had to be related to the early-morning invasion of her home. Why else would the base commander ask to see them?

She walked into the kitchen, surprised to be greeted by the enticing scent of coffee. Isaac stood leaning against the counter, sipping from a mug. He eyed her cautiously over the rim.

"Did you talk to Justin?"

She nodded and helped herself to a cup of the steaming brew. "You, too?"

He nodded. "I didn't want to leave without making sure you were up, but I need to get home to shower and change."

"Understood. Do you want to meet here in thirty minutes?"

He hesitated, then shrugged. "Sure. Half an hour is a lot of time. It won't take us that long."

"I just don't want to be late for a meeting with the top brass." She grimaced. "That would be a CLM for sure."

He lifted a curious brow. "A what?"

"Career Limiting Move."

Isaac chuckled. "Okay, then. Thirty minutes it is." He downed the last of his coffee and set his mug in the sink. "See you soon."

"Sure." She carried her mug and followed him as he took Tango and left through the front door. Aiden wasn't out there, but was in the backyard, working with the puppies.

Her brother really seemed to have a connection with the animals and she couldn't help wondering once again if it was possible that he could get reassigned to the K-9 training center. She made a mental note to discuss the possibility with Westley James, although she knew it wasn't completely up to him. Aiden was on medical leave and he needed permission from not only his current captain, but Lieutenant Colonel Flintman's recommendation, as well.

"Hi, Aiden," she greeted him, then turned and nodded at the cop stationed outside the door. "How are the national parks doing this morning?"

"You should see how well trained they are," Aiden gushed over the progress the puppies had made. "Even with their mother recuperating at the vet, they're getting the hang of this. They're truly amazing."

"Because of you," she reminded him. "You're doing an awesome job with them. Hey, I have a meeting at Base Command at nine. What time is your doctor's appointment?"

"Um, not sure. Maybe three this afternoon?" Aiden answered distractedly. "Why?"

"You asked me to watch the pups, remember?" She wondered if her brother was suffering from lapses in memory, which was not unheard of in cases of PTSD.

"Oh, yeah. Right. Aw, good girl, Shenandoah, you're managing to keep up with your brothers and sister." Aiden lifted the runt of the litter and snuggled with her for a moment.

She smiled. "I'll make sure I'm back well before fifteen hundred, okay?"

"Uh-huh."

She left him with the pups, and made a quick breakfast. After eating her omelet, she made one for Aiden.

She worried about him. He was so focused on the puppies, she wasn't sure he was taking care of himself.

Isaac arrived in exactly thirty minutes as promised and they left for the meeting. She brought Eagle with her, for added protection and so Aiden would have one less animal to worry about. Her loyal and protective K-9 jumped into the back of the SUV without any trouble.

Impeccably handsome in his dress blues, Isaac smiled and nodded as he slid into the passenger seat.

"Where's Tango?"

"I left him at home." Isaac slid into the passenger seat and closed the door. "If there's time, I'd like to stop by the vet on the way back, to check on Beacon."

"Have you heard from Kyle?"

"Not yet." Isaac's expression was troubled. "I'm hoping no news is good news."

"I agree. I'm sure Kyle would let you know if there was a change for the worse."

Isaac nodded, but didn't say anything further. A strained silence filled the car, making her wonder what was going on in Isaac's mind.

She told herself he was probably reviewing the sequence of events from yesterday. The gunfire at the Winged Java, followed by the nightmare and the attempt to steal the puppies, were probably replaying over and over in his head.

Hopefully, he didn't regret their kiss—or worse, agreeing to go to church services with her.

She parked on the street and slid out from behind the wheel, releasing the back so Eagle could jump down. Clipping the leash to Eagle's collar, she walked beside Isaac.

Because they were a few minutes early, they were shown into a small reception area to wait for Captain Blackwood. Eagle sat tall beside her and she scratched the Doberman between the ears.

She'd gotten Eagle a few months ago, when events had escalated on base. The top brass had agreed that anyone targeted by the Red Rose Killer could keep their K-9s at home with them at all times. The smart Doberman had accepted her without a problem, and she was thrilled to have him as a guard dog.

Ten minutes later, the door opened and Justin beckoned to them. "Lieutenant General Hall is ready for us."

Vanessa felt unaccountably nervous, second-guessing her decision to bring Eagle along for this meeting. She'd wanted to be sure the general knew she was taking the threat seriously, but she wished now she'd left Eagle behind.

She entered the room first, greeting Lieutenant General Nathan Hall with a sharp salute. "First Lieutenant Vanessa Gomez, sir."

Isaac mirrored her salute. "Captain Isaac Goddard, sir."

"At ease," the base commander said after returning their salutes. "Have a seat."

Vanessa sat and gave Eagle the hand signal to sit, too. The dog dropped onto his haunches, sitting tall, ears perked forward as if awaiting his next command.

"I understand there was a break-in at your home early this morning." Lieutenant General Hall steepled his hands together, gazing at them intently. "A civilian wearing a black mask was killed at the scene."

A civilian? She risked a quick glance at Isaac.

"I stumbled upon the masked intruder attempting

to steal a box of puppies from Lieutenant Gomez's home," Isaac said. "He threw them at me and pulled a knife. He ran after I disarmed him, so I gave chase. Unfortunately, he attempted to cross the road right in front of a large semitruck delivering supplies, and he was hit and killed on impact."

Base Commander Lieutenant General Hall nodded. "Lieutenant, does the name Ricardo Meyer mean anything to you?"

Vanessa blinked. "No, sir. Is that the identity of the civilian?"

"He apparently worked at the hospital as a janitor," Lieutenant General Hall continued without directly answering her question.

Instantly she thought of Joseph Kramer, the janitor who died of a Tyraxal overdose. Did these two men know each other? Was it possible that Ricardo blamed her for Joseph's death?

"Lieutenant Gomez?"

She snapped her gaze to meet the commander's. "Sir, I don't know a Ricardo Meyer, but I took care of a civilian janitor named Joseph Kramer who died of a drug overdose a couple of days ago."

The commander's eyebrows levered upward. "You think they're connected?"

"Honestly, sir? I don't see how. Even if we assume the two men were friends, why would Ricardo blame me for Joseph's death? And even if he did, why go after the puppies instead of me personally?"

"Lieutenant, we know Boyd sent you a rose, but we can't find a connection between Ricardo Meyer and Sullivan, either. Is there anyone else who may be upset or angry with you?"

"Captain Leo Turner." The name popped out of her mouth before she could stop it. Her cheeks flushed and she avoided Justin's blatantly curious gaze. "I broke off my relationship with the captain several months ago."

"Has he been harassing you?" Justin asked.

She forced herself to meet his gaze, hoping her embarrassment wasn't too obvious. "No, he hasn't. However, he's the only other person I've argued with over the past few months. I don't believe he hired someone to invade my home, but I wanted to be completely honest about who might be upset with me."

"Thank you, Lieutenant, we will take that information under advisement," Lieutenant General Hall said.

"Sir, may I ask whether or not you believe Ricardo Meyer is linked to the Olio Crime Organization?" Isaac asked.

There was a heavy pause before the commander spoke. "We don't have any evidence of that at this time. Captain Goddard, I assume you also don't know Ricardo Meyer?"

"No, sir."

"Well then, thank you for coming in on such short notice." Lieutenant General Hall rose to his feet, so she and Isaac stood, too. "You're dismissed."

They saluted the commander and waited until he left the conference room. Then Justin shrugged his shoulders. "I'll be in touch," he said before following his boss out.

Vanessa released her pent-up breath, glancing down at Eagle, who'd behaved admirably during the meeting. "Doesn't look as if they're going to tell us anything more."

"Guess not," Isaac agreed.

They left Base Command and returned to Vanessa's SUV. She opened the windows to air it out before asking Eagle to jump in the back.

She headed back down Canyon Drive. "Do you want to stop at the veterinary clinic?"

He hesitated, then nodded. "I'm sorry to hear about your relationship."

"Yeah, well, trust me—I'm happy I learned about his cheating before things got too serious." She glanced at him. "I felt like an idiot when I realized everyone else suspected long before I found out."

"He's a jerk, not worth your time."

"Thanks, I appreciate that."

He shifted uncomfortably in his seat. "I was in a relationship before the crash, but Amber couldn't handle the way I'd changed after the traumatic event." He glanced at her. "I'm not good relationship material."

It was on the tip of her tongue to argue, but then she realized what he was really saying. This was Isaac's way of warning her off. His way of telling her not to expect anything from him, despite their amazing kiss.

Her stomach knotted and she tightened her grip on the steering wheel. She didn't agree with Isaac's assessment. That was something he needed to figure out for himself.

Isaac inwardly grimaced as his statement hung like a radioactive force field between them. He hadn't intended to come across so blunt, but it was probably better in the long run.

He'd spent what had been left of last night wide-awake in a vain attempt to keep Vanessa from invading his dreams. He couldn't ever remember feeling so tied up in knots over a woman.

She pulled over to the curb in front of the veterinary clinic and parked in one of the short-term slots. He almost wished she wasn't coming in with him but he needed to remain with her, refusing to go back on his promise to protect her.

He went around back and stood in front of her, casting a glance up and down the road. "Ready?"

"Of course."

Keeping her and Eagle in front of him, he entered the clinic and caught Airman Fielding's eyes. "Is Captain Roark busy? I'd like to check on Beacon."

"He was examining Beacon earlier. Let me get him for you." The young woman left the main desk, returning in less than a minute. "Captain Roark has Beacon settled in exam room number three."

It was frustrating to have to see Beacon in the exam rooms, but sensed it would be better than touching him through the metal bars of a kennel. He entered the exam room, suddenly feeling an odd sense of peace that Vanessa was beside him.

Kyle stood next to the table, holding Beacon's collar. The German shepherd lifted his head and thumped his tail as Isaac approached. "Hey, buddy. You're looking better today." He bent over to bury his face in Beacon's neck.

"He is better today," Kyle confirmed. "The area of hemorrhage has shrunk considerably, which is a good sign."

The news was a balm of relief. "I'm glad to hear it."

Kyle stroked Beacon's fur. "He was definitely feisty last night, giving Airman Fielding a hard time."

"I'd apologize except that's Beacon's normal nature, which makes me happy," Isaac said with a wry smile. "It must mean he's getting better."

"I think so, too." Kyle gave a nod of satisfaction. "In fact, if the CT scan looks good tomorrow, I'm inclined to send him home with you."

"I'd love it," Isaac said. "As long as you think he'll be okay."

"I wouldn't discharge him if I wasn't sure of that." Kyle stepped back. "I'll give you a few minutes, then I need to get him back to the kennel."

Isaac murmured reassurances to the animal, much the way he had when they were stranded on the edge of a mountainside. Vanessa didn't say anything, but having her there was more than enough.

"Ready to go?" he asked her a few moments later, breaking the silence.

"Sure," Vanessa agreed.

As they walked outside to where Vanessa had left her SUV, he noticed a brunette walking beside a medium-size Belgian Malinois. There was something familiar about her facial features...

Then it hit him. She was Jacey Burke, Jake's younger sister. He remembered Jake telling him how they'd both joined the Air Force out of high school and had both become dog handlers.

Jake's lifeless eyes flashed in his memory, accompanied by a flash of panic. He shoved the image away with an effort.

By the time he'd gotten himself under control, Jacey was within arm's reach. He reminded himself that this was his best friend's sister and that she deserved his respect and support.

"Hi, Jacey." He forced a smile.

"Captain Goddard," Jacey greeted him with a salute, including Vanessa in that. "Greta, sit."

The Malinois sat.

He returned the professional courtesy with a salute, then waved a hand. "No need to be formal, and please, call me Isaac. And this is First Lieutenant Vanessa Gomez."

Her smile was sad, but she nodded. "How are you?"

"I'm good." Early in the process of getting Beacon home, he'd called Jacey and asked if she minded his taking her brother's dog and she'd gladly approved. "Beacon is here on base, but there was a small accident, so he's being watched by the vet for a few days."

"Oh, I hope he's okay." Her brow furrowed with concern.

"He will be," he assured her. "I'm surprised to see you here, though. I'd heard you were overseas."

Her deep blue eyes, so much like Jake's, were shadowed with grief. "I returned from my tour in Afghanistan two weeks ago," she informed him. "Greta and I have been assigned to the training center for the foreseeable future."

"Really? I'm glad to hear it," he said. "Master Sergeant Westley James could use the help."

"That's what I've been told," Jacey agreed. Her expression remained troubled. "It's nice to be stateside for a while."

The way she avoided his direct gaze bothered him. He'd always been able to tell when something was bugging Jake, too. "Are you okay?"

"Of course." Her smile didn't reach her eyes. "Greta

is scheduled for a checkup, so I figured I'd take her my-self." She hesitated, shrugged. "She had a rough tour."

Isaac understood that meant Jacey had likely suf-fered a rough tour, as well. Dog handlers did every-thing with their K-9 partners.

"If you need something, let me know." He glanced at Vanessa, who hadn't said anything during the brief meeting.

"I will." Again, she avoided his direct gaze. "Nice to see you, Isaac. Lieutenant Gomez."

"It was nice meeting you," Vanessa agreed.

"Good day, Captain." Jacey gave him a quick nod, then gave Greta a hand signal that brought the beauti-ful animal to her feet.

Jacey walked around them and disappeared inside the veterinary clinic.

"She looks upset," Vanessa said.

"Yeah." Isaac gazed after her, sick with the real-ization that Jacey blamed him for her brother's death. Six months ago, when he'd called about Beacon, she'd sounded friendly enough, but her reaction face-to-face proved otherwise.

And he couldn't blame her.

If only he'd reacted quicker, had found a spot to land the damaged chopper sooner. Maybe Jake and his co-pilot would have survived.

Her brother's death was his fault. And how ironic that Jake's K-9 partner, Beacon, had been the one to save his life.

TEN

After dropping a silently brooding Isaac off at home, Vanessa battled a deep sense of loss that weighed heavily across her shoulders as she parked the SUV in her driveway and let Eagle out. Justin had arranged for additional protection after the shooting incident at the Winged Java, so she wasn't surprised to see a cop at the door. He saluted, and she returned the acknowledgment. She waited for the Doberman to do his business before taking him inside.

She gave Eagle food and water, glad Aiden was preoccupied with feeding the puppies in the bathtub. The last thing her brother needed was to notice the lingering hint of despair in her eyes.

She told herself it was ridiculous to be this upset over a man who'd kissed her. Leo's cheating on her was a much bigger betrayal. Although to be honest, Isaac's withdrawal hurt worse than Leo's cheating.

Was that messed up, or what?

She gave herself a mental shake. She wasn't interested in a relationship, so why did it matter? Still, the rest of the day loomed empty before her, and it struck her just how much time she'd spent with Isaac over the past few days.

If she wasn't needed to watch the puppies this afternoon during Aiden's therapy appointment, she would have called the hospital and offered to work a partial shift to help keep her hands and mind busy.

She blew out a heavy breath. Okay, since heading to the hospital was out of the question for now, maybe she should work with Eagle a bit more, refreshing the training the handlers had walked through with her a few months ago.

Outside, she put Eagle through the paces, pleased with his response. When her cell phone rang, her heart leaped.

Isaac?

No. Recognizing the number as from within the hospital, she grimaced and answered, "Lieutenant Gomez."

"This is Lieutenant Colonel Flintman. I apologize for my delay in returning your call."

"Lieutenant Colonel Flintman, I'm so happy to hear from you." Finally, the doctor had called her back.

"I'm sorry to hear about these drug overdoses," he said in a concerned tone. "It's horrible to learn Tyraxal is being abused like this."

"I agree, sir. Three overdoses are three too many."

"Lieutenant Gomez, I'm proud of how you identified this issue and raised the alarm," he said warmly. "Nice job. Do you remember the patients' names? I need to file a report about these adverse drug reactions with the Food and Drug Administration. The FDA tracks this sort of thing very closely."

She was relieved to hear Lieutenant Colonel Flintman was taking her concerns seriously. She readily gave him the three names, each patient's face burned into her memory. She could hear him clattering on a keyboard.

"Lieutenant Colonel Flintman, what do you think of the fact that Joseph Kramer was a civilian working as a janitor at the hospital?"

"I find it very disturbing," he replied. "I can only assume that one of the airmen I'm treating has decided to sell his or her prescription."

"Yes, that's the same conclusion I came to, as well." Vanessa thought again of her brother, secretly relieved he wasn't taking Tyraxal. He was doing so much better now that he'd been caring for the puppies, she hoped he wouldn't need the medication moving forward, either. She silently thanked God for watching over him. "I'm glad you're planning to report this to the FDA. I think the addictive effect of Tyraxal clearly outweighs the benefit."

"Well, now, I don't know if I'd go that far," Lieutenant Colonel Flintman said, a hint of steel in his tone. "You know as well as I do, Lieutenant, that each patient responds differently to medications. Some of my patients have found Tyraxal very beneficial. Unfortunately, like many medications, they don't each help everyone in the same way."

"You're right," she agreed, properly chastised. Flintman had a good point; she knew firsthand that every patient responded differently to medications and treatments. It happened in the critical care setting all the time. "Let's hope that we don't see any more overdoses."

"Agreed."

"Thank you again, sir, for returning my call."

"Of course, Lieutenant. After all, it's nurses like you that are the key to our hospital's success."

"Thank you, sir."

There was a pause before the psychiatrist spoke again. "Lieutenant Gomez, I don't want to overstep my bounds here, but may I ask how your brother is doing?"

She was surprised by his question. "He's doing great, sir."

"Good, good." He coughed, then continued, "I must say, I'm a little concerned because Aiden has canceled his last two therapy appointments, including the one we had scheduled for this afternoon. He claims he's far too busy taking care of a litter of puppies to come in to see me."

Vanessa was shocked by the news of the canceled appointments. "I had no idea," she managed.

"It's good he has something like the puppies to help him through this," Lieutenant Colonel Flintman continued. "But you know as well as I do how important therapy is. After all this great progress, I'd hate to see him suffer a relapse."

She didn't want that, either. "I'll talk to him, sir."

"Thank you, Lieutenant."

She disconnected the call and, summoning Eagle, headed inside. Her timing was good, because Aiden was emerging from the bathroom, carrying the box of puppies.

"Hey," he greeted her with a broad smile. "I didn't realize you were back."

"I was working with Eagle outside." She tried to think of a way to broach the subject of Aiden's missed appointments. "How are the puppies doing today?"

"They're amazing." Aiden's voice was full of pride. "I can't believe how far they've come over these past few days."

She nodded, thrilled at how her brother had taken the task of fostering them so seriously. "I'm caring for them this afternoon, right? I think you mentioned having a therapy appointment."

Aiden's smile faded and his gaze skittered from hers. "No need. I rescheduled that."

"Rescheduled? Or canceled?"

"What difference does it make?" Aiden asked, bristling. "I'm doing fine."

"You're doing incredibly well," she acknowledged, stepping toward him. "And I'm truly thrilled about your progress. But, Aiden, ongoing treatment is important. I'm asking you to please, please reschedule your appointment. Don't keep skipping them entirely."

Aiden shifted the box in his grasp and edged around her. "I'll think about it."

She didn't want to let him go without a firm commitment. "I've heard the doc is taking appointments on Saturday," she pressed. "I'm working tomorrow, but I'm sure Isaac would watch the puppies for an hour or so. And if that doesn't work for some reason, I'm off Monday."

Aiden didn't answer for a long moment. "Okay," he finally agreed. "I'll call and schedule for Monday."

She drew in a deep breath and let it out slowly. She would have preferred Saturday, but wasn't going to argue. "Thank you," she murmured. "I hope you realize I only want you to get better."

"I know, Nessa." Aiden flashed a crooked smile.

"Speaking of helping me, how about lending a hand with the next bout of housebreaking?"

"Do I have to?" she asked with a mock grimace. "That's not exactly my favorite job."

"Mine, either. But it's still rewarding when they get it right."

She chuckled in agreement. "I'm in."

The afternoon passed pleasantly enough, but she could feel her stomach knot with tension as evening approached. She'd committed to attending a homecoming party for some returning airmen, promising her best friend, Margie Campbell, that she'd come. But she knew now she needed to cancel. It wasn't worth the risk. There had been too many attempts to kill her.

She found herself growing angry with Boyd Sullivan. She'd helped him that night all those years ago and this was how he repaid her? By trying to strangle her? Shoot at her not just once, but twice? Convince people to do dirty deeds on his behalf, like trying to steal the puppies? From the very beginning, Boyd has demonstrated weird and erratic behavior.

The worst part of it all was not knowing what he'd do next.

Isaac tried to forget about the pain and sadness in Jacey Burke's eyes and to focus on what was going right instead. Kyle had reassured him that Beacon was doing much better and may be released as early as the following morning.

After picking up lunch at Carmen's, he headed home. For some reason, the food didn't taste quite as good as it had when he'd eaten it with Vanessa and Aiden.

As if sensing his mood, Tango came over and rested his head in Isaac's lap. He smiled and scratched Tango behind the ears. The golden had been a reliable companion for him over the past few months, while he'd dealt with the red tape of getting Beacon returned home. And now that his time with Tango was coming to an end, he knew he'd miss the dog's calming presence.

Maybe he should head over to see if Aiden was interested in taking Tango as a therapy dog. The kid deserved a second chance, and he'd appeared to enjoy the golden.

He was halfway to the front door when he abruptly stopped. Who was he kidding? This wasn't about Aiden at all. No, this was nothing more than a pathetic excuse to see Vanessa.

Idiot.

He belatedly remembered there was an airmen's homecoming party scheduled for early evening. Was Vanessa planning to go? He didn't know, but after everything that had happened recently, he thought not.

Which was too bad, because he wanted to go with her. Very much. Even though he shouldn't.

He dropped onto the sofa and buried his head in his hands. This emotional Cuban Eight aerobatic maneuver his brain was doing was driving him crazy. What was wrong with him that he wanted what he couldn't have?

The reasons he needed to stay away from Vanessa were murky at best, like flying through a thick storm cloud with zero visibility.

Vanessa wasn't Amber, so why was he constantly comparing the two?

Because he was afraid the end result would be the same.

And why wouldn't it be? He still didn't know what his future held. If he couldn't be a pilot because of his PTSD, then what sort of job could he do?

There was no denying the possibility that his future may not include remaining in the Air Force.

With abrupt determination, he surged to his feet and pulled out his phone. He dialed Justin, hoping his former Air Force Academy buddy wasn't still tied up in meetings at Base Command.

"Blackwood."

"Hey, Justin. I'm sorry to bother you, but do you have a minute?"

"Yeah, my next meeting isn't for a half hour. What's going on?"

"This isn't about Boyd," he reassured Justin. "It's personal."

"Related to a beautiful petite brunette?" Justin teased.

"No, I'm looking for some career advice." He didn't bother to add that part of the driving force behind the sudden phone call was, in fact, Vanessa. "I'm due to reenlist and I'd like to discuss possible career options."

"Of course," Justin agreed. "Oops, there goes my phone. Listen, it's a little crazy right now with all this stuff going on, but I promise we'll find some time to talk, okay?"

"Great, thanks." Isaac felt better for having broached the touchy subject that had been secretly weighing him down for months now. "I appreciate your time."

"We'll set something up soon," Justin promised.

Isaac disconnected from the call. "One step at a time," he said to Tango.

The golden thumped his tail on the floor.

Sitting around at home was driving him crazy. Was

Vanessa feeling the same way? He remembered how she'd bristled at the thought of being confined to her house. Going to the airmen's homecoming party might be a welcome distraction. Not as a date, but as a way to get out of the house for a while.

Once the idea took hold in his mind, he couldn't shake it loose. He was going to do it. Within a couple of hours, he was showered, shaved and changed into a fresh set of dress blues. With Tango on a leash at his side, he left his house a good thirty minutes before the party to walk over to Vanessa's. He didn't have her number, so he would have to ask her face-to-face.

His pulse kicked up a notch with anticipation, as if it had been days rather than hours since he'd seen her last.

Yep, he had it bad.

He strode up to the front door, returning the cop's salute. "Is Lieutenant Gomez inside?"

"Um, yes, sir." The cop moved over, allowing him to enter.

"Isaac." Vanessa's expression indicated surprise when she saw him walk in. "What are you doing here?"

"I thought you'd be going a little crazy sitting around, and you might want to get out of here for a while. We could stop in at the airfield and watch the homecoming."

Her eyes flashed with anticipation, but then she frowned. "I would, but it's too dangerous."

"We won't stay long." He didn't understand why he was suddenly so desperate to go with her. "You deserve to have a little fun, don't you?"

"I don't know…" Her voice trailed off. Then she shrugged. "Okay, why not? Give me a few minutes to change."

"Happy to wait." He hoped his relief wasn't too obvious. He really needed to pull himself together.

Ten minutes later, she returned in her dress blues. "I'll drive."

He didn't argue, but followed her out to the SUV in the driveway. He didn't see anyone around, but the sense of being watched had returned. His PTSD paranoia? Or true danger?

They made it to the landing strip with time to spare. As they made their way through the crowd, he noticed a tall blonde waving at them.

"Hey, Margie," Vanessa called. "How are you?"

"Great." Margie glanced at him, so he stepped forward.

"Captain Isaac Goddard," he said, introducing himself.

"First Lieutenant Margie Campbell," the blonde returned. "Vanessa and I work together. Nice to meet you, Captain," Margie said with a smile. She turned toward Vanessa. "I'm supposed to meet Tristen here. Have you seen him?"

"Not yet. But you can hang with us for a while," Vanessa offered.

"Oh, I don't want to intrude." Margie glanced around, then stood up on her tiptoes. "I think I see Tristen over there. See you later, okay?"

"Sure thing." Vanessa looked a little embarrassed when her friend left. "Don't let Margie make you uncomfortable. She's a ridiculous matchmaker."

Isaac cleared his throat, feeling awkward. "I'm never uncomfortable around you, Vanessa. Quite the opposite."

"Oh." She blushed and looked away.

"I would have called to formally invite you to attend this with me, but didn't have your number."

She arched a brow. "Why would you want it? After all, you're the one who told me you weren't relationship material."

"I'm not," he agreed. "You know, more than anyone else, how I've been struggling since returning stateside."

Her dark gaze filled with compassion. "Oh, Isaac, struggling with an illness doesn't prevent you from having a relationship."

"It does," he insisted. "Especially when I have more questions than answers about my future."

Understanding dawned in her eyes. "I see. Okay, then why did you change your mind and ask me to come?"

He hesitated, shrugged. "I couldn't stay away."

She muttered something that sounded like *men* under her breath, then wrapped her arm around his waist in a brief hug. He returned the embrace, enjoying the sweet, calming honeysuckle scent that clung to her.

Someone jostled them from behind, forcing him to release her. He lightly grasped her hand, cherishing the connection. "I can't believe how many people showed up for this."

"I know. Any reason to celebrate, right?"

"You got it."

"There's the plane," someone shouted.

Isaac lifted his gaze to the sky, momentarily overwhelmed with a sense of loss. Would he ever make it back up in the pilot's seat? Or was he doomed to be grounded forever?

The C-130 Hercules aircraft slowly grew larger as

it approached the runway. The sound of the dual engines was incredibly loud, but that didn't keep him from smiling with appreciation as the pilot leveled the plane, bringing the aircraft in for a smooth landing.

"Nice," he said.

"If you say so." Vanessa shrugged. "I wouldn't know a good landing from a bad one."

"Trust me, you would if you were a passenger inside," he joked.

The plane taxied in toward the hangar. The crowd waited patiently for the plane to stop and for the returning airmen to disembark.

The crowd surrounding them seemed to be holding its collective breath. The C-130 came to a stop and the hatch opened up, dropping to the ground with a loud clang.

After another long moment, the five returning airmen appeared from within the depths of the plane, waving as they descended.

"Hey! There's Boyd Sullivan!"

Just like when Beacon arrived on base, chaos erupted. Some people screamed, others pushed and shoved as if attempting to escape, while others dropped to the ground as if afraid of impending gunfire.

"Stay down," Isaac commanded, pulling Vanessa close. He thought for sure this was nothing more than a ruse to get at Vanessa.

"No! Look. I think I see him over there!" Vanessa pulled away from him and took off running in the direction from where the shout had come from.

"Wait! Vanessa!" Isaac kept pace with her, weaving through people with Tango close to his side. He desperately searched the male faces for Sullivan's familiar features.

Vanessa slowed and stopped, looking around in confusion. "He was here, Isaac. But now he's gone."

"Are you sure?"

"I think so." A hint of doubt invaded her tone.

"Let's join the search." He kept close to her side as they joined other Security Forces officers combing the area for a sign of the Red Rose Killer.

But after frantic searching, they came up empty-handed.

If Boyd Sullivan had in fact been there, he was gone now.

Evading capture once again.

ELEVEN

Hours later, after fruitless searching, they were gathered at Base Command. "Are you absolutely sure you saw Sullivan?" Captain Blackwood was frowning at Vanessa as if she'd personally allowed Boyd to escape.

She glanced around the group seated around the table. Several of the members of the task force assigned to catching the Red Rose Killer were in attendance, including Tech Sergeant Linc Colson, First Lieutenant Ethan Webb and Master Sergeant Westley James, none of whom appeared antagonistic, but Yvette Crenville, the base nutritionist, was staring at her suspiciously.

Because Yvette still believed she was guilty of the false claims the anonymous blogger had made about her helping Boyd?

Or because Yvette had noticed Vanessa keeping a close eye on her recently? Justin Blackwood had asked her to watch Yvette while they were both at work, so she had. But the woman had yet to do anything the least bit suspicious.

"No, I can't be absolutely sure I saw him." Vanessa tried to keep her impatience from showing. "Everyone heard the shout and when I looked in that direction, I caught a glimpse of dark hair and narrow eyes. In that brief moment, I thought the man was Boyd."

"Anyone else see him?" Justin asked.

A strained silence fell over the group and those around her all shook their heads.

"We may not have, but someone did," Isaac pointed out. "Someone shouted his name, causing instant pandemonium."

Vanessa wished she'd kept the flash of recognition to herself. The glimpse had been so fleeting, and looking back, she could admit the dark-haired, narrow-eyed man could have been anyone.

Justin blew out a frustrated breath. "Great. This is just perfect. What I'm hearing is that we don't know if Sullivan was really there or not," he said. "In fact, it's highly likely the person who shouted Sullivan's name saw the same guy Vanessa spotted."

Once again, all eyes turned toward her. She really, really wished she'd kept her mouth shut. "But haven't there been other sightings of Boyd on base? Why is it so hard to believe he was in the crowd this evening?"

"Because if he was smart, he'd stay hidden," Westley James said. "And while Boyd may not be the most brilliant criminal we've come across, he's had us chasing our tails for months now. We've seriously underestimated him."

She couldn't argue with the master sergeant. "But if Boyd is on base, then there must be a methodical way to find him. Have we gone through all the videos and checked out every possible person who might be helping him? I promise it's not me." Her voice came out more vehemently than she intended.

"No one suspects you, Vanessa," Isaac said. "You

were attacked at the hospital and have the bruises to prove it, not to mention being shot at several times."

While she appreciated Isaac's support, the collar of her dress uniform hid the bruises from view. Justin had seen her bruises that first night, but no one else had. And so far, no one could prove that the gunshots had been directed at her.

Deep down, she could understand some of the skepticism. Being targeted by Boyd didn't make any sense. She'd helped him that night in the alley all those years ago. There was no reason for him to come after her now.

"Now that you mention other helpers, I have noticed something odd," Gretchen Hill said. Vanessa was relieved when all eyes turned toward the female cop.

"Like what?" Justin demanded.

Gretchen tipped her chin and met Justin's direct gaze. "One night I worked late with our newest dog, Abby. After returning her to the kennel, I found one of the trainers, a guy named Rusty Morton, acting very strangely. He was pacing and texting, looking worried. The night was cool but he was sweating and appeared nervous. When he saw me, he tucked his phone away and left the training facility." Gretchen shrugged. "I thought it was odd."

Justin's gaze was skeptical, but then Westley James nodded. "You know, I've noticed him acting weird, too. I found him sitting outside the other day, his head in his hands as if he didn't know what to do. I asked if he was okay, and he admitted he wasn't feeling well, told me he'd caught a bug of some kind. Then he hurried away."

Justin looked thoughtful. "It's strange behavior, but

have you considered the possibility that he was just trying to hide his illness?"

"Why would he hide something like that?" Gretchen asked.

"As a nurse, I know many people don't like admitting they're sick," Vanessa said slowly. "And one conclusion could be that he's afraid Westley will take away his position as a trainer. But all of that aside, I don't think we can ignore the possibility that Morton might be helping Boyd. After all, someone let all the dogs out of their kennels as a diversion."

There was a long moment of silence.

"Rusty loves those dogs," Westley said. "But I've had the same concern."

Justin swept his gaze over the room. "Since we don't have any other leads, I'll assign a cop to keep an eye on Morton for the next few days." Justin paused, then asked, "Anything else going on that I should know about?"

More silence, then a round of *no sirs* echoed from the group.

"Good. Dismissed." Justin rose to his feet.

Vanessa happened to be seated closest to the door, so she gratefully slipped out ahead of the group.

"Vanessa, wait!" Isaac's voice rose above the din of departing airmen.

She slowed down enough to let Isaac catch up, but continued making her way outside the building, breathing the fresh autumn air.

"Vanessa, you can't go off on your own." Isaac's voice was tense with alarm.

"I know, I'm sorry."

He stood beside her for a moment, Tango at his side.

She greeted the dog with a quick rub, glad to see him, considering she'd left Eagle at home.

But hearing Boyd's name and the subsequent chaos had made her wish she'd brought her protective K-9 along.

"What's wrong? You seem upset." Isaac's gaze searched hers intently.

She sighed. "It's difficult feeling like I have to constantly profess my innocence."

"You're not a suspect," Isaac assured her.

"I am," she insisted. "And being the only one who claims to have seen Boyd at the landing strip doesn't help my case. I know Justin has told me I'm not a suspect, but that's just words. I won't feel truly vindicated until Boyd is caught and arrested."

"You may be right to some extent," Isaac agreed. "But I know you're innocent."

She was touched by his show of trust. "Thank you."

"Let's walk back to your car."

She nodded and he fell into step beside her, keeping Tango between them. He grimaced. "I should have made you bring Eagle along."

"I know, but after the scare with the intruder, I didn't feel right leaving Aiden home alone with the puppies."

"Justin still has a cop posted at your door," Isaac said.

"Yes, but that didn't help last time, did it?"

"No."

"Exactly." Vanessa shrugged. "I figured being with you would be enough and that Eagle was needed more at home."

"Boyd sent that rose to you, Vanessa. Not to your brother."

She knew that, but the break-in had shaken her confidence. No way was she going to allow Aiden to be hurt because of her.

"You really think Rusty Morton might be involved?" she asked.

"His behavior is off. Could be he's in some kind of trouble," Isaac said. "Makes sense to me that it could be Boyd."

"Maybe he is guilty of something. If he was the one who let the dogs loose, maybe that was only the start and now Boyd is holding that over his head."

"Justin will keep an eye on Rusty. If the trainer is guilty, we'll find out soon enough."

They walked for a while in silence and she wondered if Isaac had put Tango between them on purpose, to keep space between them. But if he wanted distance, why had he showed up at her doorstep to take her to the homecoming? It confused her.

When they reached her SUV, they exchanged mobile phone numbers.

"Does this mean that you're still attending church services with me and Aiden on Sunday?"

She didn't imagine the slight hesitation before he said, "Yes, of course."

There was no *of course* about it, but she didn't push. Just because Isaac wasn't interested in a relationship, she still wanted him to find a way back to his faith.

Believing in God and leaning on His grace and wisdom was important. Far more precious than anything else.

They were both silent on the ride back to her place. He walked with her up to the sidewalk, then stopped. She glanced over her shoulder questioningly.

"I'd like to spend the night on your sofa."

"That's not necessary," she said with a nod to the cop at the door. "I'm sure we'll be fine. Besides, I have to work a twelve-hour shift tomorrow, so I'll be up super early."

"Please." Isaac took a step closer. "Humor me. I promised to keep you safe and after the possible sighting of Boyd, I can't stand the thought of leaving you."

"If it makes you feel better, why not?" She saluted the cop at the door, then went inside, Isaac and Tango right behind her.

Aiden was sitting on the kitchen floor, surrounded by the puppies. "Hi. How was the party?"

"Nothing special." Vanessa didn't want her brother to worry about Boyd. "Isaac is going to bunk on the sofa if that's okay with you."

"Sure. I'll keep the puppies in my room tonight." Aiden's expression turned grim. "I'm not going to risk letting anything happen to them."

"Good idea." Vanessa couldn't help but smile when Tango went over to sniff the pups, making Aiden laugh.

It had been so long since her brother had laughed.

She stood awkwardly for a moment, secretly wishing for an opportunity to be alone with Isaac. But it was probably better to give Aiden and Isaac some time alone, in case they wanted to talk. "Well, good night, then. Don't forget, I'm working a full twelve tomorrow."

"I know." Her brother's voice held a note of annoyance. She needed to remember that despite everything he'd gone through, he wasn't a little kid anymore. At twenty, he was far from the boy she'd helped raise with their aunt Millie after their parents had died.

She left the two men alone, hoping and praying that Aiden was truly on the road to recovery.

Isaac wasn't sure why he was torturing himself by sleeping on Vanessa's sofa, surrounding himself with her honeysuckle scent. Wasn't one night of no sleep enough?

Or maybe he was hoping that he wouldn't suffer another nightmare if he was here at her place, rather than alone in his house.

He made a mental note to seek out Jacey Burke again to at least apologize for his role in her brother's death. If she couldn't forgive him, that was fine, but he at least needed to let her know he held himself responsible.

The way any good pilot would.

He sat with Aiden for a while. They didn't talk about their respective nightmares, but he sensed the young man was beginning to trust him. Maybe over time, Aiden would feel comfortable opening up to Isaac.

Ironic that the only person he'd opened up to was Vanessa.

Eventually, Isaac slept better than he'd hoped. When he woke, it was to the tantalizing scent of coffee. He pried open one eye and peered into the kitchen.

Vanessa looked lovely, her golden skin glowing from her shower, her dark hair pulled away from her face in a ponytail that made her look years younger. His heart stumbled in his chest and he had to force himself to stay where he was or risk kissing her again.

"Hey," he said, drawing her attention. "Let me know when you're ready to go. I'll walk with you to work."

"I have about five minutes, but that's not enough

time to walk, so I'll drive." She finished her cup of coffee and then set it in the sink. "Actually, now that I think about it, maybe you should drive me to work? That way I can keep Eagle here with Aiden."

"You need Eagle more than Aiden does." He shot to his feet.

"He can't stay in the ICU all day and besides, Aiden needs protection, too."

He recognized the stubborn glint in her eyes. "Please?"

"Not happening." She narrowed her gaze and thrust out her chin. "Will you drive with me or not?"

"Okay." He sensed arguing wasn't going to get him anywhere and felt a twinge of resentment that she was pushing the issue of driving after he'd already told her about his concern of triggering a flashback. "But I'm going to leave your car at the hospital. Kyle is going to release Beacon today, so I'll hang around the Winged Java for a while until the clinic opens."

"Okay." She picked up her purse and her stethoscope. "Let's go."

"Will you stop in and check on Aiden later today?" she asked as she glanced at him. "I'd feel better knowing he has someone around while I'm working."

"I can do that." He cleared his throat and cast a look at Tango in the rear. "Maybe I'll leave Tango, see if he'll bond with him."

"That's great. And I'm really happy to hear about Beacon coming home, too. You've certainly waited long enough for this day."

"You have that right." Isaac still had trouble believing it for himself. "Park close to the door, okay? And call me after your shift so I can come meet you."

She nodded, and obliged him by pulling into the first available space close to the building. He slid out of the passenger seat as she emerged with her purse over her shoulder and her stethoscope slung around her neck. He escorted her to the door.

"Have a great day." He gave her a quick hug, releasing her before he could act on his temptation to kiss her. "See you later."

"Bye."

He stood on the sidewalk, watching as she hurried inside. When the door closed behind her, he led Tango toward the Winged Java.

After purchasing a coffee and blueberry muffin, he headed back outside to one of the tables along the sidewalk.

The clinic didn't open for over two hours yet, so when he finished his muffin, he settled in for a long wait.

A familiar female figure approached on the sidewalk, dressed casually in her battle-ready uniform. He recognized Greta, her Belgian Malinois, walking at her side.

"Jacey?" He quickly stood. "Hey, do you have a minute?"

"Oh, hi, Isaac." Her smile was strained. "Um, sure, I guess."

"I won't keep you long," he promised. Now that she was here, he tried to formulate the best approach. "Do you want coffee or tea?"

"No, thanks." She sat stiffly in the seat across from him, glancing warily over her shoulder. He frowned, wondering what she'd been through in Afghanistan.

"Listen, Jacey, I just wanted a chance to apologize to

you." Isaac swallowed hard and forced himself to meet her startled gaze. "I know it's my fault your brother is gone and I feel terrible for letting you down."

"You were under attack by enemy fire," she said. "I don't hold you responsible for Jake's death. We signed up to serve our country and that's exactly what you and Jake were doing."

He stared in shock. "I—I thought you hated me."

For the first time, her smile brightened her entire face. "I don't hate you, Isaac. Never have." She tipped her head to the side. "Are we okay now?"

"I— Um, yeah, sure." He was flabbergasted at her response. "I'm glad to hear it."

"Are you picking up Beacon today?"

He nodded and finished off his coffee. "Yes, but the clinic doesn't open for a while yet." He grinned. "Somehow, I don't think Kyle will be surprised to find me waiting at the doorway."

She laughed and shook her head. "Probably not." Her smile faded and she glanced again over her shoulder. "Well, I'd better get going. I have some work to do with Greta here."

Isaac's instincts were spinning. "Hey, Jacey, is something wrong? Someone giving you trouble?"

"What?" A flash of guilt shadowed her blue eyes. "Oh, no. I'm fine, truly. Just adapting to life back on US soil, that's all."

He knew what it was like to go from one world where you feared for your life on a daily basis to one where most of the people around you weren't dangerous at all.

Well, except for Boyd Sullivan.

"Jacey, I know Jake would want me to take over the

role of big brother to look after you," he said. "Call me if you need something, okay?"

"I will." She bobbed her head in agreement, but he wasn't convinced. "See you later."

The two hours slipped by slowly. Thankfully Kyle Roark arrived ahead of schedule and readily took Isaac back to see Beacon.

The dog lifted his head and let out a sharp bark from his kennel. Then his tail began to wag and his entire body shimmied with excitement.

"He'll be fine, Isaac." Kyle opened the kennel and handed Isaac the leash. He clipped the tether to Beacon's collar and then knelt down to greet the dog the way he'd been wanting to since they'd parted.

"Good boy," he said, chuckling as the dog tried to climb into his lap and lick his face. He rubbed Beacon's coat and buried his face against the dog's neck. "Welcome home, buddy. Welcome home."

Kyle watched the reunion with satisfaction. "It's obvious you two belong together."

"I agree." Isaac finally rose to his feet. "Come on, Beacon. Let's get you home."

Beacon didn't seem to mind Tango, which was a little surprising, since Beacon wasn't what anyone would call a warm and fuzzy animal. He was a warrior.

A warrior that had saved his life.

The morning went by fast, so he didn't make it over to Vanessa's to check on Aiden until after lunch.

"You really want me to watch Tango for a while?" Aiden seemed unsure when Isaac told him his plan. "He's your therapy dog, isn't he?"

"He was, but I have Beacon now. We're a team, and I'm worried that Tango will feel left out."

He spent some of the afternoon getting reacquainted with Beacon, though their connection was so strong, he didn't need the extra time. So he decided to head back to Vanessa's to see how Aiden was doing with Tango.

In no time it was nineteen thirty, the time Vanessa's shift ended. She'd warned him that sometimes she had to work late, but he thought about heading over to meet her, even though she hadn't called yet to say she was finished.

Before he could decide, his phone rang. He grinned when he recognized her number. "Hey, Vanessa."

"Isaac? Someone smashed my driver's-side window and left a red rose on my seat."

TWELVE

Vanessa rubbed her arms, feeling chilled to the bone as she stood beside the cop who'd escorted her to her vehicle. The Security Forces cop had introduced himself as Staff Sergeant Sean Morris and had been happy to provide an escort to her car.

She should have called Isaac, the way they'd initially planned. But she'd thought she'd be safe enough with a cop escort.

And now, she was glad she hadn't been alone when she'd found the damage and the crushed red rose. The implied threat was all too real. Sean Morris had instantly called his boss, while she'd contacted Isaac.

Just hearing Isaac's calm voice had reassured her.

"Captain Blackwood will be here any minute, Lieutenant," Morris said, his blue eyes full of concern. "Are you sure you're okay?"

"Of course," she replied, wishing she could stop shivering. "Frankly, I'm glad it's only my SUV that's been damaged."

Morris didn't look convinced, but he didn't say anything more as twin headlights cut through the darkness. She tensed, until she realized the driver was Justin. He got out of the car and then let his dog, Quinn, out before coming over.

"Captain," Morris greeted the officer with a sharp salute.

"At ease, Sergeant." Justin returned the salute, then his gaze sought hers. "You're not hurt?"

"Sergeant Morris escorted me outside after work and we found this." She gestured to the broken driver's-side window. "Unfortunately, I worked a twelve-hour shift, so I have no idea when this happened."

Justin surveyed the damage, looking grim. "It's a threat all right. Seems to fit in with the way he initially picks his victims, sending a rose then following up with violence. But why is he repeating that pattern now?"

Vanessa battled a helpless wave of anger. "I don't know. None of it makes any sense. He's done so many things, from stealing uniforms, killing people, letting the dogs loose, firing into crowds and leaving threatening notes in all sorts of random places. But the biggest mystery is why he's targeting me in the first place."

"He obviously is carrying a grudge against you," Justin said. "Are you sure you don't know why?"

"No clue." She sighed, then glanced over as Isaac jogged over with Beacon at his side.

He surprised her by pulling her into his arms. "Are you sure you're all right?" he asked in a low, husky voice.

His clean, masculine scent was incredibly soothing. "Yes," she whispered. Oddly enough, now that Isaac was here, she felt much better.

Safer. Which was crazy, since Sergeant Morris was armed and Isaac wasn't.

Isaac held her for another long moment, before releasing his hold so he could examine the damage to her car. "This ridiculousness has gone on long enough," he muttered.

"You don't have to tell me." Justin's tone was laced with frustration. "I hate the way we always seem to be one step behind him."

"We need to check the video cameras, sir," Sergeant Morris said.

"We will, but they haven't helped us so far," Blackwood pointed out. "Sullivan apparently knows where the cameras are and is always wearing a mask or hoodie, keeping his face averted from view. He's managed to avoid motion sensors and other security measures we have, as well."

"Then this fits with Sullivan's previous attempts." Vanessa waved a hand at her broken window.

"Yes, it does," Justin admitted. "Although again, I don't see why he's repeating the pattern, going from attempted murder back to a scare tactic like a brick through a window and a red rose."

"Like the phone call," Vanessa said.

"Phone call?" Blackwood echoed.

She inwardly winced when she realized she'd failed to mention it. "I'm sorry, I forgot to tell you. After the gunshot at Beacon's landing, I received a phone call from an unknown number. All the voice said was, 'Next time, you won't get away.'"

Justin sighed. "You should have told me."

"I know. But I couldn't identify the voice, either. I can't say whether it was Boyd's voice or not." She felt bad about the lapse. Isaac slipped his arm around her shoulders as if to reassure her.

"Sir? Is it possible Sullivan knew that Lieutenant

Gomez has had a security detail escorting her anytime she's outside the ICU and decided to leave the brick and rose as a warning instead?" Sergeant Morris asked.

Three pairs of eyes swiveled to stare at the staff sergeant in surprise. The guy was roughly her age with dark hair and kind eyes, and she found herself impressed by his insight.

"It's possible," Justin acknowledged. "At this point, I'm open to any and all reasonable theories. Which reminds me, what about the ex-boyfriend you mentioned the other day? Maybe this is his work?"

"It's not Leo's style," she insisted.

Justin didn't look convinced. "In the meantime, let's get a tech out here to check for fingerprints or other evidence."

Vanessa knew that the likelihood of finding fingerprints on the brick or the smashed rose was slim to none, but understood it was part of the process. "Is it okay if I go home?"

Justin glanced at Isaac, then nodded. "Sure. We'll let you know when we're finished processing your vehicle."

"I'll take them, Captain," Sergeant Morris offered.

"That's good," Justin agreed. "When you're finished, I'll need your report."

"Yes, sir." Morris gestured toward his car, which was parked beneath one of the bright lights scattered across the lot. "This way."

Isaac dropped his arm from her shoulders, but reached for her hand. She clutched it tightly as they followed Morris to his vehicle. Isaac opened the front passenger door for her and dropped to one knee, bringing Beacon close.

"Friend," he said to Beacon, putting his hand on Vanessa's knee. "Friend."

Beacon sniffed her legs, then wagged his tail. She tentatively scratched his silky head, staying clear of his healing incision, glad that the animal accepted her touch.

"Good boy," Isaac praised. He rose, closed Vanessa's door then slid in behind her.

Morris started the car and drove toward the exit.

"I live off Webster, just past Viking," she said.

"Yes, ma'am."

She winced. "Please, just call me Vanessa."

The cop flashed a smile. "Okay."

"And I'm Isaac. No need to stand on formality at times like this."

Morris nodded. "I'm sorry about your car."

"Me, too." She glanced over her shoulder at Isaac. "Does Aiden know?"

"Yes, I was with him when you called. I left Tango behind. Your brother agreed to keep him for a while."

She was relieved to hear it, although she still didn't like the idea of Aiden being at her place alone. The cop posted at the front door hadn't prevented a break-in, or the additional attempts to harm her. Something had happened almost every day.

Fear threatened to close her throat, making it impossible to breathe. Every day.

Would it continue until he succeeded in killing her?

Ten minutes later, Sean pulled into her driveway. She pulled herself together, barely making it out of the jeep when the front door flew open and Aiden came rushing out.

"Nessa!" He greeted her with a hug. "I've been worried."

She returned her brother's hug, feeling the sting of tears in her eyes. Despite all the horrible things happening to her, there was one good thing to come out of all this. Aiden was acting like the kid brother he'd been before he was sent overseas.

"I'm fine," she assured him, subtly wiping her eyes. "Easy enough to fix a broken window."

"I know." Aiden stepped back, revealing Tango at his side.

"Need anything else?" Sean asked.

"No, but thanks again." She flashed him a smile as Isaac and Beacon came to stand beside her.

"I was glad to be there. Keep calling for escorts while you're at work," Sean cautioned. "Each and every time you leave the ICU."

"I will."

Sean offered a quick salute and climbed back into his car. The three of them walked inside, nodding at the cop at the door.

"Isaac, are you going to sleep on the sofa again?" Aiden asked.

She was touched by her brother's protectiveness. He'd come a long way from that first night he'd met Isaac, glaring at him with suspicion.

"I will if Vanessa doesn't mind."

The pressure of being exposed to nonstop danger had her nodding quickly. "I'd like that."

Isaac didn't hesitate. "Done."

"Good." Aiden seemed satisfied with the added layer of protection. "I'll keep the puppies and Tango in my room." He glanced around the interior. "We are definitely outnumbered by the dogs."

That made Vanessa smile. Right here, right now, she felt safe. "'We'? I'll have Eagle in my room, Beacon will stay out here with Isaac. You're the only one outnumbered by the dogs."

"I don't mind." Aiden picked up the box of puppies, his grin making him look young and carefree. He spoke to the puppies and to Tango as he disappeared into his room, shutting the door behind him.

Then she and Isaac were alone.

"He's really coming along," Isaac said, gazing thoughtfully at Aiden's door.

"He is," she agreed. "Fostering the puppies has done him a world of good."

"I'm sure being here with you helped some, too." Isaac took a step closer and her heart quickened with anticipation. She longed for his reassuring presence.

"You've given him an unofficial chance with Tango," she pointed out, tipping her head back so she could meet his gaze. "And without Tango, we wouldn't have found the pups. Let's call it a group effort."

"Yeah." Isaac reached up and pushed a strand of hair behind her ear. "I missed you today."

Her heart melted at his frank admission. "I missed you, too."

"And I hate that you're constantly in danger." He cupped her cheek, then bent down slowly, lightly brushing his lips against hers. The kiss was soft and fleeting, making her yearn for more.

"Good night, Vanessa," he murmured, stepping away.

Disappointment stabbed deep. She couldn't deny

she was getting tired of Isaac's mixed messages. One minute he was holding her and kissing her, the next he was pulling away.

As she returned to her room, she tried to let go of her fear and focus on the fact that they were attending church together in the morning.

Wasn't helping Isaac rediscover his faith more important than her feelings for him?

Of course, it was.

But the knowledge didn't help her sleep any better. Not until she closed her eyes and lifted her heart and hope to her Lord.

Please help me guide Isaac back to his faith and Your loving arms. If all we can have is friendship, help me to accept Your plan, Amen.

Why had he kissed her?

Isaac turned on the narrow sofa, wondering if he'd ever get a full night's sleep again. Beacon was home where he belonged. He'd finally fulfilled his promise to Jake. He should be satisfied, but he wasn't. Being close to Vanessa and keeping their relationship on strictly friendly terms was killing him.

He wasn't sure he could keep it up. He'd almost clutched her close and kissed her long and deep, the way he'd wanted.

Tomorrow was Sunday, and he wished he could renege on his agreement to attend church services with Vanessa and Aiden.

But that was yet another promise he refused to break.

His eyelids fluttered closed and almost instantly he was back in the cockpit of the chopper, the sound of gunfire deafening.

Mayday! Mayday? We're under fire!

Abruptly he awoke from the dream to see Beacon licking his face, his paws planted on his chest. His breath came in pants as his pulse thundered in his ears.

He'd hoped the nightmares wouldn't return now that Beacon was home but he'd been wrong. Beacon had helped, but he was forced to admit that the nightmares might never stop.

Swinging into a sitting position on the edge of the sofa, he scratched Beacon behind the ears, drawing strength from the animal's presence.

Good thing the top brass had agreed to honor Isaac's request to retire Beacon from active duty. Losing his handler and then being separated from Isaac had caused the dog to exhibit all kinds of bad behavior.

If only they could see Beacon now.

Isaac couldn't sleep, fearing the nightmare would return. Dawn brightened the horizon, so he padded into the kitchen to start a pot of coffee. As it brewed, he took Beacon outside, startling the cop at the door.

When Beacon finished his business, Isaac headed back inside and helped himself to a large mug of coffee. The caffeine helped clear the cobwebs from his brain.

Aiden got up first, yawning as he carried the box of puppies outside. Tango followed as if knowing it was his job to assist.

Isaac remained inside to cook eggs for breakfast, although they were cold by the time Vanessa emerged, a good thirty minutes later. She looked lovely and fresh after her shower, especially the way her dark hair framed her face. His mouth went dry as he noticed her short-sleeved, burned-orange sweater and a billowy flowered skirt.

"Wow," he managed. "You look amazing."

"Thanks," she murmured with a blush. Then her brow furrowed. "You look exhausted."

"Yeah, well, as usual I couldn't sleep." He tried to downplay the symptoms of PTSD, although he knew as a nurse Vanessa probably understood. Better than Amber had.

"All the more reason you should come to church services with us," she persisted.

Again, he hesitated, then reluctantly nodded. "I guess I better get home to change into something decent." Isaac glanced down at his battle-ready uniform with a grimace. He didn't have a lot of formal clothes, other than his dress blues.

She glanced at the clock on the wall. "You have plenty of time. No need to rush."

Maybe not, but he needed some distance from her enticing honeysuckle scent or he might do something foolish like kiss her again.

She didn't need a guy like him, bogged down with nightmares and mood swings.

Isaac warmed the eggs in the microwave and set the plate before her. Vanessa bowed her head and clasped her hands. "Dear Lord, thank You for providing the food I'm about to eat. Please continue guiding me on Your chosen path, Amen."

He felt guilty for not praying before his meal, although it wasn't second nature to him, the way it was for Vanessa.

They discussed their plans, agreeing to meet thirty minutes before the service, allowing plenty of time for them to walk, since Vanessa's car still hadn't been released. Isaac had also placed a call to Justin, requesting a second cop to be stationed at the house in case there was another attempt to get to the puppies.

When she finished breakfast, he helped with the dishes before heading home with Beacon. He hoped the pastor was open to airmen bringing their dogs to church services.

He spent some time with Beacon, grateful the dog didn't show any hint of weakness from his injuries and appeared content to be there with him.

The feeling was mutual.

An hour later, Isaac was showered, shaved and wearing his crisp dress blues. He walked back down to Vanessa's, struck again by her beautiful smile as she came down the steps toward him. It wasn't easy to persuade Aiden to leave the puppies behind with Tango, even though it was only for a little over an hour, but he finally agreed. The cop stationed at the door accompanied them as a second cop arrived to watch the puppies.

As they approached the church, Isaac was relieved to see that a few of the other airmen had their dogs with them, too. At least he wouldn't look completely out of place. At the threshold of the building, Isaac noticed a tall, light brown–haired man cheerfully greeting people as they entered.

"Good morning, Pastor Harmon," Vanessa said when it was their turn to enter. "I'd like you to meet Captain Isaac Goddard and his K-9, Beacon."

Isaac held out his hand and the pastor shook it.

"Welcome to God's house, Isaac. May you find peace and serenity within your faith."

"Thanks." Isaac followed Vanessa and Aiden inside, grimacing as they went directly to the front of the church. As much as he would have preferred hovering in the back, he reluctantly slid in beside Vanessa.

Sitting there, he wasn't sure why he'd agreed to come. Because of the recurring nightmare? No, because he'd promised. He stared down at his hands, finding it difficult to accept God's will after suffering the terrible loss of his closest friend, Jake. Who knew if God really had a plan? Maybe they were all on their own to flounder or flourish.

Vanessa picked up a small hymnal, offering it to him. He shook his head.

Pastor Harmon seemed to be looking at him through the entire service, making him shift uncomfortably in his seat. Another reason he preferred sitting in the back and well out of sight.

Then the pastor said something that struck close to home. "'In him was life, and the life was the light of men. The light shines in the darkness, and the darkness has not overcome it.'"

Isaac looked up and caught Pastor Harmon's gaze, stunned at the gentle knowledge and understanding reflected there. Isaac gave the pastor a brief nod, realizing that what the Bible said was true.

He'd used Jake's death as a way to avoid the light, as an excuse to stay in the darkness. But God was the light and he should never, ever have turned away from the Lord.

A sense of joy swept over him, and he reached over and picked up one of the small hymnals. When the choir broke into song, he joined in, his voice low and hoarse and rusty, yet true.

Vanessa wrapped her hand around his and he was suddenly glad she was with him.

For the first time since the horrible crash, he wondered if this moment, right now, really was part of God's plan.

If so, he would be an idiot to let her go.

The peace he'd gained in church offered a keen sense of hope. It didn't take long for them to leave the building, separating themselves from the crowd as they crossed Canyon Drive.

A dark pickup truck with tinted windows picked up speed as it headed toward them. "Look out!" Isaac shouted.

He released Beacon's leash to grab Vanessa and Aiden with each hand. The cop beside them turned to point his weapon toward the oncoming truck.

The sound of gunfire was deafening and sent him to his knees.

Mayday, Mayday! We are under fire... In a heartbeat he was sucked back into the nightmare of his crash.

THIRTEEN

The truck bounced up and over the curb, then crashed into a tree. Staring in horror as the events unfolded, Vanessa caught a glimpse of the driver, slumped over the wheel.

Boyd?

Her mouth went dry and she took a step toward the truck. "I have to check on him."

"Isaac? Are you okay?" Aiden's voice had her turning toward Isaac. He was on his knees, his hands cradling his head.

"Stay with him," she told her brother. "I'll be right back."

The cop who'd taken the shot accompanied her to the truck. Bracing herself, she peered inside, expecting to see Boyd. But it wasn't. The driver was a stranger to her, just like the other guy, the one who'd tried to steal the puppies, had been.

She released her pent-up breath. The guy didn't move, and there was quite a bit of blood covering his chest. She put her fingers to his neck to check for a pulse, but found nothing.

He was dead.

"I had to shoot, or he would have hit us," the cop said in a low tone.

"I know." She bowed her head for a moment, asking God to have mercy for the man who'd tried to kill them. Then she turned away, heading back to Isaac and Aiden.

Isaac was pale, but on his feet. "The driver?" he asked.

She shook her head. "He didn't make it."

"I'm sorry," Isaac whispered, drawing her into his arms for a hug.

She soaked in his warm strength.

The sound of sirens filled the air, and she was grateful help was on the way. It wouldn't take long for Justin Blackwood to find out about this, either.

"He was going to kill us," Aiden whispered. "Just like that kid in Afghanistan."

She belatedly realized that her brother could very well suffer a setback after this. The truck coming at them was eerily similar to what had happened to Aiden in Afghanistan. Isaac loosened his grip, realizing she wasn't going anywhere, and she quickly pulled Aiden close in a sisterly hug.

"I'm sorry, Aiden. This is my fault. I shouldn't have gone to church with you. I should have known better. Everywhere I go brings danger."

Her brother clutched her close for a long moment. "It's not your fault, Nessa. It's that stupid Boyd Sullivan."

Two Security Forces vehicles pulled up to flank the crashed truck. She lifted her tortured gaze to Isaac. "I need to get Aiden home."

"Soon," he promised. "We'll need to give our statements to the Security Forces first."

She couldn't bear to look at the truck, knowing the driver was dead. *Why, Lord? Why is this happening?*

There wasn't a good answer. She knew it was God's will, but at times like this, it was difficult to simply accept that and move on.

Captain Blackwood joined them a few minutes later, his face pale and grim as he surveyed the scene. "What happened?"

"The truck came at us out of nowhere," Isaac said. "The cop had no choice but to shoot."

A muscle ticked at the corner of Justin's jaw. "I understand, I'm not blaming him for protecting you. But is there anything else you can tell me? Did either of you recognize the driver?"

"No, but I can tell you he's not Boyd," Vanessa said. "Not that it matters, I'm sure Boyd was behind this attack, the same as the other attacks. And I don't think he'll stop until he kills me."

"That's not going to happen," Isaac said forcefully.

Brave words, and while she appreciated Isaac's promise, she was beginning to lose faith. Not in God, but that she'd escape Boyd's next attempt.

"We got a license plate. The vehicle doesn't belong to anyone on base," Justin said. "We'll put his fingerprints through the system, see what pops up."

"Another fall guy?" Isaac asked. "Just like the one who tried to steal the puppies?"

"That's my take on it," Justin agreed.

Vanessa shivered. Isaac moved closer and she gratefully leaned against him.

"By the way, we're finished with your car," Justin told her.

"Did you find any prints?"

"Unfortunately not." Justin glanced between them. "I also looked into Captain Turner's alibi for the time frame in question. He has a rock-solid alibi."

"Are you sure?" Isaac demanded. "For the entire twelve-hour shift Vanessa worked?"

"We were able to pinpoint the time frame on the surveillance cameras," Justin explained. "The video angle isn't great, but we can see a shadowy, bulky shape of someone wearing a dark hood and ski mask slamming the brick through the window at eighteen thirty, almost a full hour before she found it. We were able to verify that during that same time frame, Captain Turner was in the ER tending to a patient."

Vanessa wasn't surprised. "I told you it wasn't Leo's style."

"Yeah, well, our investigation has stalled once again. We know Boyd is the prime suspect but haven't found him on base."

"Probably because he's using other people to do his dirty work," Isaac said in a flat tone.

"Did anything come from following Rusty Morton?" Vanessa remembered how Gretchen Hill had mentioned the trainer's suspicious behavior.

"Not yet, but we're keeping an eye on him." Justin turned back to the truck. Two airmen had placed the driver's body on a stretcher. "This guy and his connection to Boyd is my priority now."

She understood and silently agreed.

"If Rusty isn't Boyd's accomplice," Isaac said

thoughtfully, "he still might be the one who sold the dogs to the Olio crime syndicate."

Justin raised a brow. "You could be right about that. I'll check him out further once I'm finished here."

It was almost an hour later before they were allowed to head home, escorted by yet another cop. Vanessa found it difficult to look the cop in the eye, knowing that being assigned to guard her was likely one of the most dangerous jobs on base these days.

No one was particularly hungry, but Vanessa made soup and sandwiches to keep herself from going crazy. Aiden immersed himself in caring for the puppies, and she hoped and prayed they'd allow him to find a measure of peace.

"Come, Beacon," Isaac said. The dog obediently crossed over to sit at his side. Isaac ran his fingers over Beacon's fur and she realized he was checking the dog for injuries.

"Is he okay?" she asked.

"Seems fine." Isaac glanced at her. "Better than you are."

She shrugged, unable to argue. This latest attempt to kill her had been the worst yet. "How old is Beacon?"

"He'll be seven at the end of the month, which is one of the reasons the top brass agreed he could retire from active duty." Isaac shrugged. "That was the first hurdle I faced in getting him home. The second was his bad behavior."

She frowned. "He's fine. I haven't seen any evidence of bad behavior."

"I did a video chat with my buddy Frank a few months ago and Beacon went nuts. Frank mentioned they were struggling with his training."

"Maybe he missed you." She leaned forward to stroke the German shepherd's head. Eagle nudged his way between them, so she turned her attention to her K-9.

"Well, now that he's home, I'm sure your nightmares will go away once and for all."

Isaac's face shut down and he abruptly rose to his feet. "They haven't, and I've accepted the fact that they never will. Excuse me, but I need to get home." He strode through the house to the front door, with Beacon at his side.

She wanted to call out to him, to ask him to stay, but sensed there was no getting through to him.

Despite the cop stationed at her front door, the house felt incredibly empty after he was gone. She put a hand to her chest in an attempt to ease the ache that was building within.

She cared about Isaac, so very much.

Yet, she understood Isaac didn't share the same depth and breadth of her feelings. Despite the heated kisses and being sheltered in his warm embrace, she could tell he was holding himself back. Treating her as a close friend, nothing more.

Had he done something similar with his former girlfriend?

She tried to take comfort in the fact that she'd helped him find his way back to attending church. Closing her eyes, she prayed that God would show Isaac the way to healing.

With or without her.

Isaac still didn't have a meeting with Justin to discuss his future, and with everything going on, his buddy likely wouldn't have time for a while yet. Maybe he should go all the way up to Lieutenant General Hall. After all, if the commander wouldn't support his attempt to transition into another role, there was no point in trying.

It being a Sunday, he made a mental note to call first thing in the morning. If there wasn't a place for him within the Air Force, he needed to start making other plans.

His future loomed empty and bleak, making the rest of the day drag by slowly. Keeping occupied with Beacon wasn't helping to keep him centered as much as he'd hoped.

It was humbling to realize how much he'd come to depend on Vanessa, too.

When his phone rang an hour later, his pulse jumped when he recognized her number. "Vanessa? Is something wrong?"

"No, but I need a favor."

Anything, he thought, but managed to hold his tongue. "What's up?"

"I was asked to come in tomorrow morning to help cover a sick call," she said. "Being at work seems to be the safest place for me to be these days, so I agreed. They need me to work a full twelve-hour shift and Aiden has an appointment at fifteen thirty with Lieutenant Colonel Flintman. Can you swing by later in the afternoon to watch the puppies?"

"Of course." He was glad Aiden was going back to therapy. "Don't worry about a thing."

"Thanks, I appreciate it. I think Aiden was going to cancel his appointment if you couldn't help out."

"I'll be there."

"I'll let him know."

"Vanessa, I'll escort you to work in the morning, and I need you to promise you'll continue to ask for escorts each time you leave the ICU."

"No need for you to be here. Justin stopped by and I now have a full-time cop to take me where I need to go."

"I see." He didn't know what else to say.

"Good night, Isaac."

"Good night."

Once, he'd liked the peace and quiet of his small house, but after spending so much time with Vanessa, Aiden and the pups, he realized how lonely it was.

Was it possible he was turning another corner related to his emotional health issues? Going back to being a pilot wasn't an option, and if he went into the civilian world, he wasn't sure what he could do there, either.

That night, the nightmare returned. As before, Beacon woke him up before he crashed. He huddled with Beacon until almost four in the morning, when he finally fell into a dreamless sleep. Thankfully Aiden's doctor's appointment wasn't until late afternoon, giving him the opportunity to sleep in.

Still, it bothered him that the nightmare had resurfaced again so soon, especially after he had Beacon home. Two nights in a row. He tried not to dwell on it, but the reenlistment paperwork mocked him from the kitchen table as he made breakfast, which technically should have been lunch, and drank two cups of coffee.

He made the call to Lieutenant General Hall anyway, feeling the need to understand his options. Or lack thereof. Pulling himself together wasn't easy, but he wouldn't let Vanessa down.

At fourteen thirty he strode purposefully to Vanessa's house to take over Aiden's puppy-sitting duties. Aiden was glad to see him and quickly reviewed the puppy's routine. Isaac assured the young man he could handle it, and sent him off to his appointment.

The four pups, especially Denali and Smoky, were becoming rambunctious, rolling around and playing, nipping at his shoelaces. Shenandoah was the smallest and seemed content to curl in the crook of his arm. He could see why being around the puppies helped Aiden relax because he felt his own burdens slip away as he played with the adorable balls of fur.

Lieutenant General Hall surprised him by promptly returning his call. "Captain Goddard? I'd like to see you as soon as possible."

"Yes, sir. I should be able to get there by seventeen hundred hours, maybe sooner."

"I expect to see you at seventeen hundred hours, then." The tone in the commander's voice didn't invite room to negotiate.

"Yes, sir."

When the door banged open sixty minutes later, Isaac was ready to go, knowing it would take time for him to go home to change and then to get across base to the Base Command offices. When he caught a glimpse of Aiden's face, he frowned. "What's wrong?"

Vanessa's brother didn't answer, didn't look at Isaac or the puppies, but wordlessly disappeared into his bedroom, slamming the door shut behind him.

Isaac quickly set the box of puppies aside, to head over to Aiden's door. He knocked lightly, but there was no answer. He tried again, harder, then turned the handle and pushed it open.

Aiden sat on the floor in the corner of the room, holding his head in his hands and rocking back and forth, clearly agitated. He was mumbling under his breath, but Isaac couldn't figure out what he was saying.

"What happened? What's wrong?"

No answer.

Concerned, knowing he couldn't leave nor could he stay until the end of Vanessa's shift without disobeying a direct order, he pulled out his phone to call Vanessa. If anyone could figure out what had happened with Aiden, it was likely his sister.

"Hi, Isaac."

"Vanessa? You need to get home as soon as possible."

"Why?"

He swallowed hard. "Aiden needs you. Something has happened and he's regressed, badly."

"I'll be there as soon as possible. Please, Isaac, don't leave him alone until I get there, okay?"

"I won't, but hurry. I have a meeting with Lieutenant General Hall at seventeen hundred hours." He disconnected the call and returned to the kitchen. Maybe the puppies would help.

He couldn't imagine what had transpired to send the thriving young man reeling backward into a pit of despair.

FOURTEEN

Vanessa was taking care of what was now her fourth Tyraxal overdose patient when Isaac called. As much as she wanted to drop everything and rush to her brother's side, it wasn't quite that easy to leave work.

She couldn't abandon her two critically ill patients.

Bothered by both the latest overdose of Tyraxal and the news of her brother's severe regression, she continued caring for her patients while at the same time calling nurses from the upcoming shift to see if anyone would be willing to come in early to relieve her.

On the third phone call, she was relieved to hear that Second Lieutenant Shelly Arron was willing to start her shift early. Knowing Vanessa had someone on the way made it easier to concentrate on everything that needed to be done.

Her patient with the Tyraxal overdose wasn't nearly as critically ill as the previous patients had been, either because Carson Baker hadn't ingested as much Tyraxal or because he'd been found earlier—she couldn't say for sure.

Regardless, she silently thanked God for sparing this young airman first class's life. And it occurred to her that maybe, once the airman recovered, they might find out where he'd gotten the medication. From the brief history the ER doc had obtained, it appeared Airman First Class Carson Baker hadn't seen any combat.

So why had he been given PTSD medications?

She made a mental note to let Captain Blackwood know about this latest overdose, then quickly finished her charting just as her colleague Shelly walked in. Over the next fifteen minutes Vanessa provided detailed information on the two patients she was handing over to Shelly, and when she finished, she was about to head straight home, when something made her pause.

Picking up the phone at the nurses' station, she called Flintman's office. His receptionist answered.

"This is Vanessa Gomez, I really need to talk to Lieutenant Colonel Flintman as soon as possible."

"He's with a patient," the receptionist told her. "But he should be finished in about twenty minutes or so."

"Let him know I'll be there. Tell him it's about my brother, Aiden."

"I will," the woman promised.

Satisfied that she had a plan, she stepped away from the desk to use her personal phone to call Isaac. "How's Aiden?"

"He's in his room." Isaac's voice sounded grim. "Are you on your way? He won't talk to me about what happened in therapy. Worse, I brought in the box of puppies and he wouldn't even look at them."

Her stomach twisted painfully. "I don't understand. He was doing so well!"

"It could be a small thing that triggered a powerful flashback. That's how PTSD works. It's rarely logical or tangible."

She knew he was right, but the possible explanation didn't make her feel any better. Fighting a wave of despair, she sighed. "Tell him the puppies need him. That Master Sergeant Westley James won't let him keep them if he can't take care of them."

"Aren't you coming home?" Isaac asked. "He's pretty bad, Vanessa. He's sitting in the corner, rocking back and forth."

She closed her eyes, wishing the image wasn't so clear in her mind. "Listen, I'm going to head up to see Lieutenant Colonel Flintman. He's finishing up with a patient and I want to catch him before he leaves for the day."

"He can't give you details about Aiden's therapy," Isaac protested. "It's confidential."

"I know that," she agreed. "But Aiden gave Lieutenant Colonel Flintman permission to talk to me about his treatment plan. I don't need specifics, but there has to be some explanation as to what sent my brother over the edge during today's session."

Isaac let out a sigh. "I guess it can't hurt. How long will you be? I'm already running late for my meeting with the base commander."

Vanessa hated the idea of leaving her brother alone. "Can't you reschedule your appointment?"

"It was an order, Vanessa. I promise to return here as soon as possible."

"Yeah, okay." She didn't like it, but understood. "Go then. But do me a favor, leave Eagle with Aiden. Tell him to protect. Eagle will stand guard over Aiden and the puppies until I get home."

"Vanessa—" he started, but she cut him off.

"Just go. Right now, I have to get up to Flintman's

office. I'll head home as soon as possible." She disconnected from the call, swallowing her frustration.

She'd been in the Air Force long enough to know that disobeying a direct order would result in a formal reprimand or worse. She tried to accept that Isaac needed to go, but there was a small part of her that felt he could have handled things better.

Seeing as he suffered from PTSD, too, she thought he'd be more understanding of Aiden's plight.

She gave herself a mental shake. Isaac wasn't important right now. Her brother was.

The psychiatrist had to have some idea of how to manage this new facet of Aiden's illness.

Because she couldn't stand watching her brother suffer.

Isaac was halfway down Canyon when he abruptly stopped in his tracks.

He couldn't do it. Leaving Aiden alone didn't feel right. Turning to head back the way he'd come, he pulled out his phone and called Base Command.

"Lieutenant General Hall's office."

"This is Captain Goddard. Please extend my apologies to the commander, unfortunately, I won't be able to make our meeting after all."

"Excuse me, Captain, but I believe the commander issued a direct order."

He winced. "Yes, I know. I would never disobey an order unless there was a very important reason. The mental health and well-being of a young airman is on the line. Aiden Gomez is in the middle of a flashback and cannot be left alone. I'm sorry."

"But—"

He disconnected the call, wondering if this was how his career was meant to end.

Quickening his pace, he shook off thoughts of his uncertain future and considered what he might say to break through the wall Aiden had built.

He knew what it was like to be trapped in a nightmare. He'd suffered several instances just like Aiden's. But he was puzzled by the impetus behind the kid's regression. What had triggered the setback? He'd told Vanessa that it could be anything, yet he found it odd that Aiden had reacted so negatively after he'd been doing so well.

The truck attack from yesterday? Could be. It wasn't unusual to see a delayed reaction. It was also possible that Aiden had witnessed something on the way home from the hospital. Sweeping his gaze over the area, he didn't see any sign of violence.

Maybe Aiden had spoken of the truck attack during his session. If so, it could be that Lieutenant Colonel Flintman inadvertently said something that had triggered a flashback.

The more Isaac considered that possibility, the more he believed it. It was the only thing that made sense.

Boyd Sullivan's attempt to harm Vanessa was causing collateral damage. To Aiden and the others who'd gotten caught along the way. Two deaths for sure—the man who'd tried to steal the puppies, and the driver of the pickup truck.

So much death.

Did Boyd Sullivan know Vanessa had a younger brother? What if he turned his attention to Aiden?

Isaac broke into a run, reaching Vanessa's house in

record time. The cop stationed outside the door looked surprised as he offered a salute.

He returned the gesture automatically. "Is Airman Gomez still inside?"

"Yes, sir."

"Good." He moved through the kitchen, feeling a sense of relief when he noticed Eagle was sitting tall at Aiden's door. Exactly the way Vanessa had said he would be.

"Good boy. Protect, Eagle," he said as he moved past into Aiden's room. The Doberman rose to his feet for a moment, sniffed around the room for a minute, then sat back down on his haunches.

Aiden was still rocking in the corner, oblivious to the puppies rolling and playing around him. Tango must have sensed Aiden's distress, because the golden retriever was stretched out on the floor beside Aiden, with his wide head pressed against Aiden's hip.

Isaac hesitated, then offered a silent prayer.

Lord, please help me find a way to get through to this troubled young man. Grant me and give me the strength and wisdom to help him, Amen.

Feeling slightly more confident, Isaac approached cautiously. "Hi, Aiden. I'm back and willing to listen if you're in the mood to talk."

The young man ignored him, keeping up his rhythmic rocking back and forth.

"I know what it's like to suffer a flashback like the one you're going through," Isaac went on. "Sometimes it was the littlest thing that set them off, too. I don't want you to feel bad if that happened to you."

Nothing.

"Aiden, did watching the truck attack bring this on?

Or was it something else? You didn't see anyone on your way back from the hospital, did you?"

More silence.

"If you did see someone, please let me know. If Boyd Sullivan is around, we need to find him before he can harm anyone else."

Aiden stopped rocking for thirty seconds but didn't meet Isaac's gaze.

"You know what Sullivan looks like, don't you?" Isaac pressed. Talking about Boyd Sullivan seemed to be causing a breakthrough. Was it possible Aiden had seen the Red Rose Killer? "You've seen pictures of Boyd, right?"

Aiden resumed his rocking, but the movements were slower now, as if the young man was indeed listening to what Isaac had to say.

His heart filled with hope that he was causing Aiden's hard barrier to crack, letting a bit of light through. But he needed to do more. He knew, more than anyone, how easy it was to build a wall to protect your mind. He racked his brain to find a way to breach Aiden's protective barrier.

"Vanessa saved him once," he went on, hoping that more discussion about Boyd Sullivan would bring Aiden back to the present. "Your sister has a kind and nurturing heart. She told me she came across Boyd when he was injured and helped him out. Apparently he didn't want to go to the hospital and risk getting in trouble for fighting, so she bandaged him up with her own personal first-aid kit."

Aiden stopped rocking for the second time, and Isaac found himself holding his breath, hoping and praying that he'd explain what had happened.

"She cares about you, Aiden, very much. In fact, she's taking the change in your condition so seriously, she headed back to the hospital to talk to Lieutenant Colonel Flintman."

Aiden's head shot up, meeting his gaze. "No." The word was hoarse, as if the young man's throat was sore from silent screams.

"Yes, she did," Isaac confirmed with a gentle smile. "But don't worry, Flintman won't discuss details of your sessions with her. She only wants advice on how to help you."

"No!" Aiden's voice was louder this time, startling the puppies playing on his lap.

Isaac frowned, trying to understand. "No, what? Talk to me, Aiden. Tell me what's wrong."

"Blood!" Aiden reached out to grasp Isaac's arm, gripping it tightly. "No! Get to Vanessa!"

He still didn't understand. "Was Boyd waiting for you outside the hospital? Is that what you're telling me? Boyd is hiding and waiting for Vanessa?"

Tango lifted his head and nudged Aiden. The young man instinctively put his arm around the golden's neck. "Flintman is a bad guy," he finally said.

"Flintman?" Isaac felt the blood drain out of his face as the puzzle pieces fell into place. "You saw blood in Flintman's office? Because he's a bad guy?"

Aiden nodded then buried his face against Tango's fur.

Isaac sprang to his feet. How much time had passed since Vanessa left to see Flintman?

Too much.

He put a leash on Eagle, grateful when the dog accompanied him without a problem. He headed to the

door, pausing for a moment when he saw the cop standing there.

"You need to stay here and guard Airman Gomez
and the puppies, understand?" he said. "That's an order."

"Yes, sir."

Without hesitation, he ran outside with Eagle keeping pace beside him, calling Blackwood as he went,
hoping and praying he wasn't too late.

FIFTEEN

Vanessa was intercepted by Captain Leo Turner on her way to see Flintman.

"How dare you accuse me of attacking you?" He approached with blazing fury in his eyes. "I know you were upset about our breakup, but this is a new low, Vanessa."

She really wasn't in the mood for Leo's theatrics. Interesting how he'd acted sweet as pie the last time they had run into each other, even asking her to meet him for dinner. There must have been some underlying ulterior motive she couldn't possibly understand.

"I didn't." She stepped to the side to move past him.

He grabbed her arm, stopping her. "You sent the Security Forces after me!"

A frisson of fear darted down her spine. Was it possible Leo was behind the attacks on her? Had he said something to Aiden, causing her brother to regress? She couldn't understand what motive he'd have for trying to kill her.

Then again, she didn't understand much about Captain Leo Turner.

Steeling her resolve, she looked down at his hand

around her arm, then back up at him, her gaze narrowing. "Let me go, Leo, or you'll have a good reason to be afraid of the Security Forces."

He met her gaze squarely, then reluctantly released her. "I don't appreciate you dragging my name through the mud. I can tell everyone is staring at me behind my back, and it's all because of you!"

She shook her head, amazed that Leo could be so self-centered. What on earth had she liked about him in the first place? Oh, he'd wooed her with sweet words and promises, but now she understood he was a jerk through and through.

Regardless, she didn't have time for this. It was already well past seventeen thirty and the hospital crowd was thinning out. Most of the people in leadership roles were gone for the day, and she needed to get to Flintman before he left, too. "In case you missed the news flash, I was attacked several times over the past week."

"And you told the cops you suspected me?" Leo asked with a sneer.

"No. I actually told them that kind of behavior wasn't your style, but maybe I was wrong about that. You did just grab my arm."

His gaze darkened with anger.

She stared at his dark eyes, wondering if he was the guilty one. Stiffening her resolve, she went on, "Even if you didn't attack me, you know those pesky Security Forces guys, they tend to follow up on every possible lead." She tsk-tsked. "So sorry they bothered you, Leo, and since you had an alibi for the most recent incident, Captain Blackwood doesn't think you're involved."

"I'm not involved," Leo said between gritted teeth. "I never did anything to hurt you."

Except cheat on her, she thought, but whatever. None of that mattered anymore. She glanced at her watch again. "You're right, you didn't do anything to physically hurt me. Let's keep it that way, okay? I have to go."

This time, Leo didn't stop her as she headed down the hall, walking fast. When she reached the elevators, she grimaced and took the stairs instead in an effort to save time.

If she missed Lieutenant Colonel Flintman because of Leo's ridiculously bruised ego over being questioned by Blackwood, she would be so ticked.

The stairwell took her up to the fourth floor. She was breathing heavily by then, inwardly annoyed at her failure to stay in shape.

When she headed down the hallway, she hesitated, realizing that this corridor was remarkably similar to the hallway from the night of her attack. The lights were set low, since it was after regular business hours. She shivered, battling a wave of apprehension as she remembered, all too clearly, the horror as strong fingers wrapped around her throat.

Maybe she should have called Security Forces to accompany her here to Flintman's office. But it was too late now.

"Give me strength, Lord," she whispered. Ignoring her fear, she quickened her pace so she didn't miss the chance to speak to Aiden's doctor.

The door to Flintman's office was closed. Worried that he'd already left, she knocked on the door and listened for sounds of activity from inside.

She didn't hear anything. Twisting the door handle, she was surprised it gave. Flintman must not have left yet for the evening, or surely the door would have been locked.

Stepping across the threshold, she entered a plush reception area. Flintman's usual administrative assistant wasn't seated at the desk, the woman she'd spoken to must have left for the day. No one was in the waiting room, either, and Flintman's office door was closed.

Did he have a patient in there? As a nurse, she knew that she couldn't just barge in and interrupt a private therapy session. She hesitated, thinking it was possible he was simply staying late to finish up some paperwork. Stepping quietly, she moved toward the door and pressed her ear against the wooden door, listening intently.

She didn't hear the sound of muted voices, but for all she knew, the office was soundproofed. She debated sitting down to wait for a bit, then realized how foolish that would be if Flintman wasn't even in there.

Gathering her courage, she sharply rapped her knuckles against the office door. After what seemed like forever, the door opened and the balding middle-aged doctor, wearing his dress uniform complete with the silver lieutenant colonel leaf on his collar, stood across from her. Flintman looked happy to see her, peering with anticipation from behind his thick glasses.

Catching a whiff of his stale aftershave, she wrinkled her nose, remembering the same icky scent the night of her attack. Her eyes widened in horror as the memory clicked. But before she could move, Lieutenant Colonel Flintman roughly grabbed her and pulled her inside his office, slamming the door behind her.

Then he reached into his pocket and pulled out a gun. What? Vanessa couldn't believe what she was seeing. Clearly, Flintman was the one who'd attacked her a week ago. Was he responsible for all the attacks? Or had Boyd done some of them?

And why would Flintman target her in the first place?

"Well, well. I knew it was only a matter of time until you figured it all out," Flintman said, his tone conversational.

"Figure out what?" she asked, trying not to stare at the gun in his hand.

"You know," he admonished, as if she was being obtuse on purpose. "Tyraxal."

"T-Tyraxal?" she stuttered, wondering how long it would take Isaac to realize she was in danger.

Too long.

Even if Isaac finished with the commander and returned to Aiden, her brother was in no shape to talk about whatever he'd seen during his therapy appointment.

Or maybe it was more what Flintman had said to Aiden. Had the psychiatrist threatened to hurt Vanessa? Was that what had sent Aiden reeling backward? She kicked herself, belatedly understanding that the reason Aiden had been doing so well was because he had been skipping his appointments with Flintman.

Until she'd forced him to return.

Oh, Aiden, I'm so sorry. I had no idea. Please forgive me.

Flintman let out a harsh laugh. "You're too smart for your own good, Lieutenant," he said, waving the gun as he spoke.

She needed to stay sharp, to stall as long as possible. "You're selling Tyraxal prescriptions, aren't you? To the highest bidder."

His expression twisted with hate. "Not selling, providing, all because of a small mistake I made—going into debt while gambling. The Olio Crime Organization set me up with the bookie and things went well for a while, until I started to lose, badly. When I tried to get out, they threatened to go to the lieutenant general if I didn't cooperate as their drug supplier. In order to pay off my debt, I had to give them Tyraxal prescriptions. Don't you see? I'm in line for a promotion to full colonel and even if I wasn't, I can't afford to lose my pension!"

Blackmail? She hadn't even considered that possibility. Even so, she couldn't feel sorry for the man who'd callously caused so much suffering. "You violated your own medical ethics as a way to protect yourself?"

He scowled and took a step toward her. "Yes, I did. I've given the government twenty-five years of my life. There's no way I'm going to stand by and watch everything I've worked for go down the drain. Besides, it's not my fault people are getting hooked on drugs. If not Tyraxal, it would be something else." He shrugged as if it didn't matter one way or another.

She shuddered with distaste.

"The people using the meds wanted more and more, so I had to get creative, making all kinds of aliases for patients so we wouldn't get flagged by the government."

She knew he was referring to the new federal regulations that closely monitored prescriptions for controlled substances. If he wasn't careful, his name would be flagged as a high prescriber in the system.

If someone bothered to look. If the people buying

scripts used a variety of pharmacies, his name wouldn't be easily flagged.

Keep him talking.

"And then your so-called *patients* started dying," she said.

He waved the gun again, as if that was nothing more than a minor inconvenience. "Not that many at first. Regardless, once you left me that voice mail message, I knew you were standing in the way of me meeting my goal. I only needed a few more months to get my promotion and retire as a full colonel. I decided it was time to get rid of you. Conveniently, you were targeted by the Red Rose Killer, so I knew your death would be pinned on Sullivan."

She swallowed a wave of nausea, remembering the words he'd whispered in her ear. *Because you're in my way.* She shook off the memory, trying to stay focused. "Okay, fine, you wanted me out of the way, but why attack Aiden?"

Flintman's expression went cold. "He saw me meeting with my contact within the Olio Crime Organization and overheard us talking. I figured, since you left the voice mail that same day, that your brother might have told you what he'd heard."

Thinking back, she realized that the day she found the puppies was the same day Aiden had been huddled in the corner of the living room when she'd come home. No wonder he'd started canceling his appointments. She wished she would have left it alone, rather than forcing Aiden to return to see Flintman.

It hurt her to realize Aiden's latest regression was completely her fault. But this wasn't the time to wallow in remorse.

Keep him talking!

"What happened earlier this afternoon?"

Flintman shrugged. "My contact came in again, only this time, we argued. I wasn't happy that these overdose cases were showing up at Canyon. He was supposed to keep the scripts off base. It was part of our deal. I demanded to speak to his boss, but he took a swing at me, so I grabbed the paperweight off my desk and hit him in the head." He shrugged. "You know how much head wounds bleed. I didn't kill the guy. He left on his own two feet. But I didn't realize anyone was near, until I heard footsteps rushing out of the waiting area." His eyes gleamed with madness. "I knew then that Aiden had heard everything."

She knew Flintman was pathologically criminal and possibly insane. She could easily picture Aiden lingering after his appointment in order to hear what Flintman and his buyer were saying, until the assault and blood transported him back in time to when he'd witnessed his buddy's death from a suicide bomber.

Poor Aiden. None of this was his fault; it was all on her. Because she'd raised the alarm about Tyraxal.

She thrust her chin forward and put on a brave front. "You bashed in my car window as a warning, didn't you?"

He shrugged. "I wanted you to be afraid of being here at the hospital. You could have easily taken a leave of absence or something. But here you are."

"And the truck that tried to hit us? The shots outside the Winged Java? Did you arrange for those events, too?"

He smiled, and the tiny hairs on the back of her

neck lifted in alarm. "It's amazing what some people will do for another prescription of Tyraxal, isn't it?"

She could barely stand to look at him. *Dear Lord, help me escape this evil man!*

"So now what? You're just going to shoot me here in your office? Talk about a stupid move. It won't take long for Captain Blackwood and his team to figure out the link between my death and Tyraxal. Especially because I've shared my suspicions about you with the team."

That information caught him off guard, and he took a threatening step toward her. "You told them about me?"

Stretching the truth didn't come easy, but her desperate situation required it. She scoffed, as if he was an idiot. "Of course. Why wouldn't I? You went overboard with all these attempts to harm me, so I had to tell Captain Blackwood everything, including my concerns about you using too much Tyraxal. Don't you see? Killing me will point the finger of guilt directly at you."

He stared at her for a long moment, then shook his head. "No way. If anyone within Security Forces knew you were here, they'd already be banging down my door. But thanks for the warning. It's time for us to get out of here." He leered at her. "And when I'm finished with you? Guess who the next victim of a Tyraxal overdose will be?"

No! Not Aiden! She tried to think of a way out of this mess. If only she hadn't left Eagle behind.

"Wait, one more question. Did you arrange for someone to try stealing the puppies from my house?"

Flintman nodded. "I convinced one of my prescription buyers to do the deed, promising to give him six months of Tyraxal for free. I wanted those puppies gone, since Aiden used them as an excuse to cancel his appointments with me. Too bad the moron got himself killed."

The way he'd tried to manipulate Aiden made her stomach burn with anger. The despicable man had attempted to hurt her brother worse than if he'd simply stabbed him.

"I tried to kill you and Aiden in one fell swoop using the truck to attack you, but after that failed, I knew I needed to take care of you myself. Thanks for calling to make an appointment with me. You really helped make things easy." He glanced around the office. "Enough talking. It's time for action."

Action? She dreaded the thought of leaving the hospital, fearing Isaac might never find her.

"Move. Now!" Flintman aimed the gun at her face. "Don't try anything stupid. We're going to walk out of here together."

She wasn't sure how to stall for more time. He'd admitted to most everything, but only because he planned to kill her and eventually Aiden, too. This man had violated his code of medical ethics all to protect his reputation, rank and retirement.

Not caring how many innocent lives he'd sacrificed along the way.

Please, Lord, help me! Give me Your strength and wisdom! Don't let this horrible man get away with cold-blooded murder!

Isaac and Eagle arrived at Flintman's office well before Justin or his team did. He hesitated, wondering if he should wait for backup, but overwhelming concern for Vanessa had him opening the door and stepping inside the plush office.

Loud voices from behind the door leading into Flintman's office indicated there was trouble. Isaac unleashed Eagle, knowing that the well-trained, protective K-9 was the only weapon he had.

He stepped toward Flintman's office door when it abruptly swung open, revealing Vanessa. For a fraction of a second her eyes widened in surprise, then she mouthed the word *gun* and abruptly dropped down to her knees.

"Attack!" Isaac ordered as he dove to the floor. Thankfully they seemed to catch Flintman off guard as Eagle went over and clamped his jaw around the man's right ankle with a low, fierce growl.

"Owww!" Flintman screamed, wildly waiving his gun. "Grab the dog off me! I'll shoot him! I'll shoot you all!"

Vanessa abruptly lunged to her feet, kicking Flintman directly in the left kneecap. He howled in pain and teetered precariously, attempting to maintain his balance. Isaac used the moment to rush forward and grab the guy's wrist, roughly twisting the gun from his hand.

Flintman cried out again then crumpled to the floor. Isaac tossed the weapon aside and jumped onto the prone figure of the doctor, pressing his face against the floor. "It's over, Flintman. You're a disgrace to your rank and profession."

"Too bad I missed when I took that shot at your stupid dog, Beacon," the doc muttered.

"What did you say?" Isaac was dumbfounded by the man's confession. Had Flintman really been the one to shoot at Beacon during the animal's homecoming? It hadn't been a shot meant for Vanessa?

"You heard me." The man struggled against his weight. "Let me up! I'm hurt! I need medical help!"

"Why?" Isaac was truly bewildered by the psychiatrist's attempt to harm Beacon.

"You chased me off the night I tried to take care of Vanessa. After that, I thought if I got rid of the dog, you'd go into a deep pit of despair." Flintman flashed an evil smile.

Isaac was shocked by the news and understood that Flintman was likely responsible for everything that had transpired in the past week. None of it had been related to Boyd Sullivan.

Flintman continued wiggling beneath him. "Get off me! She broke my knee and the dog bit me! I demand to see a doctor!"

"Roll him over," Vanessa instructed, dropping down to her knees beside Flintman. "I need to take a look at his injuries."

Isaac reluctantly did as she requested. "One false move and I'll kick your other knee," he warned as he released his hold on the older man. "Eagle, guard."

The Doberman came over and sat right next to Flintman's head, showing his teeth. Vanessa smiled weakly, then leaned over to examine the man's injuries. "Does this hurt?" she asked as she gently palpated his swollen knee.

"Yes." Flintman peered up at her, his glasses sitting askew on his face. "I knew you cared."

"What?" Vanessa reared back, staring at Flintman as if shocked by his statement.

"Something wrong?" Isaac crouched beside her.

"Oh, no." She shook her head. "It's just that Boyd Sullivan said the exact same thing to me when I provided first aid to him in the dark alley all those years ago."

He nodded, still not understanding her reaction. But at that moment, the door to Flintman's office burst open. Justin and his K-9, Quinn, led the way inside, followed by other armed cops.

"You're late to the party," Isaac said, relieved that the danger was over. "I disarmed Flintman. His weapon is in the corner."

"I've got it," one of the cops announced as he carefully picked up the gun between two fingers and dropped it into an evidence bag.

"You'll want to test it for ballistics," Isaac said. "Flintman admitted he was the one who took a shot at Beacon at his homecoming. It's likely he was also the one who tried to shoot Vanessa at Winged Java."

"He was the one who attacked me, broke my car window, hired that guy to steal the puppies and hired the man who tried to run us over with a truck," Vanessa added. "All because I raised the alarm over the recent Tyraxal overdoses. Apparently, he's being blackmailed by the Olio Crime Organization and as a result has been giving them Tyraxal prescriptions."

"Unbelievable," Justin muttered.

"Oh, and you might want to go through his office, too," Vanessa added. "He mentioned assaulting one of his contacts with a paperweight. He claims he didn't kill the guy, but the paperweight may still have trace evidence on it."

"We'll go over the place carefully," Justin assured her, his expression bleak.

Isaac understood that finding evidence against Flintman and arresting him for the recent events meant the Security Forces team was no closer to finding Boyd Sullivan.

For all they knew, Sullivan may not even be on base.

"I want a lawyer," Flintman said. "I'll give you evidence against the Olio Crime Organization if you'll cut me a deal."

The thought of Flintman getting a deal made Isaac furious, but he understood how the system worked. Besides, at this rate, the guy would be too old to be a threat by the time he got out of jail.

"Oh, don't worry, you'll get a lawyer." Blackwood stood over Flintman, looking down at the guy with disgust. "But don't pin your hopes on getting a deal. If I can link you to the recent overdoses, you'll be on trial for murder."

Flintman went pale at the threat, and Isaac nodded with satisfaction.

The immediate threat against Vanessa was over, but that only meant Boyd Sullivan was still out there, somewhere.

And there was no way to know the identity of his next victim.

SIXTEEN

Vanessa wanted nothing more than to get back home to check on Aiden, but she had to wait until Justin had finished taking her statement.

"I need to make sure I understand his motive," Justin said. "Did Flintman mention any details about why he was being blackmailed?"

She thought back to what he'd revealed. "He said he was set up by the Olio Crime Organization who encouraged him to gamble. He apparently won at first, then began to lose. When he got further into debt, they used that as a way to blackmail him. They threatened to end his career if he didn't pay them back by writing prescriptions of Tyraxal." It made her sick to her stomach to realize Flintman had saved himself at the expense of ruining young people's lives. "When I noticed the pattern of Tyraxal overdoses, he decided he had to eliminate me."

"Why go after your brother?" Isaac asked.

"Aiden overheard Flintman meeting with his contact within the crime ring on the same day I left him the message about my concerns regarding the Tyraxal overdose." She swallowed against a tight ball of guilt.

"Aiden did the right thing, putting distance between himself and Flintman by canceling his appointments. Until I forced him back."

"Vanessa," Isaac said, his voice low and husky, "it's not your fault. You had no way of knowing Flintman was being blackmailed into writing prescriptions for Tyraxal."

"No, I couldn't know that. But I should have left Aiden alone. He was doing so well after not seeing Flintman for several days, but now…" She let her voice trail off, battling back the sting of tears.

It was her fault and that was something she'd have to live with for the rest of her life. Who knew how long it would take Aiden to recover this time? Remembering how Isaac had said he was rocking in the corner, suffering so badly, the adorable puppies hadn't been able to break through his wall of despair.

She sent up a silent prayer that God would help Aiden find his way back to being healthy.

"Anything else?" Justin asked.

"Not that I can think of at the moment," she said. "If you don't mind, I'd like to see my brother now."

Justin nodded, glancing down at his K-9, Quinn. "That's fine. If I need anything more I'll let you know. My next job will be to pry information about the Olio Crime Organization from Flintman."

She wanted Flintman to be held responsible for the Tyraxal overdoses, as well as the multiple attacks on her, including the young cop's. And she especially wanted him to be held accountable for the way he'd attempted to destroy Aiden's mind, his very being.

It wouldn't be easy to forgive him for what he'd done to her, to other innocent people and to her brother. God would want her to try, and she would, but not yet. It was too soon. Not until she'd talked to Aiden for herself.

Her brother had already been through so much.

"Oh, one more thing," Justin said as she made her way to the doorway.

She glanced at him over his shoulder. "What?"

"Isaac mentioned that Flintman said something that triggered a memory about the night you helped Sullivan."

"Yes, that's true," she reluctantly agreed.

"Tell me what happened."

"When I knelt down to provide first aid to Flintman he said, 'I knew you cared.' Back when I treated Boyd, he said the same thing while trying to kiss my cheek. I instinctively shied away to avoid his kiss, and told Boyd that as a nurse, I cared about everyone. At the time, he seemed fine. He even thanked me for helping him out when no one else would."

Justin nodded thoughtfully. "Interesting. Looking back at Sullivan's pattern of killing those who rejected him, maybe he wasn't as okay with the way you avoided his kiss as he seemed."

She shook her head in amazement. "I assumed it was kind of a brotherly thing, because that's how I felt toward him. He reminded me of Aiden, of how I had to take care of my brother after our parents died." She knew that Aiden's decision to follow her into the Air Force had been made in part because he didn't want to be too far away from her. "It's crazy to think that shying away from him was enough to target me as a person to kill."

Justin's expression went hard. "Trust me, most of the so-called transgressions against Sullivan were nothing more than a word or action that hurt his pride. The interaction you just described explains why he sent you a red rose, despite the fact that you helped him out by offering first aid."

She felt foolish for not having mentioned the brief interaction sooner. "I'm sorry, but at the time, I didn't think much of it. But when Flintman said the same thing, I instinctively shrank away, the same way I did that night with Boyd."

"It's not your fault, Vanessa," Isaac said again. "But at least now we understand what drove Sullivan to seek revenge against you."

It was incomprehensible to her that Boyd would send her a red rose just because she'd avoided his kiss. And if Boyd hadn't sent the stupid rose, Flintman wouldn't have had that threat to use as a cover for attacking her.

Her temple throbbed with the effort to think. She was exhausted, and her entire body felt as if she'd been battered by a group of ninja warriors. "I need to see Aiden."

"I'll take you home." Isaac handed her Eagle's leash and she took a moment to kneel beside the K-9, giving him a grateful hug for the role he played in saving her life.

She owed Isaac her gratitude, too.

She rose to her feet and followed Isaac out into the hallway. Isaac fell into step beside her, staying protectively close. Part of her wanted to lean on his strength and support, especially since he'd come running with Eagle to her rescue.

"Wait a minute. How did you know I was in trouble?" she abruptly asked, frowning in confusion.

Isaac waited for the elevator doors to open, then

ushered her inside, hitting the button that would take them to the main level. "I called and canceled my meeting with the commander, so I could head back to your place to continue talking to Aiden."

Had he really blown off a meeting with Base Commander Lieutenant General Hall?

"Oh, Isaac, I'll feel terrible if you get in trouble over this."

He shrugged, avoiding her gaze. "It was worth it."

She was touched by his change of heart, then glanced up at him in surprise. "Are you saying Aiden talked to you?"

"Not right away," Isaac said with a grimace. "I did all the talking, reassuring him that we'd be there to help him through this. I can't remember everything I said, except that when I mentioned how you had gone to talk to Flintman, his fear for your safety helped bring him back to the present. He mumbled about blood and then finally told me that Flintman was a bad man."

"Aiden actually said that?"

"Yes. He told me to get to you, to save you from Flintman." Isaac put his arm in front of the elevator door, letting her and Eagle step out first. "I called Justin as I ran here with Eagle."

"You ran?" she echoed in surprise. "I can't believe you beat Justin here."

"Part adrenaline and part God's strength," Isaac said as they walked outside. "I prayed the entire way."

Darkness had fallen and Vanessa couldn't stand the idea of her brother being home alone in the dark. She quickened her pace, heading straight for her SUV. She opened the back for Eagle, who knew the routine enough that he gracefully jumped in. She closed the hatch behind him.

"I'm thankful I made it in time," Isaac added, opening the passenger-side door for her.

"Me, too." She stood beside him, offering a wan smile. "Thank you, Isaac, for saving my life."

"Anytime," he said in a low voice. He gently pulled her close and she hugged him, resting her cheek against his broad chest.

She ached to kiss him but knew there wasn't time, so she reluctantly pulled away. "I'm sorry, but we need to hurry home. I can't bear the thought of Aiden being there with a cop he doesn't know."

"Of course." Isaac's expression was troubled, but he nodded, taking her car keys and sliding in behind the wheel. Surprised that he'd decided to drive, she sneaked a glance at his handsome profile, wondering if they'd drift apart now that she was no longer in imminent danger.

Sure, Boyd was out there, somewhere, but the recent attacks had all been Flintman's doing. Justin would no doubt get rid of the cop stationed outside her door, and honestly, she couldn't blame him.

No point in wasting resources that could be better used to track down Sullivan.

Isaac didn't say anything more as he drove her home. Plagued by a sense of urgency, she barely waited for him to stop the car before leaping out and rushing up the sidewalk past the cop at her door, to head inside.

She stumbled to a stop when she saw Aiden was sitting at the kitchen table holding Shenandoah in his arms, with Tango's head in his lap.

"Nessa!" Aiden staggered to his feet and lurched

toward her. She hurried over to meet him, wrapping her arms around her brother's shoulders, making sure not to crush the puppy.

"Shh, it's okay. I'm safe, Aiden, and so are you. Lieutenant Colonel Flintman has been arrested by Captain Blackwood. I promise you, he won't hurt anyone again."

"I was so scared," her brother whispered hoarsely.

"I know, and I'm sorry." She loosened her grip so that she could look into her brother's dark eyes. "I never should have forced you into making another therapy appointment. I didn't know he was doing bad things, Aiden, or I wouldn't have made you go back. I was wrong, so very wrong. I should have trusted your judgment."

"My judgment hasn't been my strength this past month," Aiden said in a low voice. "I thought what I'd overheard was nothing more than another waking nightmare."

Her heart squeezed in her chest for everything he'd suffered. "Oh, Aiden. I'm so sorry for what that man did to you. Will you please forgive me?"

"Hey, there's nothing to forgive," her brother responded. He placed his free hand on Tango's head. "In fact, I'm relieved Flintman has been arrested. It helps knowing that I wasn't totally losing my mind. To know the heated argument and the blood was real."

She nodded, giving him another quick hug before stepping back and subtly wiping at her damp eyes. Eagle came to stand beside her, as if sensing her distress. She glanced at where Isaac stood near the doorway.

"Thanks again, Isaac. I appreciate everything you've done for me and Aiden."

He frowned. "Can we talk outside for a moment?"

She hesitated, glancing at Aiden. The way her brother had looped his arm around the golden's neck, pressing his face against Tango's soft fur, warmed her heart. Between Tango and the puppies, she firmly believed her brother would soon be back on the path to healing.

Although, it wouldn't be long before Westley would want to reunite the puppies with their mother, especially since she'd heard during her lunch break that the puppy's mother was doing better. No doubt he'd want to begin training the national parks as future K-9 military officers.

As she followed Isaac outside, she felt as if she knew what was coming. This was the goodbye speech. Isaac wouldn't need to stick around. In fact, she realized they'd never spoken about the future.

She knew she would be on base for at least the next year, since she'd already done a tour overseas.

What was Isaac planning to do?

She knew he'd been through a lot in Afghanistan, suffering the loss of his copilot, his best friend, then Beacon. It made sense that he'd offered to protect her as a way of making a difference.

She only wished their closeness over the past eight days had been built on something other than Isaac's desire to be needed.

That he cared about her the way she deeply cared about him.

Not just cared, but loved. She'd fallen in love with him.

No sense in worrying over things she couldn't change. Isaac would always be a good friend. Nothing more, nothing less.

It was time to say goodbye.

* * *

Isaac stood for a moment, waiting for Vanessa to join him on the sidewalk outside her house. When she came over to stand beside him, he noticed how the glow of moonlight bathed her skin.

Her beauty, inside and out, took his breath away.

"I'm sorry," he said, deciding to cut straight to the point.

She lifted a shoulder, shivering a bit in the cool night air. Vanessa hadn't changed out of her thin scrubs, and he had to battle the urge to once again pull her into his arms. "It's okay, I understand. Disobeying a direct order isn't something to take lightly."

"No, but it's not just that." He wasn't sure how to explain that he'd initiated the meeting.

That it was his future on the line.

Her smile was sad. "I really do understand, Isaac. It took me a while to realize just how important it is for you to keep the people around you safe from harm. Perfectly natural after everything you've been through during your last deployment."

Deployment? Now he was confused. "Everyone? Who is everyone?"

"Me and Aiden for starters. And I think there will likely be others. As soon as you find the next person who needs assistance, you'll be there to step up in the role of protector." She crossed her arms over her chest. "But obviously now that Flintman is under arrest, I don't need your protection anymore."

"You're not making sense," he muttered, wondering if his own fatigue and lack of sleep from the night before was getting to him. "It's not just about helping people, it's about having a future. A career. Don't you understand? PTSD will always be a part of my life."

She tipped her head to the side. "I'm a nurse, Isaac. I think that's one thing I do understand. But this isn't just about your illness. It's about something more. I believe you have a hero complex. A deep, desperate need to come to people's rescue."

"Hero complex?" he repeated, feeling stupid. "How about a guilt complex? My best friend is dead because of me!" His voice seemed overly loud even to his own ears, so he did his best to calm down. "I witnessed someone attacking you and wanted to keep you safe. All of this—" he swept his hand out encompassing the space around them "—is a way to atone for my sins."

"What sins, exactly?" Vanessa asked, her expression perplexed. "You were flying a chopper that was under fire by the enemy. Help me understand why that's your fault. What sin caused your buddy's death?"

A heavy pressure built in his chest, suffocating him. This was something he hadn't admitted to anyone. Not his therapist, not his CO. Not even himself.

Until now.

It was time he faced the truth, no matter how painful.

"Arrogance," he admitted. "My sin was arrogance."

She arched a brow, her expression skeptical. "I doubt it."

"It's true. I heard distant gunfire, and should have immediately gotten us out of there, but I waited too long." He tried to swallow but his throat felt as if he were being choked by a big black anaconda. "I thought I could steer the enemy in the wrong direction, before finding a way out of the tight spot we were in, the way I always had before. But that's not what happened. The chopper took a direct hit, I crashed and my copilot and Jake died." He was glad for the darkness that surrounded him when he added, "There were plenty of times I wished I'd died, too."

"But you didn't," she reminded him. "Beacon saved your life and you saved his in return. Not to mention the way you rushed to my rescue tonight. Don't you see? This is all part of the plan God had in store for you."

Was it? He wasn't convinced.

"God forgives us our sins," she went on. "Remember Pastor Harmon's service? When he spoke about walking in the light and forsaking the darkness, he meant we need to believe in God's word. To accept His truth. To follow His plan."

The tightness in his chest abruptly eased as the truth sank deep. A sense of calm swept over him, making him relax.

She was right. He would choose light over darkness. God's light.

"I'll try to remember that," he said.

"I'm glad. It means a lot to me that you found your way back to your faith and to God." Her expression softened and once again, he wanted nothing more than to pull her into his arms.

Yet everything that had transpired between them gave him pause.

It was time to be brutally honest with himself.

What sort of a future did he have to offer Vanessa? Especially now that he'd disobeyed a direct order from Lieutenant General Hall? No clue. He hadn't touched the reenlistment papers on his kitchen table. And if he did decide to sign them and turn them in, he couldn't avoid the possibility the Air Force would recommend a full physical that could easily end up with him facing a medical discharge based on his mental health issues.

He knew, better than most, that you couldn't have a pilot flying choppers while suffering PTSD. Driving Vanessa home tonight from the hospital had been the first time he'd been behind the wheel since Flintman fired a gun at Beacon, and he'd sweated every second of the short drive.

Despite the strides he'd made in the past few months, and being reunited with Beacon, he couldn't say that he was cured.

Quite the opposite.

There was no cure. Only a variety of strategies he could utilize in order to deal with his symptoms.

"Isaac?" Vanessa's voice brought him out of his thoughts. "Something wrong?"

"Nothing," he said, while thinking, *Everything*.

It was one thing to tell yourself to follow God's plan, but another to actually put the words into action. He could easily accept that God had saved his life, and Beacon's, for a reason. That he'd come back to Canyon to help Vanessa and Aiden.

But was that all God had in store for him? Probably not, but from where he was standing, his future still looked bleak and empty.

"Well, I guess I should go inside." Vanessa's voice broke into his thoughts.

He had no idea what to say, so he nodded. "I'll check in on you and Aiden tomorrow."

"I'm sure Aiden will appreciate that. I'm hoping he doesn't have nightmares over this." She hesitated, then added, "Good night, Isaac."

"Good night."

Type here to search

She disappeared inside, leaving him with the keen sense that whatever closeness they once shared was gone. Possibly forever.

SEVENTEEN

Over the next forty-eight hours, Vanessa remained glued to Aiden's side, refusing to let him deal with his nightmares alone. Especially since Westley from the training center had called to let them know the mother was about to be discharged to Westley's care and it was time to reunite the mother with her pups.

Frankly, Aiden took the news better than she'd hoped, although he clearly didn't want to let go of Shenandoah, his favorite little runt of the litter. Putting on a brave face, Aiden accompanied her to the training center. As Aiden sat beside Tango and watched the mother sniff and lick her babies, she edged Westley aside for a personal conversation.

"I need two favors," she said in a quiet voice so Aiden couldn't overhear.

He grimaced. "Okay, but no guarantees."

"Isaac doesn't need Tango anymore now that Beacon is home." She gestured to the way Aiden sat with his arm looped around the golden's neck. "Look at how Tango and Aiden have bonded. Don't you think they're the perfect match? I know he's failed one pairing, but this one looks promising. I'm hoping you'll give them a chance."

Westley nodded slowly. "Yeah, I can see that. Okay, sure, I can approve switching Tango from Goddard's therapy dog to Aiden's. I'll submit the paperwork right away."

"Thank you." She'd sailed over the first hurdle, but the second one was higher and far more difficult. "I know you're planning to train the puppies as future military dogs, and I'd like you to consider allowing Aiden to assist."

The master sergeant was shaking his head no, before she'd finished her sentence. "He doesn't have any experience with dog training," Westley protested.

"I know," she agreed. "But you said how impressed you were with the amazing job he did fostering the puppies. Notice how attached he is to Shenandoah?"

Westley didn't answer but watched her brother for a long moment.

"Aiden needs a purpose, something to look forward to. It's not fair for him to end up booted out of the Air Force because he's struggling with the aftermath of a suicide bomber that killed his best friend." She smiled as the four national parks fell all over themselves in excitement at seeing their mother. "He can start at the bottom, Westley, cleaning kennels, feeding and watering the dogs, or whatever. But please, please consider giving him this opportunity. I truly believe this is his calling."

Westley let out a sigh and stood watching her brother for several minutes. The puppies ran back and forth between Aiden and their mother, clearly exuberant. Shenandoah, in particular, lingered by Aiden's side.

He gently lifted the puppy, nuzzled her for a moment then gently urged her toward her mother.

She held her breath, waiting, hoping, praying.

"Yeah, okay," Westley relented. "I'll take Aiden under my wing, assign him to work with the kennel manager, but he better not balk at the manual labor because I can promise that cleaning kennels is definitely part of the job description."

"He won't. Thank you," she whispered. "This means the world to me. To us."

"He has a connection to the pups already, so if all goes well, involving him in the pups' training helps me, too."

Training? She threw her arms around Westley in a quick hug. "You're awesome."

He shuffled about, looking uncomfortable yet pleased. "Yeah, yeah. That's what Felicity says."

Vanessa chuckled, but then experienced a sense of sadness. She remembered seeing Westley and his wife, Felicity, together on base and realized that's what she wanted. The closeness of a partnership, of leaning on each other, drawing strength from their love.

But Leo had been a complete and total jerk, and Isaac… Her chest tightened. Isaac was still wrestling with his own issues.

She hadn't heard from him, and doubted she would. Hopefully she'd see him at church services this next weekend. The only solace she had about everything that had transpired between them was that he'd embraced his faith.

She was happy to have had a small role in that reunion.

And if that was the only role God wanted her to have in Isaac's life, so be it.

She'd find a way to get over him, no matter how much it hurt.

Staying away from Vanessa wasn't easy, but Isaac couldn't in good conscience go see her when he didn't know what his future held.

Lieutenant General Hall hadn't been pleased with his canceling the meeting, but thankfully hadn't taken formal action against him. Isaac hoped that didn't mean his career in the Air Force was already over.

Instead, Isaac had tried to meet up with Justin for a personal, off-the-record discussion. Today, Justin returned his call, saying he was heading home for the day, inviting Isaac to meet him at his place at noon.

Isaac didn't need to be asked twice. He took Beacon with him and picked up a pizza along the way.

"Thanks for the grub," Justin said, pulling paper plates out of the cupboard. "Looks good."

"It does." Isaac was amazed at how much his appetite had improved over the past ten days.

Since meeting Vanessa.

As much as he hated to admit it, her claim that he was looking to rescue women wasn't entirely untrue. For the past eight years he'd been a battle-tested combat pilot. Now that he was grounded, it was no surprise that he needed something else to focus on.

But just because he felt better having something constructive to do didn't mean he didn't have feelings for Vanessa. She was wrong about that.

The problem was that he cared about Vanessa. Too much. His feelings for her were deep and complicated.

He admired her strength, her intelligence, her dedication to her brother and to her patients. Even her stubborn nature. When he'd understood how much danger she was in, he knew that his life would never be the same without her.

Because he loved her.

"Isaac?" Justin's voice snapped him from his pensive thoughts. "You claimed you had something important to talk to me about."

He finished his helping of pizza and nodded. "I need career advice."

Justin's expression turned solemn. "Okay, shoot."

"I received my reenlistment paperwork and I'm not sure what to do. I doubt I'll be medically cleared to fly combat anymore. The risk of suffering flashbacks after my last crash is too great. I need something else to do."

"I see." Justin nodded thoughtfully, leaning his elbows on the table. "What are you considering?"

He stared at Justin for a long moment. "Don't laugh," he warned, "but I'm seriously considering a career in intelligence."

Justin's eyebrows levered up. "You mean Security Forces intelligence?"

Isaac nodded. "Exactly."

"Okaaay," Justin said slowly. "But if you want me to be honest, I need to tell you it won't be an easy transition. Most of our Security Forces candidates aren't coming in at entry level with the rank of Captain. I'm not sure that will fly with the brass."

"I know, and I'm willing to give up pay and accept a demotion if it means I have a career I'm proud of." Isaac spread his hands. "I don't want to leave the Air Force, and I think that I have something to offer by way of intelligence work. I was leaning that way when I first entered the Academy, remember?"

"I do," Justin agreed. "I was a year or two ahead of you but remember how they discovered your gift of flying and steered you toward being a pilot. After that, we went our separate ways."

"And here we are now," Isaac said with a smile. He wiped his damp, nervous palms against his BDUs. "Do you have any advice on how I should approach this with Lieutenant General Hall?" Isaac rose to his feet and began clearing the table.

"Why don't you let me talk to him first?" Justin suggested. "Considering your service record, I think I can convince him to grant you special dispensation to transfer without a demotion."

"Really?" Isaac tried not to get too excited about the possibility, but he couldn't help thinking that with Justin on his side, he stood a good chance at being accepted for a career transition. "I'd really appreciate anything you can do."

"Hey, what are friends for?" Justin asked. His phone rang, and he frowned at the number. "I have to take this. Rusty Morton is missing, can you believe it? Your instincts were right on target. He was most likely the one who sold four of our dogs to the Olio crime syndicate and now he's missing. Give me a minute, okay?"

"Sure." Isaac moved out of the kitchen, wandering down the hall as he attempted to give Justin the privacy he needed. He wondered how things were going with Justin's teenage daughter, Portia. As a single dad, Isaac knew that his buddy didn't have it easy raising a teenage daughter, especially since he hadn't been very involved in her life at the beginning.

Between being the captain of the Security Forces in charge of finding Boyd Sullivan and being a dad to a troubled teenager, Isaac wasn't sure which role was more difficult.

But he suspected the latter.

He glanced in her room, inwardly grimacing at the mess. Clothes were strewn everywhere, including her unmade bed. He imagined the chaos in here drove Justin crazy.

The glimpse of a red rose caught his eye, and he frowned, moving farther into the room. A red rose was taped to the frame of the laptop sitting open on Portia's desk, the only surface that was relatively clean.

What on earth?

Beneath the rose was a white note card. Printed in black where the words: *I'm coming for you.*

"Justin!" Isaac shouted to his buddy, while standing rooted to the spot, unwilling to tamper with evidence. "Get in here now!"

"What?" Justin sounded annoyed until he joined Isaac. Seeing the red rose and the note, he paled. "Sullivan was here? How? Why?"

"I don't know, but I think the computer is part of the message." Isaac nudged the mouse with the side of his hand. The screen flickered on, showing a half-finished anonymous blog post railing once again at the stupidity of the Red Rose Killer.

"What?" Justin's face went starkly pale as he lifted a trembling hand toward the note. "Portia? My daughter is the anonymous blogger?"

"Easy," Isaac said, putting his hand on Justin's arm. "I'm sure she didn't mean any harm."

"She's been leaking information for months!" Justin's pale face flushed red. "Things she must have over-heard from me! I can't believe it. My own daughter!"

Isaac tightened his grip on his buddy's arm. "This isn't the time to be angry."

"You're right! This note means Sullivan knows Portia is the blogger. She's his next target!" Justin looked panicked. "I need to pick her up at school now! Before he can find her!"

"Go," Isaac agreed. "I'll wait here for the crime scene techs."

Justin was already calling in the team as he left the house. Isaac was shocked and stunned to learn that Justin's own daughter was the anonymous blogger. She'd leaked information, no doubt hearing tidbits of the investigation from her father, but it was her most recent post that worried him. The one that had almost taunted Sullivan, calling him a fool and worse.

Isaac sent up a silent prayer for his buddy and his troubled daughter.

The crime scene was processed with amazing efficiency, no doubt because no one wanted to risk their Captain's wrath. The idea of Justin's daughter being the next target for Sullivan was enough to keep every cop on their toes.

When the crime scene was secure, and Justin had returned with Portia, Isaac left. He stopped at home long enough to complete his reenlistment paperwork and submit it to Base Command, feeling good about the possibility of a new career, especially since Justin had offered his assistance.

And he made another phone call to Lieutenant General Hall, begging for a second chance. He was surprised and grateful when the base commander agreed to another meeting first thing in the morning.

Feeling better about his future, he sat for a moment, contemplating his next step. Thinking back over his relationship with Vanessa, he felt as if the kisses they'd shared were promising.

He needed to convince her that he wasn't a hero, but a man determined to do better with his life moving forward.

With her.

He picked up his grandmother's heirloom and tucked it into his pocket. Maybe he was rushing things, but he needed her to know his feelings for her were serious.

As he approached Vanessa's house, it was odd not to see the familiar cop stationed outside her door. He understood that Flintman was behind bars awaiting his court-martial, but also knew that Sullivan was still on the loose. And the guy was obviously on base, considering the note and rose he'd left for Justin's daughter.

He knocked at the door, waiting patiently for Vanessa. She answered the door wearing casual clothes— jeans and a gold sweater that complemented her golden skin.

"Isaac." She looked surprised to see him. "Is something wrong?"

"I—uh, wondered if you wanted to get a bite to eat. Maybe at La Taquiera." He felt like an awkward teen asking the prettiest cheerleader to go to prom. "If you're not fond of Mexican, we can go to Carmen's. The atmosphere there is a little nicer."

"Oh, sorry, Isaac, but I already picked up burgers for me and Aiden," she said. "We just finished eating. There aren't any leftovers, or I'd offer them to you."

He couldn't tell if she was avoiding him on purpose, or if it was nothing more than his rotten timing. What did it matter? He wasn't leaving, not like this. "Do you have time to talk?"

She glanced over her shoulder, then reluctantly opened the door and stepped outside. "I want to thank you again for giving up Tango. Westley has agreed to transfer him to Aiden as his therapy dog. The two of them have seriously bonded."

"I'm glad," he said, pleased that he'd been able to help. "What about the puppies?"

"Westley reunited them with their mother, and they're doing amazingly well. He's agreed to allow Aiden to help with training."

"That's incredible news," he said, even though he hadn't come here to talk about Aiden. He'd come to talk about them.

Specifically, the two of them together.

"It is," Vanessa agreed. "Aiden is thrilled to know that once he's cleared from medical leave, he'll be able to see the puppies every day, and between his new role at the training center and Tango, he's doing much better." She met his gaze head-on. "Thanks to you, Isaac. I want you to know how grateful I am for everything that you've done for us."

"You're welcome, but I don't want your gratitude." He searched her gaze, trying to gauge what she was thinking. "You accused me of having a hero complex, and maybe to some extent that was true. I'm a lot like Aiden, battling my emotional issues while searching for the key to my future."

Her expression softened and she reached out to rest her hand on his arm. "Oh, Isaac, I'm sorry. Surely you have a future here in the Air Force. The top brass would be foolish to let someone with your skills and reputation go."

He covered her hand with his, reveling in the softness of her skin. "Maybe. I've asked Justin for his support. I'm hoping to transition to working intelligence within Security Forces here on base. I even have another meeting with Lieutenant General Hall in the morning."

"Really?" Her eyes lit up. "That's fantastic."

He nodded. "To be honest, not knowing anything about my future was difficult. My PTSD symptoms have limited my options. I needed to have at least a plan of some sort before coming over here."

Her expression was full of chagrin. "I understand."

"Good. Because I need to make something perfectly clear. My feelings for you don't have anything to do with my so-called hero complex and need to protect you because I couldn't save Jake. I care about you, Vanessa. Very much. So much that being away from you over the past few days has been torture."

She hesitated, then smiled. "It's been hard for me, too," she confided. "I missed having you around."

His heart swelled with hope. "Vanessa, I know you deserve someone better, someone without the baggage that I'm carrying around, but I love you."

Her eyes widened. "Love?" she echoed hoarsely.

"Love," he repeated firmly. He took her hand and tugged her toward him. She readily walked into his embrace and as he hugged her close, he felt complete. He pressed a kiss to her temple, filling his head with her honeysuckle scent, then said, "I know you'll need time to assimilate this, but I'm begging you to give me a chance. I truly believe God's plan is for us to be together."

"Oh, Isaac." She tipped her head back, her gaze quizzical. "Are you sure? So much has happened—"

"I'm sure," he cut in. "More certain about how I feel toward you than anything else. I promise I'll never hurt you, cheat on you or lie to you. I love you, Vanessa." He swallowed hard, trying not to overreact. "Please give me a chance to show you how important you are to me."

"Yes." A broad smile bloomed on her face and she wrapped her arms around his neck. "I'll give you a chance if you grant me one in return. Because I love you, too, Isaac."

He sealed their agreement with a long, deep kiss that left them both breathless. He continued to hold her close, unwilling to let her go.

"We should probably tell Aiden, don't you think?" Vanessa asked, breaking their intimate cocoon of silence.

"In a minute." He eased away and took a deep breath, sensing the time was right. Subtly reaching into his pocket, he removed his grandmother's dainty engagement ring. An heirloom, the one that his mother had passed down to him before her death.

Holding Vanessa's hand in his, he dropped to one knee and presented her with the intricate gold ring. "Vanessa Marie Gomez, will you do me the honor of becoming my wife? This ring belonged to my grandmother, but if you don't care for it, I'm happy to replace it with whatever you choose."

"Yes! Yes, I'll marry you, Isaac." Her hand trembled as he slipped the ring on the fourth finger of her left hand. She stared at the ring with awe. "It's beautiful and fits perfectly. I'm humbled you chose to give me your grandmother's ring and I promise to cherish it forever."

"You deserve it." He stood and caught her close, swinging her in a circle as she laughed. "That and more."

"I deserve you," she said, going up on her tippy-toes to kiss him. "We deserve each other."

He couldn't disagree. The bright October sun rippled off the red, yellow and gold leaves on the trees, showcasing God's beauty.

In that moment, he knew he didn't have to worry too much about his future. Nothing else mattered but this moment.

They were blessed. Blessed with faith and God's love.

* * * * *

Aside from her faith and her family, there's not much **Shirlee McCoy** enjoys more than a good book! When she's not hanging out with the people she loves most, she can be found plotting her next Love Inspired Suspense story or trekking through the wilderness, training with a local search-and-rescue team. Shirlee loves to hear from readers. If you have time, drop her a line at shirlee@shirleemccoy.com.

Books by Shirlee McCoy

Love Inspired Suspense

True Blue K-9 Unit

Sworn to Protect

FBI: Special Crimes Unit

Night Stalker
Gone
Dangerous Sanctuary

Mission: Rescue

Protective Instincts
Her Christmas Guardian
Exit Strategy
Deadly Christmas Secrets
Mystery Child
The Christmas Target

Visit the Author Profile page
at Harlequin.com for more titles.

VALIANT DEFENDER

Shirlee McCoy

How excellent is thy lovingkindness, O God!
therefore the children of men put their trust
under the shadow of thy wings. They shall be
abundantly satisfied with the fatness of thy house;
and thou shalt make them drink of the river of
thy pleasures. For with thee is the fountain of life:
in thy light shall we see light.
—*Psalms 36:7–9*

To my continuity buddies, Dana, Laura, Lenora, Lynette, Mags, Terri and Val, with much affection and admiration. And, most especially, to Emily, who puts up with all our writing shenanigans.

ONE

Canyon Air Force Base was silent. Houses shuttered, lights off. Streets quiet. Just the way it should be in the darkest hours of the morning. Captain Justin Blackwood didn't let the quiet make him complacent. Seven months ago, an enemy had infiltrated the base. Boyd Sullivan, aka the Red Rose Killer—a man who'd murdered five people in his hometown before he'd been caught—had escaped from prison and continued his crime spree, murdering several more people and wreaking havoc on the base. He'd released two hundred highly trained military dogs from the base kennel and created a feeling of unease among the community. Sullivan wanted to destroy everyone and everything that he blamed for his failures.

Justin planned to stop him.

"What are your thoughts, Captain?" Captain Gretchen Hill asked as he sped through the quiet community. A temporary transfer from Minot Air Force Base, Gretchen had been in Texas for several months, observing the way Justin, himself a K-9 handler, commanded the Security Forces. When she returned to her post, she'd help set up a K-9 unit there.

"I don't think we're going to find him at the house," he responded. "But when it comes to Boyd Sullivan, I believe in checking out every lead."

"The witness reported lights? She didn't actually see Boyd?"

"She didn't see him, but the family that lived in the house left for a new post two days ago. Lots of moving trucks and activity. She's worried Sullivan might have noticed and decided to squat in the empty property. Since she lives on the same court, she's terrified."

"Based on how easily Boyd has slipped through our fingers these past few months, I'd say he's too smart to squat in base housing," Gretchen said.

"I agree," Justin responded. He'd been surprised at how much he enjoyed working with Gretchen. He'd expected her presence to feel like a burden, one more person to worry about and protect. But she had razor-sharp intellect and a calm, focused demeanor that had been an asset to the team. She didn't shirk duties, didn't complain about long hours, didn't stand back and take notes while others did the job. She'd thrown herself into her temporary assignment wholeheartedly.

As much as Justin had dreaded her arrival, he was going to miss her when she was gone.

"Even if he decided to spend a few nights in an empty house, why turn on the lights? He knows this base. He knows that everyone on it is on high alert and searching for him."

"If he's there, he wants us to know it," Justin responded. It was the only explanation that made sense. And it was the kind of game Sullivan liked to play—taunting his intended victims, letting them know that he was closing in. He left red roses and notes before he struck. *I'm coming for you.* He loved to kill, but terrorizing people was his drug of choice.

He needed to be stopped.

Tonight. Not in another month or two or three.

For the sake of the people on base and for Portia's sake.

Just thinking about his sixteen-year-old daughter being targeted by Sullivan made Justin's blood run cold. A year and a half ago, Portia had come to live with him unexpectedly and reluctantly, forced to give up her school and friends after her mother died in a car accident. The loss had hit her hard. A shy teenager who seemed to have trouble connecting with her peers, she'd turned to the internet for comfort and amused herself by blogging. Unfortunately, she'd chosen the wrong topic, and had been unmasked as the anonymous blogger on the Red Rose Killer.

She'd had no idea, of course, that Justin and Boyd had crossed paths long before Boyd's escape from prison. She'd had no idea just how much danger she was putting herself in.

While Justin and his team had struggled to find Boyd and identify the anonymous blogger, Portia had been quietly listening to their conversations and gathering information that she'd posted online. Worse, she'd mocked Boyd—a man who was as arrogant as he was dangerous. That, along with being Justin's daughter, had put her in the crosshairs of the killer. She'd received a threatening note from Boyd a week ago, and that terrified Justin.

If anything happened to Portia, Justin would never forgive himself.

Please, Lord, help me keep her safe.

The prayer flitted through his mind as he turned

into a cul-de-sac and eyed the darkened windows of the houses there. This was the quiet residential area of the base. Single-family homes that housed the larger families of airmen and officers.

"It's the brick two-story, right?" Gretchen asked, leaning forward as he approached the house.

"Yes."

"And our witness was certain of what she saw?"

"Yes. She said the house was lit up like a beacon. Almost every room in it. She noticed when she brought her dog out for a walk. Her husband is deployed, and she didn't want to check it out herself, so she called it in."

"It could have been a cleaning crew. That is a nice-size house, and there are plenty of air force personnel with big families who'd love to have it. I doubt it's going to stay empty long," Gretchen suggested as Justin pulled into the driveway of the two-story brick home. Currently there were no lights in any of the windows. The front door was closed, as were all the visible windows. Someone may have been there, but the place looked empty now.

"That thought crossed my mind, but I want to check it out, anyway." He turned off the engine, and his K-9, Quinn, shifted impatiently in his travel crate. The Belgian Malinois loved his work, and he was anxious to get out and do it. Trained in suspect apprehension, he had a great nose and a strong prey-and-play drive that made him easy to train and a pleasure to work with. When they'd first been partnered together, Quinn had reminded Justin of Scout—a German shepherd he'd found as a puppy and fostered until he was old enough to enter the K-9 training program. At the time, Justin already had a K-9 partner. Scout had been partnered with another officer and earned a reputation for being a superstar on the team, but he'd remained one of Justin's favorite dogs.

Now he was missing, along with two more of the four superstar German shepherds that had been released from the kennels by Sullivan.

"Ready, boy?" Justin asked his K-9 as he climbed out of the SUV.

Quinn shifted again, whining softly.

"What's the plan?" Gretchen asked, following him to the back of the SUV.

"Quinn and I will do a perimeter search. He'll know if someone is here."

"You and Quinn? And I'm supposed to wait here and twiddle my thumbs?"

"You are going to keep your eye on the front door. I don't want anyone escaping out the front while Quinn and I are around back."

"Come on, Captain. You know that's not going to happen."

"When it comes to Boyd Sullivan, I know we need to expect the unexpected." He opened Quinn's crate and hooked the dog to his leash.

"When it comes to Sullivan, you'd be happy if you could keep everyone away from him. Admit it. You want me to stay here so I don't get anywhere close to the guy we're after."

She was right, but he wasn't going to argue the validity of his feelings. The fact was, he was Boyd's target, and he didn't want Gretchen to be collateral damage. "Stay here, Captain."

He headed around the side of the house, Quinn heeling beside him. The dog was nearly prancing with excitement, his nose in the air, his tail high.

And Gretchen, of course, was following, her boots thudding softly on the grassy side yard.

"I told you to stay with the vehicle," he said, not glancing in her direction. His focus was ahead—the dark backyard and shadowy corners.

"Unfortunately for you, we're of equal rank and equal authority. This is your base, so usually I do things your way, but going into a situation like this without backup is dangerous. So, this time, I'm doing things my way," she said, and he couldn't argue. If Boyd weren't a factor, he wouldn't have told her to stay at the SUV.

They were both well-trained military police officers.

They'd both reached the rank of captain.

She was as capable as Justin.

He was still worried.

Quinn turned a tight circle at the corner of the house, his ears twitching, his scruff raised.

He'd caught a scent. Justin released him from the leash.

"Find," he commanded, and Quinn barked once, excited. Eager. He bounded toward the back door of the house, head high, obviously detecting a scent.

Please, God, let it be Boyd, Justin prayed silently.

He wanted this over. He wanted Boyd behind bars, his victims finally receiving the justice they deserved, their families finally receiving closure.

Portia safe.

Quinn snuffled an old mat that had been left near the back door, turned a quick circle and bounded away. He worked silently, nose to the ground, trotting along an invisible trail. Left. Right. Toward the back of the house and then away.

No bark of alert. No sprint back to indicate that someone was nearby. They'd been doing this together for years, and Justin knew his dog well enough to know that the Malinois sensed no danger.

His skin crawled, anyway.

He had a feeling about this. One he couldn't shake. Boyd might not be there now, but Justin's gut said he had been.

"What do you think?" Gretchen asked quietly.

"Whoever was here is gone," Justin responded, watching as Quinn ran back to the door. He nudged it with his nose, and it swung open, creaking on old hinges.

Quinn didn't enter. He just glanced back over his shoulder to see if Justin was following.

"Front!" Justin called, and Quinn sprinted back, stopping short directly in front of him and sitting there, tongue lolling, a happy smile on his face.

"Why would Boyd enter an empty house and then leave?" Gretchen asked, her gaze focused on the open door. "He's been keeping pretty well hidden. He obviously has safe places to go to ground."

"I was wondering the same thing," Justin admitted, walking to the door and shining his flashlight on the opening. He was looking for signs of a booby trap, evidence that Boyd had left something dangerous behind. He wasn't the kind of criminal who did things without careful planning and thought. He was smart, meticulous and, thus far, one step ahead of Justin and the base police.

"A booby trap, maybe?" Gretchen suggested what

he was thinking. "Or a bomb?" She crouched, peering into the dark house.

Justin continued his search of the door. From what he could see, there was no trip wire and no evidence that the door had been booby-trapped.

"If he was here, he had an agenda, and it wasn't just finding a place to hang out for a couple of hours," he responded. "I'll call in our explosive detecting team. Nick Donovan and his K-9, Annie, can check things out before we go in and look around."

Quinn snuffled the ground nearby, then made a circuit of the yard. It wasn't large, but someone had planted several trees. At one point, there had been a garden. Now old vines and dead plants filled a weed-choked patch of cleared land. An old swing set sat near the edge of the property. Beyond that, thick woods spilled out into deep forests. It would have been easy for Boyd to reach the house without being seen. The fact that he was on base, stalking victims again, infuriated and worried Justin.

His phone buzzed, and he pulled it out, expecting to see a text from someone at headquarters. The entire Security Forces was on high alert, ready and anxious to face off with Sullivan.

Instead, he saw Portia's number. Read the text. Felt the blood drain from his head.

I've got your daughter. Three guesses where I'm hiding her.

"What's wrong?" Gretchen asked, leaning in close and eyeing the message on his phone.

"It was a setup! He has Portia," he said.

"Boyd? How? Didn't you hire twenty-four-hour protection for her?" Gretchen asked, but Justin was already running back to the SUV, Quinn loping beside him.

He had to get back to the house.

He had to find Portia.

Nothing else mattered but keeping his daughter safe.

There weren't a lot of things Gretchen was afraid of. Snakes, mice, spiders, the dark. She could face any of those things without blinking an eye or breaking a sweat. She knew how to take down a man twice her size, how to disarm an adversary and how to keep her cool in just about any situation. Being raised in a military family with four older brothers had made her tough, strong and—she hoped—resilient.

So, fear? It wasn't something she was all that familiar with.

Right now, though, she was afraid.

Portia was a kid. Sixteen years old. At that strange age where childishness and maturity seemed to converge into a mess of impulsivity. This was the age where kids experimented with drinking, smoking, drugs.

Portia had taken another route.

And it had turned out to be an extremely dangerous one.

Blogging about Boyd Sullivan anonymously and thinking she wouldn't get found out had put her in the crosshairs of a very deliberate and cold-blooded killer.

One who wouldn't hesitate to kill again. If Boyd really had her, if he wasn't just playing a sick game, Portia was in serious danger.

"Are you sure he has her?" Gretchen asked, hoping against hope that Justin wasn't.

But she knew him.

She'd worked with him for months, and she'd never seen him panic. Until now.

"He texted from her cell phone," he responded as he secured Quinn and jumped into the driver's seat. When he gunned the engine, she let the silence fill the SUV. She knew he was heading back to his place.

She called headquarters, explaining the situation in a succinct and unemotional way. Not because she didn't feel desperate, but because she was a military police officer. She was also a woman. Two things her old-school father had never thought should go together. She'd had to prove herself as much to him as she had to any of her fellow officers—not just being good at her job, but being exceptional. Always in control. Always following protocol. Seeking justice. Capturing criminals. Pretending that she wasn't shaken by the depravity she saw.

Boyd Sullivan was beyond depraved.

He was a psychopath. If she had to choose a word to describe him—one that her fellow officers would never hear—she'd call him evil.

He had no empathy, no remorse. He was his own law. Probably his own god.

And if he had Portia...

Please, God, let her be safe, she prayed, surprised by her sudden need to reach out for divine help. It had been a long time since she'd prayed.

She hadn't given up on God.

She hadn't stopped having faith.

Not during Henry's illness. Not during the hours

she'd spent sitting beside him during chemo. Not while she'd been planning a wedding she'd known would never happen. Not when she'd held her fiancé's hand while his breathing became shallower. Even when she'd stood at his graveside listening to the pastor talk about hope during heartache, she'd trusted in God's plan.

She'd believed in His goodness.

She still did, but something in her had broken when Henry died. Four years later, and she wasn't sure if it would ever be fixed.

Tires squealed as Justin took a turn too quickly, and she eyed the speedometer. They were going too fast for the area and for the vehicle. She understood Justin's desire to get back to his house quickly, but if he didn't slow down, they might not get there at all.

"Getting into an accident won't help Portia," she said calmly.

"I'm aware of that," he muttered.

"So, how about you ease off the accelerator, or pull over and let me drive?"

"We don't have time to pull over." But he eased off the gas and took the next turn more slowly. "I should never have left her alone."

"She wasn't alone," she reminded him. "You had twenty-four-hour protection for her."

"Which failed."

"Have you heard from her bodyguard?"

"No, and I'm not foolish enough to think Boyd somehow slipped under the radar, grabbed Portia and slipped out without being noticed."

"So, you think the bodyguard has been…?" She didn't finish the question. They'd turned onto Justin's street, and she could see his house. The windows were dark, the front door closed. Everything looked locked up tight and secure.

"It looks quiet," she commented as he pulled into the driveway.

"When it comes to Boyd Sullivan, that doesn't mean anything." He braked hard, threw the car into Park and jumped out, opening the back hatch and freeing Quinn.

No discussion. No plan. This wasn't the way Gretchen operated. She liked to be methodical and organized in her approach to the job. In a situation like this—one where a serial killer could be lurking nearby—that was especially imperative.

She knew Justin felt the same.

She'd worked with him for several months, observing the way he led the Security Forces, how he approached dangerous situations, how he and his K-9 partner worked together and the way he interacted with his subordinates. He seemed to have unlimited energy and a passion for justice that was admirable.

But right now, he was running straight into danger without thinking the situation through.

She had two choices: sit in the car and wait for him to return, or run after him.

She opted for the second. She couldn't let a comrade face danger alone.

She sprinted after him, snagging his arm and yanking him to a stop. He was taller and heavier, packed with muscles he worked hard for. But she had decades of experience dealing with four older brothers who were also taller and more muscular than she was.

"Hold on!" she whispered, keeping her voice low. "We need to call for backup."

"Go ahead." He yanked away and headed around the side of the house.

"Captain, this is what Sullivan wants—you panicked and not thinking."

"I don't care what he wants. I care about Portia, and I need to see if he left anything behind. Any hint of where he took her."

"This could be a trap," she cautioned, following him into the backyard, the hair on her nape standing on end. She didn't think Boyd Sullivan would hang around waiting for Justin's return, but she couldn't guarantee that he wouldn't. He was a psychopath, extremely intelligent and determined to seek revenge for perceived wrongs that had been committed against him. Based on the file of police reports she'd read and the crimes he'd committed since escaping prison, Gretchen knew he was capable of anything.

"It's not a trap, but if you're concerned, go back to the vehicle."

"Justin, you need to slow down and think things through." She tried using his first name, speaking to him the way she did when they were off duty. He glanced in her direction, but didn't slow down. Quinn was just ahead, snuffling the ground, his ears back and his tail low.

The dog looked tense, and that worried Gretchen.

Quinn was good at finding people. She'd been with him and Justin when they'd tracked down a kid who'd vandalized the school. She'd also been with them when Quinn tracked a guy who'd beaten his wife black-and-blue and then fled the house. She'd observed the dog several times, and she knew the posture he was displaying indicated someone's presence.

He barked and took off, running to the edge of the property, Justin on his heels. She was close behind, staying just far enough back to give them space to do their work.

They pushed through the thick foliage that surrounded the property. Gretchen followed, twigs catching at her short dark hair and scratching her face.

When Justin stopped short, she nearly slammed into his back, her hands coming up automatically, grabbing his shoulders to catch her balance.

"What—" she began.

"Quinn found the bodyguard," Justin said, crouching and giving her a clear view of what lay in the bushes in front of him. A man sprawled on the ground. She pulled her Maglite and turned it on, wincing as she saw blood trickling from the back of his head.

"Gunshot wound?" she asked, crouching beside Justin as he checked for a pulse.

"Yes. Just one to the head."

"Pulse?"

"No."

She eyed the fallen man as Justin radioed for backup and medics. The bodyguard had been dragged into the shrubs. She could see the trail his body had made—empty of leaves, dirt scraped up by his shoes. His jacket was hiked up, and his firearm was visible. Still holstered.

"He didn't have time to pull his weapon," she commented as Justin straightened.

"Boyd doesn't give people time. He doesn't play by rules. He doesn't care who he hurts. Stay here until backup arrives. I'm going inside." He called for Quinn and took off, racing back the way they'd come as if he really thought she'd stay where she was.

But he wasn't the only captain on the team.

And he wasn't thinking clearly.

That was an easy way to get killed.

Especially when someone like Boyd Sullivan was around.

She ran after him, the faint sounds of sirens drifting on the velvet night air as she sprinted across the yard, up the porch stairs and into the dark house.

TWO

Quinn didn't sense danger.

Justin was as certain of that as he was of the fact that the house was empty. He could feel it—the silence, thick and unnatural. Up until Portia had come to live with him, Justin had lived by himself. He'd been used to returning to a house that was empty and quiet. Since his daughter had arrived, things had been different, better in a way he hadn't anticipated. He'd always been a loner. He'd never thought he needed what so many of his friends had—a wife, children, family.

He'd known, of course, that if anything happened to Melanie, Portia would live with him. They'd discussed that after the death of Melanie's mother. That had been six or seven years ago, and Justin had been quick to agree that he would step in if Portia needed him. He and Melanie had been high school sweethearts. They hadn't married, but he'd still cared about her. And he'd certainly wanted to be there for her and Portia. He'd obviously also wanted to be the custodial parent if something were to happen to Melanie. He just hadn't expected it to happen. Melanie had been young and fit, health-minded and cautious. He hadn't expected her to suddenly be gone. Portia hadn't, either. Her mother's death had been a shock. Being forced to move from Michigan to Texas had meant giving up everything she knew and loved.

For the first few months, they'd tiptoed around each other. Mostly silent. Uncertain. He'd been a little too eager to build a bridge between them. Portia had been resistant. Recently, though, they'd begun to relax around each other, and he'd begun to enjoy the music drifting from her room, the quick tap of her fingers on the laptop keyboard while he made dinner.

He couldn't remember when she'd begun sitting at the kitchen table while he cooked, but he knew he enjoyed having her there. Even when he didn't know what questions to ask or how to ask the important ones, it was nice to have a house that felt like a home. It was nice to return from work to the very real and unmistakable feeling of not being alone.

Now the house was empty, and the terror he felt at the thought of his daughter being with the Red Rose Killer stole every thought from his head. Except one: finding her.

"Portia!" he called, knowing she wouldn't answer.

Boyd had her phone. He had her.

Justin was surprised that his voice wasn't shaking, surprised that his legs were carrying him upstairs.

Quinn loped ahead of him, following a scent trail into a narrow hall that opened into three bedrooms and a bathroom. The Malinois beelined to Portia's door, scratching at it with his paw.

It opened silently, swinging inward.

"Portia?" Justin repeated, stepping inside.

The room was empty.

Just like he'd expected.

Tidy. Portia liked her things neat and organized. Just like Justin. She liked an uncluttered environment. Also, like Justin. Funny how those traits had carried genetically. Melanie had been creative and disorganized, her house filled with knickknacks and art projects. The few times Justin had been there, he'd had the urge to declutter and organize.

Had Portia felt that way?

Had her bedroom at her mom's house been as neat and tidy as this one? He hadn't asked her. The topic had felt too fraught with emotion—a minefield he wasn't sure either of them was ready to walk through.

"I'm sorry, Justin," Gretchen said, stepping into the room behind him.

"This is my fault. I should have sent her somewhere safe."

"Nowhere would be safe. Not if Boyd wanted to get his hands on her. You know that."

He did, but that didn't make it easier to stomach.

"And the only person at fault here is Boyd," she continued, turning a slow circle, taking in all the details of the room. "There's no sign of a struggle."

"I don't think she'd have tried to fight someone who had a gun," he said, trying not to imagine the terror Portia must have felt, the fear that must have been in her eyes. She might be organized and meticulous like Justin, but she felt things deeply like her mother. She was a writer. Of journals. Of blogs. All the things she didn't say, she poured into written words and sentences and paragraphs. He didn't have to be father of the year to know that about his daughter.

"It looks like she was on her computer." Gretchen

walked to the bed, moving past Justin and Quinn. He let her lead the way, because his judgment was clouded by fear. He was a good enough officer to know that, and she was a good enough one to take control of the scene.

He'd noticed the laptop, and now he noticed a note taped to it as he approached the bed. He could read it easily, the words printed in bold red ink: *Now the formerly anonymous blogger of CAFB will really have something to write about.*

"I need to find her." He called for Quinn, planning to run outside. If Quinn could find a scent trail, they might be able to follow it to Boyd's location.

"You need to slow down, Justin."

"That's an easy thing to say when it's not your daughter in the hands of a serial killer," he responded, regretting it immediately. He knew Gretchen cared deeply about the work she did and about the people she worked for. She took the job as seriously as he did, and she was as eager as he was to find and stop Boyd.

"Maybe. Probably. But we have a job to do here, and the first step in that is figuring out where he took her."

"That's what Quinn and I are going to do."

"Find!" he commanded, and the Malinois took off, sprinting downstairs and out the door. Sirens were blaring, lights flashing on the pavement. Backup had arrived, but Justin ignored everything but his K-9 partner.

Please, God, don't let it be too late for Portia, he begged silently as he followed Quinn around the side of the house and across the backyard. The night was cool, the moon high, and he could see Quinn easily, loping toward the woods at the edge of the yard. Confident, excited, tail up, ears alert, nose dropping to the ground every few yards.

The scent trail was fresh.

They were right on the heels of Boyd and Portia. With a dog as well trained as Quinn, it would be easy to overtake them. Portia would be moving slowly. At least, he thought she would be. She'd be dragging her feet, trying to slow progress, because she was smart, and she'd know just how much she could push before Boyd reacted.

That was what Justin was telling himself.

He didn't know if it was true.

Sure, his daughter was smart—an A student who excelled at both math and English—but their bond was still tenuous and new, their knowledge of each other limited, and he really had no idea how she'd react to being kidnapped.

They reached the tree line, and Quinn trailed back toward Justin, then circled around a place where the grass seemed to have been smashed down and trampled.

"Looks like someone fell," Gretchen said, flashing her light on the spot. He hadn't expected her to stay at the house and wasn't surprised that she'd followed him. Her methods of approaching crime scenes were spot-on. She'd been an MP for six of her nearly eight years in the air force. He'd seen her military record. She was well-known for her dedication and professionalism, and he'd seen both during her time at Canyon Air Force Base.

Right now, though, he didn't want to spend time discussing the crime scene or working out the details of a plan. He wanted to find his daughter.

"You know that you can't approach this any differently than you would if we were searching for someone else's child," she added, as if she'd read his thoughts and knew exactly what he intended.

"*Kidnapped* child," he replied, but she was right. If he were searching for anyone other than Portia, he'd be meticulous as he surveyed the scene, approaching the situation logically rather than running on emotion and adrenaline.

He frowned.

Gretchen was right. He needed to slow down. He also needed to start thinking like a military police officer rather than a panicked father.

"But your comment is noted. I need to approach this like I would if it were any other case."

"Do you think she fell on purpose?" Gretchen asked, her light dancing over the crushed grass and darting toward the woods that stretched out beyond his yard.

"Maybe. Portia knows what he's capable of. She might have been trying to slow him down so that Quinn and I could catch up."

"Smart girl," she murmured, meeting his eyes. Hers were a dark rich chocolate, her features delicate and pretty. With her height and slim build, she wouldn't have been out of place on a fashion runway. A few weeks ago, a drunken airman had made the mistake of underestimating her. She'd been trying to arrest him for disorderly conduct, and he'd taken a swing at her, laughing about how he wasn't going to be taken down by a pretty little girl.

Seconds later, he'd been on the ground and in cuffs.

"Not so smart when she decided to blog about the Red Rose Killer," Justin said, "but in every other area, she seems to have a good mind. Let's hope she's slowed him down enough for us to catch them."

"He's going to be expecting us to use Quinn. You know that, right? He'll be watching, making sure that we're not coming up from behind."

"We don't have any other option," he said, watching as Quinn nosed the ground near an old spruce.

"What did he say in his text?" she asked.

"That he had her, and he'd give me three guesses as to where they were."

"So, he thinks you'll know where he's taking her."

"He likes to play games. You know that, Gretchen."

"You two have a history together. I know he was here before he was dishonorably discharged. Did you have any run-ins with him? Maybe something happened in a particular location that stuck out in his mind?"

"We had plenty of run-ins. I was beginning as an MP. He was a cocky, insubordinate bully."

"You had a high opinion of him even then, huh?"

"I don't have time for a trip down memory lane."

"You don't have time not to take the trip. He said he'd give you three guesses. He must think you'll be able to find him. It's what he wants, right? Not Portia. You."

She was right. Again.

"Right. We had a few run-ins. He was in a couple of fistfights with weaker recruits, and I broke things up. I caught him drinking once when he should have been in the barracks, and I wrote him up for that. I'm sure he can remember more incidents than that. He's proven his memory and his ability to hold a grudge."

"Is there any particular incident that stands out?

Maybe one that got him into more trouble than any other. Or had the potential to."

There was. He hadn't thought about it in years, but his last run-in with Boyd had led to an investigation into his conduct. Eventually, his commanding officer had filed a complaint of insubordination because of Boyd's attitude and inability to take orders. That had led to his dishonorable discharge, but Boyd had always blamed Justin.

"Yes," he responded. "I caught him torturing a puppy once. He had free time on a weekend. I happened to be off duty and was hiking in the woods on base. I heard something yowling, and I followed the sound, thinking that maybe a fox or coyote had gotten itself into trouble. There's a cabin about a mile from here. Hidden in the woods."

"I've been there," she said. He wasn't surprised. The cabin had been on the property before the base existed. A hunting cabin or a rustic home built in the early 1900s, it had been left standing by the air force and was sometimes used as a hiding place during K-9 scent training.

"The sound was coming from there. I wasn't trying to be quiet when I approached. I figured if there was an animal that wanted to get out before I arrived, I'd rather have it gone. Boyd walked out the door as I was crossing the clearing. He had a knife in a sheath on his thigh, and for a couple of seconds, I thought he might pull it on me. I asked what was going on, and he said he'd found a dog trapped in the chimney and freed it. He walked away. I went in the cabin, and found the German shepherd puppy. He was really young. Maybe nine or ten weeks old."

"Was it dead?"

"No. His fur was singed, though. Like someone had been holding a match to it. I had no idea how he'd gotten there, and I still don't. I brought him to the base vet and found out the poor guy had a broken hind leg and a couple of cracked ribs. He survived, and I fostered him until he was able to go into our working dogs training program. Scout is now one of the best German shepherds on the team, one of the four superstar K-9s. Or he was until Boyd released the dogs."

"Scout is one of the three still missing?"

"Unfortunately, yes."

"I'm assuming you turned Boyd in to your commanding officer after you found Scout?"

"Yes. He said nothing could be done without proof. I wasn't satisfied with that. A guy who'd hurt an animal is just as likely to hurt a human being. I went to Boyd's commander and told him the story. Boyd already had a history of insubordination. A couple of days later, he was dishonorably discharged."

"And he blames you."

"He blames everyone but himself," he responded, his mind on that day and the cabin, his thoughts suddenly clear. "The cabin has to be where he took her."

"That makes sense. So, how are we going to approach it? He's probably waiting to ambush you. Based on his history, I doubt he's going to give you a chance to strike. He'll be expecting Quinn to move in first—an early-warning system for him. Maybe we hold Quinn back?"

"*We* aren't going to do anything. You're going to stay here and inform backup."

"Backup is on the way and radios work well. I'll

call in the information, but I think you know I'm not standing down."

He did, but he'd had to try. He'd lost a partner before. That was a loss he never wanted to experience again.

He glanced back the way they'd come and could see lights dancing along the ground as Security Forces officers headed toward the edge of the property. He could wait for them, but had to get to the cabin. He knew how long it would take to get there.

He knew that Portia was waiting for him to arrive. That she was scared and in danger.

That was all he could think about. All he could focus on.

He shrugged his agreement, hooked Quinn to his leash and stepped into the forest.

She was moving slowly, following Justin and Quinn as they wound their way into the woods. What Gretchen wanted to do was run. She'd been to the cabin a few times, and she had an excellent sense of direction. Probably thanks to her parents' deep love for adventure, she'd learned young how to find her way through the wilderness. The moon was high, the stars bright. She could navigate using the sky, and she could move a lot more quickly while she was doing it.

Justin seemed content to walk at a steady reasonable pace, Quinn on the leash beside him.

"We're not that far from the cabin, are we?" she asked quietly, searching the moonlit forest for landmarks.

"Less than two miles."

"So it wouldn't have been difficult for Boyd to get Portia there."

"Not difficult, but not easy, either. Not if Portia was trying to slow him down. This forest can be hard to navigate during the day. At night, it's more challenging."

"I'm sure he had the route timed and took into consideration his kidnapping vi—Portia."

"Victim. You can call her what she is. Let's just make sure she stays a kidnapping victim and nothing more."

Quinn pranced a few feet ahead, his tail and ears up, his nose to the ground.

"It looks like Quinn is on Sullivan's trail," she commented.

Justin nodded. "His or Portia's."

"What's the plan for when we reach the cabin?"

"We keep Portia and ourselves alive and apprehend Sullivan."

"I was hoping for a few more details."

"We'll assess things when we get there."

She would prefer to assess things now.

She liked to know what she was going into and how she was going to get out of it. Not just in work. In life.

She'd enjoyed working with Justin these past few months because he was the same. Careful. Methodical.

"I think we'd be better off stopping for a couple of minutes and coming up with a solid plan about how we're going to approach the cabin. Boyd Sullivan is—"

"I know what he is." He stopped suddenly, and she realized that Quinn had stopped, too. The dog was just a few feet ahead, stiff and alert, staring through thick undergrowth.

"What does he see?" she whispered.

"The cabin."

"Where?" She moved closer, stepping up beside Justin. He was taller than her by several inches. That had surprised her when she'd met him. She was used to being eye to eye with her male coworkers.

He pointed but didn't speak, his arm brushing hers, the fabric of his uniform rasping quietly. The forest had gone silent except for the distant sounds of backup moving through the woods. She'd spent enough time outside at night to know what she should be hearing. Animals scurrying through the trees. Deer picking their way through the forest. The rustle and sigh of leaves as predatory birds searched for prey.

Moonlight filtered through the thick tree canopy, bathing the world in its green-gray glow. Tall evergreens and shorter, thicker oaks stood as silent sentinels, guarding a clearing that Gretchen could just see through the foliage.

The cabin was there. Four walls. A thatched roof. Empty holes where windows and doors had once been. She couldn't see the details—just the right angles of the old exterior walls—but she'd explored the woods and seen the cabin. She'd also been on training exercises with K-9 puppies. She could picture the building— its size and shape and access points for the interior. It would be easy to get inside, but not as easy to do so undetected.

"This way," Justin said, his words more breath than sound.

He led the way through the undergrowth, bypassing the thickest sections. Quinn moved silently in front of them, disappearing for a few seconds, then reappearing. He didn't need to be commanded to remain quiet. He'd been trained well. He knew his job and seemed to have endless enthusiasm for it.

He stopped at the edge of an overgrown clearing, moonlight glinting in his tan fur, scruff raised, ears forward and down. He sensed danger, and he was letting Justin know it.

Gretchen tensed, eyeing the clearing and the old cabin that sat in the center of it. She could see it plainly now. That meant anyone inside could possibly see them.

Light danced across a window opening, disappearing as quickly as it appeared.

"He's there," Justin muttered as if it had ever been a question in either of their minds.

She grabbed his arm, pulling him back a few steps. "You aren't planning to step out into that clearing, are you? Because if we can see the cabin, anyone in it can see us."

"My daughter is in there," he responded.

That didn't answer the question.

It didn't make her feel any better about the situation.

"I'm aware of that," she replied, keeping a tight grip on his arm. "If he takes you out before you reach the cabin, what's going to happen to Portia?"

"If he takes me out, it'll ruin the game. Sullivan isn't about that. He wants to see my face and know that he's got me where he wants me—scared and helpless."

"You're not either of those things."

"I'm not *one* of those things, but let him think what he wants. It'll keep me alive until I can free Portia."

"Until? What about after?" she whispered, but he pulled away, breaking her grip easily.

"Stay here and stay hidden. He's got nothing to lose by taking you out."

He stepped into the clearing with Quinn, and she almost followed.

But Justin was right.

Sullivan had no grudge against her, no game he wanted to play with her. He had no reason to want to watch her suffer. If she stepped out into the clearing, the first bullet he fired would be at her.

He'd save the next for Quinn. Then Portia.

Finally, after he took everything Justin cared about, he'd kill him.

She slipped back into the woods, skirting around the clearing, listening to the eerie silence and the wild beat of her heart. She wasn't afraid for herself. She was terrified for Justin and for Portia. Boyd Sullivan had come to Canyon Air Force Base to seek vengeance for perceived wrongs, and Justin was probably at the top of the list of people he wanted to destroy. The fact that Portia was in danger seemed to be clouding Justin's judgment, and clouded judgment could easily get a law enforcement officer killed. Especially in a situation like this.

She stepped out of the woods near the back of the cabin and moved silently across the clearing. She could hear Justin moving on the other side of the building, his footsteps crunching on dead leaves and twigs. He wasn't trying to be quiet. He probably figured there was no reason. Boyd knew he was coming but had no idea Gretchen was there, too.

She'd use that to her advantage.

She crept close to the light-colored log walls of the cabin. There'd been two windows cut into the facade, and she approached one, freezing as she saw the flash-light beam sweep across one of the openings and then the other.

"I know you're out there," a man called in a sing-song voice that made her blood run cold.

For a moment, she thought she'd been seen, that somehow Boyd had realized Justin wasn't alone.

She dropped to her stomach, her left side pressed close to the cabin, her right arm free to pull her service weapon.

"Blackwood!" the man continued. "Move a little faster, or your little girl is going to die."

"Dad! No!" Portia called, her voice wobbly with tears. "He's going to shoot you!"

"Shut up!" Boyd yelled in response, the quick hard crack of flesh against flesh ringing through the night.

For a moment, there was nothing but silence, and then the soft pad of feet on the ground. Justin was moving again, and Gretchen wasn't going to let him go into the situation alone. She crept toward the window, staying low to the ground as she moved toward the old cabin, the sound of Portia's terror still ringing in her ears.

THREE

Justin had spent most of his adult life keeping his anger in check. His father had been a raging alcoholic with a mean and violent temper. The day Justin had left home for basic training, he'd vowed he'd be a better man. He liked to think he had been. He'd avoided the trap of alcohol and anger. He'd treated people with empathy and kindness. Even on the job, even with known criminals, he'd focused on justice rather than revenge.

Right now, though, he wanted to drag Boyd from the cabin and make him pay for putting his hands on Portia.

His muscles were tight with anger and tension, his movement stiff as he approached a gaping hole that had once been a door.

"Leave the dog outside, Blackwood," Boyd commanded.

Boyd thought he had the upper hand, and he seemed happy to let the game play out for a while longer. That was fine by Justin. He could hear Security Forces officers moving through the woods. It wouldn't be long before the cabin was surrounded.

"Down," he commanded, and Quinn dropped to

his belly, growling deep in his throat as he eyed the doorway.

"Good boy," Boyd said, laughing coldly. "You. Not the dog, Blackwood."

If he wanted to get a rise out of Justin, he was going to be disappointed. Having his judgment clouded by emotion wasn't going to help him get Portia out of this situation alive. That was his goal, his mission and his focus. Boyd's games were incidental.

"Nothing to say to that?" Boyd taunted. "I guess you're not as big a man as you pretended to be when I was in basic training."

"Let Portia go," Justin responded, ignoring the taunt. "She's a child."

"She's a teenager. One who likes to post junk on the internet she knows nothing about."

"I'm sorry," Portia said. "I shouldn't have written any of those things about you, Mr. Sullivan."

"Do you think an apology is going to save your dad?" Boyd replied.

"I just—"

"It's not!" Boyd snapped. "Me and your dad go way back, and there's nothing good between us."

"I'm sorry," Portia repeated, and Justin wondered if she was trying to keep Boyd's focus away from him.

"Shut up! Blackwood, get in here!"

Justin stepped across the threshold and into the cabin's main room. Decades ago, the place may have been someone's home. Now it was nothing more than a carcass made of old logs. In addition to the missing windows, the door and part of the roof were missing. Moonlight illuminated the interior, and he could see Portia sitting on the ground a few feet away. Her face was pale, her hair falling across her cheeks. She looked more like Melanie than she did Justin—her build delicate, her cheekbones high.

Boyd stood beside her, tall and lean, his eyes gleaming with dark amusement. He had a gun in his right hand and a flashlight jutting from his jacket pocket. If he were worried about being captured, he wasn't showing it.

"Well, well," he said. "Here we are. Finally face-to-face. After all these years, you probably thought you were going to get away with what you did to me."

"I don't recall doing anything," Justin responded, taking a step in Portia's direction.

"Don't," Boyd said, his voice cold with rage. "I would hate to kill your daughter before the party even got started."

"This isn't the kind of party I like," Portia said, and Boyd's gaze cut to her.

"No one asked you, Ms. Bigmouthed Blogger."

"If that's the best insult you can come up with—"

"That's enough, Portia." Justin cut in before she could say more. Goading Boyd would only anger him, and right now, Justin wanted things to stay calm.

"Good call, Blackwood. Now, how about we all take a little walk?" He grabbed Portia's arm and dragged her to her feet.

To her credit, she didn't resist, and she didn't cry out.

She looked terrified, though—her eyes wide and filled with fear.

"It's going to be okay, Portia," Justin said.

Boyd laughed. "That depends on what side of the gun you're standing on. Speaking of which…" He lifted his gun and pressed it to Portia's temple. "What's it feel like to come face-to-face with the guy you called inept, blogger-girl? Do you still think I'm stupid?"

Justin's heart stopped.

He stared into Portia's eyes, trying to convey a sense of control and comfort that he didn't feel. Trying to discourage her from giving a flip teenage response.

Boyd could and would pull the trigger.

He'd done it before.

"Let her go, Boyd," Justin said, keeping his voice calm. He didn't want to escalate things.

"You don't call the shots anymore, Blackwood." Boyd chuckled, the pistol easing away from Portia's temple but still aimed at her. "Get it? Call the shots? You're not laughing. I guess you're as boring and up-tight as ever. Man, it's been a long time, hasn't it?"

"Not long enough."

"I disagree. I'd have been happy to take you out months ago. I should have thought about her before now." He jabbed the gun closer to Portia. "Seems you'll do anything to keep your kid alive."

"I will," Justin agreed, and Portia shook her head.

"Dad—"

"This is a grown-up conversation, blogger-girl," Boyd growled. "You keep your mouth shut. Where's the dog, Blackwood? We're leaving, and I don't want him coming at me when we step outside."

"He won't bother you." Not until Justin called him. Once he did, Quinn would be on Boyd like a missile— quick and deadly accurate.

"He'd better not. Your daughter's life depends on it. She sure is a pretty little thing." He flicked Portia's hair with the muzzle of his pistol, chuckling when she flinched.

"She's a kid. A little girl," Justin said, his voice gritty with banked anger.

"A teenager who knows her way around a computer. Not a kid. I don't kill kids," Boyd spit. "But I do kill annoyances, and you're both that."

"She wrote a few anonymous blog posts. What's that matter to a guy like you?"

"It matters. It all matters." The gun swung toward Justin and then back in Portia's direction. "You did this, Blackwood. You did all of it. I might have pulled the trigger and fired at those people, but you called the shots. Do you regret it? Do you have any remorse?"

"Maybe if you tell me what I did—"

"You know what you did! I would have done just fine in basic training. I would have excelled. I would have been top of the class. Except for you."

"I don't like bullies, Boyd. I don't let them prey on people weaker than they are. I don't allow them to hurt defenseless animals."

"Everyone there was weaker. That wasn't my fault. I was taking my rightful place as the leader of the pack. You work with dogs. You should understand how that goes. And as for that puppy, I didn't do anything but save his life, and look at him now—one of the top dogs on your team." The pistol was slipping again, the muzzle dropping.

Portia noticed. She met Justin's eyes, shaking her head slightly. He knew the message she was sending him silently. She didn't want him to act, didn't want him to try to disarm Boyd, but that was the only way to save her.

"He was. Now he's missing. Thanks to you."

"Right. Consequences stink, don't they?" He grinned.

"I guess you'd know about that more than I would. You were insubordinate in basic training, and you got a dishonorable discharge. You went home and killed five people, and then got sent to federal prison. You escaped and started killing again, and you're going to be thrown in prison again," Justin said, purposely riling him up, getting him angry, trying to keep him from thinking, from noticing that Justin was edging nearer.

A few more steps, and he'd be close enough to lunge for the weapon.

"I'm not going back to prison, Blackwood," Boyd said coldly. "Men like me never do."

"Like you? You think you're too smart to get caught?" he asked, taking another step forward. "You made a mistake tonight. You should have come after me and left Portia alone."

"I don't make mistakes!" he screamed. The gun moved, and for a split second, Justin thought he'd won, that Boyd would release his hold on Portia and go after him.

But as quickly as Boyd's anger appeared, it was gone.

"Good try, Blackwood," he said. "But I know what you're trying to do."

"Maybe you could explain it to me?"

"Put your gun on the ground. Now. And do it slowly. You so much as make me think you're taking aim, and I kill your daughter."

Justin played along, taking his handgun from its holster and setting it on the floor.

Something moved in the window behind Boyd, a flurry of shadows that coalesced into a figure climbing silently through the opening. Slim. Tall. Graceful and quick.

He had about two seconds to realize it was Gretchen.

He wanted to tell her to stop, but it was too late.

Boyd must have sensed her presence. He swung around, firing a shot almost blindly.

Justin grabbed Portia, yanking her away and thrusting her through the doorway, shouting for Quinn.

The dog was there, snarling and snapping, rushing toward Boyd, who still had his gun in hand.

"Call him off or she dies," he yelled shrilly, his firearm aimed at Gretchen.

She lay still.

Stunned or injured or afraid to move.

"Quinn, off!" Justin shouted, and the dog backed off, still growling, still snarling. Unhappy to have been called off his prize.

Justin moved toward Gretchen, freezing when Boyd dragged her to her feet and pressed the gun into her side. She was a rag doll, limp and helpless in his grip.

"Don't move," Boyd commanded. "Don't even breathe."

The world went silent.

Not a breath of sound.

And then chaos reigned again. Gretchen moved suddenly, thrusting her hand under Boyd's chin, slamming her elbow into his gut. The firearm discharged, the bullet slamming into the dirt floor.

Boyd backhanded Gretchen, propelling her toward Justin.

He caught her, lowering her to the ground and grabbing his gun at his feet. He came up and fired a shot as Boyd jumped through the window. He wanted to follow, but Gretchen was injured and Portia was standing in the doorway, her soft sobs filling the cabin. Obviously, she'd been too terrified to make a run for it. He didn't dare leave them alone. Not with Boyd on the loose.

"It's okay, Portia," he said quietly, holstering his weapon. "He's gone."

She'd been shot. That was Gretchen's first thought. Her second thought was that Boyd Sullivan was escaping. She pushed herself to her knees, surprised when someone took her arm, holding her steady as she got to her feet.

Not someone.

Justin.

He'd shrugged out of his jacket and was pressing it to her shoulder. She brushed it away. "I'm fine."

"You're bleeding a lot, Gretchen," Portia said, hovering a few steps away, her eyes wide with fear, her face pale.

"You call this bleeding?" She scoffed, offering the teen an encouraging smile. "You should have seen me when I fell out of the tree my brothers dared me to climb. I hit my head on the way down and bled so much they thought I was dead."

"You have brothers?" Justin asked, pulling the fabric of her jacket and shirt away so he could see the wound. The bullet had grazed her upper arm, and dark blood bubbled from the wound. She didn't feel any pain. All she felt was anger. That Boyd had struck again. That a man was dead. That a teenager had been terrorized. That a man who killed indiscriminately was escaping again.

"I have four brothers." She brushed Justin's hand away. "Stop fussing. I'm fine."

"Sure you are. If fine is having a bullet take a chunk out of your upper arm," he responded, pressing his jacket to the wound to try to stanch the bleeding.

She felt that. The pressure on the open wound made her grimace, but she wasn't going to admit that she was in pain. She brushed his hand away again. "The bleeding has almost stopped, and Boyd needs to be captured. Take Quinn and go after him. I'll watch Portia until backup arrives."

He hesitated, and she knew he was torn. He didn't want to leave his daughter, but he knew how important it was to apprehend Boyd.

"I'll make sure Portia is okay, Justin. I promise," she assured him.

"It's not just her I'm worried about," he replied, but he'd moved to the window Boyd had escaped through. "You're pale and still bleeding. You probably need stitches."

"I can get stitches with or without you nearby."

"Dad, please don't go," Portia cut in, grabbing Justin's arm as he leaned out the window opening.

"Portia, he needs to be stopped. Tonight. Before he hurts anyone else. Gretchen will make sure you're okay—"

"I'm not worried about me," the teen protested. "I'm worried about you."

"Your dad is going to be okay, too," Gretchen said, putting a hand on Portia's shoulder and wishing she were better at this part of the job. She'd gone into military police work because she'd believed in justice, and because it had seemed like the thing to do. Her father had worked as an MP until he'd retired. All four of her brothers were military police officers, and from the time she was old enough to remember, she'd wanted to follow in their footsteps. She'd been the youngest by nine years. A surprise that had pleased her parents and her brothers. She'd been encouraged to pursue her dreams, and military life had been the only one she'd had.

Until Henry.

He'd made her want the things she'd written about in her adolescent diary—love and romance and forever. By the time she and Henry met at an on-base church, she'd already established herself as a tough no-nonsense military police officer. Tough was a necessity when you were a woman in a man's world. Showing empathy, sympathy and sorrow were not. Henry had appreciated that. He'd been Airman Second Class, back from Afghanistan and training new recruits. They'd hit it off immediately.

If things had worked out, Henry would have finished out his final year in the military and then applied to the FBI. Gretchen would have spent another four years working and then left the air force to start a family with him.

But things hadn't worked out.

And now she was in an old cabin in the middle of the woods with a teenager who needed the kind of nurturing support Gretchen hadn't had any practice with.

Portia still had Justin's arm, her eyes dark in her pale face. "Dad! Really! You can't go after him. He wants to kill you."

"Gretchen is right. I'm going to be fine. Quinn is smart and quick, and he always has my back."

"He's a dog, and he can't stop a bullet. You know Boyd Sullivan will shoot you as soon as he gets a chance."

"I'm not going to give him a chance," Justin assured her.

"That's what you think is going to happen, but you can't know for sure that you can stop him. Look what happened to Mom. She was going to work. Just like she did every Wednesday night. She should have made it home, and she didn't." Portia swiped at a tear that was sliding down her cheek, and Gretchen wanted to pull her close, tell her again that everything was going to be okay. That her father would return. That Boyd would be caught. That life would go on, and that she'd continue on with it. That, one day, she'd think of her mother, and she'd be happier for the times they'd had than sad for the times they'd missed.

But those were big concepts. Difficult ones.

Gretchen was nearly thirty, and she struggled to accept her loss. Even four years after his death, she missed Henry and what they'd planned together.

Portia was a kid.

One who'd lost her mother. It wasn't surprising that she was terrified of losing her father.

"I wish I could stay here with you," Justin said, pulling Portia in for a hug.

She went stiff, her arms down at her sides.

"If you really wished it, you'd stay," she muttered.

"I have a job to do, Portia. And if I don't do it, you'll never be safe." He stepped back, his voice as stiff as Portia's hug had been.

"If you die it's going to be my fault. Just like—"

She stopped and stepped back, her expression tight and guarded.

"Just like what?" he asked.

"Nothing." She was lying. Gretchen didn't know much about teenagers, but she knew a lie when she heard one.

Justin hesitated, staring into his daughter's eyes as if he could find the secret she was keeping.

Outside, a dog barked and dry leaves crackled. Lights bounced across the clearing. Help had arrived. Finally.

"I need to go," Justin said. "We'll discuss how none of this is your fault later. Stay with Gretchen. Do whatever she tells you without arguing."

"But—"

"It really is going to be okay, Portia," he said, and then he issued a command to Quinn, waited for the Malinois to bound through the window and follow him. He had to find Boyd. He had to stop him.

Tonight.

Before he had the chance to hurt anyone else.

FOUR

He didn't want to leave.

That was a problem that Justin hadn't anticipated.

He'd spent his military career as a bachelor. He'd never worried about returning home, and he'd never thought about what would happen to Portia if something had happened to him.

He'd known that she'd be okay. Melanie had been a wonderful, caring mother. He had never realized how much peace of mind that had given him. Until now.

He followed Quinn across the clearing, nearly running to keep up. The Malinois was focused and intent. He didn't seem to notice the men and women in military uniform who were swarming out of the trees. Every member of the base Security Forces wanted Boyd Sullivan caught, and they were desperate to cut off his escape.

Justin wanted to believe that would be enough, but they'd been in this position before—so close to Sullivan that his capture had seemed inevitable. Every time, he slipped through their fingers.

And now he'd gone after Portia.

Justin had been anticipating that. He'd tried to keep

her safe, but even an armed bodyguard hadn't been enough.

He frowned, pushing through thick undergrowth, his heart heavy with the knowledge that another person had died. Another life lost, and Sullivan was still free.

"Captain!" a woman called.

He glanced over his shoulder and saw Ava Esposito jogging toward him, her yellow lab, Roscoe, on a leash beside her.

"Airman Esposito, what are you doing out here?" he asked. Ava was a K-9 handler with Search and Rescue who'd had a personal run-in with Sullivan while she'd been searching for a missing child.

"I heard about your daughter. I thought Roscoe might be able to help find her."

"She's been located."

"I heard that, too. Since I'm here, I thought we'd lend a hand in the search for Sullivan." She tucked a strand of hair behind her ear and gestured toward Quinn. "He's got the scent?"

"Yes."

"How much of a head start does Sullivan have?"

"A few minutes." He ducked under a low-hanging branch, his attention on Quinn again. Justin had worked with other dogs, but he'd never worked with one that had as much enthusiasm for the job. Quinn's tail was wagging, his head down as he made a circuit around a large tree. This was a game to him. Boyd Sullivan was the prize. He was eager and anxious to find him.

"A few minutes is a long time in Boyd Sullivan's world," Ava murmured.

"Unfortunately, that's true."

Quinn's head popped up, his ears twitching.

"Find!" Justin commanded, and Quinn took off, racing through the woods.

Justin raced after him, sprinting across a dry creek bed and up a steep ravine. He knew Ava was behind him, her K-9 still on his leash. Roscoe was trained in search and rescue, and he had the sweet temperament of his breed.

Quinn's training was in apprehension.

He knew how to take down the enemy, and he'd done it dozens of times. God willing, he'd do it tonight.

Please, Lord, Justin prayed silently, *help us stop him.*

He wanted a clear sign that God had heard, that He was ready and willing to step in and stop the carnage that Sullivan had been causing. He wanted to listen and hear some internal voice telling him that God was there, that He was working everything out for His good.

All he heard was his panting breath and heavy footfalls as his boots slapped against dead leaves.

Where are You? he wanted to ask.

Where have You been?

Years ago, he'd prayed just as desperately when his partner had been shot while they'd been responding to a domestic violence call. Justin had been a rookie military police officer. He'd been assigned to work with Corbin Williams—a twenty-year veteran of the Security Forces. They'd been partners for four years, and in that time, they'd become good friends. Corbin had included Justin in family events, invited him to church, helped him mature as a Christian.

And then they'd gone on the call that had changed everything.

One shot fired by a drunken airman and Corbin had fallen. The bullet had punctured his lung and lodged in his liver. He'd lived long enough to see his wife and his kids at the hospital. During surgery to remove the bullet and repair the damage, his heart had stopped.

Justin's desperate prayers hadn't saved him.

His prayers hadn't eased the heartache of Corbin's family.

If Corbin had been around, he'd have told Justin that God works even the difficult times into good things.

And maybe he'd have been right.

Justin had gone into K-9 work because he hadn't wanted to lose another partner. Corbin had been his first and last human partner. Over the years, he and K-9 partners had stopped a lot of criminals and saved a lot of lives.

Corbin's widow, Alexis, reminded Justin of that when he visited. She lived in Houston now. The kids were grown. She had grandkids. And she never doubted that God was with her. That He loved her.

Justin tried to have that kind of faith.

More often than not, he failed.

Right now, though, he wished he could hold on to the promises that Corbin had so often quoted when they were on the job together. He wished he could access the kind of belief in God's divine plan that didn't waver. No matter the circumstances.

Instead, all he managed were quick, desperate prayers that seemed as ineffective as umbrellas during hurricanes.

Up ahead, lights gleamed through the trees. Not house lights. Streetlights. Sullivan was running toward an escape vehicle.

The thought left Justin cold.

He'd been hoping they had him boxed in.

"He has a vehicle waiting," Ava said, echoing his thoughts.

"Radio in our location. See if we can get some manpower here. We'll want to block the road..." His voice trailed off as Quinn suddenly appeared. The Malinois ran to him, jumping up and planting his feet on Justin's chest. One quick bark, and the dog was off again.

"He's found him," Justin yelled, racing after the dog.

The trees thinned out and the forest opened up into a grassy field. Beyond it, he could see a brick building and an empty parking lot.

The church.

He and Portia attended every Sunday, and it didn't surprise him that Boyd would go there. He loved instilling fear. This was a place Justin felt comfortable and at ease. Boyd wanted to change that.

Behind Justin, Ava was speaking quickly, relaying their location, calling for police presence at the church and on the streets surrounding it.

Too little too late.

Sullivan had planned this well. He'd parked far enough away to have built-in escape time. He'd parked close enough that walking had been easy.

And he'd made a stop at the empty property, broken in, turned on some lights. Stretched the Security Forces thinner by giving them another location to search.

"I want this guy. Tonight," Justin muttered as he raced across the field. He could see Quinn, moonlight glinting in his fur, his body tense as he loped through the grass.

He was heading straight toward the church, not

sniffing, not searching. He'd seen his prize, and he was leading Justin to it.

A car engine revved as Quinn reached the parking lot, and Justin's pulse jumped, his hair standing on end.

Quinn was heading into the fray, ready to take Sullivan down. But a car was a deadly weapon, and Justin wasn't willing to lose another partner.

"Front!" he yelled, and Quinn's ears twitched, his powerful body jerking to a stop.

He swung around, running back toward Justin as a vehicle raced around the side of the building and sped straight toward them.

Justin pulled his firearm, aiming for the car's windshield. His first shot shattered the glass.

The car spun to the left, the engine revving again as Sullivan fled. Of course he wouldn't stand his ground. He was a coward. Just like most bullies.

Justin fired another shot, taking out a back tire. The car fishtailed but kept going, crippled but still functioning. Hopefully not for long.

He radioed in a description of the vehicle, offering a partial plate number and asking that gate security officers be made aware of the situation. He doubted Sullivan would attempt to drive off base, but he wanted to be prepared if it happened.

Quinn whined, still sitting in front of Justin, staring into his face as if he had some secret message to convey.

"What is it, boy?" Justin asked.

Quinn jumped up, front paws on Justin's chest for a second before he sat again.

"That's his indication," Ava commented. Not a question, but Justin nodded. Sullivan was gone, but Quinn had something else he wanted to go after.

"Go get it, Quinn," he commanded.

The dog bounded away, running into the parking lot, away from the pebbly pieces of glass that glinted in the moonlight. He reached the church, rounded a corner and disappeared from sight.

"Do you think we should call in the bomb unit to check the church?" Ava asked. "I wouldn't put it past Sullivan to use something like that as a distraction."

"I don't think he planned on being followed back here, so I think we're in the clear."

"He's been excelling at staying a step ahead of us, Captain," she reminded him. "Anything is possible."

"I agree, but he had no reason to believe I'd be able to follow him here. He planned to kill me in the woods, and he isn't used to failing. He'd have assumed he was going to get the outcome he was looking for."

"He is cocky and arrogant, so you could be right. That will work out well for us. Arrogant, cocky people tend to make mistakes."

"And mistakes get criminals caught."

They rounded the corner of the building to find Quinn standing beneath a streetlight. Ears back, muzzle down, he stared at something that lay on the ground.

"Off!" Justin commanded. Quinn was well trained. He wouldn't touch the item. He wouldn't eat it.

But Sullivan was familiar with the K-9 team. He'd been observing it for months. He had to know how tight the bond was between handler and K-9 partner. Justin wouldn't put it past him to try to poison the dogs. He certainly hadn't cared about releasing the well-trained dogs from their kennels.

"Heel," he said as Quinn reached his side.

The dog did as he was commanded, stepping into heel and matching his pace with Justin's.

Justin motioned for Ava to stay back, then approached the streetlight. After a few steps, he could see the item clearly. *Items.* A long-stemmed red rose lying on top of a piece of paper. He crouched beside it, pulling out his phone and snapping a few photos.

"What is it?" Ava asked, approaching cautiously.

"A rose."

"Sullivan's signature," she murmured. "Is that a note?"

"Yeah. It says, *'You're next.'*"

"Did he think you hadn't already figured that out? He did kidnap Portia to get to you."

"He's enjoying the game. He won't be for much longer," he responded grimly.

"Let's see if we can track the vehicle," Ava suggested. "He won't get far with a blown-out tire. Once we find the car, we should have no problem tracking him from there."

"You are Search and Rescue, Ava," Justin pointed out. Ava had been key in helping to locate many of the dogs Boyd had freed from the base kennel, and she continued to search for the ones that remained missing. A few months ago, she'd helped find a child who'd been missing from a school trip. During her search, she'd come face-to-face with Sullivan. Since then, she seemed determined to be part of the team efforts to bring in the serial killer.

"And?"

"Security Forces will handle searching for Sullivan."

"We're all part of the same team, Captain," she reminded him. "And Roscoe's got a great nose. The scent is fresh. Now is the time to go."

She was already walking toward the street, Roscoe beside her.

"He's not trained in apprehension or attack, and Sullivan won't care whether he takes out a mild-tempered Labrador or a high-energy Malinois."

She hesitated. He'd known she would.

K-9 teams were strongly bonded, and no handler would put a dog into a situation he hadn't been trained for.

"Are you taking Quinn?"

He wanted to, but three Security Forces vehicles were speeding into the lot, officers jumping out and running toward him. He could count on his MPs to do everything in their power to apprehend Sullivan, but if Sullivan slipped through their fingers, he knew where he needed to be. At the hospital.

Portia was there with Gretchen, who was injured.

The thought of either of them coming up against Boyd made his pulse race.

"I'm going to the hospital. I need to make sure Portia and Gretchen are okay," he responded, his attention on the officers who were moving toward them. Tech Sergeant Linc Colson was there, opening the back hatch of his vehicle and letting his rottweiler out.

Good.

Star was a trained attack dog. She'd be able to take Sullivan down easily. If they were able to track him down.

"Captain," Linc called, raising a hand in salute. "I hear there's been another run-in with Sullivan."

"He killed a bodyguard and kidnapped Portia."

"Does he still have her?"

"Gretchen and I managed to free her, but Sullivan

slipped through our fingers. Again." He filled Linc in on what had transpired, giving a description of the car and the direction Sullivan was heading.

Hopefully it would be enough.

The Red Rose Killer needed to be brought to justice before anyone else was hurt or killed.

"We'll do everything we can to bring him in," Linc assured him. "Are you heading to the hospital?"

"Yes."

"Take my vehicle. I can catch a ride back to head-quarters and grab the SUV later." He tossed keys in Justin's direction, issued a terse command to Star and jogged away.

Justin wanted to believe they'd find Sullivan.

He wanted to believe tonight was the night that this months-long nightmare would end, but Sullivan had eluded them over and over again. He'd killed an airman, stolen his uniform and used it to blend in while he was on base.

He was smart, and he had no conscience, no remorse.

If he got his hands on Portia again...

Justin shook the thought away, calling to Quinn and loading him into the back of Linc's vehicle. He shut the door with a little too much force, angry with himself for allowing Sullivan to escape again. Angry with God for not ending things.

Corbin had believed that there was a reason for everything. He'd often told Justin that God's plans weren't always clear, but they were always good.

Maybe he'd been right.

Probably he had been.

But Justin could see no reason for people being murdered. He could think of no good plan that involved innocent lives being lost. He'd become a military police officer because he'd believed that justice should always prevail. He'd believed that good should always win. He'd wanted to make a difference in the world, and he supposed that he had. God had used him to help dozens of people. He'd used him to solve hundreds of crimes. Justin acknowledged that, and he was grateful for it.

But this case?

It was eating him alive, because no matter how much time was put into it, no matter how many hours were spent pursuing leads, no matter what they did to try to stop him, Boyd Sullivan remained free.

"Not for long," he promised himself as he started the SUV and pulled out of the parking lot.

God was always good.

Even in the tough times.

Henry had said that often during the years they'd been together. He'd lost his father in a car accident. He'd been diagnosed with an aggressive cancer. He'd gone through chemo and radiation and been so sick he couldn't get out of bed.

And, to him, God was still good.

Funny how Gretchen had forgotten those words, forgotten how confident Henry had been when he'd said them. He hadn't been afraid to die. He hadn't been afraid to be sick. He'd lived life to the fullest until the very end.

She remembered that.

Just like she remembered his smile and his laughter.

He'd be smiling now if he were there. Joking with her while she waited for the doctor to stitch the wound in her upper arm. He'd always been happy and confident and fun. Without him, she'd become too somber and too focused, too intent on her work.

At least, that was what her closest friends said.

That may or may not have been one of the reasons she'd agreed to take the assignment at Canyon Air Force Base. She'd been at Minot Air Force Base for several years. The community there was small and tight-knit. People knew each other well, and most of them cared a lot about the happiness of their comrades.

Over the past couple of years, Gretchen had been invited on double dates, set up on blind dates and encouraged to step out of her comfort zone by friends, coworkers and acquaintances.

Apparently, there was a timeline for grief, and she should have reached the end of hers.

And in some ways she had.

Grief had faded into quiet sadness for what she'd lost and into bittersweet joy for what she'd had. But that didn't mean she wanted another relationship. She'd tried to tell her friends that. She'd tried to explain it to coworkers, but Gretchen's single status was a constant source of discussion on base, and frankly, she'd had enough of it. When she'd been asked to take a temporary transfer and train for a leadership position at another command post, she'd jumped at the opportunity.

In the months since then, she'd missed her friends and community in Minot, but she hadn't regretted the decision to leave. Even now, sitting on an exam table, arm bandaged, waiting for the doctor to return with a suture kit, she wasn't sorry she'd come to Canyon Air Force Base. She'd learned a lot, and would continue to do so for the next four weeks. At the end of that time, she'd return to Minot and begin putting together the new K-9 unit there.

Or leave the military.

She'd almost completed eight years of active service. Her commanding officer had reminded her of that when he'd offered her the temporary transfer: *You're young. You can move up the ranks and make a name for yourself, or you can leave and start a new career. The choice will be yours. Either way, we'll expect you to spend the last six months of your assignment setting up our new K-9 unit and putting airmen in place who will be an asset to it.*

She'd agreed, because she'd needed a change of pace, because the transfer had seemed interesting, because she was always willing to learn something new.

But she'd had no idea whether she'd return to take the post as head of the Minot K-9 Unit. If she did that, she'd be committing to another four years in the military. By the time she left, she'd be thirty-two. Which shouldn't matter. She loved being an MP, but the truth was, she'd never intended to make a lifetime career of it.

"Are you okay?" Portia asked. She'd been brought to the hospital triage room at Gretchen's insistence. Anything else had been out of the question. No separate rooms. No being interviewed by the MP who was waiting in the corridor. Gretchen planned to keep Justin's daughter within arm's reach until he arrived and could take over her protection.

"Right as rain," she responded, offering the teen a bright smile.

Portia didn't seem convinced.

She tucked a strand of blond hair behind her ear

and frowned. "This is all my fault. I should never have blogged about the Red Rose Killer."

"You shouldn't have blogged about him, but that doesn't make this your fault."

"You don't have to be nice to me, Gretchen. I know that everyone my dad works with is mad at me for what I did."

"Who gave you that idea?" she asked, looking into Portia's bright blue eyes. She was a quietly pretty girl. No makeup. No oddly colored hair. Just a sweet-looking kid with dark circles under her eyes and sorrow in her expression.

"No one. It's obvious. I was writing things that my dad discussed with the team, and I was putting everyone at risk."

"Is that what your dad said?"

"Yes, and he's right."

"You're a kid. Kids make mistakes."

"My mother always said that mistakes happen. It's what we do after we make them that defines us as people."

"Your mother was a very wise woman."

"Yes. I wish…"

"She was here?" she guessed, and Portia shrugged, her gaze dropping to the floor.

"I guess that's the way every kid who loses a parent feels."

"That doesn't make it an easy feeling to have."

Portia met her eyes again. "No. You're right. It doesn't. Do you think my dad is okay?"

"Your dad is really good at what he does."

"And I'm really good at knowing when someone

doesn't answer my question. I may be a teenager, but I'm not stupid."

"I think your dad is okay," she said, because she did. But she'd seen Sullivan's handiwork. She knew what he was capable of. If he had an opportunity to kill someone he thought had wronged him, he'd take it. And he was convinced that Justin had been a big part of his dishonorable discharge.

"For now?" Portia guessed.

"We're going to capture Boyd Sullivan, and once he's in jail, everyone will be safe."

"And until he's in jail, no one will be."

"You're a smart young woman, Portia. What are you planning to do when you graduate high school? College?"

"That wasn't a subtle change of subject," Portia muttered.

"No. It wasn't, but there's not much I can say that wouldn't be a lie, and I don't lie."

"So, you're admitting my father isn't safe?"

"I'm admitting that Boyd Sullivan is dangerous. But you knew that when you were blogging about him. You did it, anyway."

"Anonymously."

"It's very difficult to stay anonymous forever. I'm sure you knew that when you started the blog."

Portia blushed. "I know it was stupid. I said I was sorry. If I could change it, I would."

"I didn't say that to make you feel bad, Portia. I said it because you decided that the blog was more important than the risks associated with it. Your father is the same. He knows the risks of his job. Every day when he goes to work, he weighs that against the importance of what he's doing. And every day he decides that what he's doing matters enough to take the risk."

"That's a good way to put it," said a deep male voice, breaking into their quiet conversation.

Gretchen turned and glanced at the open door.

Justin was standing at the threshold, Quinn sitting calmly beside him.

"Has the search ended?" she asked, hoping that he'd say it had and that Boyd was in custody.

"No. We've still got teams on the ground, but I wanted to see how you and Portia were doing." He crossed the room and took a seat in a chair next to Portia. "Are you okay, sweetheart?" he asked his daughter.

"I'm not the one who got shot," she responded, her gaze skittering away from Justin. She seemed intent on looking at the floor, the ceiling, the walls. Anywhere but at her father.

"A person can be physically fine and mentally struggling," he responded.

"I'm fine. Mentally and physically," she said, crossing her arms over her chest and staring at her feet. All the worry she'd had for her father, all her concern about him coming up against Sullivan, was hidden beneath a facade of teenage indifference.

Justin seemed to take it in stride.

He patted Portia's shoulder and turned his attention to Gretchen. "How about you, Captain?" he asked. "Are you okay?"

"I'll be better once the doctor gets in here and stitches me up. The sooner I can get back on Sullivan's trail, the happier I'll be," she answered, looking straight into his eyes the way she had dozens of times during their months working together.

This time shouldn't have been any different.

He was the same guy she'd met a few months ago. The captain who'd showed her around, who'd introduced her to the other MPs, who'd welcomed her to the team. At the time, she'd been aware of his height and strength, of his confidence and his excellent communication skills. The people he worked with had seemed to respect and like him, and she'd noticed that, too.

She hadn't noticed how blue his eyes were. She hadn't paid attention to the smile lines at the corners of his mouth or the thickness of his lashes. He was a coworker, a mentor, a guy she'd know for a while and then walk away from. She'd had no interest beyond that.

But right now, she was noticing his eyes. His lashes. The faint smile lines. She was thinking about how concerned he looked and how intent. Not just focused on the job, but on her well-being.

She stood abruptly, swaying a little as the blood flowed out of her head.

"Whoa! Careful," Justin said, holding her arm while she regained her balance. "You don't want to fall and knock yourself."

"What I want is the twenty-five stitches the doctor promised me," she muttered, avoiding his eyes, because she was done noticing how striking they were in his tan face.

"You're the first person I've ever known who was eager to have a needle poked through her arm," he said as she walked to the door.

"I'm eager to get back to work." And away from

him, because noticing anything aside from Justin's work ethic seemed wrong. They were coworkers who were becoming friends, but that was it. For now and forever.

"You don't really think you're going straight back to work, do you?" he asked, and she knew he was watching her. She could feel the weight of his gaze, but she didn't turn around. She didn't meet his eyes. She took the cowardly way out and stared into the hall.

"I don't see why I shouldn't. Someone has to write up tonight's report."

"I can do that. I think the best thing for you to do is take some time off. Maybe a week or two."

Surprised, she swung around, realized he'd moved closer. She was tall, but she still had to look up to meet his eyes. "You're kidding, right?"

"Why would I be?"

"This is barely an injury, Captain." She raised her arm, ignoring the fact that the gauze was stained with blood.

"It looks like one to me. I may not be your commanding officer, but I do send him weekly reports. I'm sure he'll agree that time off is a good thing."

"I only have four weeks left on base. I still have a lot to learn, and I'm not going to do that if I'm stuck at home for half the time."

"I wasn't thinking you'd be at home." He glanced at Portia. "I've already asked my commanding officer to arrange for Portia to go to a safe house."

"No way!" Portia jumped up, her hair flying around her face, her eyes dark with anger. "I'm not going."

"You're not going to have a choice," Justin said

calmly. "Sullivan wants me dead, and you're the perfect way for him to get to me. Now that he knows it, he's not going to stop going after you."

"I'm sixteen. I should have some say in what happens to me."

"You can choose how you want your hair cut and what you want to eat, but you're not going to choose whether or not to stay on base when a serial killer is after you," he responded firmly. No anger. No frustration. Just a statement of fact.

Portia looked like she wanted to argue, but Justin had turned his attention back to Gretchen. "Since we're setting that up, I thought it would be a good place for you to stay while you're healing."

"Let me make sure I have this right," she said, finally understanding. "You want me to go to a safe house until Sullivan is caught?"

"I didn't say that."

"And you're not saying it's not the truth."

"You could have died tonight," he said quietly, glancing at Portia.

"You aren't the only one who weighs the risk and then reports to work every day, Captain. I didn't become an MP to stand down when there's danger."

"I'm not asking you to do that."

"Sure you are, and I'm not sure why. Is it because I'm a woman?" she asked, because there had been men who'd thought her gender made her weaker and less capable.

She wouldn't have expected it from Justin. She'd never seen any hints of gender bias, but it was possible he'd learned to hide it during his years in the military.

"No," he responded. Flatly. Bluntly.

"Then what is it?"

He glanced at Portia again. "Not something I want to discuss right now."

"Then how about we discuss it after you transport your daughter to the safe house?"

"We'll transport her together. We can discuss the rest later," he responded, stepping to the side as the doctor finally arrived.

Gretchen was tense now, her muscles taut, and when the doctor began stitching her, the needle hurt more than it probably would have if she'd been relaxed. She'd never minded stitches, and she'd never been overly sensitive to pain, but she felt woozy, her ears buzzing as the doctor worked.

She'd lost a lot of blood.

That was for sure, but there was no way she was taking the time off that Justin had suggested.

She wasn't hiding in a safe house, either.

She'd come to Texas to be a member of Canyon Air Force Base Security Forces. That meant keeping the men and women who worked and lived on base safe. No one would be safe as long as Sullivan was free.

She had four weeks to continue her training.

Four weeks to help Justin find the serial killer who'd made the base his hunting ground.

Four weeks to make sure that Sullivan didn't strike again.

She could only pray it would be enough time, because she wanted to be there when Boyd was captured. She wanted to watch as he was handcuffed and led away. When she returned to Minot, she wanted to know that Justin, Portia and all the people she'd met and worked with could go on with their lives, free from the fear that had been dogging them since Sullivan escaped from prison.

FIVE

Portia wasn't happy.

Justin didn't have to know much about teenage girls to know that. She sat silently in the back seat of Linc's SUV as he drove to Security Forces HQ, her eyes closed, head back, ignoring everything and everyone.

He could see her in the rearview mirror—angry and withdrawn. He was tempted to try to explain how important she was to him, how worried he was about her. But he'd done that before, outlining the situation from his perspective in an attempt to convince her that he was more concerned than angry after he'd found out she was the anonymous blogger.

She'd listened, but he doubted she'd believed him.

They had enough history together to understand a little about each other, but not enough to have an unspoken understanding about their relationship. He was her father, but he was certain she saw him more as a stranger. He wasn't someone Portia could turn to when she was upset. He wanted to be. He'd tried to be. But trust had to be earned, and all he seemed to be earning was her contempt.

He'd had no idea being the parent of a teenager was

this complicated. If he'd had, he'd have thanked Melanie more than a few times a year for being such a great mother to their daughter.

He frowned, glancing in the rearview mirror again. He owed it to Melanie, to Portia and to himself to keep reaching out, to keep trying, to keep being there. Even when Portia didn't seem to want him to be.

"I know you're upset, Portia," he began.

Her eyes flew open, and she met his gaze.

"That's an understatement," she responded, turning to look out the window.

"I'm sorry. I understand that you don't want to go to a safe house, but your well-being is my top priority. I've already tried hiring bodyguards and keeping you on base. That didn't work. Now we've got to take more drastic measures."

"*You* have to take more drastic measures," she corrected. "I have nothing to do with that decision."

"You're sixteen, Portia. There are a lot of things you don't understand."

"At sixteen, I could be legally emancipated and living on my own," she retorted, her tone a little flip and a little haughty.

He tamped down irritation, trying to get to the heart of the matter rather than the emotions of it. "Reminding you that you're sixteen and that there are a lot of things you don't understand wasn't meant to be an insult."

"I didn't take it as one," she said.

"But you did mention becoming an emancipated minor," Gretchen cut into the conversation, shifting in the front passenger seat so she was facing the teen. "Is that something you've been considering?"

"No," Portia muttered. "My best friend suggested

it. She thought I could become emancipated and come back to Michigan and live with her family until I graduate."

"Addie Windsor?" Justin asked, telling himself that it didn't bother him that she'd been looking for ways to get out of living with him.

She was a kid.

She'd had friends and a school and activities back in Michigan.

When Melanie died, she hadn't just lost her mother. She'd lost everything.

"It isn't about not wanting to live with you, Dad," Portia said quickly. She might be teenager with all the attitude that went with it, but she had a heart of gold. "It's about not wanting to be away from home."

"I understand," he said, because he did. The day Portia entered kindergarten, Melanie had purchased a craftsman-style home in the little town where she and Justin had grown up. He'd helped her with the down payment, and he'd requested a few days of leave to help her move in. That was the only home Portia remembered. All her memories of her childhood, her mother, her friends were there.

"Like my room. Mom let me decorate it myself last year. She let me pick out the paint color and new bedding," Portia continued, the words spilling out quickly as if she'd been holding them in for too long and finally had to release them.

"I remember," he said. He'd sent Melanie extra money to help with the cost of redecorating. She'd texted photos of the finished room with Portia and her friends sitting on the bed, beaming at the camera. He'd had no idea when he'd opened the text and seen the photos that Melanie would be gone within the month.

"Addie and Jordan came over to spend the night after it was done, and we made a dream board that showed what we wanted to accomplish during our last two years of high school," she said with a quiet sigh.

"A dream board?" Gretchen asked. "Did you bring it with you? I'd love to see what you and your friends came up with."

"I tossed it in the trash," Portia muttered. "Three of the things were about me and Mom going places. We had a trip to the Grand Canyon planned for my senior year. And we were going to visit five colleges this year. She was excited because—" She stopped abruptly.

"She told me you were thinking about attending Michigan State. Just like she had. She was really proud of you, Portia."

Portia didn't respond.

Which was pretty much how things always went when he mentioned Melanie.

The silence stretched out for a few moments too long, and Gretchen shifted again, her injured arm bumping Justin's shoulder. "You said there were three things that you and your mother were supposed to do together," he said. "What was the third?"

"Buy my prom dress. Mom was really excited about that. I didn't even have a boyfriend, but she said going with friends would be even more fun. She never got to go to prom, because she was pregnant with me. I guess she wanted to have the experience." Her voice broke.

"I'm sorry, honey," Gretchen said. "I know how much it hurts to lose someone you love."

"Did you lose your mom?"

"No. My fiancé. Three weeks before our wedding."

Surprised, Justin glanced her way, trying to see her expression through the dark interior of the vehicle.

"Wow," Portia said. "I'm so sorry."

"So am I," Justin added. He'd never been engaged. Except for the first few days after Melanie had discovered she was pregnant, marriage had never been on his radar. He dated, but he kept things light. Dinner. A movie. He'd made it clear to any woman he'd been out with that he didn't want more. Not because he didn't sometimes think about having someone to go home to. But because his father had been an abusive alcoholic. Justin had memories of his mother being beaten black-and-blue. She'd left when he was ten, abandoning him to his father's rage. Sometimes, he could understand that. Sometimes, he couldn't. Either way, he hadn't had good examples of love when he was growing up, and he'd had no desire to see if he'd do any better.

Until the choice had been taken from him, he hadn't wanted to be the custodial parent to his daughter. He'd been afraid of what he might do, of the things he might say. He'd worried that he'd open his mouth and speak the words his father had, that he'd tear down rather than build up. That he'd create the same unforgiving and hate-filled environment he'd grown up in.

Somehow, though, that hadn't happened.

Portia had been living with him for over a year. He'd had plenty of opportunity to lose his cool and act like a raging lunatic. He hadn't. So, maybe nurture wasn't the only thing that shaped a person. Maybe faith and commitment and compassion trumped learned behaviors.

"Yeah. It was rough," Gretchen said, her voice soft and filled with emotion. "Henry and I had a whole life planned out. No dream boards, but I could picture it all in my head."

"When did he die?" Portia asked, leaning forward, apparently eager to hear the story.

"Portia, Gretchen might not want to talk about it," he cautioned, turning onto a side street that led to Security Forces headquarters. Portia would need to be interviewed by someone other than Justin. Once she'd given her statement, she'd be transported to a safe house, according to the base commander.

"I don't mind talking about it," Gretchen said, downplaying his concern. "Henry died four years ago. A little more than that actually. If things had gone the way I'd planned, I'd be retiring in six months, and Henry and I would be starting our family." She sounded matter-of-fact, but he detected a hint of something in her voice. Longing for what she might have had. Sorrow for what she'd lost. He'd assumed she was a die-hard military officer, but maybe becoming an MP had been something to do while she waited to pursue other dreams.

He didn't ask, because Portia was hanging on to her every word, nearly hanging over the seat in her eagerness to get the story. "So, you were going to have kids and everything?"

"Sure. Just because a woman is in the military doesn't mean she doesn't want those things."

"Oh, I know that," Portia said. "I've seen plenty of female officers on base who have kids. I just thought that because you were so old and not married—"

"Portia!" Justin said. "She's not old."

Gretchen laughed. "I think that depends on what

side of twenty you're standing on. What are you, Justin? Thirty-two?"

"Thirty-four," he corrected.

"I'm twenty-eight. Portia is sixteen. I'm sure, from her perspective, we're both ancient."

"Actually, I didn't mean old," Portia explained. "What I meant was that a lot of women your age are already married and have children."

"Right. How about we change the subject?" Justin suggested, and Gretchen laughed again.

"You seem more uncomfortable than I am, and I'm the one she called old."

"Really, Gretchen," the teen said, "I didn't mean that. My mom always used to say I needed to learn to think before I spoke. I guess I haven't mastered that yet."

"That's okay. Neither have I," Gretchen responded. "But since your dad wants to change the subject, how about we talk about the safe house again?"

"What about it?" Portia asked suspiciously.

"Your father is right to be concerned for your safety, and you aren't going to be safe on base."

"I can go back to Michigan for a while. I'm sure Addie and her parents will let me stay there for a few weeks. Maybe I can even take classes at the high school. Until it's safe to come back."

There was a hopeful edge to her voice that Justin didn't miss, and if he could have agreed to the plan, he would have.

"Sullivan is extremely dangerous. He's killed innocent people. Some of his victims were people he had a vendetta against. Some were just in his way," he said. "If he followed you to Michigan—"

"Don't even say it, Dad. I'd never forgive myself if something happened to Addie or her family."

"Then you understand why I can't let you do that."

"I understand, but I still want to go home," she said so quietly he almost didn't hear.

"How about we plan a trip for winter break?" he suggested, glancing in the rearview mirror. The street was empty. No cars. No people. Nothing that would lead him to believe that Sullivan was nearby. But his skin was crawling, his nerves alive with warning.

"A trip where?" Portia asked, oblivious to the danger that might be stalking them.

"To Michigan. The management company I hired to rent out your house is doing a good job, but I'd like to a do a walk-through of the property. Just to make certain everything is being maintained."

"You'd really bring me there for Christmas?" Portia asked.

"As long as this thing with Sullivan is settled, yes. Otherwise, it might have to wait until spring break." He glanced in the rearview mirror again. This time, he thought he saw a car in the distance. Lights off. Moving slowly.

"What is it?" Gretchen asked.

"Probably nothing."

"Then why do you keep looking in the rearview mirror?"

"Just a feeling."

She turned to look out the back window, her arm brushing his again. "Is that a car?"

"I think so."

"It's moving slowly. No lights. You think it's Sullivan?"

"Is it?" Portia asked, her voice shaking. "Do you think he followed us?"

"No," Justin responded. But he wouldn't put it past Sullivan to figure out where they were headed or to try to keep them from getting there. It would be a risky move. Security Forces were already out searching for him. Sullivan had to know that, but he hated making mistakes and he hated losing.

In basic training, he'd talked big, bragging that he was the best and the brightest. The strongest. The most capable. If he hadn't been a psychopath with no regard for others, he would have done okay and had a good air force career.

But he *was* a psychopath.

When he'd made mistakes during training, it had always been someone else's fault. Justin had broken up several fights that Boyd had started because he'd believed another recruit had sabotaged him or made him look bad.

No doubt, the mistake he'd made tonight, the fact that he'd almost been captured, was Justin's fault. Or Gretchen's. Or even Portia's.

Boyd would want his revenge, and he'd want it quickly. He wouldn't care who he had to hurt to get it.

Justin accelerated, driving above the speed limit.

The car behind him did the same.

Now there was no mistaking it. The car was tailing them. And whoever was driving it meant business.

Deadly business.

Gretchen called for backup as Justin swerved onto a busier street, and then unhooked her seat belt and crawled into the back with Portia.

"It's going to be okay," she assured the teenager, her attention on the car that was still behind them.

"Is it him?" Portia asked, levering up beside her.

Gretchen grabbed her arm, pulling her down. "Keep your head down. Let's not give him a target."

"Your head is up," Portia argued, but she'd dropped low, her forehead to her knees.

"I am being paid to get a good look at the vehicle. You are not." Only she couldn't see much. Just the outline of a car flying through the red light at the intersection they'd just passed through. "He's going to kill someone," she muttered, radioing in the location and the direction they were traveling.

This section of base offered plenty of places to hide, she noted as they sped past. Several small businesses lined the streets, all of them closed at this time of night. There were alleys and Dumpsters and doors that could easily be jimmied and opened. Fences. Delivery trucks parked beside buildings.

If she were trying to elude the police, she'd be taking cover somewhere. Whoever was in the car didn't seem to have the same idea. The driver accelerated, flying through a stop sign and speeding after them. Not gaining on them but not falling behind.

"He's still there," she said even though she was sure Justin already knew that.

"It's Boyd," he replied, taking a turn a little too quickly. The SUV squealed in protest, and Quinn whined. He was either scared or eager to be out of the vehicle and on the hunt. Based on what she'd seen during the past few months, Gretchen was confident it was the latter.

"If you slow down, I may be able to get a positive

ID. I don't want to shoot until I'm certain of who I'm shooting at." She opened the window anyway, leaning out and trying to get a look at the vehicle's license plate.

The driver slowed the vehicle, bumped over the curb and rolled to a stop. The door flew open, and the driver jumped out. She saw the flash before she heard the gunshot.

One. Two shots.

She had her firearm out and was pulling the trigger, protecting Portia and Justin, keeping her focus on the shooter, as Justin took another turn.

Headquarters was just ahead, and he sped into the parking lot, pulled up to the front doors and braked hard.

"Get her into the building," he shouted, hopping out of the SUV and opening Gretchen's door.

"You aren't planning on going back there," she protested as she ran around the side of the car, gun in her right hand, left arm throbbing and nearly useless. She managed to open Portia's door, anyway, grabbing the teen's hand and nearly dragging her out.

"Yeah. I am. I want Boyd behind bars. Tonight is as good a time as any to make sure that happens." Justin opened the back of the SUV and released Quinn, giving the dog the command to find and taking off before Gretchen had the door to HQ open.

"Dad!" Portia called, yanking away.

Gretchen tucked her gun into its holster and snagged the back of Portia's shirt. "We need to get inside."

"But—" The crack of a gunshot interrupted whatever she planned to say. The bullet wasn't fired from close enough to be dangerous, but that didn't mean anything. Boyd knew his way around the base, and no doubt he was working his way near enough to shoot Justin or Portia.

"Inside. Now!" Gretchen opened the door and shoved Portia into the building. An MP was running toward them, boots pounding on the tile floor.

"Take her to a room without windows and keep her there," Gretchen ordered, and then she closed the door and ran in the direction Justin and Quinn had gone. Right at the shooter.

SIX

Quinn was on the hunt, moving quickly and without hesitation. Ears up. Stride long. Focused but not sniffing the ground. Not trying to find a scent. He knew what he was after, and he knew where to find it. The question was, would they get there before Boyd escaped? Or fired off a round that hit its target?

Justin raced after the Malinois, praying that these would be Boyd's last moments of freedom. He wanted this over. Too many people had been killed. Too many people were still in danger.

As far as he was concerned, no one on base would be safe until Boyd was behind bars.

He rounded a street corner and his heart dropped.

Three MP cars were parked at the curb, lights flashing. But there was no sign of Boyd's car, and no sign of Boyd.

Someone raced up behind him, feet pounding the ground.

Gretchen.

He knew it before he turned. Knew absolutely that she'd done what he'd commanded—made sure Portia was safely inside the building.

And then she'd done exactly what he'd hadn't wanted her to do.

She'd followed him.

"I wanted you to stay with Portia in the building," he said as she reached his side. They were still running hard, Quinn suddenly pivoting away from the MPs' vehicles.

"I belong here," Gretchen responded. Not panting. Not struggling.

She had to be in pain, though.

She'd removed the sling the doctor had given her at the hospital, and he could see blood on the gauze bandage that covered the wound. "You're bleeding again."

"How about we focus on what we're here to do?" she replied. "Do you think Quinn has his scent?"

"It's possible. We've tracked vehicles before, but it will be difficult for him to follow the trail if we get to a more heavily trafficked area." And that was where they seemed to be heading. There were a few bars and restaurants in this area, most opened late.

"Which is exactly where we're headed."

"Right."

"He's done his research."

"Boyd takes pride in his intelligence. When I knew him, he loved to throw random facts out to impress people. It wouldn't surprise me if he spent months researching military working dogs and the way they work."

"Too bad he didn't take pride in his compassion for others."

"I doubt he knows what compassion feels like. He certainly wouldn't see it as a strength."

Quinn was trotting back, nose to the ground. He'd

lost the scent and was trying to pick it up again. They could continue, or they could return to headquarters. If Portia hadn't been there, Justin might have been tempted to keep working the trail and letting his K-9 try to find the scent.

But the likelihood of success was small, and he was worried about Portia.

He wanted her off base and in a safe house.

The sooner that happened, the better.

"Heel," he commanded, and Quinn loped to his side.

"Good work, buddy," Justin said, scratching the dog behind his ears and under his chin.

"He looks disappointed," Gretchen said as they turned back.

"He is. He likes to win the game, and this time he didn't."

"I get the impression that you like to win, too," she commented, folding her left arm and using her right hand to support it.

"Depends on the game. When it comes to my job? Yeah. I want to win every time. Hold on." He touched her shoulder and stopped.

"You want to keep searching for him?" she asked, her attention on the road and the few cars that were driving by.

He could have told her that Boyd had probably already abandoned the car and was running as far and as fast as he could. He might want revenge, but he also wanted his freedom. Free, he could continue to terrorize people, and the desire to do that seemed to be his driving force.

"No. We'll go after him again. After I get Portia taken care of." He unbuttoned his shirt and shrugged out of it. His kept a uniform at the office, and he'd be able to replace it when he got there.

"What are you doing?" Gretchen asked as he fashioned the shirt into a makeshift sling, his white T-shirt nearly glowing in the streetlight. If Boyd were anywhere nearby, Justin would make an easy target.

"Here." He looped the makeshift sling around Gretchen's neck, then lifted her left arm gently and slid it into place. "See? Perfect."

"Did you learn creative uses for your shirt while you were in basic training?" she asked, her cheeks pink.

He'd never seen her blush, and he found himself studying her face—high cheekbones and delicate features, full lips and flawless skin. He'd never thought of her as more than a comrade, an airman, a partner, but she was a woman, too. One who'd been in love, who'd nearly gotten married, who'd lost her fiancé.

He started walking again, because if he let himself, he'd keep staring into her face and into her eyes, and that was no way to keep things professional.

"I learned how to make a shirt sling the summer I turned eleven," he said, determined to not feel awkward or discomfited. He liked Gretchen as an airman and a person. Noticing that she was lovely didn't mean that he'd crossed some well-marked line. It just meant that he'd noticed.

It was his job, after all, to pay attention.

He could have kept telling himself that until the cows came home, and it wouldn't have changed the fact that he'd worked with a lot of women and he'd never paid attention to their hair or eyes or skin.

"Were you one of those outdoorsy types? Always prepared for whatever happened?" she guessed.

"No. My father pulled my arm out of the socket. He popped it back in himself. He didn't want to bother with doctors and medical bills. So I made a sling out of an old shirt and used it until the shoulder felt better." It wasn't a story he'd ever shared, and he wasn't sure why he was sharing it now.

"Were you roughhousing?"

"That's one way to put it."

"So, he did it on purpose?" she asked, and he could hear the surprise in her voice.

"I wouldn't say that. He was trying to drag me into the house, and I didn't want to go."

"Oh."

"You say that as if you get it," he commented.

"I don't. I was very fortunate. My parents were and are great people, but I understand what you're not saying. And I'm sorry. It sounds like your childhood was hard."

"It could have been easier."

"You've made sure Portia's is. You're a really good dad, Justin."

"You've seen me with Portia a handful of times. You don't have much to base that on."

"She's here. Living on base with you. You could have sold her mother's house and used the money to help raise her."

"Melanie paid off the house a few months before she died. She was always really good with money," he replied, because it was the truth. They might not have worked as a couple, but he'd liked Melanie. Maybe even loved her in the way people loved long-distance family.

"All the more reason to sell it. At least, some people would think so. You could have a nice little nest egg sitting in the bank. Instead, you're paying a management company to rent the place out so that Portia can have it one day."

"That doesn't make me a good father. It just makes me a decent human being."

"Why are you so opposed to the idea that you might actually be good at parenting?" she asked.

He could tell her that his parents had been poor examples and that he felt pretty certain he would mess up like they had, but they'd reached the cruisers, the strobe lights flashing across the pavement and nearby buildings. Three patrol officers were standing near the street, and they were as good an excuse as any to pretend he hadn't heard the question.

"I'd better go talk to them. See if they saw anything. Maybe we can get surveillance footage of the vehicle." He pointed at security cameras attached to the eaves of the corner store.

"Good thinking," she replied. "I'll go check on Portia." She took off, not running, but not walking, either.

Maybe she'd felt what he had—lines being crossed, too much personal information being exchanged.

It wasn't uncommon for partners to share the details of their lives. He'd known just about everything there was to know about Corbin's family, his childhood, his hobbies. They'd been partners when they were on duty and buddies when they weren't, and there hadn't been anything strange or awkward about it.

After Corbin was killed, Justin had worked with a few other MPs while he was training as a K-9 handler. He'd never worried that lines were being crossed with his female partners. He'd hung out with them after work sometimes, gone to their houses for dinner if they had husbands or kids. He'd been a brother to some of them, and to some he'd just been the guy they worked with.

In all his years as an MP, he'd never wondered what would happen if he was partnered with someone he was attracted to, because he'd never expected to be attracted.

So, this strangeness with Gretchen? It had to be a glitch. A product of fatigue or adrenaline. Worrying about Portia was getting to him, and he wasn't focusing the way he should.

That had to be it, because anything else was out of the question.

She wasn't running away from Justin.

Not really.

She was running to his daughter, because someone had to check on the teenager. Sure, Portia was safe at headquarters, guarded by MPs and far away from Boyd Sullivan, but she was probably scared and worried about her father.

That was as good an excuse as any for Gretchen to hurry away. She probably should have given back Justin's shirt before she left, but all she'd been thinking about was what she'd seen in his eyes—a flash of something that reminded her of midnight walks and candlelit dinners. Girlish dreams and adolescent crushes.

If he'd been anyone else, she'd have wondered if something was growing between them, if a bond was forming that went beyond work and friendship. But Justin wasn't just anyone. He was the guy she'd worked with for months. He was the captain of the Security

Forces, a man she admired for his integrity, his honesty and his love for his daughter. There couldn't be anything but work between them, because he was the kind of guy she could fall for if she let herself.

She didn't intend to let herself.

Her heart had shattered when Henry died. She'd slowly been piecing it back together again, learning to go on without him, to accept that the life they should have had would never be.

That was enough for now.

She didn't need to add a relationship into the mix. At least, not a romantic one.

Friendship was fine. If they kept things light and easy. That was how it had been for months. She had no intention of changing things.

Sometimes, though, you didn't get to choose how life went. Sometimes you put your all into doing the right thing and being the right person, and ended up in an unexpected and unwanted situation.

Sometimes good intentions weren't enough.

Sometimes even prayer didn't seem to help.

Sometimes God's way wasn't a road that a person ever expected to travel, and all she could do was hold on tight and trust in His promises.

"But sometimes we do have the power to decide things," she muttered as she reached headquarters. "Sometimes we can stay on course. This is going to be one of those times."

Because she wasn't going to risk her heart again. Whatever direction she went after this assignment, she would be going alone.

She opened the door and stepped into the building. This time of night, the corridors were usually empty, the MPs who were on duty out on patrol. Tonight, though, the building seemed to bustle with activity. MPs. Dogs. The constant thud of boots or pad of paws on the floor.

She strode through the hall, waving at a few MPs, but not stopping to speak to any of them. She was eager to find Portia. At sixteen, she wasn't a baby or even a young child. But she'd been through a lot, and she had to be terrified.

Gretchen approached the desk sergeant and asked what room Portia had been taken to. The MP typed information into a computer and scanned the screen. "Interrogation Room One. Do you want me to have someone take you, ma'am?"

"I'm familiar with the building and can find the room, but thank you." She stepped away, then stopped. "If Captain Blackwood reports in or radios in, let him know that I'm with his daughter."

She hurried away, walking through a set of doors and deeper into the building.

"Gretchen!" a woman called. "Hold up!"

Gretchen turned, surprised to see Felicity James and her new husband, Westley, hurrying toward her. Now a base photographer, Felicity had been a trainer with the Canyon K-9 training program her husband led. Unlike his extroverted wife, the master sergeant was quiet and somber, but he had a reputation for being a dog whisperer—the kind of trainer who could get the best out of every K-9 he trained.

She greeted Felicity and Westley as they approached. "It's good to see you. I guess you heard that Boyd Sullivan has been spotted on base again." Like all the members of the investigation team, the two had been deeply involved in trying to apprehend Boyd.

"We did," Westley responded. "But that's not why we're here. We got a call from Special Agent Oliver Davison. He has some information he wants to share and asked us to meet him here."

"This is late for a meeting," she said, and Felicity nodded.

"We're hoping he's in a hurry to meet with us because he has information about the dogs that are still missing."

It was possible. The FBI has been working to infiltrate the Olio Crime Syndicate, and the CAFB K-9 team believed the syndicate might have purchased a few of the German shepherds that had been released, including the four superstars. The well-trained, missing K-9s—Glory, Liberty and Scout—should have been easy to recall, but despite months of searching they remained missing. Two months ago, Patriot—the fourth phenomenal shepherd—had been found at the base gate wearing a collar that had been attributed to Olio. The team had asked the FBI to investigate, and Special Agent Oliver Davison had been leading the efforts.

"Do you really think that's what this is about?" Gretchen asked, hoping for the sake of the team and the dogs that it was.

"If the dogs were, as we suspect, purchased by Olio, it's very possible," Felicity said.

"I hope they know what they've got," Westley said. "If they understand the value of the dogs, they'll take better care of them."

"Rusty knows the value of the dogs, and I'm certain if he was responsible for selling them to the crime organization, he charged an exorbitant fee." Rusty Morton was a K-9 trainer who was suspected of being responsible for the missing dogs.

"I agree, Gretchen," Felicity said. "But until we find Rusty, we have no idea whether he was actually involved."

"He was involved," Westley said, his voice hard.

"We'll let a judge and jury decide that," Felicity responded, hooking her arm through his. "We'd better get to the meeting. Are you joining us, Gretchen?"

"I will once I've checked on Portia."

"Is she here?" Felicity's eyes were wide with surprise. "I thought they'd have transported her to a safe house by now. We heard that Sullivan kidnapped her."

"He did. We need to get her statement before we move her."

"I can't believe Sullivan had the gall to walk into Justin's house."

"He didn't just walk in the house. He murdered the man Justin hired to guard Portia," Gretchen said, the image of the security guard lying on the ground suddenly filling her head. He'd been ambushed, shot from behind, not given even a fighting chance to defend himself. That was a reminder of what they were up against.

Because *that* was the kind of killer Sullivan was. No guilt. No remorse. Very few mistakes.

He'd made one tonight, though.

And she was going to pray that he continued to do so.

A criminal's mistake was a police officer's miracle. At least, that was the way she saw it.

"Another victim," Westley said grimly. "Sullivan needs to be stopped before more people die."

"We'll catch him," she assured the master sergeant.

"How many people are going to die before then, Gretchen?" he asked, rubbing the back of his neck and sighing. "Felicity is right. We need to go. See you at the meeting when you finish with Portia. If not, we'll fill you in."

"I'd appreciate that," she said as they turned to walk away. They both looked tired. The past few months had taken their toll, Sullivan's games escalating as he targeted four people he believed wronged him. Felicity was one of them. Justin was another. The stress of being in a killer's sights had to be intense.

Gretchen had come to Canyon Air Force Base to shadow Justin and to learn from him. She'd had no idea that she'd become part of a team tasked with the job of capturing an elusive serial killer. This wasn't her hometown or her territory. She had nothing but military ties to the people who lived on base, but those ties were strong.

As much as she was ready to move on with her life, to go back to Minot and make her decision about leaving the military or staying, she couldn't go until Sullivan was caught and the people she'd begun to care about were safe.

She sighed, turning a corner and walking into a narrow hall that led to the interrogation rooms. There were several unmarked doors lining the corridor. She didn't need a number to find Portia. She could hear her high-pitched voice drifting through the hallway, the words muffled.

Gretchen followed the sound to an open door. Portia was sitting at a small table in the center of the room, talking on the phone that was on the table beside her, twisting the chord as she held the receiver to her ear. Across from her, an MP sat with his legs stretched out, his arms crossed.

He jumped up as Gretchen entered the room, offering a sharp salute. "Captain, I've taken the victim's statement and filed the report."

"Thank you, Airman."

"Would you like an escort back to Captain Blackwood's house?"

"We'll stay here until he returns," she responded, not bothering to mention the safe house or the plans to move Portia there. The fewer people who had the information, the better. "You can head back to whatever you were doing. I'll take over guard duty," she added.

"Yes, ma'am." He didn't hesitate. Obviously, listening to a teenage girl's phone conversation wasn't his idea of a good time.

Gretchen lowered herself into the chair, her arm throbbing in time with her heartbeat, her head just woozy enough to make her wonder how much blood she'd lost.

Probably more than she should have.

Portia was still twirling the chord and still talking.

She met Gretchen's eyes and offered a shaky smile. "Hold on," she said. Then she covered the receiver with her hand and whispered, "I'll only be a minute."

"Take your time. We can't leave until your father gets here."

Portia nodded and went back to her conversation. Something about proms and dates and the best place to buy dresses. Maybe talking about these normal teenage topics gave Portia a sense of normalcy.

Portia finally hung up, her hand shaking as she

smoothed her hair and fiddled with the sleeve of her sweater.

"Have you heard from my dad yet?" she asked without meeting Gretchen's eyes.

"Not yet, but I'm sure he'll be here soon. Was that someone from Michigan?"

"No. It was Natalie. She's in my physics class."

"So, you're friends," Gretchen said, hoping to keep the conversation going and keep Portia's mind off her father.

Portia shrugged.

"You're not?"

"Why do you care?" It was a typical teenage answer. One that Gretchen might have offered at the same age. Not meant to be particularly rude, but not meant to be polite, either.

"Because we're both sitting here, and if we don't discuss your father or Boyd Sullivan, then there's not a whole lot to talk about unless I ask questions."

Portia met her eyes and smiled. "You're not what I expected, Gretchen."

"No?"

"Most of the bodyguards Dad has left me with try to be too nice. Like I'm fragile and I might break if they aren't."

"You've been through a lot, Portia."

"Lots of people go through difficult things. Mom worked as an emergency room nurse. She saw the results of horrible things happening to people every day."

"That's a hard job."

"Maybe, but Mom loved it. She didn't care that I wasn't interested in following in her footsteps, though. She wanted me to pursue my dreams."

"Which are?"

"See? That's what I mean. You're not pretending that my life is just going to skate along for a while because my mother died. You're assuming I still have goals and dreams."

"Your life hasn't ended. It's just changed. That doesn't change you. At least, not the part of you that has goals and dreams."

"Right. Like I said, you're not like the other MPs."

"And you still haven't told me what your plans for the future are."

"I want to be a journalist."

"Is that why you started the blog?"

Portia hesitated, and Gretchen thought she might refuse to answer.

Instead, she sighed. "Maybe. I mean, I considered myself to be doing investigative reporting, but I got caught up in things and started poking the bear with a stick instead of reporting on what it was doing."

"Is that what your father said?"

"My father is really busy trying to catch the Red Rose Killer. And he doesn't want to put a wedge between us. Like, he doesn't want to come down too hard on me, because we don't know each other all that well yet. So, he hasn't said much. Except that I should haven't done it. That it was dangerous. That I made myself the killer's target. He's right about all of that, but I came up with the bear analogy myself."

"It's a good one."

"Yeah," Portia said, leaning back in the chair and sighing. "I've had a lot of time to come up with it. I haven't been allowed to leave the house alone since he found out."

"This will be over soon," Gretchen said, hoping she was right.

"Maybe. Or maybe not. Either way, I guess I'm going to some stupid safe house."

"A safe house isn't stupid," Justin said as he stepped into the room, buttoning the top button of a crisp uniform shirt.

Gretchen stood, surprised that he'd returned so quickly. Surprised, too, by the quick jump of her pulse when she looked in his eyes.

She glanced away, focusing her attention on Quinn. He looked happy, his tail thumping as he lay beside Justin.

"The idea of missing school is stupid," Portia corrected. "The idea of staying with people I don't know is stupid. The idea of being safe isn't stupid."

"I'm glad you feel that way, honey, because there's an FBI agent here, and he was able to get a safe house approved for you. We're going back to the house, and you'll have a few minutes to pack before you leave."

"Before I leave?" Portia asked. "You're not coming with me?"

"We found one of the vehicles Sullivan used, and a couple of the dogs are on his scent trail. Quinn is the best apprehension dog on the team. He needs to be out there. And so do I."

"But, Dad—"

"There's more to it than that, Portia. I'm the person Boyd is after. If he's going to watch anyone tonight, it's going to be me. I want you moved out of the way while he's distracted. I don't want him to have the slightest chance of following."

"And I don't get a say in this?" Portia asked, shoving away from the table and standing. Right then, her eyes blazing and her chin up, she looked as strong and indomitable as her father. Gretchen could imagine her in a few years—graduating from college, heading into a career as an investigative reporter. From the look of things, she had the guts for it. She also had the writing ability. Like everyone else involved in the case, Gretchen had read her blog.

"No," Justin answered firmly.

"That's totally not cool."

"I'm not going for cool. I'm going for keeping you alive."

"Fine. Whatever. Where's the person who's taking me to the house? I want out of here." She stomped into the hall, and Justin shook his head.

"Apparently, I am exceptionally good at upsetting her," he said, talking to Gretchen but eyeing the doorway.

"At that age, everyone upset me."

"Really?" he asked, turning his light blue gaze in her direction.

She lost her train of thought, forgot what he'd said, what she'd said, what they were talking about.

This was not good.

Not at all.

"We should probably go after her. The sooner you and Quinn get on the trail, the sooner we can have Sullivan in custody," she said, because she wanted to be back on the move, back on the job. Not standing in a small interrogation room with a man who made her pulse jump.

"I'm praying we get him tonight. He needs to be stopped. Not just for Portia's sake. For everyone's. The bodyguard he murdered tonight has a family. He has people who love him." Justin shook his head, his fist clenched just like Portia's had been.

"I know, and I'm sorry."

"Me, too, but sorry isn't going to mean anything to his family. They're going to want justice, and I plan to make sure they get it. Come on. Let's head out." He strode into the hall, Quinn beside him, and Gretchen followed.

This was what she was here for.

To do a job that mattered.

To be part of a team that was dedicated to justice.

Everything else was secondary.

And the quick, hard beat of her heart when she looked into Justin's eyes?

That didn't matter at all.

SEVEN

It didn't take Portia long to pack her things.

She tore through her room, tossing clothes and books into a suitcase, grabbing a photo of Melanie from her nightstand and a Bible from her dresser. She didn't even glance in Justin's direction as she worked.

He tried not to be bothered by that.

Gretchen had said that everyone had upset her when she was Portia's age. Maybe so, but Portia didn't seem to be upset with anyone but him.

She asked Gretchen to grab a sweater from the closet, thanked an MP who offered to carry the suitcase downstairs. She even smiled at Special Agent Oliver Davison.

But Justin, she ignored.

"Are we set?" Oliver asked, his gaze skirting across the bed.

The laptop Portia had been using was gone, along with the note. Justin knew who the perpetrator was. What they were hoping was to find some evidence of where he'd been holing up.

"I think so." Portia whirled around, grabbed another photo from her dresser. This was one that had been taken in the summer—the two of them at a church picnic. She had a sunburned nose and a broad smile. He had his arm around her shoulders.

He remembered the day and the feeling that they were finally connecting, that he was beginning to understand her. That maybe they were going to be okay.

A couple of months later, he'd learned that she was the anonymous blogger. Since then, it seemed as if they were back at square one. Tiptoeing around each other, trying to figure out the steps of a dance that neither of them had ever learned.

"If you get there and find out that you forgot something, I'll have someone bring it to you," he offered, and she finally looked at him.

Her face was pale, her eyes red-rimmed with fatigue. She looked determined, though. Stoic. Like someone who knew what had to be done and planned to do it. No matter how much she didn't want to.

He understood that.

He'd been that type of teenager.

"I don't want to do this, Dad," she said, grabbing her backpack and hoisting it onto her shoulder.

"I know."

"I don't think you do."

"Then how about you explain it to me?"

"You think I don't want to go because I don't want to be in some weird house with a bunch of people I don't know."

"It's not a weird house," Oliver offered, taking a duffel bag that Portia had filled and zipped. "It's nice. Your room is big, and you'll have a nice computer setup. No internet access, but you can play games or journal. I read your blog posts. You're a gifted writer."

"If you're trying to remind me that this is my fault, and that I wouldn't have to leave if I hadn't been so stupid, don't bother. I think about how dumb I was every day. If I could go back and *not* write the blog, I would."

"Hey, it was just a comment," Oliver said calmly. "I'm not trying to do anything but make the safe house sound like a nice place to spend some time. Which it is."

"Nice would be going back to Michigan. Nice is not going wherever we're going," she responded, turning to look at Justin. "But I'm not worried about the house or how things will be there. I'm worried about you, Dad. With Mom gone, you're all I have left. And if I'm at the safe house, I can't make sure you're okay."

"Portia—"

"I know it doesn't make sense. You're an air force captain and a military police officer, and you know how to take care of yourself." She shrugged. "But I still have this feeling that if I'm with you, you'll be safe, and if I'm not…maybe you won't be."

"You know what?" Gretchen said, stepping forward. "How about Special Agent Davison and I meet you two downstairs?"

She hurried out of the room, and Oliver followed.

Obviously, she was trying to give Justin a few minutes to say what needed to be said, to reassure Portia that he'd be okay. That she wasn't going to be left alone.

"Don't worry about it, Dad," she said before he could speak. "I'll go. I know you and Quinn have to go find Sullivan."

She would have left the room, and he could have let her go. It would have been the easy thing to do. It was what he wanted to do. He couldn't promise her he'd be okay. His job was dangerous, and every day that he did it, he took risks.

She knew that, and she wouldn't believe any platitude he might try to feed her.

But he couldn't let her go without offering some reassurance.

"Wait." He touched her arm, and she stopped.

"What?" she asked, exasperated or trying to act like she was—bangs hanging in her eyes, hand on her hip, eyes shooting daggers.

"I know you're scared."

"Glad you finally figured that one out." She started walking again.

"I'm scared, too."

She stopped.

"Not about the situation with Boyd. Not about my safety," he continued. "I'm afraid I'll mess this up. That I won't be the parent you need. That you'll finish growing up, and I still won't know your favorite color or what size shoe you wear. I've tried to be a good long-distance father—"

"You have been," she said, all her exasperation and attitude gone.

"But now it's time for me to be the kind of parent that's right in the middle of all of it. The daily problems. The school troubles. The teenage—"

"Drama?" she cut in, brushing the bangs out of her eyes.

"That wasn't quite the word I was going to use," he said, and she offered a half smile.

"It's what Mom always said. That teenage drama was going to give her a head full of gray hair."

"Your mom did a great job with you, Portia. You've

turned into an intelligent, strong, independent young woman. But you still have a lot of growing up to do, and it's my job to make sure that you're safe while you do it. The easiest and best way for me to do that is to have you in a location that Boyd can't find."

"But he can still find you, Dad. What if he ambushes you or makes a bomb or hires someone to hurt you?"

"I have an entire team of people who are working with me to make sure that doesn't happen, but as long as my focus is on your safety, I'm not going to be able to concentrate like I should. You going to a safe house will keep us both safe, because it will free the part of my mind that is currently focused a hundred percent on making sure Boyd doesn't get to you."

She frowned. "I don't want to be a distraction. I just want to help keep you safe."

"So go to the safe house. Follow the rules. Cooperate with the people who will be guarding you. Trust me and the team to capture Boyd."

"And trust God to keep you safe?" she asked quietly. "I did that with Mom and look what happened."

"Sometimes we can't understand His plans, Portia. But we can always count on the fact that He'll take difficult situations and use them for our benefit. If we let Him," he responded, repeating words Corbin had said to him years ago.

"Mom used to say that, too—*God can make the toughest times into the biggest blessings.* If she were here, I'd ask how her dying could ever be that." She sniffed, a tear sliding down her cheek.

He wiped it away, pulled her into his arms. "Honey, I'm not going to pretend that I understand God's ways. But I know this—faith is never wasted. Your mother was one of the most faith-filled people I know, and she wouldn't want you to doubt God's goodness because of what happened to her," he said, knowing it was true. Justin had admired Melanie's work ethic, her drive, her parenting skills, and he'd admired her faith. She'd become a Christian after Portia's birth, and she'd never wavered from the conviction that God had used one of the hardest times in her life to show her the truth about His love.

"I don't. I just want to know that He's not going to let you be taken from me, too."

"He's not."

"Do you really believe that?" she asked.

"Yes. Like I said, faith is never wasted. Whatever happens, you're going to be okay. I promise." It was the best he could do, the most honest he could be, and he could only hope the truth was what she wanted.

She nodded, stepping away. "I know. I love you, Dad. I'll follow whatever stupid rules they have at the safe house, and I'll pray for you every day. And when this is all over, we're going to plan that trip to Michigan. Okay?"

"Okay."

"See you later, alligator." She offered the words they'd said to each other when she was in elementary school.

"In a while, crocodile," he responded, surprised and pleased that she'd remembered.

She grinned, kissed his cheek and walked away, her backpack bouncing, her shoulders straight. She was her mother's daughter.

But she was his daughter, too.

He might not have spent as much time with Portia as

he'd wanted during her formative years, but he'd supported Melanie's parenting in every way he could. Not just with finances. He'd been a willing ear, a second opinion. He'd been there when Portia had ear tubes put in, and when she'd had her tonsils out. There had been dozens of times when he'd taken leave to be there for her and Melanie, and he'd like to think that the confident young woman who'd just walked out of the room had learned some of her strength from him.

Maybe his father hadn't rubbed off on him.

Maybe he *could* be what he'd wanted when he was a kid—the kind of parent who listened and who really heard, who offered support and encouragement along with the parameters for right living.

He called Quinn to heel and walked out of the room, closing the door behind him.

Gretchen had never liked goodbyes. When she was a kid, her father's air force career had meant a lot of them. Her brothers had grown up and gone into the military, and she'd found herself saying goodbye to them, too.

She preferred *hello*.

Or *see you later*.

She tried not to watch as Portia threw her arms around Justin one last time. She tried not to listen when she made him promise to be careful. But, of course, they were all standing in the foyer of Justin's house, crowded together, and she couldn't help but see and hear father and daughter say their goodbyes.

She had a lump in her throat, and she wasn't even going to pretend that she didn't.

"You'd probably better go, Captain. If Boyd is

watching the team that's tracking him, he'll notice if you're not there. We don't want him to realize we're moving Portia," Special Agent Davison said, putting a hand on Portia's arm. "I'll get her to the house safely. I've got three agents there, and your team is sending in some MPs. She'll be safe."

"I'm counting on that," Justin said. "Follow the rules, Portia. It's the only way to stay safe."

"I will, Dad," she promised, sniffing back tears.

"Ready?" Gretchen asked, opening the door and letting cool air drift in. She didn't want to rush Justin, but Oliver was right. Sullivan knew the team's routines. He'd been observing them for months. If Justin wasn't around, he'd wonder why. The last thing any of them needed or wanted was for him to return to Justin's place looking for him. If he saw Portia leaving, he'd follow. Maybe he'd be spotted. Maybe not. The guy was slick, and he was smart. He might launch an attack before the transport reached the safe house.

She frowned, stepping out into the darkness, a cold breeze ruffling her hair. She scanned the yard, her arm throbbing in time with the beat of her heart. She still had the makeshift sling Justin had given her, and she adjusted her arm to try to ease the pain.

There were still several MP vehicles parked near the curb. Yellow crime scene tape had been strung around the bushes where the bodyguard had been found. An MP was taking photos of the area, and the evidence team was still working. She'd like to think that Boyd would keep his distance. Most criminals would. But Boyd wasn't most criminals. He was a psychopath and a narcissist. A guy who believed he was too smart to be caught.

"And that's going to be your undoing," she murmured.

"What is?" Justin asked, and she swung around to face him.

"I was just thinking about Boyd's arrogance, about the fact that he doesn't believe he can be caught. That's what's going to lead to his capture."

"You're worried he's coming back here, aren't you?"

"I don't think he will while all this activity is going on, but I do think he'll be back if he doesn't see you out searching for him."

"He may be off base, Gretchen."

"Maybe, but everything I've learned about him says differently."

"What do you mean?" He walked down the porch stairs, calling for Quinn to follow.

"You're his main target, and he wants to see you suffer. Knowing that Portia is in danger is fear inducing, and Boyd is the kind of person who revels in instilling fear. He's going to want to know that he's accomplished his goal—that you're terrified for Portia, that maybe you're even losing your focus."

"If that's what he wants, he's going to be disappointed. I may be afraid for my daughter, but I haven't lost my focus," he said, popping the hatchback of his SUV and giving Quinn the signal to jump in. "Let's head out. If he is hanging around, I want to get him away from Portia."

He closed the hatch and opened her door, waiting as she climbed in.

"I know your shift ended an hour ago, Captain," he said, leaning down so they were eye-to-eye. "I can take you back to the station if you want to clock out. I don't expect you to work 24/7."

"I expect it." She buckled her seat belt.

"You got twenty-five stitches in your arm. I think a little time off is in order."

"I think the guy who caused me to get the stitches needs to be in jail, so how about we not waste time arguing about whether or not I should go home?"

"We're not arguing. I was stating a fact."

"So was I."

He stared into her eyes, and at first it was nothing. Just the two of them looking at each other. Like any other time during any other shift.

But then, she felt it again. That shift in the air, that strange feeling that they were connecting in a way she hadn't expected and didn't want.

He frowned, backing away and closing the door. Not speaking as he started the engine and pulled away from the house. They were both professionals, and they both behaved in ways that reflected that. But there was tension that hadn't been there before. Some unspoken thought that filled the space between them.

She didn't break the silence, and when they finally reached Boyd's abandoned vehicle, she was relieved.

She exited the SUV before Justin turned off the engine and hurried to the abandoned vehicle. It was a small Dodge. Two doors. Dark colored. Nondescript. The front license plate was in place, and she walked to the back of the vehicle, noting the blown-out tire.

An officer was walking around the car. Tall, with dark hair and broad shoulders, he had a bloodhound beside him.

"Lieutenant Donovan?" Gretchen called, recognizing the explosives expert and his dog, Annie, immediately.

"Captain Hill," he responded, saluting as she approached.

"Find anything interesting?"

"We didn't find explosives," he responded. "That's generally the most interesting thing to me and Annie."

"You searched the vehicle?"

"The front and back seat are clear. Console has been cleaned out. Nothing in the glove compartment. We found a single red rose in the trunk." Nick opened it, stepping back so that she could look inside.

A rose had been left there. Dark red petals. Long stem. No note, but Boyd might not have had time to leave one. He'd been on the run, but he'd still wanted them to know that he was in control.

"He was taunting us," she said, taking out her flashlight and shining the beam into the trunk's dark corners.

"He definitely wanted us to know it was him," Nick agreed.

"It's not like we had any doubt," Justin said as he joined them, Quinn at his side. The Malinois didn't approach Annie. Both were too well trained to do more than look at each other.

"I searched the cabin, your house and the empty property. Not even a hint of explosives or accelerants anywhere," Nick said. "I'm thankful for that. Put enough explosives in a residential area, and you can injure a lot of people."

"Currently, Boyd's focus seems to be on injuring just me." Justin glanced in the trunk, then walked around to the driver's door and opened it with a gloved hand. "You said the interior is empty."

"Yes. He cleaned out any identifying documents. There's no title. No insurance. Not even a crumb on a floor mat. I thought maybe he'd stolen it from a used car lot, but we ran the plates. It belongs to an airman who lives a couple of miles from here. She'd left the keys in the ignition when she went inside with some groceries. He stole it from her driveway."

"When?" Justin asked, signaling for Quinn to find the scent and search. The dog sniffed the front seat, the steering wheel and the door.

"Two nights ago," Nick replied.

"So, he's been on base and ready to take action since then." Gretchen wasn't surprised, and she wasn't happy. He'd planned the kidnapping, and he'd executed it perfectly. His error had been in playing games with Justin. Giving clues. Drawing him into the woods and assuming that he'd go there alone.

"Looks that way." Nick said something to Annie, and the bloodhound sat, her long ears swinging gently as she moved. "Now he's on the run, but I have a feeling he's not going far."

"Why do you say that?" Justin asked as Quinn sniffed the ground near the car. Nose down, tail up, he seemed to catch the scent immediately.

"I was in basic training with him, remember? He never liked a challenge. He liked things to be easy, and when they were, he bragged that it was because he was superior to the recruits who were struggling. When they weren't, he wanted to quit."

"And you think things are getting difficult for him?" Justin asked.

"Definitely. We're closing in, and he knows it. I don't think he's going to enjoy the feeling of us breathing down his neck, and he's going to be very unhappy about losing his kidnapping victim." He frowned. "Sorry. Losing your daughter, Captain."

"She was a kidnapping victim, Lieutenant. No need to dance around that, but I agree. He's been sloppier tonight. His emotions are getting the better of him."

"Emotions? I didn't think he had any," Nick said.

"Sure he does. All the dark ones—hate, anger, malice," Gretchen replied.

"Those and the need for revenge. Quinn is on the scent. We're going to see what we can find." Justin gave the command and Quinn darted forward, nearly flying down the center of the street.

Justin raced after him.

Leaving Nick and his K-9 to their work, Gretchen followed, adrenaline pumping through her, thoughts focused. All her worries about Justin were gone. There was nothing in her head right now but the mission and the goal: find Boyd Sullivan and take him into custody.

They searched for hours, working their way from one street to the next. When Quinn lost the trail, they worked a grid pattern, covering several miles of the business district before heading into the residential area.

But the trail had gone cold, and finally Justin called Quinn to heel.

Gretchen didn't plan to admit it, but she was glad. Her arm had been throbbing for hours, the pain intensifying as the night wore on.

"We'd better call it," Justin said wearily. "He's slipped through our fingers again."

"Tomorrow is a new day," she replied, too tired to think of anything profound or uplifting. She was disappointed, too. They'd been close to capturing Boyd in the cabin. Maybe closer than anyone had ever been.

"It *is* tomorrow," he responded. "The sun will be up in a couple of hours. How about we go back to headquarters, file our report and get a couple of hours' sleep?"

She nodded, then thought better of it. "Unless you think we missed something at the cabin or at your place. A clue that will lead us to his hiding place."

"The evidence team is exceptional. If there was something to find, they'd have found it." They'd reached the street where Boyd had abandoned his car. It was quiet now. No sign of Nick and Annie. No sign of Boyd's vehicle.

"Looks like they've already impounded the Dodge," she commented as they reached Justin's SUV.

"The team is trying to process evidence quickly and thoroughly. We're all hoping something was missed during the initial search."

"Like what? A map with an X marking Boyd's hideout?"

Justin grinned, his face softening with amusement as he opened the hatch and let Quinn jump in. "Wouldn't that be nice?"

"It would be," she replied, sliding into the passenger seat, her cheeks hot for reasons she refused to acknowledge. It wasn't a crime to notice Justin's smile, how handsome it made him, and there was nothing criminal about thinking he should do it more often.

"What's the plan? Aside from both of us getting a few hours of sleep?" she asked, determined to keep

the conversation flowing. No more awkward silences.
No more unspoken thoughts. They'd been working together for months, and there'd never been any of that
before.

Nothing had changed.

Nothing was going to change.

She'd make sure of it.

"Both of us staying alive." He started the engine
and pulled into the road.

"Good plan, Captain. Now, how about we go into
the details of how that's going to happen?"

"You could go back to Minot," he suggested, and
that was enough to chase any thought about his smile
out of her head.

"You're kidding."

"No. I'm not," he said.

"I can't cut my training short," she replied.

"I can speak to your commanding officer. I'm sure
your safety is his priority."

"His priority is launching a K-9 MP team on base.
My safety, like the safety of every airman under his
command, is a matter of God's grace and my ability
to do my job well." The words were stiff, but she managed to keep emotion from her voice.

"You're angry," he guessed. "And that wasn't my
intention."

"Of course I am. You've seen me work. You know
I'm good at my job. Yet, somehow, you don't think I'm
capable of helping you solve the Red Rose Killer case."

"We're not solving anything." He pulled into the
parking lot at headquarters and parked his vehicle
close to the front door. "We're chasing a killer. One

who would put a bullet in your head as quickly as he would mine."

"And?"

"I want you out of here, Gretchen." He turned off the engine and turned to face her. "Not because you're not capable. Because Boyd will hurt anyone he thinks matters to me."

"We're work partners. Not—"

He raised his hand, cutting off the words.

"The truth isn't going to matter to Boyd, and I'm not willing to lose another partner. I want you to go back to your assignment in Minot. I'll tell your commanding officer that I've taught you everything I can."

"Lose *another* partner? What does that mean?" she asked, and he tensed.

"It's not open for discussion."

"You're the one who brought it up," she pointed out.

"And now I'm shutting it down."

"You know that I can find out, right? Easily."

"Why would you want to?"

"Because you're trying to send me back to Minot before I finish my assignment here, and I want to know why."

"I'm not trying to send you anywhere. I'm making a suggestion. For your safety."

"You mentioned speaking to my commanding officer," she retorted, frustrated and unable to hide it. "I'm not Portia. I don't need your protection."

"I am very aware of that," he muttered.

"Then stop trying to keep me from doing my job."

"Your only job here was to learn. You've done that." He climbed out of the SUV and released Quinn from his crate.

She thought the conversation was over, that her frustration would continue to simmer. *Good.* She shouldn't like Justin as much as he did. She needed to start viewing him in the light of his flaws rather than his strengths. But that went against the grain. She liked to find the good in people and focus on that, but it was for the best.

"This isn't something I talk about often," he said as he hooked Quinn to his leash, "but you have a right to know since it's impacting our relationship."

We don't have a relationship, she almost said, because she wanted to remind them both of that.

She kept her mouth shut. Something any of her four brothers would have been surprised by. She wasn't known for keeping her thoughts to herself. She'd been raised to speak the truth, and she'd found her bluntness to be an asset in the military where she seemed to be in a constant battle to prove herself to her male counterparts.

"My first partner was killed in the line of duty," Justin continued. "We'd been working together for four years. Corbin trained me. He mentored me. I spent holidays at his place, and his family became mine. His wife was like the sister I never had. His kids were like nieces and nephews. And Corbin was my brother. In every way that mattered."

"Justin, you really don't have to tell me this," she said, because she knew where this was going. She knew how the story would end, and she could already feel her heart breaking for Justin and for the family Corbin had left behind.

"You asked, Gretchen, so I'm going to tell you. Corbin and I responded to a domestic violence call.

The airman who was involved had a son who played football with Corbin's oldest son. He and Corbin had seen each other at sporting events. They'd talked a few times."

"Corbin thought he wasn't violent?"

"I don't know. I've never figured it out. He got out of the car and was heading for the front door before we'd discussed any kind of strategy. He rang the doorbell, and the suspect fired on him through the door."

"I'm sorry, Justin," she said, her voice breaking on his name.

She hated that sound of weakness, hated that he'd heard it.

The last thing she wanted him to do was view her as weak or emotional. She'd worked hard to attain a reputation for being tough, reasonable and strong.

He studied her face, his light-colored eyes nearly glowing in the exterior building lights. He had chiseled features and a strong physique, but she'd seen the softness in his face when he looked at his daughter. And when he smiled.

"I'm not going to cry, if that's what you're wondering," she managed to say in her best annoyed-younger-sister voice.

She didn't feel like his younger sister, though, and maybe that was the problem. She'd begun to see him as a man rather than an air force captain.

"Everyone cries, Gretchen. Even the most hardened soldier. But I didn't give you the information to make you sad. I didn't give it to you to make you sorry. I gave it to you because I want you to understand my position. I spent years after Corbin's death asking myself if I could have saved him, wondering if I could have prevented his death by walking to the door ahead of him or insisting that we go around the back of the property."

"You couldn't have," she said.

"At this point, it doesn't matter. What matters is making sure it doesn't happen again."

"I'm not Corbin, Justin. And I'm not planning on dying. If I do, it won't be your fault. I'm glad you shared the story. It does help me understand, but it doesn't change anything. I still plan to stay for the entirety of my temporary orders. I'm going to start our report. See you inside."

She strode across the parking lot, telling herself that nothing had changed between them. She knew it was a lie.

Personal stories were great. She'd shared lots of them with coworkers, but the story Justin had told was one that defined him. It had been a catalyst that had shaped and changed the airman he'd been into the captain he'd become.

He didn't have to say that for her to understand it. She'd heard the pain and regret in his voice, and she'd understood just how deeply the grief and guilt had gone. She'd struggled with the same since Henry's death. She'd gone to a therapist, who'd told her that holding on to guilt wouldn't bring Henry back and would only stunt her ability to be in other fulfilling relationships. Gretchen still hadn't been able to let go.

Deep in her heart, she believed that a person should always be able to save the people she loved. Even knowing in her head that it wasn't true couldn't change the way she felt.

She opened the door and stepped into headquarters, her heart heavy. She'd wanted to do more than tell Justin she was sorry. She'd wanted to explain that she understood. That she lived with the same guilt and the same regret, but they were getting dangerously close to crossing boundaries they shouldn't.

She wasn't sure how she felt about that.

She liked Justin. A lot. She respected him.

And hearing his story? It had made her feel close to him in a way she hadn't before.

"Gretchen!" someone called.

She turned and was surprised to see the base nutritionist, Yvette Crenville, standing in the cafeteria doorway.

"Yvette! What are you doing here?" she asked.

Yvette smiled. Tall, with blond hair and delicate features, she was as pretty as she was sweet.

"I work here."

"Not at this time of day."

"I heard there'd been another Boyd sighting, and I figured you'd all be out working. I wanted to make sure you had nutritious snacks when you returned. I made dark chocolate oatmeal bars. Interested?"

"You said the word *chocolate*, so I'm definitely in."

Yvette giggled. "Good. Great. I set up a table. There are a few different types of juices, too. Coffee, if you must. Decaf if you want to sleep."

"It sounds like you thought of everything."

"I try." She glanced toward the exterior door. "Did you find him?" she whispered.

"Boyd?"

"Who else?"

"Not yet."

Yvette's face fell, and she rubbed the back of her

neck. "That's too bad. I was really hopeful that this nightmare was finally going to end."

"I think we all were."

"Captain Blackwood more than any of us, I'm sure. I heard Boyd kidnapped his daughter."

"He did," Gretchen responded. Yvette worked at headquarters, creating and prepping nutritional meals. She wasn't part of the team that had been going after Boyd, but she was apparently one of his targets. She'd dated him during basic training and publicly broken up with him. Months ago, she'd received a red rose. Since then, she'd been cautious and nervous.

"Wow! That poor girl. She's just a kid. You'd think Boyd would find it in his heart to leave her alone."

"I'm not sure Boyd has a heart," Gretchen said.

Yvette tensed, her angelic features suddenly pinched and tight. "Everyone has a heart."

"It was a joke, Yvette. Not meant to be taken literally."

"Right. Sorry." Yvette rubbed the back of her neck again and smiled sheepishly. "My parents always told me I was much too literal. I do understand what you're saying. Boyd is rotten to the core. I can't believe I dated him during basic training. He was a total dud. The kind of guy that only wants to be with someone he can use." There was a hint of venom in her voice.

She didn't look angry, though.

She looked sweet and placid and eager to please.

Gretchen wasn't buying the facade. She'd met people who really were as sweet and kind as they seemed, but something about Yvette rubbed her the wrong way. Maybe it was how she seemed to show up every time the Red Rose Killer case heated up. Maybe it was the subtle changes in her facial expression when she was talking about Boyd.

The two *had* dated.

According to people who'd been there, Yvette had made a show of breaking up, but that didn't mean her feelings for Boyd had died. A couple of months ago, Gretchen and another team member, nurse Vanessa Gomez, had followed Yvette, watching her every move, trying to see if she and Boyd were together.

They'd found nothing out of the ordinary.

Yvette did what everyone did—shopped, went to work, went to the gym, went to church. No secret side trips into the woods. No suspicious excursions off base. No packages delivered to her house or tossed into Dumpsters. Nothing that would indicate she was aiding and abetting a criminal.

But looks could be deceiving, and Gretchen wasn't convinced Yvette was as innocent as she appeared to be. Since she had nothing but her gut to go on, she'd been keeping quiet and staying alert. Eventually, every criminal made a mistake. If Yvette were somehow aiding Boyd, she'd be found out.

"What?" Yvette asked, smoothing her hair and swiping at her cheek. "You're staring at me like I have something on my face."

"No. I was just thinking about your relationship with Boyd."

"That was a long time ago." Yvette laughed nervously. "It was destined to fail from the beginning. He loved fast food." She shuddered. "Who would put junk like that into his body?"

"I might," Gretchen responded honestly.

"Oh! I hope not. I know you're not thirty yet, but you

know what happens to women when they reach that age, right? The metabolism slows, fat starts to build up, the thyroid begins to struggle. What you want to be doing is detoxing every first week of the month. Follow that with the eighty-twenty approach to eating. You remember that, right?"

How could she forget? Yvette mentioned it every time she saw Gretchen with anything that smacked of unhealthy. "Yes. I do."

"I can go over it with you again, Gretchen. What we put into our bodies is so important to our health."

The exterior door opened, and Justin entered the building with Quinn.

"There's Justin… I mean, Captain Blackwood. I'd better run," Gretchen said, turning on her heel and nearly flying back down the hall.

Justin saw her coming and offered a quick smile that made her heart skip a beat.

"Everything okay?" he asked, his gaze shifting to Yvette and then back to Gretchen.

"We were talking about the eighty-twenty eating plan and detox," she whispered.

"Poor you," he said in a rumble of laughter.

"You don't know the half of it. I seem to be her favorite target. Last week, she cornered me two times to tell me that healthy eating was imperative as I reach middle age."

"Middle age? You're nowhere near middle age!"

"Maybe you should tell her that," she murmured, glancing over her shoulder. Yvette was still at the cafeteria door, smiling in their direction.

"I made dark chocolate oatmeal squares, Captain Blackwood," she called. "I've set up a nice snack table for your officers. Make sure you get something to eat. It looks like you've had a long night."

"Thanks, Yvette. I'll do that," he said.

He touched Gretchen's shoulder. "Ready?"

"Sure," she replied, allowing him to steer her back toward Yvette.

She could feel the warmth of his fingers through her shirt. Could feel the way her heart responded to his light touch. She could have moved away. Maybe she should have, but it had been a long day, a long few months. Really, it had been a long few years, and it felt nice to have Justin's hand on her shoulder.

She let it stay while they walked past Yvette and entered the cafeteria. A few MPs were there, milling around a table set with trays of cookie bars and pitchers of juice.

One of the MPs glanced their way, his gaze going to Justin's hand before shifting to Gretchen's bandaged arm. Finally, his attention drifted away, and he grabbed a cookie, munching it while he talked to one of his buddies.

He'd probably forget what he'd seen before he left the cafeteria. And why wouldn't he? It wasn't uncommon for military comrades to pat one another on the arm or shoulder. Hugs and back claps weren't unheard-of, and offering support was common even among airmen of differing genders.

But gossip ran rampant on military bases, and Gretchen didn't want to be fodder for the rumor mill.

She stepped away, nearly running to the table. She grabbed a napkin and two of the treats, but didn't bother trying to pour juice into a cup. Her left arm ached, and she doubted she could coordinate the movement without help. She wasn't going to ask any lower-ranking airman, and she wasn't going to ask Justin.

"I'm heading into the office," she announced a little too loudly, and then she nearly sprinted out the door and up the stairs. It might have been childish to run away, but the alternative was sticking it out and faking comfort in what had become an uncomfortable situation. Not because of anything Justin had done, but because of her own traitorous heart.

As much as she wanted to deny it, to protest it, she had to face the truth: she was attracted to Justin Blackwood.

But it—they—could never be.

"Get your act together, Hill," she muttered, dropping into her desk chair and turning on her computer. Writing reports was her least favorite part of the job, but right now, it was the perfect excuse to keep her head in the game and off the blue-eyed captain.

EIGHT

The sanctuary was silent when Justin walked into Canyon Christian Church. Not surprising. He was a half hour early, his dress shoes spit polished and squeaking as he walked to the front of the church and took a seat in a pew. He hadn't slept well the last few nights, and he'd been up before dawn, following his Sunday morning routine, hoping that Boyd would make the mistake of coming after him. He was prepared for it, even praying for it, as he'd run his normal five-mile route and sat on the front porch with his coffee.

Daring Boyd.

Taunting him the way Boyd had taunted the team.

But, of course, Boyd hadn't shown up, and Justin had finally given up and showered. During the months that Portia had been living with him, he'd gotten into the habit of making a hot breakfast before church. It was the one morning they were both free. No school. No work. No obligations other than to themselves.

With Portia gone, there'd been no reason to cook, and he'd found himself with a little too much time on his hands. The house was empty without Portia. No music drifting from her room. No muffled complaints as she picked through the clothes in her closet or attempted to style her hair.

He hadn't realized how much those things had filled the house and made it into a home.

"I guess I'm not the only one who couldn't sleep." Gretchen's voice echoed in the empty space, and Justin turned, surprised and pleased to see her walking up the aisle. She wore a dress. Light blue and soft looking, it clung to her slender curves and fell just past her knees. No high heels. No makeup. She was beautiful, and he wasn't sure why he hadn't noticed before.

He'd seen her at church many times.

He'd seen her on base, wearing jeans and sweaters or running gear. Always with perfect skin and dark lashes and a half smile on her face, but all he'd noticed was Gretchen. The woman he worked with, partnered with, brainstormed with.

She wasn't smiling now.

She looked tired and a little unsure. That surprised him. From the day she'd arrived on base, Gretchen had been confident and filled with energy. She threw herself into her work, never seeming to doubt her abilities.

She slid into the pew beside him, setting her Bible next to her hip.

"You miss Portia," she said before he could offer a greeting.

"The house is too quiet without her."

"I'm sure. I remember when I finally moved into my own place. It was difficult getting used to the silence. Even when it was just me and my parents at home, there'd been noise and people to fill the emptiness. They entertained a lot, and it always seemed like we had someone staying at our place. Then, suddenly, I was on my own, coming home to a house that no one was in, and it felt very empty and lonely," she said as she tried to shrug out of her jacket. It caught on her bandaged arm, and he helped her, tugging gently until she was free.

"You mentioned four brothers the night you were shot. Your parents' home must have been really busy."

"First of all, I was grazed by a bullet. Not shot," she corrected.

He nodded, conceding the point. "How's the arm?"

"You've asked me that a hundred times since the incident, Justin. My answer remains the same. It's fine." She touched her arm. The sleeve of her dress covered the bandage, but he could see it bulging beneath the fabric. "And you're right. The houses I grew up in were loud. My brothers were nearly teenagers by the time I came along. They always had friends over and they kept my parents on their toes. It was a fun childhood. Loud, busy and crazy. But fun. Especially with the Ping-Pong table in the basement and a rock climbing wall in our backyard."

"You're kidding?"

"About the rock climbing wall? Nope. It's still there. My nephews and nieces love it." She dug into her purse and pulled out her phone, scrolling through until she found a photo she wanted to show him. "See?"

She handed him the phone, her cool fingers sliding across his warmer ones, and he wanted to capture her hand, look into her eyes, ask her what was wrong. Because something was.

He studied the photo—three kids and an older gentleman standing near a rock wall. All of them smiling.

One of the girls looked like Gretchen—dark hair, dark eyes, slim body and wide smile.

"She looks like you," he commented, handing the phone back.

"She's my oldest brother's kid, and he always says she looks and acts just like me. He especially says it when she's getting into trouble. Which she apparently does often." She smiled, dropping the phone into her purse. "She's nine. I keep telling him it's the age and the fact that she has three older brothers."

"Lots of boys in your family."

"Yes. I was the first girl in three generations on my dad's side. There were major celebrations when I was born. Followed by major disappointment when my grandmother realized I was a tomboy."

"Was your mother disappointed?"

"No. My mother has always given me a hundred percent support in my choices. As long as they aren't illegal or immoral, she's happy."

"It sounds like you have a great family."

"I do. I've been missing them a lot lately."

"Are they back in Minot?"

"Upstate New York. My parents grew up there, and after I was born, they bought a house near his parents. My dad was an MP for most of his air force career. We moved a lot, and he and my mom wanted us to have a home base. For a while, it was just a place to stay when we were visiting family. Now it's their year-round home. Henry and I—" She frowned. "Sorry. Not work-appropriate conversation."

"We're not at work."

"But we're coworkers, Justin."

"Is that what this is about?" he asked.

"What?"

"Whatever is bothering you."

"Who said something was?"

"We've worked together for months, Gretchen. We've spent hundreds of hours together. I know you."

"You know Captain Gretchen Hill. There's a difference." She crossed her arms over her stomach and stared at the front of the church. If she hoped the pastor would appear and begin the service, she was going to be disappointed. They were still twenty minutes from the start of the service. People would begin trickling in soon. Until then, Justin and Gretchen were alone, and he wasn't planning to stop asking questions. Tension was never good for a team, and unspoken issues had a way of festering.

"You *are* Captain Gretchen Hill. I may not know the private details of your life, but I know that you like your coffee black and your work station neat. I also know that you run every morning and have a fondness for sweets and french fries. You're a straight shooter. Which I like. You're tough. You don't put up with fools. You don't party on the weekends, and you're wondering if you want to keep working as an MP or if you're ready to leave the military and do something different."

She met his eyes and frowned. "Who told you that?"

"Which part?"

"The part about me wondering if I should leave the military."

"No one."

"Then why would you say it?"

"Am I wrong?"

She shrugged, the fabric of her dress pulling taut across her narrow shoulders.

"So, I'm right," he pressed, because he wanted to know. If Gretchen was struggling with making the decision, if she was struggling with the job, if she felt life was passing while she worked a job she no longer loved, he wanted to help her figure things out, come up with a plan, create a future that she could be happy with.

"Why does it matter, Justin? I'm going back to Minot in a few weeks. We'll both move on with our lives, and whatever I decide to do, it won't matter to you one way or another."

For some reason, her blunt and truthful statement rubbed him the wrong way. He didn't bother hiding his irritation.

"If you think that, you don't know me very well."

"That's the point. We don't know each other. We have a working relationship, and that's all either of us wants."

"I don't recall being asked if that's what I want." He was irritated by her assumptions. That he didn't care deeply about the people he worked with. That he wouldn't bother following up and keeping in contact with them. That he'd never be interested in more than a professional relationship with someone like her.

She was intelligent, funny and driven. She worked harder than just about any MP he knew. There wasn't anyone on the team who didn't enjoy spending time with her. Male. Female. K-9. She was charismatic without trying, drawing people to her without effort.

A person would have to be blind not to notice.

He wasn't blind. He wasn't hard-hearted. He wasn't so consumed by work that he didn't think about long-term relationships. If he were a different kind of person, with a different kind of background, he'd absolutely be thinking about Gretchen in more than a professional way. There was no military rule about dating someone of the same rank, and he knew plenty of men and women who had done it, fallen in love and gotten married.

Happily-ever-after happened. Even in the military.

It just wasn't going to happen for him.

"I wasn't trying to be rude, Justin. I'm just being… practical," she said, smoothing her dress over her thighs, her fingers trembling.

"You're nervous," he said, lifting her hand and giving it a gentle squeeze. He should have released it immediately, but they were side by side, inches away from one another, and he could see the confusion and fear in her eyes. "Why?"

"This has never happened before," she replied.

"Nothing has happened."

"Not to you," she muttered.

"Not to either of us. We're sitting in an empty church having a conversation about your decision to leave the military or continue in it."

"I haven't even spoken to my family about that." She slipped her hand from his. "It's not something I'm ready to share."

"I'd think with a family like yours, you could share anything," he said, thinking about that picture—the obviously happy kids and their grandfather. No bruised cheeks. No tears. No angry scowls. They were what he'd wanted to be when he was a kid.

"In theory, yes. I should be able to share anything. But I come from a long line of military heroes. My father served as an MP for thirty years before he retired. My older brothers are all career military. My grandfather was. My grandmother was a navy nurse. The list goes on."

"I don't know your family, but I doubt they're going to boot you out of the fold if you decide you've had enough of military life."

"They won't. I just don't want to disappoint anyone. Especially not myself. The thing is, I always wanted to be an MP, to follow in my father's and brothers' footsteps. My mother was a teacher, and that seemed so boring in comparison that I stood on a chair at my ninth birthday party and announced that I planned to follow in my father's footsteps. I even put my hand on my heart." She smiled at the memory. "My father has the video of it."

He laughed, imagining her as a child earnestly insisting that she was going into the military. "I'd like to see that one day."

"Trust me, if you ever meet him, that'll be the first thing he drags out. Anyway, I made the announcement, and I never stopped believing it was going to happen. I had it in my mind that I was going to join the military and spend my life devoted to being the best MP I could. Then I met Henry in basic training, and everything changed. Suddenly, I wasn't just thinking about a career, I was thinking about a family. Kids. All the stuff that was difficult when I was growing up in a military family."

"You wanted something different?" he asked, and she nodded.

"I wanted my kids to have friends that they didn't leave every few years, and a mom who wasn't away more than she was home. Henry and I had everything planned out, and I had a whole timeline worked out in my head, and then he was diagnosed with cancer."

"That had to be devastating for both of you."

"I think I was more heartbroken than he was. He had this unbelievable faith that God was in control, and that he had nothing to worry about. He died a few weeks before our wedding, and I still haven't figured out what I want to do with the rest of my life."

The door at the rear of the sanctuary opened, and a group of parishioners walked in, laughing and talking as they made their way into the church.

He wanted to continue the conversation, but Gretchen seemed finished, her focus on the empty pulpit, her hands fisted in her lap.

Whatever boundary she'd set for their relationship, she seemed to think she'd crossed it. Her muscles looked so tense he thought they'd snap if she tried to move.

"Relax," he whispered in her ear. "I'm not the enemy, and I'm not going to use your secrets against you."

"You shouldn't know my secrets," she hissed. "I'm not even sure why I told you any of that."

"Because we're friends?"

She met his eyes. "We are, Justin, and I really value that. So let's try not to ruin things."

He would have asked what she meant, but the sanctuary was filling now, and Pastor Harmon appeared, walking through a doorway to the left. He waved at Justin and Gretchen, hurrying toward them and offering a greeting.

"How are you, Gretchen? Is the arm healing up?"

"It's nearly good as new, Pastor," she responded, and he smiled.

"Good. That's what I like to hear. And how about Portia, Justin? I heard she's been taken off base."

"She's in a safe location until Boyd Sullivan is caught."

"Poor kid. I know she's had quite an adjustment this past year. Is she okay? Is there anything my wife and I can do for her?"

"Just pray for her. I know she'd appreciate it."

"Of course, and if you need anything while she's gone, let us know. I'm sure the house is quiet without her in it."

"It is," he agreed, imagining going home after church to the emptiness. Making lunch without her sitting at the table. Spending a long day alone.

Which was something he'd done hundreds of times before.

It felt different now. It felt like a loss.

"My wife and I always have room at the table for a few friends. Why don't the two of you have lunch with us?" Pastor Harmon said as if he'd read Justin's mind.

"As much as I appreciate the offer," Justin said, "I think it would be safer for your family if I stayed away."

"Safer...? Oh. Right. Boyd. Don't worry about him, Justin. God is in control, and we trust His divine protection."

"I'd still feel better staying away, Pastor."

"And I'd feel better knowing that you weren't going home to an empty house," Pastor Harmon responded.

"I've gone home to an empty house hundreds of times. I'll be fine."

"How about you, Gretchen? We'd love to have you."

"I'll have to take a rain check, too. I have some work that needs to be done at my apartment, and today is the only day I have free."

"What kind of work?" Justin asked as the pastor stepped up to the pulpit.

"My mother sent me the supplies to make four hundred wedding favors for my brother's wedding."

"Wedding favors?"

"Yeah. The cheap little gifts the bride and groom give to their guests?"

He laughed at the description. "Sounds like something everyone wants to go home with."

"I think half the guests leave them behind, but it's a tradition, and since it's not my wedding, I'm not going to argue with it."

"So, your brother is having four hundred guests, and you're making a gift for each of them? That sounds like a lot of work. When's the wedding?"

"New Year's Eve."

"That's right around the corner."

"Yeah. I know. The wedding favors are jars of candy kisses. Each one has to have a personalized note attached that reads *'Hugs and Kisses from the Mr. and Mrs.'*"

He laughed. He couldn't help himself. "That's…"

"Corny? Yeah. I agree."

"How did you get roped into making them?"

"My brother Micah is at Goodfellow Air Force Base. The wedding is going to be at the chapel there. Shelby—his fiancée—is finishing a residency at a hospital in Massachusetts and won't be down here until right before the ceremony. Since I'm in Texas, my mother thought it would be easier for me to make

them and transport them to San Angelo than for Shelby
to have to transport them from New England."

"That worked out nicely for Shelby."

"I don't mind. Shelby is a great person, and I'm
really happy she's marrying my brother. But things
have been busy here, and I'm behind. Today is the day,
though. I'm getting the favors done so poor Shelby has
one less thing to worry about." She grabbed a hymnal
and stood as the pastor invited the congregation to sing
the opening hymn.

He joined her, leaning close and whispering, "Since
I'm the reason you've been so busy, I'll help you with
the favors."

"That's not necessary."

"Yes, it is."

"Justin—"

"Shh. You wouldn't want the old ladies in the next
pew over to start frowning the way they do when the
pastor's son is too loud."

She laughed and didn't continue the argument.

She might have thought he was joking, that there
was no way he was planning to go to her house and
spend the afternoon making wedding favors. If so, she
was going to be surprised. He hadn't been joking. He
might not know anything about wedding favors, but he
knew four hands working a task were better than two.

He also knew that spending time with Gretchen
seemed like something he wouldn't mind doing a lot
more of.

They'd spent six hours making wedding favors. Six
hours talking and laughing. Six hours that Gretchen refused to regret. She liked Justin. She enjoyed his com-

pany, and she was glad he'd insisted on helping out. Jobs were more fun when done with friends.

And that was what he'd said at the church.

That they were friends.

She could handle that. She could even appreciate it.

Being raised in a military family had meant making and losing friends often. She'd always been outgoing, and the process of meeting new people had never been difficult.

So, yeah. Calling Justin a friend was a natural extension of her life story.

Making sure he stayed in that category? That might be more difficult. He was too easy to talk to, too comfortable to be with. When she was around him, she forgot that her heart was broken. She forgot it needed to be protected. She forgot that loving someone meant risking losing him.

She packed a favor into the last unfilled box, tucking it in carefully. The label was completely dry, the handwritten calligraphy unsmudged.

"These looks great," Justin said, handing her another jar. He'd filled it with chocolate kisses and screwed on the lid and wrapped a ribbon around it. "Your calligraphy skills are impressive."

"I'll have to tell my ninth-grade art teacher you said so. He was a master at it, and I wanted to learn, so he taught me."

"I'm sure you're regretting it right about now." He gestured at the boxes of favors that sat against the living room wall.

"A cramp in my hand is a small price to pay for my brother and sister-in-law's happiness," she deadpanned.

"I hear that fresh air is good for hand cramps," he said, handing her the last favor.

"Really?" She chuckled.

"No, but how about we take Quinn for a walk, anyway? Maybe grab a coffee. There's a place right around the corner."

She could think of a dozen reasons why that would be fun, and she couldn't think of one reason to refuse.

"Quinn would enjoy it," Justin added, and the Malinois lifted his head, his ears twitching. They'd picked him up after church, and he'd seemed content to lay on the floor or stare out the window. Now, though, he looked eager to get up. Get out. Do something. His tail thumped as Justin grabbed his leash and hooked it to his collar.

"I can't say no now. He'd be too disappointed." She grabbed her coat from the closet and handed Justin his. He was still wearing his dress clothes—black slacks and a blue shirt that matched his eyes. Polished shoes. He'd taken his tie off when he'd arrived, and his hair was mussed from running his hands through it.

Her palm itched to smooth the strands.

She handed him his jacket instead, opening the apartment door and stepping into the corridor.

Justin's phone rang as they walked to the elevator, and he answered quickly. "Hello? Yes."

He glanced at Gretchen and mouthed, *Ava Esposito.*

"Do you have GPS coordinates?... Send them to me and clear out. Don't go in. If Rusty is there, Sullivan could be there, too... Yeah. You're right. Olio's operatives are probably more likely. I still want you to stand down and wait for backup to arrive."

"Rusty Morton?" Gretchen asked, her heart thumping wildly.

He nodded, stepping away from the elevator and pulling her back to her apartment as he finished his conversation with Ava.

She unlocked the apartment door and ushered him in, leaving him in the living room as she ran to gear up. If Rusty had been spotted, she'd need to be ready to go to work.

The team was eager to speak with him about the still-missing dogs. Like many on the case, she felt confident he'd somehow been involved in their disappearance. She wanted to know where he'd taken them, whether he'd sold them to the Olio Crime Syndicate and where they were currently located.

She wanted them returned.

The three missing German shepherds were financially valuable, but they had intrinsic value, as well. They'd been part of Canyon Air Force Base since they were puppies, and they needed to be returned home.

It didn't take long to change into her uniform, take her service weapon from her gun safe and grab her backpack. As always, she kept it ready with water, food rations and a first-aid kit, along with everything she needed to stay warm and start a fire. Extra ammunition. Tactical gear. She wouldn't need all of it on this mission, but she didn't have time to repack.

She ran into the kitchen, grabbing a box of dog treats she kept for Quinn and other K-9 guests and shoving them into the pack.

"What are you doing?" Justin asked.

"Preparing. If Rusty is around, it's possible some of the missing dogs are, too."

"I hope so. I'm ready to reunite them with their military family. I'm also hoping to see Scout again. He's a phenomenal K-9. I'd love for you to get a chance to meet him." He scratched Quinn's head. "Ready to work, boy?"

The dog barked once, rushing to the door and staring at Justin expectantly.

"Looks like you are," he commented. "I need to stop by my house and grab my gear, Gretchen. I'm not sure what we're going to find, but I'm going to assume we won't be walking into a friendly situation."

"Where are we heading?"

"A cave. From what Ava said, it's off the beaten track. She was out hiking with Roscoe and heard someone walking through the woods. She thought it was Boyd and took cover. When Rusty appeared, she decided to follow him rather than attempt apprehension."

"And he led her to a cave?"

"Ava said it's really hard to see. If she hadn't watched Rusty walk into it, she's not sure she would have known it was there."

"Should I radio in for backup?"

"No. I want to keep radio silence. Just in case."

She didn't ask what he meant. She knew he was worried about a leak, concerned that someone might be feeding information to the enemy.

She understood the concern. Boyd was smart, but the way he slipped through every trap they'd set for him was uncanny and defied logic. "We could make some phone calls."

"It's Sunday evening, Gretchen. If we start pulling people away from their families and activities, the community is going to notice."

"How about Oliver Davison? We don't have any worries about the FBI being tied to Boyd or to Olio, and most people on base aren't familiar with him," she said. "I could give him a call. If we're right about Rusty selling dogs to Olio, it's possible he's meeting some of their operatives."

"Give him a call, and let's hope that's what's going on. If we can catch a few high-level Olio operatives, we might be able to bring the entire organization down."

"That would be a good day's work," she said, pulling out her phone and dialing Davison's number as they hurried into the hall and onto the elevator.

NINE

The sun set early this time of year, and by the time Justin changed into his military uniform and grabbed his tactical gear, it was dusk, the sky dark with evening clouds. Raindrops splattered the windshield, and he turned on the wipers. A storm would be a blessing—the sound of falling rain and thunder masking their approach to the cave.

He was curious to find out why Rusty was at the caves.

The dog trainer had been missing from base for a couple of weeks. He wasn't suspected of freeing the dogs, and if he'd stuck around and answered some questions, he'd probably have been removed from the person-of-interest list. After all, the team had no doubt that Boyd was responsible for the deaths of the two trainers who'd been at the kennels the night the dogs were released, and they were certain he'd been the one to let the dogs go. The team had planned to question Rusty regarding his whereabouts that night.

But he'd run. Innocent people generally didn't do that.

They usually assumed that justice would prevail,

that truth would win, and that no matter what the authorities believed, their innocence would be proven.

Rusty had gone into hiding, and he'd had a reason.

Justin was eager to find out what it was.

If, somehow, the trainer was connected to Olio, it was possible the FBI would use him to close down the crime ring.

"What are you thinking?" Gretchen asked as he pulled into the lot where Ava had left her vehicle. He could see it—a white SUV parked beneath a streetlight. He pulled up beside it and parked, switching off the ignition and turning to face Gretchen. They'd spent the afternoon together—laughing and making labels for jars of candy. Talking. Sharing. And now they were going to spend the evening bringing in criminals.

Something about that felt right and good, as if all the pieces of his life had finally come together.

He wanted to tell Gretchen that, but time was ticking, and Ava was in the woods, waiting for backup to arrive.

That had to be his focus and his priority.

"I'm thinking that this is the break we've been waiting for."

"Are we going to wait for Oliver?"

"I sent him the coordinates. He'll be here as soon as he can. Right now, it's just us. And Quinn." He jumped out of the SUV, and she did the same, standing beside him as he opened the hatch and released Quinn.

The Malinois sensed Justin's excitement and adrenaline. He lunged against the leash, eager to get into the woods and onto the trail. But Justin didn't release him. He didn't want Quinn giving away their presence.

Rusty knew the dogs who were part of the K-9 unit.

He'd worked with Quinn on several occasions, and he'd know an alert bark if he heard it.

He'd know any bark was bad news, but hearing Quinn would set off more than alarm bells. It would send him running.

Justin wanted him to stay put, dry and cozy in the cave. Oblivious to the fact that he'd been found.

He glanced at his GPS, adjusted his trajectory, heading up a hill and through a thicket filled with brambles. Gretchen was right behind him, moving almost silently, the only sound the soft crack of branches and the quiet thud of her feet on the muddy earth.

As they walked, rain poured from the sky, falling in cold, fat drops. They slid down his head and his cheeks, pooling in the hollow of his throat and sliding under his coat and shirt. The temperature had dropped dramatically, and he wouldn't be surprised if a few snowflakes fell.

They walked three miles, crossed a creek that he remembered from one of his longer treks into the woods, and then down a steep slope.

It was quiet here. Cut off from the houses, business and traffic. Far enough away from roads to seem almost prehistoric in its beauty—thick vines hanging from old trees, rotting logs lying across sapling trees. Mushrooms and other fungi growing out of tree stumps. No hint of civilization. No trash. No broken bottles or plastic bags. The ground almost marsh-like, the air filled with the pungent scent of rotting leaves.

According to the GPS coordinates, the cave should have been a hundred yards ahead. He moved in that direction, the rain muting his footsteps and Quinn's soft whine. The dog's ears were down, his tail up, his scruff raised.

He smelled another dog.

Justin couldn't see one.

And he still couldn't see the cave.

A shadow moved to his right, and he whirled to face it, relaxing when Ava stepped into view. Roscoe was beside her, his blond fur dark with rain, his eyes bright. He looked happy to see friends, but stayed by her side, quietly moving through the foliage.

"You made it," Ava whispered as she reached Justin's side.

"Anyone else arrive?" he asked quietly.

"I'm afraid not."

"That might not be a bad thing," Gretchen said. "If the cave is big enough for him to hide in, it's big enough for firearms and explosives to be stored in. He could be well prepared to defend his position."

"*If* he's been hiding there," Ava responded. "I'm pretty certain he was carrying dog food. He had a bag over his shoulder. I couldn't get close enough to see what it was."

"This would be the perfect place to keep the dogs," Justin murmured. The area was remote enough to keep them from being heard and discovered. "Where's the cave?"

"This way." Ava led them through the woods, confident and relaxed. No sign that she'd been afraid or worried. Justin wasn't surprised. She had a reputation for being one of the best on the K-9 Search and Rescue team.

She stopped near a huge oak, standing beneath its

thick limbs and pointing to the west. "There. See where the boulders are piled up?"

He did. Three large boulders, sitting against the face of a small hill. "Yes, but I don't see a cave."

"It's behind the boulders. Which is probably why none of us has ever been in it. This place isn't exactly easily accessible."

"No, but it sure does make a great place to keep something you don't want anyone to find," Gretchen said quietly, taking a step forward.

"You two stay back," Justin told them. "Quinn and I are going to take a look."

"I'm not sure that's the best idea, Captain," Ava said. "It might be better to call for some tear gas. I'd rather have him come to us than go to him when we have no idea what's he's got in there."

"I'd consider that if I were certain he didn't have any of our missing K-9s in there."

"Justin," Gretchen said, grabbing his wrist. "I agree with Ava. It's too dangerous. You have no field of vision. No way of knowing how many people might be in that cave."

"I have Quinn," he reminded her. "He'll be my eyes and ears."

"I'll go with you, then. There's strength in numbers."

"Any other time, I'd agree," he said, "but we don't know if he's meeting someone here. We don't know if Olio has operatives heading in this direction, and we don't know if Boyd is around. I want you to stay here and stop anyone who tries to enter the cave after I go in."

"Justin—" she began, but he cut off her argument.

"We're moving ahead with my plan. Stay here. If I

need help, you'll know it." He unhooked Quinn's leash and gave him the command to heel. They moved side by side, stepping between ancient pines and younger oaks. Visibility was limited in the rain and dusk, and he was glad. If he was having difficulty seeing what he knew was there, Rusty would have trouble seeing something he wasn't expecting.

And Rusty had no reason to expect someone to be approaching.

Not unless he was meeting someone.

And, even then, he wouldn't have reason to be standing watch.

Justin approached the cave cautiously, keeping to the tree line until he had a clear view of the boulders. As Ava had said, there was no visual of the cave beyond. It really was the perfect place to hide something or someone. If the team's theory was correct, Rusty had sold Patriot to the Olio Crime Syndicate. If the other dogs were in the cave, he'd either had second thoughts or he'd been bargaining for more money.

Justin had a feeling the latter was unlikely. Rusty was a good K-9 trainer but hadn't had a commanding enough personality to move quickly up through the ranks. It was doubtful he'd want to bargain with a syndicate that might decide they'd had enough and kill him.

On the other hand, Rusty had always seemed to care about the dogs. He'd spoken highly of the German shepherds who were missing, and he'd seemed legitimately upset about the trainers who'd been killed. It seemed more likely he'd seen the freed dogs as an opportunity to make some extra money and had then come to regret the deal and had brought the dogs to the cave while he tried to figure out how to rectify his mistake.

As far as Justin was concerned, there was no time like the present to find out the truth. He reached the boulders, Quinn heeling so closely they were almost touching. This was how they worked when they were moving through enemy territory. Pressed together and ready to defend one another.

Light danced on the ground to the left of the boulders. A high-powered lantern rather than fire. The air was chilly and damp, filled with the scent of rain and wet earth. Not a hint of smoke.

A dog barked, the sound muted but clearly audible.

Not Roscoe. The sound had come from the other side of the boulder. If Justin hadn't been so close to the cave, he'd have radioed Gretchen to tell her that they might have located the dogs.

Quinn growled, his hackles raised, his muscles tense.

Down, Justin signaled, and the dog immediately dropped to his stomach.

Crawl, Justin signaled again, and Quinn inched along on his stomach until they reached the edge of the boulder.

This was it. They had to breach the cave, and they had to do it before Rusty and anyone he might be with could react.

Justin pulled his firearm, met Quinn's eyes. The dog was staring at him. Eager. Ready.

One quick signal, and the dog was off, bounding into the cave, teeth bared and growling.

Justin ran in behind him, keeping low and close to the rock face, the sound of a man's scream filling his ears.

* * *

Someone was screaming. A man.

Gretchen could hear him over the sound of Quinn's growls and barks. Not Justin. It had to be Rusty. She didn't hesitate. She didn't think it through. She knew when it was time to hold back, and she knew when it was time to move in.

"Stay here." She tossed the words at Ava as she sprinted to the boulders, rounded them and found the cave. It was deep, but well lit by a lantern. She stopped short when she saw the scene before her.

Justin kneeling over Rusty Morton, hiking his arms up behind his back and slapping on cuffs. Quinn right beside them, growling, his jaws snapping. Bags of dog food on the ground, one of them spilling kibble across the dirt. Food and water dishes. And three large German shepherds chained to stakes that had been hammered into the ground.

"Do you need help, Captain?" she asked, moving toward him, her focus on Rusty.

The trainer wasn't even trying to fight. He lay with his cheek pressed to the ground, his body lax. It seemed almost as if he were glad to have finally been found.

"No. I'm good." Justin pulled Rusty to his feet. "Good to see you again, Rusty. We've been worried about you," he remarked, pushing him into a chair.

"Worried about the dogs, you mean," Rusty said quietly. He looked…broken. His head down, his hair disheveled.

"We've been worried about you, too. It isn't like you to be AWOL. Want to tell me what's going on?" Justin asked calmly.

"I made a mistake. I was trying to fix it."

"By keeping these dogs in a cave?" Justin asked.

"By not selling them to Olio."

"So, you *were* responsible for Patriot being used by the crime organization," Gretchen said, and Rusty finally looked up. He met her eyes, and she didn't see any anger or hatred in his gaze. Just remorse.

"Yes, and I regretted it almost immediately. I love these dogs. I just wasn't thinking clearly. An Olio operative had been contacting me for months, offering me major dollars to grab one of the dogs and hand it over. When I realized someone had freed the dogs, it seemed like a perfect opportunity to get some extra cash." He swallowed hard, his skin pale and pasty, his eyes shadowed.

"And you brought them here?" Justin prodded.

"No. I put them in my van and drove off base. A friend of mine was looking after them while I worked out the details of their sale. He lives out in the country but has a nice fenced yard and experience with dogs. I went and checked on them every few days." He shrugged.

"Does your friend happen to work for Olio?" Justin asked.

Rusty hesitated.

"You may as well tell us," Gretchen said. "Eventually, it's all going to come out, and it'll be better for you if we don't have to work too hard to make that happen."

"Yes. We grew up next door to each other, and we've been friends for years. He knows what I do on base, and he was the one who suggested to the crime ring that military dogs would be perfect guards for drug and illegal weapon caches."

"So, he's your contact with Olio?" Justin asked.

"Yes. When I changed my mind about selling the rest of the dogs, I went out to his place and got the dogs who were still there. Patriot had already been sold. Olio's head honcho wanted to see how effective he was before he paid for the other dogs."

"That worked out well for you," Justin said. "It would have been difficult to get them back to base if they were already in Olio's hands."

"I know, and I can't tell you how much I regret what I did, but it wasn't criminal. It *wasn't*. I found a few stray dogs and I sold them. There's no crime in that."

"You knew they belonged to the US Air Force," Gretchen said, scratching the muzzle of the closest German shepherd. He was large and handsome, his eyes bright and alert. He'd obviously been well taken care of.

"I made a mistake. That doesn't make me a criminal, and it doesn't mean I should go to jail."

"I think the court will have something to say about that," FBI Special Agent Oliver Davison said as he walked into the cave, Ava right behind him with Roscoe.

"I can't believe it," Ava breathed, hurrying across the room and looking at the shepherds. "They're here. All of them."

"We'll have to check the microchips to be sure of that," Justin said. "But it does look like these are the missing shepherds."

He crouched near the one Gretchen was petting. "This is Scout. I'd know him anywhere."

The dog licked his cheek, and Gretchen smiled. "I guess he knows you, too."

"We do go way back, don't we, buddy?" He scratched

the dog behind his ears and stood. "Gretchen, can you radio Dispatch? Have someone let Westley know that we have the dogs. He may want to come in and help transport them out. Or he can meet us back at the kennel."

"Sure." After she'd done so, she walked deeper into the cave. She could hear Oliver interrogating Rusty and the trainer giving up his friend's name and contact information.

But that wasn't all she wanted to hear. She felt a sense of failure, of frustration because there was still a loose thread that needed to be tied.

"You okay?" Justin asked, falling into step beside her. Quinn was lying on the ground, staring at Rusty as if he'd like to make a meal of him. He didn't seem aware of the other dogs, although she was certain he'd noticed them. His focus was on the cuffed man, and she knew he'd continue to watch Rusty until he was told to back off.

"I'm fine. I'm just wondering what else Rusty is hiding in here."

"Drugs, you mean? Firearms? Because I believe his story. I think he took an opportunity and regretted it. I don't think he has anything to do with Olio's criminal operations."

"I agree. I was thinking more along the lines of roses or notes. Something that the Red Rose Killer uses." She purposely said it loud enough for Rusty to hear. The team had been leaning toward him being an opportunistic criminal, but it was still possible he'd been in league with Boyd Sullivan. The cave would certainly make a great hiding place for the serial killer.

"I had nothing to do with Boyd Sullivan's crime spree," he yelled, jumping to his feet.

Quinn growled in response, the sound terrifying enough to send a chill up Gretchen's spine.

"Really?" she asked as he dropped back into his seat, his focus on the dog. "Because you benefited a lot from his crimes. How much were you paid for Patriot? A couple thousand dollars?"

"Ten thousand," he muttered. "But I would never hurt anyone."

"You hurt the team when you took those dogs," she said.

"I would never physically hurt someone," he corrected. "I didn't even have it in me to steal a dog. I waited until they were already loose, and then I grabbed them, because I figured a few dogs missing out of hundreds wasn't going to be a big deal."

"You were wrong about that," Ava said, scratching Roscoe behind his floppy ears. "Our dogs are family. I thought you understood that."

"I did. I *do*. But I had gambling debts to pay." He swallowed hard. "I realized as soon as I made the deal that I shouldn't have. That's why I brought these dogs here last month. I was trying to figure out a way to get them back to the kennel without having them traced to me."

"You should have asked for help," Justin said. "There isn't a person on the K-9 team who wouldn't have been willing to give it."

"I'm sorry. I really am."

Gretchen didn't want to, but she believed him.

As disappointing as it was, they'd found the missing dogs, but they were no closer to finding the Red Rose Killer.

She ran a hand over her damp hair. He should have

been caught months ago. Canyon Air Force Base had one of the best Security Forces in the nation. The K-9 team was top tier. The men and women who worked there were driven by the need for justice.

And God was on their side, right?

Surely, He wanted Sullivan caught as much as they did.

So, why the wait?

Why the months of chasing leads and hitting dead ends, of trying desperately to stop a killer, only to find another victim?

There'd been too many lives lost.

Too many people hurt.

But God was good. He was love. He was righteousness.

And yet evil still existed in the world.

She strode to the mouth of the cave and stepped outside, desperate for fresh air. She let the rain fall down her cheeks like tears.

When your job meant constantly looking for criminals, sometimes it was hard to see the good in the world. Sometimes, it was difficult to see God's work going on around you.

She acknowledged that and her own jaded viewpoint.

There were plenty of people who walked through life without ever coming up against someone like Boyd Sullivan. There were wonderful things happening every day. Even during the most difficult trials, joy could be found.

She and Henry had shared a lot of sweet and funny moments during his cancer treatment, and if he'd lived, he'd probably say the tough times had strengthened his faith. He'd been the kind of person who'd focused on the positive, and she wanted to be like that, too. Not just to honor his memory, but to honor God.

No matter what, she believed He was there, and that the way she moved through the world would lead people toward Him or away.

She walked past the boulders and away from the lantern light. In the distance, a dog barked. The K-9 trainers and their dogs must be on the way. Probably with extra hands to help bring the German shepherds out of the woods.

It would be good to have them back where they belonged.

Even with Boyd still free, the returned dogs would raise morale and give the team something to celebrate.

She'd focus on that and on doing everything she could to make sure they found Boyd before he struck again.

"Are you okay?" Justin asked, walking around the bolder and heading toward her. His hair was glossy with rain, his expression hidden by the darkness.

"I just needed some air."

"You were hoping we'd find Boyd here."

"Weren't you?"

"Yes, but not finding him isn't the end of the road. Eventually, he'll make a mistake, and we'll be there when he does."

"Hopefully, he'll do it before someone else is hurt."

"It's unlikely anyone will. He's after me, Gretchen. He's made that very clear."

"That's what I'm worried about."

For a moment, he was silent. Then he tucked a strand of hair behind her ear, his fingers lingering against her skin. His eyes gleamed in the darkness, the softness in them making her throat tight.

"What?" she said, stepping back because she was afraid she might step forward. Into his space. Into his arms.

"You're worried about me," he said, and she could hear the smile in his voice.

"Of course I am, and it's not funny."

"I'm not laughing."

"You're amused," she accused.

"I'm...touched."

"Don't be. I'm always concerned about the people I work with." She just happened to be a little more... invested in Justin.

They'd worked countless hours together.

They'd shared stories and told jokes and treated each other to coffee when the days were long. They'd made wedding favors, and she'd looked in his eyes, and she'd felt things she hadn't felt in years. Hope. Excitement. Attraction.

"You don't have to worry, Gretchen. I'm not planning on letting Boyd win," he said.

"It's not your plans I'm worried about. It's Boyd's. Maybe even God's. It's not like we know what He has in store."

"'All things work together for good to them that love God,'" he replied. "Corbin used to quote that all the time. I can't remember the chapter and verse, but it seems appropriate to the situation."

"It's easy to quote Scripture. It's not always easy to believe the words."

"I know." He put his hands on her shoulders, and she could feel the weight of his palms, the strength of his fingers. She could feel his warmth seeping through her soaked jacket, and for a moment, she felt like she'd finally found that sweet place called home. The one she missed so much when she was away from her family. The one she'd felt like she'd lost when Henry died.

She would have stepped away, but he was studying her face, his eyes gleaming in the darkness, and she wasn't sure what he was looking for, wasn't sure if she wanted him to find it.

"We've both been hurt, we've both lost, we've both struggled to hold on to our faith," he said as if he'd read that in her face. As if, somehow, he had looked in her eyes and seen all the questions and worries she hid from the world. "And we're both standing here, knowing we might just have found something we weren't even looking for. That's a scary thing. Don't think I don't know it and feel it. Don't think I'm not just as worried about it as you are."

"We were talking about Boyd," she pointed out, her voice raspy with emotion. She'd always been a straight shooter, quick to speak her mind. Right now, though, she couldn't make herself agree. Even though everything he'd said was true.

"We were also talking about faith and God's plan. The way I see things, it all ties together." He wiped rain from her cheeks, and she could see his smile through the darkness. "So, how about we spend less time worrying and more time trusting that things will be okay?"

She nodded, because she was afraid to speak. Afraid that the emotion in her voice would give away all her fear and anxiety and hope and excitement.

"Good," he said, leaning down so that they were eye

to eye. She could feel his breath fanning her face, see the tenderness in his expression.

When he kissed her, it felt right. Like sunrise after the darkest night. Like the first rays of light after a storm.

When he broke away, she was breathless, her hands clutching his arms.

"Justin—" she began.

"Let's not ruin the moment by overthinking it, okay?" he said gently.

"I just don't want to have my heart broken again," she admitted.

"I would never break your heart," he promised.

"Henry didn't plan to, either," she said, her voice raw and hot with emotion.

A quiet click broke through the sound of rain splattering on leaves and splashing on the ground.

Gretchen recognized it immediately. Pulling her gun from the holster, she swung in the direction of the sound.

She didn't have a chance to fire.

Justin was on her, tackling her to the ground as he fired into the trees.

TEN

Justin was on his feet before the sound of gunfire faded to silence, pulling Gretchen to her feet, asking if she was okay. Listening to the crash of someone fleeing through the woods.

Not someone.

Boyd. He knew that the same way he knew that the click of the safety being released was another game. Sullivan might have been average in basic training, but he'd been an ace at target practice. If he'd been willing to do the work, he'd have made an excellent sharpshooter. Even if his skills were rusty, he'd have been able to hit a target.

It wasn't like Justin and Gretchen had been on the move. They'd been sitting ducks, waiting for the bullets to fly.

But Boyd hadn't taken the shot.

He probably had a list of offenses that had been committed against him, and he wanted to explain every one of them before he ended things. He wouldn't be happy to kill someone from a distance. He wanted to take the shot close-up. He fed off the fear of others.

Justin fed off locking people like him away.

"That was close," Gretchen said, straightening her pack. Her voice was shaky, but he didn't think that was because of Boyd.

The kiss had upset her.

Because she didn't want her heart broken again.

That was what she'd said, and he'd planned to ask if she were willing to risk it, anyway. Now wasn't the time, though. Boyd was on the move, and he planned to go after him.

"Not as close as he'd have liked," he replied, un-hooking Quinn's leash. The dog lunged toward the woods, straining against the hold Justin had on his collar.

"Is everyone okay?" Oliver called, rushing out of the cave, Ava and Roscoe behind him.

"Fine. Quinn and I are going after him." Justin released the collar, snapping the command that freed Quinn to do what he did best.

The dog took off, racing into the woods, barking wildly.

More dogs took up the cry. The team was closing in, and he'd have plenty of backup if he needed it, but Justin wasn't going to wait around to give instructions. He set off into the woods.

"Can you see Quinn?" Gretchen asked as she ran up beside him.

"No, but I don't need to. I've already given him his command. He knows what to do."

"What if he finds Boyd and is hurt?" she asked.

"That's the risk I take every time I release him to apprehend a criminal."

"I'm not sure I could do it," she admitted. "I'd worry too much."

"Then you're better off doing the kind of work Ava does. Search and rescue is dangerous. But not like this."

"Does it ever get to you? Or are you really as unaffected as you seem?"

"It gets to me all the time. I've had Quinn for three years. I got him straight out of his K-9 training. He's family. I'd give my life to save his, but this is his job, Gretchen. He loves it. So I tell myself that it's no different than you or me walking into a dangerous situation. We're well trained. If something happens, it won't be because of anything we did wrong."

"At least, we hope not," she said, panting slightly as they crested a hill.

Lights flashed in the distance. One. Then another and another.

It took a moment for him to realize he was looking at cars.

A road.

Boyd's escape route.

He radioed the team, asking for the road to be ID'd and MPs to be dispatched to the area. They needed to set up blockades to keep Boyd from fleeing in a vehicle.

If they could keep him on foot, their chances of capturing him were better.

Up ahead, Quinn was bounding down the hill, his body a black blur in the darkness. He wasn't barking. Wasn't growling. Which meant he was closing in on his prey.

Justin raced after him, feet sliding on muddy ground and wet leaves, heart racing. The road was close. He could hear cars speeding past, but the trees were thicker near the bottom of the hill, the brambles catching at his clothes.

He finally broke through thick undergrowth, stumbling onto the breakdown lane of a four-lane highway.

"Is this the interstate?" Gretchen asked, still right on his heels and keeping pace.

"It's a state highway. Unless I've gotten turned around, the north entrance to the base is a few miles to the right."

"Quinn is heading in the opposite direction," she pointed out.

"Then Boyd must be, too." He took off, running full-speed down the road, Quinn a swiftly moving shadow in front of him.

They rounded a bend, and he saw a small sedan idling on the side of the road. He saw Boyd next, his blond hair nearly white in the streetlight, his long legs eating up the ground.

He glanced over his shoulder, probably trying to see how close Quinn was.

"Police! Stop and keep your hands where I can see them," Justin called, but Boyd had reached the vehicle, was yanking open the passenger door and jumping inside.

Quinn reached the car seconds later, jumping up against the window and door, snarling and snapping.

"Off!" Justin called, afraid Boyd would shoot through the window.

Quinn backed off reluctantly, his attention on the car.

"Heel!" Justin yelled as the engine revved and the vehicle jumped forward.

Quinn spun away, racing back to Justin and pressing close to his left leg. They moved in tandem, sprinting after the car. Sirens screamed in the background.

Justin wanted to pull his gun and take a shot, but there were cars filled with civilians passing by, and he couldn't risk injury to one of them.

When the taillights of the sedan disappeared, Justin finally stopped running.

Disappointed.

Frustrated.

Angry that he hadn't been just a little faster.

He'd been minutes away from capturing Boyd, and once again, the killer had slipped through his fingers.

"I got a partial plate," Gretchen said, panting as she pulled out her phone and typed something into it. "Were you able to get the make or model of the car?"

"It was a Toyota. I'm not sure what model. Four-door. Black or dark blue. That's about all I saw."

"How about the driver?"

"Nothing. The interior lights were off."

"Too bad."

"Why do you say that?"

"I think it's someone from the base. Someone we know. We need to contact gate security and ask them to keep an eye out for the car. Did you use the secure radio frequency when you called headquarters?"

"Yes." And that meant only Security Forces officers and dispatchers had access to the communication. As much as he hated to admit it, Gretchen was right.

"Make the call," he said. "I'm going to talk to the MPs who are arriving." He gestured toward a cruiser that was speeding toward them, lights flashing, sirens blaring.

She nodded, already speaking into the radio.

From running in the rain, her hair was hanging across her cheeks, thick wet strands clinging to silky skin.

He was tempted to brush it away, but the cruiser had parked, and two officers were getting out. They'd see any gesture he made toward her. He didn't care, but he knew Gretchen would.

So he walked away, Quinn still on heel beside him. The fact that Gretchen had gotten a partial plate impressed him, but he wasn't sure it would bring them any closer to Boyd. The killer had a predilection for stealing cars and using them when he was on the prowl. More than likely, the Toyota had been stolen.

That didn't mean that the person driving it wasn't military personnel. Gretchen's assessment had been spot-on. Someone with inside information was helping Boyd.

Justin's mission was to find out who.

It was 3:00 a.m. when Gretchen finally finished writing up her report, shut down her computer and grabbed her backpack from the floor beside her chair. She and Justin had been back at the office for several hours, going over lists of possible leaks, attempting to obtain phone records for everyone who'd been working in the building when Justin made radio contact.

That would take time.

Until Gretchen had them in hand, she'd have no idea who had made the call that had sent Boyd to the cave.

She lifted her coffee, sipping the last dregs of her fifth cup.

Or was it her sixth?

She should have been wired from the caffeine. All she felt was bone-deep fatigue.

"All set?" Justin asked, pushing away from his desk and standing. They'd been alone in the office for at least an hour, the quiet hum of their computers muffling the sound of people walking through the hallway outside. She'd done her best to ignore him, but her thoughts seemed to constantly move in his direction. She'd wanted to talk to him rather than work in silence, but the things she'd had to say had nothing to do with the case and everything to do with the kiss.

If she let herself, she could still feel the warmth of his lips against hers.

Her cheeks heated, and she stood. "Yes. Finally."

She sounded normal, she thought. She *hoped*.

"Quinn and I will take you home." He grabbed her coat from the back of the chair and draped it around her shoulders.

"That's not necessary, Justin. I can walk from here."

"I'd rather you not. Boyd was watching us tonight."

"So?" She brushed a crumb from her desk, moved her pen so that it was neatly centered on the computer keyboard. Anything to avoid meeting his eyes.

She was falling for him.

Hard.

And she didn't want him to see the truth of that in her eyes. She was too afraid of what it would mean, too afraid to commit herself to tumbling headfirst into something new and exciting and terrifying.

"So, he might have seen me do this." He tucked a strand of hair behind her ear, his fingers drifting from her cheek to her ear, and then down to the column of her throat.

"I don't remember you doing that," she murmured, but she didn't move away. She *should* have. Of course she should have.

Because she didn't want a repeat of the kiss.

She *didn't*.

"Okay, so maybe it was more like this." He shifted his hands so that they rested on her shoulders, and she found herself moving closer. Not because he asked or demanded it. Because she couldn't seem to stop herself.

This time, his kiss was as gentle as a warm spring breeze. Soft and tender and filled with promise of things to come.

"Either way," he murmured as he pulled back, "Boyd may have seen it, and he may have decided you're the perfect way to get to me."

"The only way he could use me like that is to kidnap me," she managed to say.

"That's my point. Let's not make you an easy target, okay? I'll take you home. You'll lock the door, and you won't unlock it until you call and let me know you need an escort." His thumb brushed the pulse point in her neck, the raspy slide of it sending heat up her spine.

"You can't escort me everywhere I need to go," she protested.

"If I can't, I'll send someone else. Just until this is over." He studied her face, his gaze intense and unwavering. "You don't have to be scared, Gretchen."

"I'm not scared. I'm terrified."

"Of Boyd?"

"Of my stupid fickle heart," she blurted out, and he smiled.

"I'm serious, Justin," she muttered. "My heart has

already been broken once. I don't think I'll survive it a second time around."

"Who's to say there will be a second time? Maybe your heart will be just fine."

"This is a dangerous job. Either of us could get injured." Or worse. She didn't add that.

He knew what she was thinking.

No one got into a relationship with a law enforcement officer without understanding the risk.

"That's true, but I'd rather give my all to something and have my heart broken than sit in a safe little bubble and never experience life," he responded.

"That's interesting. Coming from you."

"What's that supposed to mean?"

"You're in your thirties and still single. Obviously, you're not all that eager to take relationship risks."

"Me being single has nothing to do avoiding risks. At least, not in the way you're thinking."

"Then what does it have to do with?" she asked, genuinely curious. Justin was a great guy. He had a good career that earned him good money. If he stayed in the military until retirement, he'd have a good pension. He was handsome, smart and funny. Any woman would consider herself fortunate to be with a man like him.

"The truth?" he asked.

"I certainly prefer it to a lie."

"I'm single because the only example of a husband and father I had was my dad. He beat my mother for fun, and he did the same to me."

His words were like ice water, cooling her blood, clearing her head.

"I'm sorry, Justin. That's horrible," she said.

"It was, but watching him taught me what being a

man wasn't. Now I'm doing everything I can to be what he wasn't. I'm not afraid of having my heart broken. I'm afraid of breaking the heart of someone I love. I'm afraid of turning into a selfish, angry monster who only cares about his own needs and desires." He paused, a frown line between his brows. "Or I *was* afraid of those things. Portia has been with me for over a year, and I haven't flown off the handle yet. I'm hoping that's a good sign."

"You don't need a sign. If you were like your father, you wouldn't be able to do this job. Being the head of Security Forces requires self-control and patience. If you didn't have those things, you'd be sunk."

"Maybe you're right. I hope you're right." His gaze dropped to her lips, and her breath caught. She was pretty sure her heart stopped, too.

"You can tell me to stop, if you want me to," he said, leaning down until they were just a hairbreadth away.

She knew she should.

She knew she was setting herself up for heartbreak, but she couldn't make herself say the words.

His lips brushed hers. Just like they had before. Gently. Tenderly.

Tears burned behind her eyes, and she pulled away, breathless, off balance.

"We shouldn't be doing this," she said, her heart still pounding wildly.

"Why not? There's no rule against it."

"It's not about rules. It's about me going back to Minot in a few weeks. It's about you staying here. It's about long-distance relationships not working."

"Your brother is in Texas. Your future sister-in-law is in New England," he pointed out.

"They're an exception."

"We can be an exception, too. If we want to be." He took a step away, watching her, waiting for a response.

But everything she thought of saying seemed trite and dishonest. Nothing seemed to match up to the magnitude of this moment and this conversation, because no amount of fear seemed insurmountable when she looked into his eyes.

She was going to tell him that.

She *was*, but the door opened, and Oliver walked into the room.

He glanced at Gretchen and then at Justin.

"Sorry," he said, starting to close the door again.

"It's okay. What's up?" Justin walked toward him, his posture stiff, his expression unreadable.

She'd hurt him.

She knew she had.

And she wanted to take it all back, tell him that she'd been stupid. That, of course, she was willing to risk her heart again. For him.

"My transport to Houston will be here shortly," Oliver said. "Rusty is already cooperating. He's given us a few names and the address of a storage unit that he thinks Patriot was guarding. He believes Olio was keeping drugs or weapons in it."

"If you find it, you may find the person who owns it," Justin said.

"Right, and we're hoping that person can give us names. We're getting close to closing the crime ring down, and I wanted to thank you both for your help."

"Thank us when Olio no longer exists," Justin said. "Until then, let me know if you need any more help."

"Thanks. I'll also keep you updated. And before I

forget…" He pulled a folded piece of paper from his pocket and handed it to Justin. "Portia gave this to one of my men and asked if we could deliver it to you. I'd planned to give it to you earlier, but things got a little crazy."

"That's an understatement."

"See you later." Oliver hurried away, and Justin unfolded the note, smiling as he read it.

"Is she doing okay?" Gretchen asked.

"Yes." He folded the note again, tucked it into his pocket without sharing any of the details.

He was putting up barriers.

That was clear, and she couldn't even be upset, because she was the one who'd demanded them.

"Justin," she began, determined to clear the air. To explain. To apologize.

"How about we discuss it later?"

"You don't even know what I was going to say."

"I know that I need to get you home. It's been a long day. We're both tired, and I have a team meeting scheduled for ten. If you're not up to attending, I'll understand, but I have to be there. I'd like to get some sleep before then."

"Since when have I ever missed a meeting?"

"I'm just giving you the option. Not implying that you'll choose it." He called to Quinn and walked out of the room.

She followed, knowing she'd made a mistake. Knowing she was the only one who could fix it. She'd have pulled Justin to a stop and forced him to hear her out, but now didn't seem like the time.

Like he'd said, it had been a long day. They were both tired.

Tomorrow would be soon enough to explain herself.

They made the drive back to her place in silence.

Justin left Quinn in the SUV and walked her to her apartment. He waited as she unlocked the door. Just like he had dozens of times before.

Only this time felt like the last time.

This time felt like the end.

She reached for his hand, but his phone rang before she could touch him.

He answered, his voice rumbling through the hallway, the words terse and a little sharp. "You're sure? Okay. I'll swing by on my way home. See if I find anything."

"What's going on?" she asked as he tucked the phone back in his pocket.

"That was the desk sergeant. An airman called. She was on her way back from furlough and thought she saw a red rose lying on the sidewalk in front of the high school."

"Another message from Boyd?"

"Maybe. Although I don't know why he'd leave it there when Portia is out of his reach."

"Maybe he wants you to panic and contact her?"

"He's not going to get what he wants. I never panic. But I will go check it out."

"I'll come with you."

"Not this time. I have Quinn, and I don't think I'm going to find anything. It's dark and rainy. Sticks look like swords in weather like this. A clump of grass might look like a rose."

She didn't argue.

He was probably right. The likelihood of Boyd leaving a rose on the sidewalk was slim.

"All right. I'll see you in the morning," she said, stepping into the apartment and closing the door.

She turned the lock and flicked on the light.

Only, the room remained dark.

Surprised, she walked across the living room and switched on the lamp. Like the overhead light, it didn't go on.

She planned to walk into the hall that led to the bedrooms and try the light there. If it didn't work, she'd call management and ask if a circuit had blown. She stepped toward the hall and stopped.

This wasn't right.

None of it.

The light in the hall outside the apartment had been on.

The last time a circuit had blown, it had been out.

This made no sense... Unless someone had entered her apartment and removed light bulbs or cut lines.

She went cold at the thought, her skin crawling as she walked to the door. She told herself not to run, because if someone was in the apartment, she didn't want him to know she suspected it.

Someone?

Boyd. If Boyd were in the apartment...

"Please, God," she whispered.

"I don't think He hears you," a deep voice responded.

She whirled around, ready to fight.

Pain exploded through her head, and she fell into nothingness.

ELEVEN

There'd been no red rose. He'd spent an hour search-ing the sidewalks near the school, and he'd come up empty. When Justin tried to find the airman who'd called in the report, he couldn't. She hadn't given her name, hadn't offered an address, and the phone num-ber she'd called from was unlisted. He suspected the phone was prepaid and impossible to trace.

Thinking about that had kept him from sleeping.

No sleep led to a bad mood that no amount of caf-eteria coffee seemed able to ease. He dumped a packet of sugar into his cup and took a sip.

That wasn't doing it for him, either.

Not that his mood would have been stellar if he'd gotten a full eight hours. He'd made a jerk of himself with Gretchen last night, taking offense because she hadn't been willing to step out in faith with him. He could blame that on fatigue as well, but he didn't make a habit of lying to himself.

Over the past few months, he and Gretchen had built a rapport and a relationship, and he'd been in-trigued enough to want to try for more. After spend-ing the afternoon with her, he'd thought she'd felt the same. They'd clicked, fitted together like two halves of a whole, and it had felt as right to him as sunrise in the morning or snow in the winter.

She obviously hadn't felt the same.

If she had, she'd have been more willing to let go of the past and step into the future. Whatever it brought.

At least, that was how he'd felt last night.

In the cold hard light of day, he wasn't as convinced.

He set his coffee on the conference room table and glanced at the clock. Ten o'clock, and, as if on cue, the door opened and Westley and Felicity walked in. They both looked tired but happy.

"Good morning," Felicity said cheerfully, grabbing a mug and pouring coffee for herself and Westley. "Any news from Oliver? I was hoping that a miracle occurred, and the FBI located the Olio kingpin. The crime ring needs to go down for what it did to our dogs."

"Were they injured?" he asked, eager for a report from Westley now that he'd had a chance to get the three German shepherds examined by the base vet.

"No, but they're traumatized. It's going to take some time for them to get acclimated." Westley pulled a chair out for Felicity and then took a seat, his dog, Dakota, settling down beside him.

"Fortunately, we can give them that," Felicity said, glancing around the room and frowning.

"What's wrong?" he asked.

"Where's Yvette?"

"She's not here?" Ava stepped into the room, Roscoe loping beside her. If she was tired from the late night, it didn't show.

"Maybe she didn't realize we were meeting?" Justin offered.

It *was* strange.

Since Boyd had been on the loose, she'd been at every meeting regarding the Red Rose Killer. The fact that she'd received a rose from him had made her a part of the group.

"How's everyone?" Vanessa Gomez asked as she walked into the room. A nurse who worked at the base hospital, she'd nearly been killed by a Red Rose Killer copycat. She'd become involved in the quest to stop Boyd when she'd thought she was his target. Even after she'd learned the truth, she'd remained part of the team. Tech Sergeant Linc Colson was right behind her with Nick Donovan. Oliver was back in Houston working on the Olio ring, so everyone on the team was accounted for.

Except one.

Gretchen hadn't arrived.

He glanced at the clock again—10:10 a.m. Not exceptionally late, but Gretchen was always early. His mood took a nosedive, the rose and the airman who'd reported it nagging at the back of his mind. He should have stopped by her apartment and offered her a ride. He had told her not to leave the house without an escort, but he'd been preparing for the meeting and time had gotten away from him.

And he'd assumed she'd call.

That she'd realize the seriousness of the situation and agree to his plan.

"Is Gretchen coming?" Linc asked, his attention on the empty seat.

"She was really tired last night. We've had a couple of long days," he hedged.

"Want me to call her?" Vanessa asked, pulling out her cell phone.

"I told her she could skip if she wanted to," Justin admitted, and the team went silent. No more quiet conversation. No more rustling papers as they looked through the case notes he'd put together for them.

"You told her she didn't have to attend?" Nick asked. "Why?"

"I already explained that," he replied, glancing at the clock again. Fifteen minutes after the meeting was supposed to begin, and she still wasn't there. And if he knew anything about Gretchen, it was that she didn't skip meetings and she never shirked responsibility.

She should be there.

She wasn't, and the team was right to be concerned.

"But you're right. It's not like her to not show." He pulled out his cell phone and called, waiting impatiently for her to pick up.

She didn't, and the unsettled feeling in his gut intensified.

"She's not home?" Ava asked.

Like Justin, the team knew Gretchen's work ethic.

"Not answering," he corrected.

"Who's not answering?" Oliver walked into the room, crossing to Ava and setting his hands on his fiancée's shoulders.

"Gretchen," she responded, looking up to meet his eyes. "What are you doing here? I thought you were staying in Houston."

"Just until we got the information we needed. And we did. We picked up Rusty's friend last night. He's

singing like a canary. We got several names and ad-
dresses. We also went to a storage unit he told us about.
We found all the equipment needed to counterfeit cur-
rency. We put out an arrest warrant for the owner of
the property, brought him in and got a list of names.
We have a dozen people in custody."

"That's wonderful!" Ava said.

It was. If the FBI hadn't completely shut down Olio,
they'd put a huge dent in its operations. Even if it managed to limp along for a while longer, it wouldn't survive.

"So, what's going on with Gretchen?" Oliver asked,
taking the empty seat.

"She's not here," Ava responded. "Which isn't typical. She's usually the first to arrive and the last to
leave."

"I've noticed that about her." Oliver frowned. "You
tried to call her?"

"Yes."

"Maybe the next step is going to her apartment.
If she's there, we can have the meeting at her place."

It was a better idea than sitting around hoping she'd
show up.

Justin stood, grabbing his coffee and notebook.
"Quinn, heel."

He left the room, the rest of the team filing out behind him.

The apartment's parking lot was nearly empty, and
Justin spotted Gretchen's car easily. Parked where it
usually was. Just a few spaces away from the lobby
door.

He jumped out of the SUV, not bothering to wait
for the rest of the team. His heart was racing, adrena-

line coursing through him, telling him something was wrong.

He released Quinn and ran into the building, bypassing the elevator and taking the stairs two at a time. He made it to the third floor in seconds, shoving open the stairwell door and running into the hall.

He realized her door was open before he reached it.

He could see a sliver of darkness beyond the well-lit hallway and his heart sank. He rapped on the door, stepping inside as it swung open.

Quinn growled deep in his throat, his shoulders hunched with tension as he lunged against his leash.

"Find," Justin commanded, releasing the dog, letting him bound through the living room. He ran down the hall and scratched at a closed door.

Justin knocked. When he got no answer, he turned the handle and walked into the room. And he saw the long-stemmed rose lying in the middle of the bed. There was a note beside it, the letters scrawled in thick black marker—*You're next.*

"He has her." He whirled around, nearly knocking Westley off his feet as he retraced his steps down the hall. Quinn was ahead of him, sniffing the floor, the walls, the couch.

"The light is out," Nick said, flicking a switch near the door.

The words barely registered. Justin couldn't think of anything else but Gretchen. If anything happened to her, he'd never forgive himself.

"This one, too," Oliver said, glancing under the lampshade, then dragging a chair into the hall and checking the light fixture there. "No bulb. Looks like someone was here ahead of her, and made sure she was in the dark."

"How about we name that someone?" Justin said through gritted teeth. "Boyd has her. I'm taking Quinn to see if we can find their trail."

"Hold on." Nick grabbed his arm before he could leave. "I don't think running off half-cocked is going to help anything."

"It's better than standing around hoping something turns up."

His phone rang, and he grabbed it, glancing at the number.

Unknown caller.

He knew, though. Before he answered. Before he heard Boyd's voice.

"Hello," he barked, and Boyd chuckled.

"You sound cheerful this morning."

"Where is she?"

"If you're talking about your girlfriend, she's in a safe place. For now."

"Let me speak to her," he demanded, his tension making Quinn pace restlessly. The dog was feeding off his energy. If they were going to search effectively, Justin needed to dial it down.

"Sorry. I call the shots now. You want to talk to her, you'll have to find her."

"I don't like hide-and-seek."

"I do. So, you have until midnight to figure this out. If you don't. She dies." He disconnected, and Justin was tempted to toss the phone across the room. Breaking it wouldn't achieve his goal, though.

And his goal was to find Gretchen.

The team had gathered around him, everyone waiting for him to make a decision or give a command.

He took a steadying breath, forced himself to focus. "He has her, and he's playing games again. He's given me until midnight to find her."

"Did he give you any clues?" Ava asked.

"Not this time. Our best option is to take the dogs out and start searching."

"Where? On base?" Nick walked into the bedroom and grabbed the pillow, holding it out for Annie to sniff.

"Could he have gotten back on base without gate security stopping him?" Vanessa asked.

"He could have if he were in the trunk of a car that belonged to someone who had ID." Justin had taken the pillow and was holding it in front of Quinn's nose. The dog inhaled deeply, his tail wagging.

He knew Gretchen.

He liked her.

Please, God, let Quinn be able to find her.

"I know we're in a hurry, and you don't have time to waste," Vanessa said. "But I keep going back to the conference room and those snacks. A couple of months ago Gretchen and I followed Yvette, remember? We were trying to see if she was helping Boyd."

"Right," Justin said. "I remember, but she wasn't caught doing anything out of the ordinary. She's clean."

"Or she overheard the plans and made sure she didn't do anything suspicious. Think about it. Lately she's always at headquarters. Always. Every time I turn a corner it seems like she's there."

It was true. Justin had noticed the same thing. "That makes her nosy. Not guilty," he said, but he was thinking about the missing snacks, too. Thinking about the phone call last night and the report of the rose on the sidewalk in front of the high school. All of it timed just right. If Boyd had been in the apartment, he'd have heard Gretchen return. He'd have realized Justin was with her, and he could have easily hidden somewhere, called someone and had the false report made.

Yvette had dated him when they were in basic training.

She'd broken up with him, but Justin remembered the relationship—how eager she'd been to please Boyd. How callous he'd been to her.

He'd been relieved when Boyd was dishonorably discharged, and hopeful that Yvette would find someone who treated her better.

Had she contacted him while he was in prison?

Or had he reached out to her after he escaped?

If so, she'd probably been a willing pawn, eager for a relationship. She was also knowledgeable about the base. Well liked by everyone.

"You're thinking what I'm thinking," Oliver said, and Justin met his eyes.

"Yvette," he said, because he knew they were on the right track. "She'd have been able to get past gate security easily. She was at headquarters when I broke radio silence, and she probably called Boyd immediately. I gave the coordinates, so he'd have had no trouble finding the cave. She drove off base in her car, met him and they drove to the state highway together. She could easily have gotten him on base in the trunk of her car. He got into Gretchen's apartment and waited for her to return."

"Then what?" Vanessa asked. "There aren't a lot of

places on base where he could hide her. Plus, transporting her wouldn't be easy. She's tall, and she knows to fight. If he managed to knock her out, he'd still have the problem of getting her out of the building without anyone noticing."

"Maybe he didn't take her out of the building," Ava said. When they all turned a questioning eye to her, she explained. "Yvette lives on the fourth floor."

"In this apartment complex?" Justin asked, his heart slamming against his ribs, his muscles tight with the need to act.

"In this building. I was there last year. She offered a healthy cooking class to people on the K-9 Search and Rescue team. She's in 418. It's on this side of the building and has a balcony that looks over the parking lot. Just like that one." She gestured toward the sliding glass door that opened out onto a small deck.

"Let's go." Westley headed for the door, but Justin grabbed his arm.

"If he hears us coming, he'll kill her for the fun of it."

"Then what's the plan?"

Good question, and Justin needed to come up with an answer. One that would keep the team safe, keep Gretchen safe and bring Boyd and Yvette to justice.

He walked to the sliding glass door but didn't open it. If Boyd or Yvette were watching, he didn't want to give them any hint that he planned to access Yvette's apartment. It was just above Gretchen's, and should be easy enough to enter. If they were careful.

Stealth was the key, and he and Quinn were good at it. They'd ascend the fire escape and cut through the sliding glass door. He had the tool in his tactical vest. All he needed was a diversion.

"We pretend to do what we'd be doing if we didn't think Gretchen was in this building. Team up. Take the dogs out. I'll take Quinn around to the east wing of the apartment complex and go in through the service door there. The basements are connected, and I should be able to access this wing easily."

"You don't think we're going to let you do this alone, do you?" Westley said. "Because that's not going to happen. You may be the captain of the team, but we plan together and we execute together."

"You're all going to be my diversion. Create plenty of radio traffic. Make things up if you have to, but make sure it sounds like we're out searching, still trying to figure out where Gretchen's being held. Unless I miss my guess, Yvette has a scanner in her apartment. She's probably been monitoring our team for months."

"What I'm hearing you say," Oliver said, "is that you're planning to do this alone."

"Quinn and I are going to climb up the fire escape and access the balcony that way. I'll need someone to go to the front door and offer a distraction. Yvette didn't show up at the office today. That's a good enough excuse to do a well check." He glanced around at the group. "But we'll need to be careful. Boyd isn't stupid. He's going to be hard to surprise."

"Isaac can do it," Vanessa said. "I texted him and asked him to bring Beacon."

Justin nodded. Her fiancé, Isaac Goddard, was a senior airman and former fighter pilot. He'd returned from Afghanistan with PTSD and the desperate desire to bring home the German shepherd that had saved his life while he was overseas. It had taken months and a lot of red tape, but Beacon had finally been flown to the base. While Isaac was waiting, he'd saved Vanessa from an attacker and had been instrumental in stopping an air force psychiatrist who had been selling drugs on the black market and treating his patients with placebos. Justin had found Isaac to be smart, tough and quick thinking. Beacon was proving to be an excellent therapy dog for him, but Isaac wasn't content to get the therapy certification. He'd been training Beacon in obedience and protection. The shepherd was as smart as any of the dogs they had in the kennel.

"Have him text me so we can coordinate the timing," he said. "Let's move out."

They stepped out into the hall, dogs and handlers moving in sync as they walked into the stairwell. They didn't try to be quiet. Justin wanted Boyd to think he had the upper hand. That, combined with his arrogance, would be his undoing.

Justin knew what needed to be done.

He knew he and Quinn could do it.

He could only pray that they'd be able to do it quickly enough and that Gretchen wouldn't be injured during the process.

Blood still flowed sluggishly from a wound in her head, and she was pretty sure she had a concussion. Her vision was blurry, her stomach churning, but she wasn't going down without a fight.

Gretchen knew what Boyd planned. She'd heard him on the phone with Justin. He wanted to draw Justin out and kill him. Once that was accomplished, he'd kill her.

She scanned the bedroom in Yvette's apartment,

looking for something that she could use to her advantage. There was a bed. A dresser. The two chairs. A bookshelf filled with books.

She shifted, trying to ease the throbbing pain in her shoulders. Boyd had handcuffed her to a high-back chair, her arms pulled through the spindles in the back. The cuffs were loose, and she could move her arms, but they were pulled so far behind her, she thought they might pop out of the sockets.

"I hope you're not trying to escape," Yvette said quietly. She was sitting in another high-back chair, staring at Gretchen as if she were afraid she'd pull a magic trick and disappear.

"How do you suppose I'm going to do that?" Gretchen asked, her head pounding with every word.

"I don't know, but the last time I watched a prisoner, he escaped. Boyd and I had a huge fight about it. We didn't speak for a month."

"Who was that?"

Yvette replied, "Why do you want to know?"

"Just curious."

"Nosiness can get a person killed," she said. "Look at you. You came here to learn some new skills, but you couldn't keep yourself from butting in where you didn't belong. Now…" She shook her head sadly, and if Gretchen hadn't known better, she'd have thought Yvette felt bad for what was happening.

"It's my job to track down criminals, Yvette. You know that." She felt dizzy, darkness edging in, but she had to keep it together. She had to escape before Boyd accomplished his goal. If something happened to her, and Justin lived, he'd blame himself. She knew that for certain. She'd feel the same if she survived and he didn't.

They both had to come out of this alive.

Please, Lord, help me figure this out, she prayed silently.

"Boyd is not a criminal," Yvette said.

"What do you call a murderer?"

"He didn't murder anyone!" she spit. "He was forced to seek vengeance on people who were trying to destroy him. If he hadn't killed them, they'd have killed him. It was self-defense."

"Do you hear yourself, Yvette? You're defending a man who took innocent lives. Who ambushed a bodyguard and killed him because he was in the way. Who kidnapped a sixteen-year-old girl and terrorized her."

"The bodyguard shouldn't have taken the job," she said coldly. "And Portia has a big mouth. She needs to learn to keep it shut. If she hadn't been blogging and saying all those hurtful things about Boyd, he'd have left her alone."

"The bodyguard needed money to support his wife and children. He took the job because your boyfriend threatened a kid."

"He's more than my boyfriend. He's my fiancé."

"Really?" Gretchen said, purposely looking at Yvette's empty ring finger.

"He's going to get me a ring as soon as he—" She frowned.

"Kills me and Justin?" She shifted again. Between the throbbing in her shoulders and the pounding in her head, she was having difficulty focusing, but she had to pull herself together.

There was always a way out.

One of her brothers had told her that when she was a kid and he'd brought her into a carnival fun house. She'd been seven, and she'd hated it. The mirrors. The noises. The oddly moving floors. She'd been certain they were going to get trapped there.

There's always a way out.

Currently, she couldn't see one.

"Look," Yvette said, leaning forward, her expression earnest and sweet. "You have to understand. Boyd is special. He's got a lot to give to the world. He can't do that from prison."

"So far," Gretchen responded, "he's taken more from the world than he's given. Those people who died? They were gifted, too. We all are, Yvette. Boyd isn't someone put on earth to rule us all. He's a human being. Fallible and fallen."

"He's everything to me," she retorted, sitting back and looking away. "And I'm everything to him. He says that I look like one of those Greek statues they have in the museums."

"You look like a petulant child." The words slipped out, and Yvette jumped to her feet.

"I'm going to tell Boyd to kill you now. You're mean and hateful, and all you've done is cause problems." She fled the room, and Gretchen could hear her high-pitched voice as she explained things to Boyd.

Hopefully, she had a lot to say.

Gretchen's tactical vest had been removed, and she could see it lying in the corner of the room. Her gun was gone, and she was pretty certain that was the weapon Boyd planned to murder her with.

He'd like the irony of that and the power it made him feel.

She tugged at the cuffs, knowing she'd never get her hands through them, but she felt compelled to try. She shoved her feet under the chair, trying to stand. If she could, maybe she could make it to the vest. She wasn't sure what she could do with it while her hands were cuffed behind her back, but at least she'd have more options.

"Going somewhere?" Boyd asked, stepping into the room, Gretchen's service weapon in his hand.

She was cold with fear, but she wasn't going to let him know it. "Trying to stretch my legs. I'm not used to sitting for ten hours."

"It hasn't been that long," he said, stopping beside her and pressing the barrel of the gun to her head.

She was helpless, and he knew it.

She was terrified, and he probably knew that, too.

But she planned to decide how she'd die. Cowering wasn't it.

"Does killing people who can't fight back make you feel like a man?" she said, moving her feet, trying to widen her stance so she could get enough leverage to throw herself sideways and knock him over.

"I'm not going to lose my cool because you taunt me. If you're hoping to make me lose my concentration, you're going to be disappointed."

"I have a feeling you lose your cool all the time. Bullies usually do."

"She wants me to kill you. You know that, right?" He flicked her hair with the gun, scowling when she didn't wince.

"I'm not surprised. I figured she was the one calling the shots. I've heard about your time in basic training. Your work was mediocre at best. If you'd graduated, you'd have been at the bottom of the class. Yvette was better. I think she was in the top ten percent. It's not surprising that she's the one who's planned this all out."

"I do the planning," he growled. "And I'm the one calling the shots. Right now, I want you alive. Later, I won't."

"Let me guess, you want to kill me in front of Justin, so you can see him suffer?"

"Good guess. Have fun thinking about it for the next few hours." He smirked, walking back out of the room and shouting for Yvette to return.

She had tears in her eyes when she sat down in the chair minutes later, and finger marks on her wrist.

Despite the fact that Yvette wanted her dead, Gretchen couldn't help feeling sorry for her.

"No one you love should ever hurt you, Yvette," she said.

"He didn't." She rubbed her wrist and frowned.

"Then why are there marks on your arm?"

"I bumped into the kitchen counter."

"You're going to want to have a lot of those excuses in your repertoire, because if you and Boyd make it off base and to wherever he's promised you, you're going to have a lot of bruises to explain."

"Shut up, Gretchen. You have no idea what it's like to be with someone like him, and you never will. You're not good enough to attract a man of his caliber."

"I'm very thankful for that," she said sincerely, her eyelids so heavy she wanted to close them and let herself drift away for a while. She rolled her shoulders in the sockets, letting the pain drive her back to wakefulness. Her fingers brushed cool wood and the heavy fabric of her military jacket. When she was a kid, she'd dreamed of having one just like it. She'd open her father's closet and stare at his uniforms and imagine what it would be like to be a hero to the world.

He used to laugh when she asked him what it felt like, lifting her up and swinging her in circles, his pockets jingling with keys.

She blinked, that last word lodging in her brain.

Keys.

Had Boyd removed them from her pocket?

He'd taken the obvious set—the one she'd had hanging from her belt—but her father had taught her to keep an extra handcuff key hidden on her person. Just in case. She'd assumed he'd meant in case she lost a set. Now she thought he must have meant in case she was ever trussed to a chair with her own handcuffs.

She bent her arms, trying to maneuver them closer to her jacket pocket. The key was in a small slit she'd made in the fabric. It would be difficult to get, but if she could, she'd be able to free herself.

"Wiggling isn't going to help you," Yvette said.

"My shoulders are in agony. I'm trying to ease the pain."

"Don't worry. In a few hours, you won't be feeling a thing." She giggled, her angelic face obviously hiding a very dark soul.

"At least my eternity is going to be spent in a much nicer place," she responded, wiggling again, using her hip to force the coat back against the spindles.

Her wrists felt like they'd snap, but she managed to get two fingers between the spindles. She used them to pull the coat taut and feel for the pocket.

There! She found the edge and shoved her fingers in between the fabric.

The key was there, the metal cool against her fingers.

"You know what your problem is, Gretchen?" Yvette asked, apparently oblivious to Gretchen's efforts to escape.

"What?"

"You think you're better than other people."

"What gave you that idea?" she asked, trying to keep the woman talking as she eased the key out of the pocket. She was sweating with fear, terrified she'd drop it, but she managed to get it out and close her fist around it.

"Boyd told me that's the way women like you are, and he's right."

"Like me? What am I like?"

"Career military. You get in and stay in and think you own the world because of it."

"I've only been in eight years."

"And you'd be in for eighty more if you lived long enough. Which you won't." Yvette laughed. "You were so busy thinking you were better than me that you didn't notice I was collecting information."

"I guess I didn't." She felt the edges of the key, tried to get it in the right position. She might only get one shot. She didn't want to waste it.

"Well, I guess you've learned your lesson. It stinks being under lock and key, right? Now you know how my poor Boyd felt when he was in prison, don't you?"

"Yes."

"Are you thirsty? I mean, I know Boyd's right about the kind of person you are, but you were always nice to me. Even if you were faking it, I appreciate that."

"Water would be good," she lied. The thought of taking even a sip made her stomach heave.

"All right. I'll get you some. Kindness for kindness, right? That's what makes the world go round." She left the room, and Gretchen shoved the key into the lock, turned it.

She felt it click, and then she was free.

The cuffs were double locked, but she didn't open the second one. She was afraid they'd fall and make enough noise to bring Boyd running. She pocketed the key and positioned her hands so that only someone looking closely would know the cuff was open.

"Here you are." Yvette said, walking into the room with a water glass in hand, a straw poking out of it. "Don't worry. I didn't drug it. Boyd says you should be awake for the festivities."

"That's really nice of him," she muttered, taking a tiny sip of the water.

"You didn't drink much."

"I think I have a concussion. I don't feel very well. As matter of fact, I might get sick." That was the total truth, and she hoped to use it to her advantage.

"As in throw up?"

"That's what it feels like."

"You do look a little green."

"Maybe you could open the window and let some fresh air in. That might help." She knew from the setup of her apartment that Yvette's window would open. She also knew that a balcony stretched the entire length of the unit. If Yvette opened the window, all Gretchen would have to do was crawl through it.

"All right. I guess that's not going to hurt anything." She flipped the lock and cracked open the window.

"Can you open it a little more?"

"You're awfully demanding for someone who's on death row."

"Death row inmates get special privileges."

She opened it wider, and Gretchen winced as the vinyl pane squeaked.

"There," Yvette said. "Don't ask for anything else."

"I won't."

The doorbell rang, and Yvette jumped, whirling toward the bedroom door. "Who's that?"

"I have no idea. Maybe you should go check."

"It can't be your friends. They're off with their dogs, hunting for you. I can't wait until they find out you were here all along."

The doorbell rang again.

"Yvette!" Boyd appeared in the doorway. "Get your butt out there and open the door."

"But what if it's Justin?"

"It's not going to be. I set up cameras at the front of the building, remember? If he came back, I'd know it." He grabbed her arm and then pointed the gun at Gretchen.

"You scream or make noise and I'll kill whoever is at the door." With that, he yanked Yvette out of the room and shut the door.

TWELVE

Gretchen stood, her legs wobbly, her head fuzzy.

She was four floors up. She'd climbed rock walls higher than that, and on any other day, she wouldn't be worried about making it down the fire escape.

Today, though, her movements felt disjointed, her gait unsteady.

She could hear Yvette speaking to whoever was at the door.

Boyd had to be hiding somewhere close enough to take out anyone who tried to enter the apartment. Which meant Gretchen had a golden opportunity to get out. She had to hurry. She had to escape. She had to warn Justin. She had to get the team to the apartment building before Boyd fled.

But it was all she could do to make it to the window. She managed it. Barely.

Once she was there, she leaned against the wall. Just for a second. Just to catch her breath.

Move it! She could almost hear her brothers shouting the orders. Or maybe it was Justin's voice.

She levered up, pushing her upper body through the window, her head swimming.

"You can do this," she muttered, pressing her hand against the siding, trying to gain enough momentum to slide through.

She closed her eyes, because the world was spinning.

Glass shattered, and for a second, she thought she'd broken the window. Then Yvette screamed, the sound raw and terrible.

Someone grabbed Gretchen from behind, yanking her back into the room, swinging her around, the cold barrel of a gun pressed to her cheek. She could see Justin in the doorway of the room, Quinn beside him. The dog lunged, growling and snarling.

"One wrong move, Justin, and I'll kill her," Boyd said.

"Don't do anything stupid," Justin replied.

"Stupid would be letting you capture me." Boyd shoved Gretchen forward, his grip tight on her upper arm.

"Let her go," Justin responded, Quinn growling deep in his throat, his teeth bared, his eyes on Boyd.

"Get out of the way," Boyd shouted, swinging the gun wildly, aiming it at Justin.

Gretchen tried to grab his arm, but her movements were slow and uncoordinated.

"I said move, Justin," Boyd screamed, the gun suddenly against her cheek again. "If you don't, I'll blow her beautiful face off."

"Calm down, Boyd," Justin said, stepping backward out of the room, his eyes locked on Gretchen.

She could see the fear in his eyes, but he wasn't panicked.

"It's going to be okay," he said calmly, and she believed him, because she believed *in* him. In the strength of his conviction and his faith, in his ability to think through the problem and come up with a solution.

And she believed in what he'd said, and what Henry had: that God was in control. That He would bring good to those who loved Him, and that no matter what happened, everything would be okay.

"Not if I don't get a car and a clear path off base," Boyd said. "You have three minutes to arrange that, Justin. You don't get it for me, and I'll shoot her in the knee. Every three minutes after that, I'll shoot her again. She's not just going to die, she's going to suffer."

"I'll get the ride," Justin said, taking another step back. He seemed to be moving toward the hallway. Or blocking Boyd's view of it.

"Good. Good," Boyd said. "That's what I like. Quick action. Come on, Gretchen. We're getting out of here." He nudged her forward, the gun slipping away from her face, and this time she was ready. She swung the handcuff, slamming it into his temple.

She expected the explosion of gunfire. Instead, she heard an angry snarl, and a large dog flew past, clamping his jaws on Boyd's leg and dragging him to the ground.

Not Quinn.

Beacon.

He must have come through the window.

She moved away from the writhing man and the dog. She'd seen Beacon the day he'd finally arrived from Afghanistan and been reunited with Isaac Goddard. He hadn't seemed vicious then. Now he was terrifying, Boyd's screams filling her ears.

She felt sick.

Really sick, and she stumbled to the couch, dropped down and pressed her head to her knees.

"Hey, it's okay. You're okay." Justin was beside her, his hand on her back, and she turned her head so she could see his face.

"Where's Yvette?"

"In cuffs out in the hall with Ava and Oliver."

"I can't believe she's been working with him all this time," she murmured, her head throbbing with every word.

"She had us all fooled." He felt her pulse, his fingers gentle on her wrist. "There's an ambulance on the way. We need to get you to the hospital."

"I'd rather stay here and see what Boyd has to say." She stood, and he grabbed her arm, holding her steady.

"I don't think standing is a good idea."

"I agree," Vanessa said, suddenly on Gretchen's other side. "Sit. Let me take a look. You've lost a lot of blood."

"Not enough to kill me," she said, sitting down again, because she still felt dizzy and off balance.

She tried not to wince as Vanessa probed the head wound, focusing instead on Justin and Isaac. They flanked Boyd, their dogs close beside them. He was cuffed, angry and as arrogant as ever.

"This isn't the end, Justin," he said, his face filled with rage. "I'm going to win. I always do."

"Not this time." Oliver stepped into the room, flashing his FBI badge at Boyd as he read him his Miranda rights, and Gretchen closed her eyes, trying to still the spinning world and anchor herself to the moment.

She was alive.

Justin was alive.

The team and their dogs were all okay.

And Boyd had been caught.

Finally. After months of hunting him, he'd been captured.

"Thank you, Lord," she whispered out loud, and someone squeezed her hand.

"I was just saying the same thing," Justin said, and she opened her eyes, realized she was on a gurney in the elevator.

She could hear someone crying, and she tried to sit up.

"Don't," Justin said, touching her shoulder and urging her to relax.

"Is that Portia?"

"No. She's still at the safe house, remember?" he asked, a note of concern in his voice.

"I got hit hard, but I haven't lost my memory. I just... Who's crying?" It wasn't a large elevator, and there was just enough room for the gurney, Justin and a medic.

None of them were crying.

She didn't think.

She touched her cheek. Just to be sure.

Justin smiled. "It's not you. In case you're wondering. Yvette is down in the lobby. She's been sobbing since I cut through the sliding glass door and took her into custody."

"I don't think many people would be happy about going to jail."

"It's not jail she's worried about," he said as the doors slid open.

Another medic was waiting in the lobby, and he helped roll the gurney out.

She thought he might be saying something to her, but she couldn't hear anything over Yvette's ear-piercing cries.

"Please!" she screamed. "Take me to the same prison. I just want to know we're close. Please, I'm begging you. Please."

"Someone shut her up!" Boyd shouted, his voice thundering through the lobby.

"Wow. Some lovebirds. They sound more like alley cats," Gretchen said as she was wheeled outside.

"I was thinking the same," Justin replied.

"She's mentally ill," she said, because she was afraid she'd close her eyes and lose the opportunity. Yvette was sick and needed treatment.

She also needed to be behind bars.

"She's being transported to a high-security VA mental facility. That's why she's screaming," he explained. "She thought they were going to the base prison together."

"Is that where he's going?"

"No. We're transporting him directly to the federal prison he escaped from. Which I'm sure he knew would happen if he was caught. That's not what he told Yvette, though. He had her convinced that they'd be brought to our holding cell, and he'd escape again. With her, of course."

"Of course. She's going to be shocked when he turns on her during the trial, and you know he will. He was planning to abandon her and leave with me as his hostage. Meanwhile, she'd been dreaming of happily-ever-after. I shouldn't feel sorry for her. She might be mentally ill, but she did ask Boyd to kill me."

"I heard. I was outside the window when you had

that conversation with her. I wanted to break the glass and climb through, but I was afraid you'd be hurt before I could get both Boyd and Yvette under control. So I followed the plan and waited for Isaac to show. It was the worst three minutes of my life."

"Really?" she asked, reaching for his hand.

"Really. I've enjoyed having you as a partner, Gretchen. But I enjoy having you in my life even more."

"I feel the same way," she said, halfway thinking she was in a dream, because the world suddenly seemed made of soft edges and gentle slopes. Nothing hard or difficult or ugly.

"Good," he said. "Because I have some plans for after you've recovered."

"What kind of plans?"

"Moonlit walks, picnics after church, sitting beside the fire and listening to Portia gab with her friends while we just enjoy each other's company."

She smiled at that, because she could picture it happening. She could picture him—walking beside her for days and weeks and years to come. "That sounds like…"

"What?" he asked, touching her cheek and looking into her eyes.

"Like everything I could ever dream of."

"Good, because all of my dreams of the future suddenly have you in them. I love you, Gretchen. I need to say that now, because when Boyd had his gun to your cheek, I realized how much I would regret it if I never got the chance to say the words."

"I love you, too," she murmured, and he smiled.

"Sir?" one of the medics said, interrupting them. "Are you planning to ride along?"

"Am I?" Justin asked her.

Two words, but it seemed like more. It seemed like the most important question he'd ever asked.

"Can his dog come?" she asked, and the medic shrugged.

"I don't see a problem with it."

"Then yes," she responded, holding on to Justin's hand as she was rolled onto the ambulance, looking into his face as an IV was started. Memorizing the curl of his lashes and the curve of his lips. The fine lines near his eyes and the ones that bracketed his mouth. Filing every detail away, because this moment was the beginning of their journey together.

And she didn't want to forget any of it.

THIRTEEN

Thanksgiving

It had been a long time since Gretchen had been part of a big Thanksgiving celebration. She'd been back home for the holidays a few times over the past eight years, but her brothers were usually in distant locations, and Thanksgiving with her parents had been a quiet, intimate event. After years of hosting airmen and their families, that was the way her mother and father wanted it.

Gretchen didn't mind, but she'd missed the controlled chaos of large holiday gatherings. She'd always enjoyed the sounds of people chatting and laughing and enjoying each other's company. Growing up in a military family had meant moving a lot and leaving a lot behind, but it had also meant making strangers family.

Today, she was going back to those roots and to the sweetest of childhood memories. She couldn't wait.

She eyed herself in the mirror above her dresser, trying to ignore the deep circles beneath her eyes and the paleness of her skin. She'd spent nearly a week in the hospital after Boyd's attack, recovering from a fractured skull and a severe concussion. Even now, three weeks after the attack, she tired easily. She'd been on medical leave since the incident. Hopefully, she'd be cleared to work following the holidays. Once she finished her required time at the base, she could return to Minot.

Her phone rang as she grabbed her purse and stepped out of the bedroom. She glanced at the caller ID and smiled. Portia had come out of her shell since she'd returned from the safe house. She'd begun making friends at school, and she seemed happier, more content with her life. She enjoyed sharing stories about her day, telling Gretchen about her new friends.

Gretchen, for her part, had been happy for the distraction. Inactivity was boring, and she'd had too much of that while she was recovering.

"Hello?" She held the phone to her ear as she walked down the hall and pushed the elevator button.

"Hi, Gretchen, it's Portia."

"I gathered that from the caller ID."

"Yeah. I had to say it, anyway. My mother drilled phone manners into my head."

"Are you missing her more today?" Gretchen asked, stepping onto the elevator.

"I miss her more every day," Portia replied, the sadness in her voice unmistakable.

"I'm sorry. I know it's hard to have Thanksgiving without her. Is there anything I can do to help?"

"Hurry up and get here? Dad said we can start the celebration once you've arrived."

"Am I late?" She glanced at her watch, worried that maybe she'd gotten confused. That had been a problem after the head injury. Although she'd been better during the past week. Clearer thinking. More focused.

According to the neurologist who was treating her, she still wasn't quite back to normal, but Gretchen could see the light at the end of the tunnel.

"No. It's still early. I just wanted to make sure you were coming. We invited the families of two of my friends from school. I don't want to act stupid in front of them."

"You're not stupid, so that would be impossible."

"I think you're forgetting that I was the anonymous blogger," Portia said with a sigh.

"Everyone makes mistakes."

"Not mistakes that almost get people they love killed. Anyway, Dad keeps saying I have to forgive myself, so I'm trying."

"Your dad is smart, too," Gretchen said.

"Would you say that if you weren't madly in love with him?" Portia giggled, obviously amused by her assessment of Gretchen and Justin's relationship.

"Madly, huh?"

"Would you call it something else?"

"I'd call it…wonderfully, beautifully, happily."

"The happy part sounds good. I love you both, and I want both of you to always be that. So, you're on the way?"

"Yes. Heading to my car now," she responded, stepping outside and crossing the parking lot.

"The doctor said you could drive, right? Because I don't want…" Her voice trailed off, but Gretchen heard what she didn't say: that she didn't want Gretchen to get into an accident.

"Yes. I got cleared yesterday, and I'm thrilled. Maybe we can go Black Friday shopping tomorrow."

"No way. You've got to rest, and that won't be restful. I'll see you in a few." The teen disconnected, and Gretchen dropped her phone into her purse.

The sun was high and warm, the air chilly. Someone had a fire burning, the warm aroma drifting on the late-November air.

This wasn't supposed to be home, but lately it had felt like it. She'd expected to come to Canyon, do what she'd been assigned and return to Minot. She'd known she'd have to make a decision about her military career, but she hadn't imagined that she'd have something even bigger to decide.

Not that there *was* a decision.

She knew in her heart that a military career wasn't for her. Just like she knew deep down where it counted that right here was where she wanted to be. Close to Justin and Portia and all the people she'd come to care about. She'd spent some time with Ava these past few weeks, watching her train puppies for search and rescue. There were several civilian search and rescue teams in Texas, and she planned to join one after her honorable discharge from the air force.

She also planned to get her master's in forensic profiling. Eventually, she'd like to use trace evidence to make cases against criminal offenders.

She and Justin had discussed it over several dinners and over ice cream and over cups of coffee. Just thinking about the conversations they'd had and the time they'd spent together made her smile. She was still afraid of heartache. She was still worried that she might be shattered again one day.

But Justin was worth risking her heart.

And God was good.

He'd brought them through so many trials and challenges, and brought them to a place where they could meet and fall in love and make something beautiful out of the tragedy.

She pulled up in front of Justin's house, her heart pounding a little harder, her pulse beating happily in her veins. She could see people in the backyard, gathered under canopies that Justin had set in place the previous day. Adults. Kids. Teens. Dogs.

Family.

Not by blood or even by legality.

There was one thing she'd learned after spending a lifetime in the military. Sometimes family was a disparate group of people brought together by God.

She got out of the car, pulling her sweater a little tighter as a cool November breeze chased leaves across the grass.

A dog barked, and Quinn was suddenly there, nudging her hand with his nose, begging to be petted.

"Hey, boy. I bet you're having a fun day."

"He's having the time of his life," Justin responded, walking across the yard. Sun glinted in his hair and his flannel shirt pulled taut across his muscular shoulders, but it was his smile that made her heart swell with dreams she'd once thought were dead.

"And are you having fun?" she asked.

"More so now," he responded, pressing a quick, warm kiss to her lips. "You're beautiful, Gretchen."

"And you're a flatterer. But I'll accept the compliment." She took his hand, Quinn falling into step beside them as they headed around to the backyard.

She could see Linc Colson and his wife, Zoe, her little boy standing between them, and Linc's rottweiler lying in a warm patch of sunlight beside them. They were talking to Isaac and Vanessa, Beacon sitting next to Isaac and leaning against his leg.

"It's good to see them together," she said aloud.

"Who?" Justin asked, his palm warm against hers.

"Isaac and Beacon."

"I agree. Beacon is being retired from the military and is training to be Isaac's obedience and protection dog."

"I have a feeling Beacon will be good at any task." That reminded her of another German shepherd. "How's Scout doing?"

"Great. Westley has given all four shepherds some peace and quiet and rehab time, but they're getting back to work, and none of them seem the worse for wear."

"I'm glad. And I'm glad Boyd is where he belongs."

"And that Yvette is getting the treatment she needs," Justin added.

"Still no link between her and his crimes?"

"She helped him get on and off base. She helped him keep you prisoner. She did admit to planting the rose and the threatening note in her apartment to throw us off her track. More than likely, she'll be court-martialed and sent to a mental hospital for the rest of her life."

"Gretchen!" Portia called, racing across the yard, two teenage girls with her. "This is Lauren and Stacia. We're all on the school's yearbook committee. We're also starting a journalism club."

"Sounds like fun," Gretchen said, greeting each of the teens, happy and excited to see Portia connecting with people who had similar interests.

"It's going to be. We're going to do some investigative reporting on what they're putting into the cafeteria meals. We're thinking it's not actually food."

"Portia, don't get into trouble trying to prove that theory," Justin warned, and Portia laughed.

"Don't worry, Dad. I learned my lesson about digging up dirt. I'm going to keep my nose clean and do this the right way. Come on, girls. You can help me bring out that surprise I showed you earlier."

The girls hurried away, and Gretchen smiled. "I remember being that age."

"It wasn't that long ago."

"Long enough," she said. "Not that I'd ever want to go back. It's hard making friends when you're the new kid."

"I hope she's happy," he said quietly, watching as Portia and her friends rushed into the house.

"She is. You're doing a great job, Justin. It's one of the things I love about you."

"So, there's more than one, huh?" He pulled her close, kissing her tenderly.

"Hey, none of that stuff," Maisy Lockwood called as she walked across the yard, a casserole dish in her hands. Chase McLear was beside her, his little girl in his arms. They made a beautiful family, his beagle, Queenie, trotting along behind.

"No?" Chase asked, leaning in to kiss her.

"I take back my protest." Maisy laughed, setting the casserole down on a long table filled with dishes. Portia had suggested a potluck, and Gretchen had agreed it would be the easiest way to feed a crowd.

Everyone who'd been invited had volunteered to bring something. Westley and Felicity had come with

several dishes of food. Lieutenant Ethan Webb and his
fiancée, Kendra, had offered to roast three turkeys.
They were both standing beside the food table, Ethan's
German shorthaired pointer, Titus, lying beneath it,
the dog's long legs stretched out, his head resting on
his front paws. Nick Donovan was on the other side
of the table, his arm around his fiancée, Heidi Jenks,
the base reporter. He was talking to Ethan, smiling as
Annie, his bloodhound, nosed around near the table.

Obviously, she'd caught the scent of food.

Fortunately, the dogs were too well trained to snatch
unattended food.

"It's pretty awesome, isn't it?" Justin whispered in
her ear, and she didn't have to ask what. She knew.
The team had been through so many trials and strug-
gles. The return of the Red Rose Killer. The murder
of Maisy's father, Chief Master Sergeant Clint Lockwood, and two dog trainers. The missing dogs. The
Olio Crime Syndicate. Each person here had perse-
vered and overcome.

There'd been sorrow, for sure. But there had also
been joy.

She could hear it ringing across the yard—kids and
adults laughing, conversation flowing. "It really is,"
she agreed.

"So, are you ready?" Isaac asked, walking toward
them, Vanessa at his side.

She thought he meant for the turkey to be cut and the
blessing to be said, but the other couples were gathering around. Kids and dogs and adults, forming a circle that she and Justin seemed to be in the center of.

"What's going on?" she asked, but then Portia
stepped into the center, carrying a basket.

"We wanted to thank you for all you've done as a member of the team," Ava said. "You've become more than just a temporary transfer. You're a friend and a comrade."

"I feel the same about all of you," she admitted, surprised when Portia set the basket near her feet. A blanket lay over it, and she thought it might have wiggled. Quinn nosed in, his snout so close to the blanket Justin gave him the down command.

"What is it?" she asked, looking into Justin's eyes.

"Six months is a long time to be away from the people you love," he said. "We discussed it, and we decided that you needed something to remember us by."

"You make it sound like I'll be gone forever."

"Like I said," he responded, "six months is a long time. Go ahead. Take a look. Everyone on the team had a hand in helping choose your gift."

"Justin…" Her voice trailed off as she leaned down and lifted the blanket. A chubby puppy lay inside. Belly up and tail wagging, he looked like a red Lab—a breed Ava had said would be perfect for search and rescue work.

"His name is Winston," Portia said.

"He is the cutest puppy I've ever seen." She lifted Winston from the basket, smiling when he licked her chin.

"Since it looks like you're not *totally* in love with him," Portia said, sliding her arm around Gretchen's waist, "you can just say so, and we'll take him off your hands."

Gretchen laughed. "Nice try, kid. I adore him."

"I kind of knew you would. I named him Winston,

because the first time I saw him, I thought he looked like a portly old man."

"A very cute portly old man," Gretchen agreed, teary eyed from surprise and pleasure.

She'd been given many gifts in her life, but this one, coming from so many people who cared, meant the most.

"Thank you all so much," she said.

"There's one more thing, Gretchen," Justin said. "But this one is just from me. To remember that I'm here for you, and that I always will be."

He took a box from his pocket and opened it.

"Justin," she breathed, not sure what she intended to say.

"I love you, Gretchen. You are everything I could ever want in a friend and life partner. I can't imagine my life without you. Will you marry me?"

The look in his eyes and on his face, the happiness and excitement and love there, filled her heart until there was no room for the past and its disappointments. There was only the future that they would create together.

"Of course!" she said, and he handed her the ring instead of sliding it on her finger.

"I hate to tell you this." Oliver chuckled. "But that's not the way it's done."

"Read it," Portia said, pointing to the words engraved inside the band.

In adversity, love blooms.

Gretchen's throat was tight, her eyes filled with tears.

"Yes," she managed to say, "it does."

Justin took the ring again, sliding it onto her finger this time. He kissed her then, deeply, passionately, their friends offering cheers and congratulations, the dogs barking and Annie baying.

Winston joined in, yipping happily and doing his best to lick the tears from Gretchen's face.

"He's already trying to make you feel better," Portia said, smiling at Justin. "You did good, Dad."

"I'm glad I have your approval," Justin said with a grin. "Now, how about we give thanks and eat?"

Gretchen set Winston back in the basket, linking hands with Justin and with Portia. One by one, they all did the same, standing in a circle beneath the pristine sky and thanking God for all the blessings they'd received. For the trouble and the triumph and the love they'd found along the way.

For His grace and His goodness in the dark times.

When they finished, Gretchen continued to hold Justin's hand, wrapped an arm around Portia and thanked Him again.

For faith, for family and for all the things that mattered most in life.

* * * * *

SPECIAL EXCERPT FROM

LOVE INSPIRED SUSPENSE
INSPIRATIONAL ROMANCE

A murder that closely resembles a cold case from twenty years ago puts Brooklyn, New York, on edge. Can the K-9 Unit track down the killer or killers?

Read on for a sneak preview of
Copycat Killer *by Laura Scott,*
the first book in the exciting new
True Blue K-9 Unit: Brooklyn series,
available April 2020 from Love Inspired Suspense.

Willow Emery approached her brother and sister-in-law's two-story home in Brooklyn, New York, with a deep sense of foreboding. The white paint on the front door of the yellow-brick building was cracked and peeling, the windows covered with grime. She swallowed hard, hating that her three-year-old niece, Lucy, lived in such deplorable conditions.

Steeling her resolve, she straightened her shoulders. This time, she wouldn't be dissuaded so easily. Her older brother, Alex, and his wife, Debra, had to agree that Lucy deserved better.

Squeak. Squeak. The rusty gate moving in the breeze caused a chill to ripple through her. Why was it open? She hurried forward and her stomach knotted when she found the front door hanging ajar. The tiny hairs on the back of her neck lifted in alarm and a shiver ran down her spine.

Something was wrong. Very wrong.

Thunk. The loud sound startled her. Was that a door closing? Or something worse? Her heart pounded in her chest and her mouth went dry. Following her gut instincts, Willow quickly pushed the front door open and crossed the threshold. Bile rose in her throat as she strained to listen. "Alex? Lucy?"

There was no answer, only the echo of soft hiccuping sobs.

"Lucy!" Reaching the living room, she stumbled to an abrupt halt, her feet seemingly glued to the floor. Lucy was kneeling near her mother, crying. Alex and Debra were lying facedown, unmoving and not breathing, blood seeping out from beneath them.

Were those bullet holes between their shoulder blades? *No! Alex!* A wave of nausea had her placing a hand over her stomach.

Remembering the thud gave her pause. She glanced furtively over her shoulder toward the single bedroom on the main floor. The door was closed. What if the gunman was still here? Waiting? Hiding?

Don't miss
Copycat Killer *by Laura Scott,*
available April 2020 wherever
Love Inspired Suspense books and ebooks are sold.

LoveInspired.com

Annalise's heart beat so fast her stomach churned with
nausea and an icy chill filled her veins. Bert was dead?
The security guard with the great smile who loved to tell
silly jokes was gone? And what two women had been
killed? Who had been in the office at the time of this...
this attack?

What were these killers doing here? What did they
want?

The sound of distant sirens pierced the air. The big
man cursed loudly.

"We were supposed to get in and out of here before
the cops showed up," the tall, thin man said with barely
suppressed desperation in his voice.

"Too late for that now," the big man replied. He
turned and pointed his gun at Annalise. She stiffened.
Was he going to kill her, as well? Was he going to shoot
her right now? Kill the girls? She put her arms around
her students and tried to pull them all behind her.

More sirens whirred and whooped, coming closer and
closer.

"Don't move," he snarled at them. He took the butt of his gun and busted out one of the windows. The sound of the shattering glass followed by a rapid burst of gunfire out the window made her realize just how dangerous this situation was.

The police were outside. She and her students were inside with murderous gunmen, and she couldn't imagine how this all was going to end.

Don't miss
48 Hour Lockdown *by Carla Cassidy,*
available March 2020 wherever
Harlequin Intrigue books and ebooks are sold.

Harlequin.com